PRAISE FOR ALAN RODGERS

"Alan Rodgers writes with style, wit, and an innate knowledge of what terrifies. Don't miss him!"

—F. Paul Wilson

"Alan's books are one of the horror field's most dependable pleasures. He's a writer with great talent, a willingness to tackle difficult (and sometimes vast) subjects, and an imagination that's as dark and fertile as cemetery earth."

—T. E. D. Klein

"Alan Rodgers is an original voice in horror who consistently rewards his readers. His name on a book guarantees a sleepless night."

—Raymond E. Feist

"The thing about Rodgers is, he takes the horror —and it's horrible, all right—and turns it into the light just a little differently than you'd ever expect and from *this* angle you realize it's more tragic than horrid, more beautiful than hideous."

—Orson Scott Card,
*The Magazine of Fantasy
& Science Fiction*

"You can depend on Alan Rodgers; he always delivers the goods."

—Mike Resnick

PANDORA

PANDORA

ALAN RODGERS

BANTAM BOOKS

New York   Toronto
London   Sydney   Auckland

PANDORA

A Bantam Book / January 1995

ISBN 0-553-56305-X

Published simultaneously in the United States and Canada

Bantam Books are published by Bantam Books, a division of Bantam
Doubleday Dell Publishing Group, Inc. Its trademark, consisting of the
words "Bantam Books" and the portrayal of a rooster, is Registered in
U.S. Patent and Trademark Office and in other countries. Marca
Registrada. Bantam Books, 1540 Broadway, New York, New York
10036.

FOR ANDREA
and
ALEXANDRA

There is a place out in the middle of Nowhere New Mexico that the federal authorities absolutely refuse to discuss. Partly they refuse on account of the fact that they get—collectively, among the twenty or so agencies who field these phone calls—forty, maybe fifty calls a week from Irate Citizens Determined to Get to the Bottom of This Irresponsible Cover-Up. Lots more calls than that in a bad week—say, when someone airs *Close Encounters of the Third Kind* on prime-time television in a major metropolitan market.

None of these agencies feels any special responsibility about these calls. They call the folks who make them cranks, or UFO-nuts, or loony-toons.

But that isn't the only reason they duck the subject. There are a couple, hidden deep in the bowels of the Pentagon, who know a hell of a lot more than they let on, on the rare occasion when some Irate Citizen finds their number and manages to dial through. But these agencies answer just as the others do, with snickers and off-color laughter. And simple denial.

And it's true, after all—the stories that Irate Citizens tell when they call aren't genuine reports with Implications that Weigh on International Security: they're urban legends. The tales people tell about Area Fifty-one (sometimes it's Fifty-two or Fifty-three, and ever so rarely a number in the sixties) and the three dead Aliens in cold storage in hangar seventeen (or nineteen, or eighteen, or thirteen)—these tales are nothing but folklore for modern times. In their own way they're little different from stories told in ancient Greece that recounted the sexual exploits of lord Zeus and his maidens.

Listen, right here, right now: it's on the radio. It's three A.M., and Barry Farber is talking on the radio, taking calls from America-at-large.

A man calls, and he says, "They're wrong, you know. About those Aliens in the hangar on the air base in Ohio. There aren't three of them."

You can almost picture Barry raising one eyebrow. "Oh?"

"Yes. There are three and a half."

Step back a moment: listen to them talking. Forget everything you know about UFO Aliens, science fiction, B-movies from the fifties, and *listen*.

The two men on the radio are passing folklore. The Aliens in hangar seventeen aren't deranged science fiction; they're a modern myth, and the fact that we tell of them speaks more of us than it does of them.

Or so they'll tell you when you call. Go ahead: make that call. You can probably find an appropriate government agency listed in your phone book—there may even be a local number listed. If they do anything at all besides laugh at you, they'll tell you that that story's been going around since the late 1950s, heh heh heh. . . .

And maybe it *is* still the late 1950s in the place where Pandora lives.

Look at it as doomed Airman Ken Estes sees it, coming now at three P.M. through the security gate: this barracks is a relic fallen through time. How long has it been since anyone used barbed wire on a military installation? Razor wire's been the rage for a decade now, at least. But look, look at the fence that surrounds this place: chain-link and barbed wire, galvanized steel poles, all of them shiny mirror-metal bright as though freshly smelted.

And the barracks itself—look how it's made up (badly) to resemble the kind of gingerbread house that every American wanted in the year 1957. Like— like something from Disney World, almost, anachronistic and impossible and here it is, right here brand-new in front of him.

Something is very wrong here.

Like: there, looming high above and behind the barracks. An airplane hangar. Big one, too. Perfect mate to all the others in this long row of hangars. (Twenty of them? No, thirty, at least. They passed at least fifteen of them on the Jeep that brought them here, and look how the line goes on and on into the distance.) Here in the foreboding shadow of the hangar the barracks is especially anomalous, since there are no other barracks—let alone barracks made up to look like fairy-tale cottages—within a mile of this one. Someone planted this barracks in the shadow of the hangar deliberately, and for reasons that are not apparent to an outsider.

Ken Estes wonders for the five-thousandth time what the hell he did to put himself in the way of a fate like this.

And he knows the answer, of course.

All last spring Ken Estes dated the wrong daughter of the wrong general.

He didn't know she was a general's daughter. If he'd known he'd've avoided her out of common caution.

And he sure didn't know she was a little on the crazy side. A little? Hell, the girl was nuts. Loon crazy from growing up under a man who ran his family the way Mussolini ran Italy; "Yes *sir!*" when her daddy was there to see, and when he wasn't, there was something wild in her eyes, something like a calamity about to shudder forth any moment. . . . That was the thing that drew Ken in, of course. Those wild crazy-sexy eyes so full of intense possibility—he should have turned away from her. Of course he should have turned away from her! And he sure shouldn't have gone and gotten her pregnant, and he wouldn't have, either, but she said she was on the pill, damn it. How was he supposed to know she was lying? And now she was away at a convent or something somewhere, a home away from home for unmarried young mothers giving their children up to charity or adoption or whatever it was they did with kids these days. His *kid,* damn it, his kid he didn't know and wouldn't ever see—!

Sometimes that was the thing that hurt most of all.

Never mind what the general did to him when she told the old man who Ken was; never mind the brooding air that surrounded everything about his new billet. What hurt most of all was the fact that no matter what, no matter what he did, Ken Estes would never see his little boy. Or girl. He was supposed to be too young to feel a thing like that, Ken being only a few weeks past his twentieth birthday. But he wasn't too young, and Ken suspected that it wasn't possible to be so young that the loss of a child wouldn't keep you awake late late at night in your bunk alone stone cold alone in spite of the fact that you could hear the guy in the bunk above you snoring.

The two APs who are Ken's escorts (murderous hulking apelike men, thugs in uniform who are nothing but nothing like the clean-cut clean-living air policemen Ken has known since the day he first enlisted . . .) Ken's escorts lead him in through the barbed-wire gate, across a short walkway that looks like someone's front-lawn sidewalk, into the barracks that is a gingerbread house.

Where a clerk sits at a desk, waiting for them.

He nods to the thuglike APs, who release Ken's arms, turn, and leave as though dismissed. Ken steals a glance at the clerk's shoulder, and for a moment he's certain that the man is an airman.

An airman. In his late forties. Ken thinks, this man, why is he still here? Has he been an airman since Vietnam, working at this desk, and won't he ever escape from this assignment? And why doesn't he try? There's only so much of his life still left to him.

And looks again at the clerk's insignia, to see that he's not an airman, but a lieutenant.

A lieutenant. Sitting a the desk of a clerk. It's a stranger thing, almost, than a forty-year-old airman. How. . . ? For a moment the sense of doom Ken has felt for days engulfs him. Turns paranoid. He imagines himself trapped in this gingerbread barracks for life, unable to escape. No one able to escape, not himself, not the clerk lieutenant, no one but the APs whose eyes all but shine with that hateful light inside them. . . . Over the course of years they'd be promoted. If they did their work, kept the people somewhere infinitely upstairs happy. Because the people, officers and politicians and bureaucrats way up there—those people aren't entirely inhumane. They can imagine what it's like to be trapped for life inside a project, and they have some sympathy.

In Ken's wild paranoid fantasy, the lieutenant's

rank is a bone that the folks on high have tossed him.

Ken's wild flight of paranoid fancy is neither wild nor paranoid, but amazingly close to the mark. He will learn this soon.

But not for a while. For now he tries to pretend that the foreboding is just a thing in his heart, a longing for things he's lost, things (maybe) that he was never meant to have.

The lieutenant clerk looks Ken in the eye, and Ken sees there's something bitter, even hostile, in his expression. And mixed in with that is a strange tenderness. There's an air about him, Ken thinks—almost as though he were a professional Santa Claus.

He shakes his head. There can't be anything about this bitter grizzled old bastard reminiscent of a Santa. It isn't even possible. Yet there it is, distinctly in his hardened eye: a twinkle.

Wonders, Ken thinks. *Will they never cease?*

The grizzled clerk frowns. "It's possible you won't be altogether happy here," he says. He holds in his hands two thick file folders full of freshly Xeroxed pages. "I don't know what you did to bring this duty down on yourself. But before you throw any tantrums, remember that every single one of us here in the Pandora Project is in the same damn boat you're in. The brass who put you here aren't around to hear you swearing. The truth is that they don't even want to know about it.

"Worse, too. Every damned one of us here is as trapped as you are. And we don't want to hear about it, either."

He waits thirty full seconds for Ken to answer. But Ken doesn't; fact is he doesn't have a damn thing to say.

What he does have is a bad feeling about those folders. They look ominous as sin, and he isn't certain but he thinks he saw his name written on the filing tab of one of them.

Could be him there on the other one, too.

The clerk gives up waiting, sighs. "These," he says, "are your briefing notes. Take them into the security lounge—" he points at a windowless, austerely-furnished anteroom "—and read them very carefully. When you're done, return them to me."

Ken takes the folders, retreats to the anteroom. He doesn't bother to close the door. Quite deliberately; he has always had a measure of claustrophobia, and this room is so narrow, so spare, so hauntingly ugly—it excites his morbid fear.

He is in the narrow room for fifteen minutes when he looks up through the door to see Pandora enter the clerk's office.

Nothing he has read to that point could possibly prepare him for the sight of her. Let alone prepare him for what happens to *him* when he sees her.

As he looks at her Ken Estes knows that he is a dead man, for his entire life flashes before his eyes. No, not his life. His life is what he's already lived, and this isn't his past but his future.

His future flashes before him.

Every single minute detail of it: day after day after day forever and a lifetime here in this tiny *wrong* barracks in the shadow of hangar seventeen. His death, alone and afraid in bed in the deepest latest part of his longest night—

And he turns, looks away to avoid the sight of what he cannot bare to learn yet already knows—

But his eyes draw back to her, draw back to the strange Alien girl who is his future and his life from that day forward, and now again he sees. . . .

Sees a future and a life that is entirely different from the first. A future filled with strange ungodly yet enticing possibility. . . .

And then, abruptly, it stops. The vision ends cold in a moment, and he still looks at her, but now she is only Pandora.

Not to say she is an ordinary sight.

She looks, well, she looks human. Mostly. But her eyes are enormous; great boöpic saucerlike things five times the size of an ordinary child's eyes. Jet-black, through and through; there is no visible distinction between pupil and iris. (Is it possible her eyes are constructed after a different plan than is the human eye? Do they fill their function differently? Do they fill the function we call sight at all?) Her skin is paler than human skin—finer, thinner than the skin of an albino. And ruddy. Chafed looking with redness—but the redness isn't irritation; it's pigment.

Hair. Her hair is palish brown, and when it catches sunlight streaming in through the clerk's big frill-curtained window, it radiates a magical-strange silvery-grey sheen.

Her arms, legs, head, neck—all of them are roughly the size and shape of those of a human girl. But the proportions are off. Her gangly arms and legs, her slender neck are all too long. Just long enough that Ken's eye senses something unnatural, but not so long that it's obvious just what about her isn't right.

"Hi, Uncle Wally!" Pandora says. Her voice is Alien and earthy both at once. The voice of a little girl—only filtered through some strange device. Ken thinks he's heard a voice distorted just that way, in a movie, maybe, or on a TV show.

The voice of a little girl.

How old? Twelve? Thirteen? Maybe younger. Ken tries to place her age by sight, but it's impossible. All the little things that allow us to measure the age of a terrestrial child are . . . *different* where Pandora is concerned. There is no way to know how old she is.

Later Ken thinks back on this conclusion many times.

Many, *many* times.

"*Hel*lo, Miss Pandora. And how are you this fine afternoon?"

Something very strange is happening. Something . . . Ken isn't sure what. But it gives him a chill that raises hairs all along his scalp, his neck, his arms.

The lights—he'd swear the lights were dimming. Or are they growing brighter? No, no, it isn't the lights but the walls themselves. The paint that covers the walls has changed its hue. Grown yellower—yellow the yellow of age, of paper decaying from exposure to air. Of paint exposed to a dozen years of smoke and grit and weather.

"I'm great, Uncle Wally. What about you? Are you feeling any better today?"

The clerk smiles patiently, warmly. "As well as can be expected, dear."

And then Pandora is gone through the side door, into what appears to be a brick-enclosed courtyard.

When she's gone Ken Estes turns to the clerk and asks, "How old is she, anyway?"

The clerk equivocates. "She was born nearly forty years ago," he says, "but she's younger than that—the scientists say she isn't moving through time the way we do. And even if she were, she's an Alien, not a human—she isn't growing up the way an earth girl would." He shrugs. "Some ways she acts seventeen. Other ways she acts like a six-year-old."

The clerk, Ken notices, looks five years younger than he did a moment ago.

That isn't possible.

Of course it isn't.

Certainly Ken was mistaken to place him in his forties. This man can be no older than thirty-five.

Late in the afternoon—after Pandora has passed twice by his desk on her way to and from the courtyard—late in the afternoon the lieutenant is a young man. A teenager; look closely at his beard and see how infrequently he needs to shave.

Ken, looking up from the dreary mystifying unsettling files spread out before him, looks up to think: *A prodigy, isn't he? Only a prodigy could earn lieutenant's bars so young.*

Later, much later in the day, when the clerk will be off duty, he'll metamorphose still again. Off duty he'll undress, climb into an uncomfortable bed in a spare room. Standard air-force-issue furniture, what little of it there is. There in the shadows his face will transform into a mask of age near death, and should anyone see him they will wonder how the man is to survive the night.

But that is much later in the evening. Now it is dinner hour and Ken collects his files to check them with the clerk.

"Your duffel," the clerk says. "It arrived on the loading dock this afternoon. It's in your bunk now."

Ken Estes nods.

"Bunk 5A. New Wing. You'll have a room to yourself. We all do. Call 'em bunks, but they're rooms. Such as they are."

Nods again.

"Galley is this way."

And the clerk leads him into the barracks.

Which transforms, as they move deep into it, from utilitarian air-force drab to. . . . Well, transforms into a home. A very *American* home, with cute little thingies on the walls, throw rugs on the floors, and aging, pleasantly tasteless furniture arranged haphazardly among its rooms.

A turn in the hall, and they're in a living room—somewhere beneath the paint and gaudiness is an air-force barracks. Ken knows this intellectually, but here and now this place is undeniably a living room—they are in a living room where Pandora sits alone on a sofa watching *I Love Lucy*.

"Pandora," the impossibly young lieutenant who is also Uncle Wally says, "this is Airman Kenneth Estes. You can call him Uncle Ken if you like." He turns to look at Ken, gestures toward Pandora. "Airman Estes, this is Pandora."

Ken blinks. Something else is wrong—with the TV, this time. What. . . ? He braces himself to see his life flash before his eyes—but that never comes.

After a moment he recovers, smiles, looks into the beautifully liquid eyes of the little girl who isn't exactly a little girl.

"Just 'Ken' is fine," he says. "I'm not ready to be an uncle yet."

Pandora giggles engagingly, and Ken finds himself taken with her, enthralled. "It's okay, Ken. You don't have to be my uncle if you don't want."

In the background someone sings a Bromo-Seltzer jingle. No, no one sings: it's the television singing. Ken turns to look—and the antique advertisement ends, and now here's that kinescoped episode—no, not kinescoped, that's a pure clear picture as though from live video. But—how. . . ? Those episodes don't *exist* on tape. There's no way this can be.

The dread comes over him again. There is something very wrong with time, Ken thinks. Time is broken, or he is losing his mind.

Maybe both.

"Come *on,* Uncle Ken. Don't you want to eat?"

Ken blinks, shakes his head. Follows "Uncle Wally" into the galley.

Which isn't a galley at all, but a family dining room where thirty, maybe forty of them sit at three long tablecloth-covered tables while the cook brings out serving dishes and they all help themselves.

As he sits Ken Estes notices that Pandora, hurrying him only a moment before, hasn't yet come to join them. Her absence worries him for no reason he can name.

She still hasn't arrived when Cookie sets the serving plate in the center of their table. Nor as Ken and the others serve themselves with the enormous slotted spoon.

Still waiting, uneasy now as though he's heard one shoe drop and waits to hear the other, Ken Estes picks at his dinner. Spicy Italian sausages with peppers and onions; and pasta with vegetables—well, there's no mistaking that dinner is the handiwork of an air-force cook. None. And still there's something more to it than that; even if it's air-force food there's an extra touch about it. Perhaps because the cook is caught up in the strange homeyness of the place, and puts a little extra care into his work?

Perhaps.

There is little talk at Ken's corner of the table at the far end of the room. This for the best, no question. He needs time to think, to digest the strangeness of this place. The strangeness of Pandora.

The bleak hints from the clerk that suggest that now that he's assigned here there is no way he will ever leave.

But most of all he needs time to digest what he has read. Because the things he saw in those files are strange and unearthly indeed.

ONE

By the time Pandora followed Uncle Wally and Uncle Ken in to eat, everyone was already sitting down for dinner. The serving dishes were out and everyone was served. A couple of people were almost done eating.

She really didn't mean to be that late. She never did. But it happened more and more lately. Sometimes she thought her sense of time was going.

And maybe it was.

She looked back and forth across the galley as she headed toward her seat at the table near the kitchen door—she was supposed to sit with Cookie and the General and the scientists, but she hated that. She never liked the General, and the scientists all kept their hearts somewhere out beyond the moon, and even though Cookie was sweet, he was never much fun at dinner.

The General made him nervous.

He made Pandora nervous, too, but she didn't let him scare her.

So she stopped in the middle of the room, just like she did lots of nights, looking for an empty seat.

She found one next to new Uncle Ken.

He glanced up when she sat down next to him, and when he saw her his eyes bugged open like Deputy Barney Fife on the *Andy Griffith Show.* He looked just awful. Confused and unhappy, like he really needed to be alone.

Most times when Pandora saw someone who looked like that she let them be, because people sometimes need a little time to themselves. But Uncle Ken, well, she liked him right from the start, right from the moment she saw him working in the little room off Uncle Wally's office. And when she saw him looking all glum she just knew that she could cheer him up if she tried hard enough.

Pandora was wrong about that, the way it turned out.

Uncle Ken got all wide-eyed and scared as Pandora settled into her seat. He turned away and tried to pretend he was okay, but Pandora could see that he was shaken. She considered trying to find another seat, then decided that would only make things worse.

She put her napkin on her lap, smiled sweetly as she could, and turned to face him.

"What kind of TV shows do you like to watch, Uncle Ken?"

He sputtered, stumbled wordlessly on his tongue, frowned, set his teeth, and looked her in the eye. After a moment he smiled.

"I guess I like *America's Funniest Home Videos,*" he said. "I don't like the guy who introduces them. But the home movies are real funny."

"When's that on? I don't think I ever saw it."

Uncle Ken spent a moment thinking about that. "Sunday night," he said. "Doesn't it show the same time as *60 Minutes?*—It's around then, anyhow."

"I always watch *The Wonderful World of Disney* when it's Sunday night. I never heard about any home-movie show." She pursed her lips. "Maybe I'll try to find it this week. It sounds like fun."

Uncle Ken turned away. He twirled his food with his fork, but he didn't eat any of it.

He looked so sad. Pandora felt so bad for him. She leaned close and whispered into his ear. "Uncle Ken," she said, "your skin is very pretty."

Ken Estes rose out of his chair like a spring cut loose, and he *screamed* like she'd scared him half to death, and Pandora wanted to cry because he made her feel rejected. . . .

Not that she had much time to feel that way. In a moment there were people all over everywhere, grabbing Uncle Ken by the arms, surrounding him like in a John Wayne movie when the crowd of friends hold John Wayne and the bad guy so they won't be able to fight inside the saloon.

But Pandora wasn't any bad guy! Heck, she wasn't even fighting. And look at poor Uncle Ken, all confused and crazy-eyed and scared like somebody was about to do something really horrible to him. . . . And she thought, *No, don't you worry Uncle Ken I won't let nobody do nothing to you!* And she got up out of her seat and started yanking at all the other uncles to get them off of Uncle Ken.

"Don't you hurt my Uncle Ken!" she shouted. She grabbed Uncle Wally's left arm by the wrist and pulled back on it, trying to get him to let go of Uncle Ken.

But Pandora knew it wasn't any use. She was just a little girl, even if she was a Space Alien. Her Uncle Wally was a full-grown man.

"Stop!" she shouted. "Stop stop stop *stop!*"

That was when somebody punched Uncle Ken in the face, probably trying to knock him out or make him stop struggling or something, and it didn't do either of those things but it made his panic worse, and now he flailed wildly at everybody, and suddenly Uncle Wally was falling over backward *slam!* right down on top of Pandora—

That was when *she* panicked.

Which was a bad thing. A very bad thing.

When Pandora panicked, things . . . happened. She didn't understand it, but she knew enough to be wary of it. She knew that when it happened it was probably for the best, usually, in some ways almost like a Guardian Angel always there to stop the world and let her get off when getting off was the thing that was absolutely needful—

Night.

Suddenly it was deep dark no-lights-on-any-where-inside night, and she and Uncle Ken were alone in the big empty dining room.

That was unusual, and even strange: almost always when this happened Pandora found herself alone.

"What. . . ?" Uncle Ken sounded afraid and confused, like a small animal suddenly confronted with unknowable danger. "Where. . . ?"

Pandora crawled over to where he lay all bruised and beaten, bleeding from the nose, and took his head in her arms to hold him, to comfort him and protect him from fear. "It's all right," she said. "We'll be back in a minute or two."

He was crying a little, which was a thing that uncles always hated to do anywhere where anyone could see. "Back where? Where are we?"

"We're in the dining room," she said, "and it's . . . tomorrow morning. After midnight. Three o'clock? Four o'clock? Everyone's gone to bed, that's why we don't see them."

"How did we get here?"

"Because of me," Pandora said. "Because I'm a Space Alien. It's like—like I've got a Guardian Angel, and when I see something terrible about to happen to me, my Guardian Angel moves me out of the way through time."

Uncle Ken looked at her kind of cross-eyed. "You mean nothing can hurt you? You're always safe, no matter what?"

Pandora laughed.

"I wish!" she said. "It only works when I'm paying attention." She held up her left hand that was still mottled white and dimply with the scar from the accident last Christmas. She'd been helping Cookie make doughnuts for the holiday morning, and she turned her back to the fryer as she joked with Uncle Wally, and when she laughed at the joke he told she waved her hands in the air, forgetting the fryer was behind her. And dipped her hand into the boiling oil. "I get hurt sometimes," she said. "Sometimes I get hurt bad."

Pandora tried to sound brave when she said that. But she didn't feel brave at all. She still got queasy when she thought about last Christmas, and the infirmary, and the doctors and scientists and everything.

Uncle Ken started to ask another question, but Pandora stopped him. "Hush," she said. "Only a moment longer and we'll be back when we started."

Then deep night opened out to early evening, and they were back in the dining room at dinner, and there were twenty, maybe thirty disheveled shaken airmen standing staring at them. How long had they been away? Not more than a moment, surely.

"He's okay now," Pandora said. "Don't pick on him." The General, pushing his way through the crowding airmen, looked like he was about to argue with that. But Pandora gave him a look to let him know how mad she was, and he held his tongue.

She looked down at Uncle Ken, whose head still rested on her lap. "Do you feel better now? Do you want to finish your dinner?"

He blinked, still confused. Hesitated a moment. Nodded.

Airmen still close in all around them. Staring at them. "Don't just stand there staring at us," Pandora said. "Go eat your dinner!"

And one by one they did. Eventually even the General stopped sputtering and went back to grouse at his scientists. When he was gone Pandora stood, helped Uncle Ken up off the floor. Led him to the table, sat him down, sat beside him, and told him to eat.

Uncle Ken stared at his food for ten minutes before he managed to eat a bit of it. And even then he hardly ate at all.

After a while he leaned close to her and whispered.

"Don't you ever feel like a prisoner here?" Very quietly; so faint that Pandora could hardly hear him. His voice was too soft for anyone else to hear, and it sounded very old. Maybe he was old—that happened sometimes. "We're all trapped, you know. None of us will ever leave here."

Pandora almost laughed. "That's silly," she whispered back. "This isn't any trap. This is home."

She could see him thinking a moment. And then he said a thing that bit her: "Don't you ever want to go out—just go out and shop? Don't you ever want to see the world?"

There was an answer to that. She knew there was. It only took her an instant to find it. "I'm a Space Alien," she said. "People outside would go crazy if they saw me. Just like they do when they see Space Aliens on the TV shows. And here—everybody here is family. Everybody loves me, 'cept for the General. And he would if he wasn't so afraid."

"If they love you so much," Uncle Ken said, "then why did they kill your parents?" Pandora could see he regretted those words as soon as they came out, but it was too late, they were said, Pandora heard them and they hurt her something awful.

"Nobody killed my parents," Pandora said. "It was an accident."

Uncle Ken didn't answer right away. He looked—surprised.

"They told you that?"

And then it was Pandora's turn to be surprised.

"Yes," she said. But it felt very wrong to say it.

"Have you been to the hangar? Have you seen . . . what's inside it?"

All she knew about the hangar was the way it cast a shadow over her play yard in the afternoon. She'd never been inside it; never even seen it up close.

"They never told you?"

Her ears rang; her eyes felt very dry. "No," she said. Then her throat constricted with unease and fear, and she had to concentrate very hard to ask the next question. "What do you mean?"

Uncle Ken looked away. He looked terrified. Was he afraid someone would hear what he was saying? It wasn't possible they would; they were too far away, and Uncle Ken spoke too quietly. "Your mother is in there, Pandora. Her body is." He wiped a drop of sweat away from his forehead. "Your mother and two others."

Pandora thought she was going to cry. Just like Lucy on *I Love Lucy* yesterday afternoon, she was going to break down and start sobbing *honk honk honk* like a goose.

"My mommy isn't in any old *airplane* hangar. She died in a spaceship. I *know.*" But she didn't know, and that was a true fact; she knew only what her uncles had taught her.

"What do you think they did with her body? Left it there?"

Pandora couldn't answer his question. No matter how she tried, she couldn't even speak. Uncle Ken stirred his food a few more times, then excused himself and left.

Pandora got so depressed that she almost missed *Hogan's Heroes*, and Hogan was her favorite. Maybe she should have gone ahead and missed it. Because all through the show all she could think were *What did he mean?* and *Why did he say such an awful thing?* and *Did he just make that up to be nasty?* None of which were questions she could answer. Worse, she knew they weren't sincere: she knew Uncle Ken better than that, just looking in his eyes. Whatever motivated him, it wasn't trickery or deceit.

She hardly noticed when *Hogan's Heroes* ended and *I Dream of Jeannie* started. A darn shame. Halfway through *I Dream of Jeannie* she looked up and realized that she couldn't remember how Hogan managed to slip all those Siberian sled dogs past Colonel Klink and she really didn't understand why Jeannie was so mad at the Master this week.

And worse still, it didn't seem to matter at all what happened with Hogan or Jeannie. All she could think was *they killed my mommy killed my mommy killed her killed her killed her.* And all the while she thought it she tried to deny it.

The moment Uncle Ken had said those words she'd known they were true. How could they be otherwise? All her life people had skirted the subject whenever it came up. No one had ever gone quite as far as to lie to her outright: when she asked they'd say, *Your mother died the day she bore you, Pandora, in a terrible accident. We never knew her because she died before we reached her. But we're sure she loved you very much. Never forget that we love you, too.*

Uncle Wally said exactly those words to her a year ago, when Pandora asked what happened to her mommy. She'd known even then that there was something important that Uncle Wally didn't want to say. Whenever Pandora heard those things she tried hard as she could to put them aside; she knew there was nothing she could do about them.

But putting them aside made only so much difference, and in the end they always came back to her, no matter where she put them.

That was what she was still thinking when she fell asleep in front of the television around ten-thirty—

how strange it was to have Uncle Ken tell her what she'd always known but couldn't admit.

How the people she loved who loved her were the ones who'd murdered her mommy.

There are only three people outside the barracks who know about Pandora.

One of them is dead.

Another has never actually set eyes on her.

There are what, now, twenty years since the last time a President was briefed on the Pandora Project? Maybe more. It's been a long time since there was any reason to bring the project to the attention of anyone not directly concerned. There are always other matters to absorb the President's attention. And besides, there's been nothing to say—the project has made precious little headway in the last twenty years. Pandora and the strange field that surrounds her are as much a mystery as they were the day her mother bore her.

The time distortion that suffuses her admits—no, *demands*—a physics that our theories and hypotheses don't imagine. Time, event, and cause all twist in her presence, and in no discernible pattern.

If the Enemy could master time and space, he could devour us.

There is no question about this.

And still, look at the price of security: sixty, maybe as many as a hundred officers and airmen tied to a project that they'll never leave—not until they solve the mystery that is Pandora.

And every single one of them knows she is a mystery that they may never solve. In the decades since the project's inception there's been so little progress toward understanding that it might just as well have been for nothing.

Frustrating.

Look how the frustration has warped and molded General Belisarius Hightower. Look at him. Closely. The General is not a well man.

He stands at the very core of the Pandora Project, and has from its very first. *Forty years!* Forty years since Colonel Belisarius Hightower led the formation assigned to intercept that unknown incoming over the skies of southeast Arizona, and in some ways that night has never ended. This project is too secret for anyone—anyone but *anyone*—to ever leave it. Not even Belisarius Hightower. Forty years stranded and stifled, imprisoned; all his ambition sealed in a barracks that might as well be hell.

As the years have passed, his ambition has grown in on itself, and festered; and now the hate and anger at the circumstances that contain him suffuse him. In due course they will rule him.

All through the night Pandora dreamed nightmares— nightmares of the General and his scientists holding her, gawking at her. Prodding her with mirror-bright knives. Someday they would use those knives to cut her apart like some piecemeal toy. That was the way their minds worked, and she knew it: in their eyes she was only another windup soldier to use and command till her only worth was in disassembly, and poking and prodding among her gears.

At one in the morning Uncle Wally—metamorphosed again and looking ancient as time—found her sleeping slouched in the big fluffy armchair. He lifted her from the chair and carried her to her room. She didn't wake to notice him, but some deep part of her brain knew him, and wove him in with her nightmare: and now she dreamed her Uncle Wally held the blinding sharp knife, and she dreamed he cut her open. . . .

At two she woke screaming and alone and afraid, and there was no one near awake enough to hear her. And she climbed from her bed trembling with fear, forced herself to quiet. But no matter how she tried she could not stop the tremor. So after a while she left her room—to walk the halls, to work away the fright.

At three, still pacing, she heard her earlier self materialize in the dining hall. Heard her own voice as she comforted Uncle Ken. She went to the dining-room entry and stood invisible in the gloom, watching with dark-adapted eye the two who could not see her.

That was the first time it came to her how beautiful Uncle Ken was:

How Alien, she thought, looking at his strangely African face, *and not alien at all.*

Ken Estes is sleeping the sleep of the damned when General Hightower bursts into his room.

Not just General Hightower. Hightower and eight, ten, maybe twelve of his blood-hungry APs.

Oh God, Ken thinks, struggling to wake, to get to his feet, to salute. *What have I done to deserve this?* But what he says as he stands lifting hand to brow is this: "Sir!"

He has never had to speak to General Hightower before. If he lives long enough, pray God, he may have to yet again. It's best, given the circumstances, to be polite.

Respectful.

He knows what he's done to deserve this. Of course he knows.

Dinner. Losing his grip at mess. Letting the little-girl Alien ward off the General in public. He should've known there'd be hell to pay. Should've, hell: he did know, and had. It is only the hour and the suddenness that surprises him.

"*Estes,*" the General says. "Who the *fuck* do you think you are, airman?"

"Ah—sir. I do not understand the question. Sir."

"Don't get cute with me, *airman.* I own your life. Do you understand me, *boy?* Two days ago you disappeared off every record file this air force keeps. And that was only half the job: by yesterday afternoon our boys had purged every solitary trace that you'd ever been *born.* No one leaves this project, Estes—not ever. Not even me. Whatever you were before, whoever you were—that's over. The minute you got yourself transferred into this project, you were mine forever. And I'll kill you if I have to. Are you real clear on that?"

"Yes *sir!*" This isn't what he thinks, of course. What he thinks is something a lot more like *Jesus fucking God what have I got myself into?* Even confused and just-waken as he is, Ken Estes has sense enough not to say this out loud.

This is wise indeed, for the General has worked himself into a fine lather. His face is puffy and red; there are welts of sweat on his temples despite the coolness of the spring night; a shiny thin line of spittle descends from the left corner of his mouth toward the epaulets of his uniform.

"I've got no idea what you were trying to accomplish in the mess hall this evening, airman. But I'll tell you one thing: you're going to forget about it *right now.*"

Right now.

Ken isn't certain whether or not General Hightower expects a reply from him. He hasn't asked a question directly, but the sort of demand he's just made generally expects acquiescence. Ken finally decides that all things being equal, it's probably better not to open his mouth.

This may be a mistake.

And may not.

The General catches his breath. "Tell me, Estes," he says. "You tell me: what the fuck was it you were trying to accomplish in the canteen?"

Ken feels his face flush with blood. Partly this is embarrassment; but much more of it is terror and the sudden certainty that an awful trap is springing shut around him.

"No, sir," he says. "Ah, sir. I wasn't trying to accomplish anything, sir. I was just afraid, is all."

"Afraid of *what?*"

Ken Estes licks his lips, hesitates. What is it that

scared him? Careful, careful what he says now—if he says the wrong thing he could die. The General could kill him for the wrong words. Or is it just a bluff, what the General said about killing and no one knowing or caring? Ken doesn't want to bet his life on it one way or the other.

He is afraid of the little girl. Afraid because . . . she is like a ghost. No, the sight of her affects him like the sight of a ghost: something about her sets every hair on his body to standing on end. Or trying to. Partly this comes from the strange alienness about her—her outline, her shadow is so little different from anyone else's. And yet to look at her . . . the subtle impossibility of the shape of her face, the strange slender length of her arms, the gentle graceful motion of her neck as she'd turned to face him. All these things so unnatural as to send off ten thousand tiny alarms in the depths of his skull.

But her appearance is only a part of the reason Ken Estes lost his grip at the dinner table.

The other part is what he read about her. That first transcript there on the top of the pile—the grotesque nature of her mother; the weird, erratic, almost dangerous way time warps around her; how the air force found her in the wreck of the UFO. (Ken tries not to picture that grisly scene, tries not to think about the screaming child ripped from the eviscerated womb of its mother— No use. Of course it's no use. The scene redraws itself despite his revulsion, and he sees as he saw yesterday afternoon. . . .) All afternoon as he read dry dull report after dry dull report, the words and images from that first transcript haunted him, as they haunt him still. And dinner, when she sat next to him and began to speak—it was almost as though he was there in the desert field in New Mexico, seeing it as the first airmen to arrive saw it.

Ken suspects that the General will not respond well if he answers honestly. Worse still if he's caught in a lie.

"All this UFO stuff," Ken says. "It scares me. Isn't natural. Sir."

The General frowns. Nods. There's a look in his eyes that suggests deep thought—he's considering Ken's answer. Then he breaks out into this shit-eating grin, and he laughs deep and long and hard.

Something nasty about that laugh. Something *evil*.

All through it—it must go on, what, five minutes? ten?—all through the General's laugh Ken stands rigid at attention in his shorts and T-shirt, waiting for the world to fall in on him. Which it absolutely and unquestionably is; Ken can feel it hung suspended from a thread just above his skull.

Finally the laughter stops. "You know, Estes, that's about the funniest thing I ever heard. Here you are, brown-skinned, moon-eyed darkie bastard, and you're ascared because UFO stuff ain't natural. What's the matter—you afraid on account of the— *Aliens?*"

And then the laughter starts again.

Ken's ears are rushing, throbbing-pounding with the flow of his own blood run amok.

"Sir," he says. "General Hightower. My ancestry has nothing to do with the fact that I'm uneasy. Sir." This isn't the worst thing he can possibly say. But it's very close. Better he should shut up now, shut up and take the abuse and live—because anything he could possibly say right now will only make matters worse.

The General stops laughing for just a moment. "Don't give me that shit, black boy," the General says. "All you Negro people all—"

That's when Ken loses it. He never consciously decides to spit into red little eyes planted down inside General Hightower's bloated, piggish face. Never decides to lunge at the General nor to hit him again and again and again to try to pound that obscene pimple of a nose flush with the quivering jowls that always glisten with sweat. . . .

But he does it nonetheless. He gets in four, five, six good punches before the APs are all over him. Just restraining him, at first. Not that he lets himself be restrained. He hurts the first two APs who try to grab him very badly—one loses balance and goes flying into a wall; the other Ken grabs by the collar and hits hard in the mouth, and over and over till they've both got blood all over them—

Still, the fight doesn't last long. Three minutes, maybe four. There are a lot of the APs, and there's only one Ken. It's not what anyone would call a fair match.

To say the least.

As they drag Ken down toward the ground the General takes a handkerchief from his pocket, uses it to clean away the blood that's smeared and spattered on his face. (Some of it comes from his nose; some from the gaping split in his lip.) Turns to the largest, meanest looking of the APs.

"Beat the fuck out of him," the General says. "I don't care how far you go. Kill 'im if you want."

And then the General leaves.

There are those who will tell you that men like Belisarius Hightower do not become generals. By and large they're right: those who swear and growl and even abuse the soldiers in their command draw the wrong attention to themselves, and with damn little exception they find their careers stalling somewhere in the middle ranks.

And Hightower's career *did* stall—years ago. *Major* Belisarius Hightower retired at the end of the Korean War. Not at all of his own volition: Hightower saw himself as a career officer, and if he'd had an ounce of decency he would have had a career, too. He was a pilot with *talent,* after all, and men with talent are always in demand.

When guns are blasting, that demand is infinite, and the air force takes talent where it finds it.

But a peacetime air force has no use for sadistic

bullies. The brass retired Hightower to light colonel
and put him out to pasture as a weekend warrior in
the Montana Air National Guard.

It was Air Guard Colonel Belisarius Hightower
whose rockets tore Pandora's mother from the sky.
He and half a dozen other Montana pilots scrambled
out of Davis-Monthan that weekend that wasn't supposed to be anything but a training exercise, and if
you believe the records not a one of them ever came
back.

But the records lie. Because Hightower came
back—to a life so classified that his existence is one
of the nation's deepest forgotten secrets. All these
years he's run the Pandora Project from the inside,
without a life, without a family, without a career. The
years have made him bitter where always he was
mean, no matter how the brass who knew of him
promoted him twice across the years—first to full
colonel, ultimately to general.

Half the soldiers he ever commanded would've
told you that his meanness and his bitterness would
be the death of him. The other half would say Belisarius Hightower is too cruel a beast to die.

And God knows they could be right: if there are
things on the face of the earth so mean that not even
death will embrace them, Hightower is one of them.

It wasn't till after the ghosts faded into time that Pandora heard Uncle Ken screaming. The instant she
heard she took off running to see what was the matter—but by then it was already too late.

She didn't know that, of course. All she knew was
the sound of him screaming, terrified like a man
about to die, and she had to find him—she ran
through the galley, through the clutter-crowded
kitchen lit only by the pilot lights of the stove-top
burners. Into the pitch-dark hall on the far side of
the kitchen and around a sudden corner, where she
ran into General Belisarius Hightower.

Full tilt and both of them blind from the darkness. The impact stunned her, and it did the General even worse.

Much worse. Her shoulder, bony-hard and sharp, found him somewhere soft and flabby. In the darkness Pandora heard him bellow with agony and rage, and she had an awful intuition that in a moment he'd lash out to strike her—

He cursed, long and loud and foul. And lunged to grab Pandora. As she pulled away from him her shoulder brushed a light switch, and suddenly the corridor went bright, and the General gaped at her, stunned and terrified as a man who's just learned he's dying, and now the General—the blubbery fat coward who could never stand to look her in the eye —the General tried to grab her.

She only barely managed to avoid him, ducking in toward the wall as his arms shot past her.

"I'm sorry," she said, "I didn't mean—"

As he fell off balance their eyes met again, and the General gasped—no, it wasn't a gasp this time, but a deep hoarse terrified sound like you'd hear from the throat of a pig as it's slaughtered—the General gasped and stood akimbo staring at her, mouth open, eyes wide—

He's having a vision. He's seen me at the wrong moment, and he's having a vision because of it.

But worse than that—worse than she'd ever seen it happen to anyone before.

Something very terrible is about to happen to him.

Something horrible.

"I'm sorry," she said. "I never meant—" And she meant to go on from there, but when she reached that last word she didn't know what was to follow.

"I'll bet you didn't, you little————" and he said a word Pandora had never heard before—but no matter that she hadn't; it was a word so hard so sharp, so full of jagged consonants that she knew there weren't many things more vile.

She had to run. Now, before the General recov-

ered from the daze the vision left on him. *Had* to—
look how he grew angrier and angrier at the thought
of what he'd seen. Look at the fine threaded veins
always visible on his nose and cheeks—look how
bright they'd grown. And there, that one—burst and
bleeding on the right side of his nose, and now a
bead of blood welled up to fall. . . .

Uncle Ken screamed again.

Uncle Ken's room—that was where the General
had come from, wasn't it?

"What have you done to him?" Pandora asked.

The General smiled.

"Done to whom?" he asked, and he gave a knowing little laugh that made Pandora's blood run cold.

Uncle Ken screamed again, and Pandora knew
that she had to try to save him, no matter if she
needed saving herself. She shoved both hands into
the General's lard-bloated-tight-to-bursting belly, and
his eyes bulged with fear and in agony—like maybe
her shove had popped lose one of his overworn intes-
tines—and he grunted, groaned, folded in on himself.
Fell to the floor.

Pandora backed up three steps, took three running strides to get momentum, took a flying leap
up—

Over the General—

Flew—

But didn't fly far enough. Up, up, way up in midair the General's good right arm shot up at her, snar-
ing her ankle.

As the General pulled her out of the air.

Pulled *down* and *out,* using her own momentum
to whirl her, slam her chest-first face-forward into
the polished-rock-slick tile that covered the floor.

It didn't seem to matter much at first; the blow to
her head shook all sense of where and when and why
she was. What did it matter to hurt when she didn't
know to ache? What was a danger when she couldn't
bring herself to be afraid?

The General laughed and laughed.

He got up, climbed up on top of her. Began to beat her and beat her, who was too stunned to realize she was getting hit.

"You won't hurt me, you hear that, you little witch? You don't scare me for a minute."

Pandora didn't answer. She scarcely heard him speak.

"It was a lie, you hear? Admit it." Spittle flying everywhere. "Admit you lied!"

Later Pandora remembered the sound of his voice as he spoke, and recognized his terror and desperation. But now she lay insensate and growing more so, and neither understood the General's motivation nor understood his question.

"Admit it!"

Here his voice broke out beyond desperation and took the tenor of a psychotic. If she'd been conscious to recognize his tone, she'd have spoken, have said anything at all just to stop him—

"ADMIT!"

But she didn't hear, and she didn't see, and she didn't know. Didn't feel when the General started pounding on her, hitting her again and again wildly with all the force of his massive arms.

Didn't even notice how he suddenly realized that it made no matter how he hurt her. Didn't see him pull away his clothes and hers.

And *touch* her. Touch her in a place that violated —violated her in a way that till that moment she'd had no idea could happen. How could the flesh so quickly conduct such violation of the deepest recess of the soul?

She didn't know, then, and it was years before she understood. But it touched her still. And finally the horror of her circumstance came through to Pandora. And her special defense enfolded her, and in a moment she was a million years away from the groaning hungry wild red-eyed man on the verge of his mortality.

• • •

For a long time she lay stunned and violated, sobbing in the prehistoric wood. An hour at least; it may have stretched to three. Something down inside her nagged to say there was a thing she needed to get up and do, something that desperately needed doing— but there was nothing in her that would hear the nag. She hurt deep down at her core. Hurt physical from things inside bruised and torn and maybe some parts broken—but hurt worse inside her *self.* She felt violated, confused; her trust was broken. How could she ever go home with the threat of him looming over her?

All her life she'd ridiculed and mocked and held him at bay with a nothing but scowl, and now . . . *I've got to run away,* she thought. *Run away run away run away.*

Of course she had to run away. How could she ever go home with—with *him* there? How could she ever go there again after what he'd done?

The dim forest afternoon turned to black night in the hall that bisected the barracks' new wing.

She was way down at the far (and not yet used) end of the hall, twenty unlit yards beyond Uncle Ken's bunk.

There were APs down there, tall strong men standing guilty and bloody-handed by the open door to Uncle Ken's bunk. Someone shouted in the distance. Pandora recognized the voice—it was Dr. Conroy, one of the scientists. *"Murder,"* Dr. Conroy shouted. "Oh my dear God someone's killed him."

Uncle Ken is dead, she thought. And a whole new wave of blackness washed over her, and her blood roared in her ears as the whole world whirled horribly around her as she ran screaming and wailing into the night.

As time and the barracks cascaded all around her, stirred by that strange and special thing almost like her Guardian Angel.

If it was an angel, its wings beat powerfully that night. Her misery, her fear and grief jolted it awake, and as it flew time all around Pandora soared wild. There were no walls before her as she ran; no fence, no wire could contain her, for the instant she grew near time dissolved the barrier; or perhaps the barrier dissolved in time.

And resolved again behind her the moment she was past.

If she'd watched where she was going—oh, if she'd watched! She would have known, she would have been prepared for the sight of what she found in the hangar waiting for her timeless!

But she didn't look, and she didn't know to look, and when she stumbled on her own shoe in the strange-lit (green, green the only light was there to the left that luminescent green) strange-lit hangar and sure and sudden time stood still around her—

And she saw her mother: saw her, and knew her the moment she saw her, despite the fact that there was no physical resemblance between them.

None at all.

Where Pandora's form was vaguely like a human's, her mother's was a fleshy horror. Head, trunk, four limbs, just as Pandora, just as a human. But there all similarities ended. Her skin was pasty, membranous, the color of oatmeal and slick wet even now dead all these years—even now the mother's skin shone damply as the outer membrane of a slug. Her hands were boneless squidlike things; her elbows lay bent in the wrong direction. Her eyes were like a spider's, but clear and wet; and where she should have had a mouth there was an insect maw full of brittle-sharp pincers.

Pandora knew the *thing* lying dead in the strange light was her mother; the bond between them was blood and circumstance and deeper things unknowable; and how could she help but know her own? But no one else—none but those who lifted her from the ruptured womb—no one else could know any such thing. They were nothing alike, Pandora and her mother.

Pandora looked carefully at her mother's midsection. Swallowed hard in sympathetic pain at the soft flesh ripped by the force—

—force—

Force of what?

The force of her mother's spaceship crashing into the ground.

Her mother's abdomen lay open to the air, wide across her middle. It was clear that she'd died by evisceration.

At the sight of her mother dead but uncorrupting in the strange green-yellow light on the hangar floor, reeling from the revelation of her mother's physical nature, Pandora fragments—shatters, shivers, shudders, and goes mad. Her eyes do not close; her body does not die: rather it's her mind that ruptures.

And so she watches mad unmoving as the vision engulfs her.

This vision comes to all who see the three dead Aliens on the floor of the hangar. It is the secret history of the Occupants of Hangar Seventeen, and it is a sight folk-famous by the whispered tales of the two dozen men and women who through the years have beheld it and snuck away to freedom.

Now, watch now with Pandora as jets fly so fast through the night to intercept the impossible radar blip hurtling north from northwest Mexico.

Impossible indeed: in the years since men have had radar to watch, they've seen nothing so large move so quickly through the skies of the earth. Almost certainly the image is a ghost. An error; a radar malfunction. Some anomaly in the electromagnetic spectrum.

Perhaps. But the object is so massive—the size and shape of a stadium, to judge by the blip on the radar screen—that there's no denying it. Several squadrons fly through the air above the desert southwest, intent on defending their nation from some unknowable attack. . . .

Closer, now, closer. The first squadron of jets draws near—there. On the horizon, fiery as a city in hell speeding down toward the earth.

A spaceship, yes dear God a saucershape spaceship hurtling burning through the air askew, and something wrong inside it, there must be something wrong inside it because it isn't flying steadily but weaving back and forth drunk as though to evade missiles in close pursuit. There are no missiles. There is nothing in the air above this isolate desert but seven fighter jets and an impossible spaceship. Only one of those—there's no pursuit from behind.

The wing commander (who will one day be General Belisarius Hightower) the wing commander thinks: *Out of his mind. Whoever's flying that thing is out of his mind.*

This may be true.

After a manner of speaking.

The Alien craft (which is nowhere near so massive as it appears on radar) is piloted by no mind at all, but a computer.

And that computer has gone awry. Only a computer run amok would bring this ship to this planet, this time, this place: here and now is as impermissible to spacecraft as a hunter to a game reserve. (A hunter to a ski resort? Perhaps that analogy is better.)

Inside the ship a strange fleshy horror of an Alien (pregnant, this Alien is pregnant—look closely at the abdomen and see the child kick the kick is plainly visible in the slick-wet mucous flesh) inside the ship a pregnant fleshy horror of an Alien stoops above a smoking sparking console and pounds on it in anger and frustration.

Something is very wrong here inside this ship.

Smoke clouds the usually modulated/filtered/pristine air. The light that should be measured steady from the ceiling flickers like some primitive fluorescent tube. Everywhere doors, panels, cabinet latches hang broken and askew.

Off against the near left wall two more Aliens (who look nothing, absolutely nothing like the first) two more Aliens stir in their bunks, rise groggy from cold sleep to see fate looming in upon them.

The larger of the two—the tall chaffed-green lizardlike thing who sometimes calls himself Blaine—shakes his head and speaks. He speaks no English, but we understand him nonetheless: "What is it?" he asks. "Where have we come?"

The fleshy horror ignores him. She's too busy staring at the video screen above her head to bother explaining the obvious.

Stares for good reason: the image up above her shows a thing the ship's instruments should have warned her of a thousand miles ago.

Jets.

Primitive Earth-style fighter-interceptor jets. "God," the fleshy horror says, "God bless us all." This isn't precisely what she's said, but it comes closer to her meaning than any other phrase our language allows.

"Where are we?" Blaine asks. "When have we fallen?"

The fleshy horror spits, annoyed. "You know as much as I do." Strictly speaking, of course, that's true. But look carefully at the crease where the fleshy horror's gill meets her maw; read her expression. She guesses more than she admits.

She has a very good idea where and when they are.

And she dreads this placetime.

Blaine hasn't the wit to parse the small clues up there on the screen; there's no chance he understands them. The fleshy horror sees no reason to waste time trying to enlighten him. She grunts, spits again.

"Where?" Blaine persists. But no matter; the question is lost as the foremost of the jets passes directly above their video feed, its wings waving, the whole plane rocking on its axis as it soars—

As though its pilot were trying to signal them.

Signal them? Signal them to what end? The fleshy horror has a dim memory regarding primitive Earthen air-signal customs, but she can recall no details.

Then the point is lost because the plane has passed above them and gone.

In a moment the plane's companions are behind them, too. Will they wheel around to pursue the ship? The fleshy horror is certain that they will. She reaches for a switch at the top of the console (still smoking, most of it so obviously dead, but the sparking now has stopped), reaches for the camera control switch, turns it once, twice, three times—and, amazingly, it works. Now the screen above them shows the hindward view. Shows the lead jet turning wide arc to follow them, and in its wake the others bank in turn.

This is of no consequence. No ordinary jet can match the ship's present speed.

The fleshy horror is confident of this.

For the entirety of three seconds.

Three seconds: three seconds and the spacetime generators—the very engines that allow the ship to warp place event and cause around itself to master the vast distances around/between/among the stars— the spatiotemporal actuators begin to fail.

Spectacularly.

The actuators, of course, have no direct effect on speed and velocity. Rather they control warp travel. Which may and may not be travel at all. But while they affect neither velocity nor inertia, they might as well: they directly control the ship's position in time and space.

This is a very dangerous virtue. More dangerous still in the well of planet, where every vanishment causes a sonic boom of atmosphere in self-collision and every reemergence displacement of equal volume.

Volume of sky, almost always. But sometimes,

some awful terrible times displacement of the planet's crust.

The sonic boom is only that, a deafening clap liable to frighten those below. But the displacement is explosive: the ship's displacement-traps instantly but temporarily convert anything the ship usurps to energy—

—raw, unfetterable matter-into-energy energy—

—exactly the energy that a nuclear explosion produces.

Oh, the traps are designed to recondense that energy in the time it takes to close an eye, and to slough off the result as so much subatomic dust. But no trap is perfect, and the fail-safe is *anything* but safe. The shock is inevitable, and hard on the ship. Far worse than that on the surrounding environs.

Which is why, when the ship vanishes only to rematerialize an instant later a quarter mile from the banking jets, it tears them from the sky.

Instantly.

Terribly.

Three of them shred in midair—in an instant they're reduced to fine unrecognizable bits of steel, aluminum, and glass. Explosive force hurls most of the others to the ground nearly whole; they slam into the rocky-sandy New Mexico soil as though hurtled from heaven by a vast terrible hand.

Crushing and pulping the pilots inside.

Only one of the pilots of the downed planes survives. He does not survive the crash by long.

But one other pilot *does* survive. His plane is the only one far enough from the emergence and explosion to escape immediate destruction.

The pilot of that plane is Colonel Belisarius Hightower.

He survives on instinct: he sees the ship emerge from nowhere to destroy the jets in his command, and he takes it for a hostile act. Which (of course) it was not. But might just as well have been, for the decaying spacetime engine would almost certainly

have next brought the ship into the exact spot Hightower's plane would occupy.

Reducing him to subatomic dust.

But it does not: instead Hightower sees the threat,
and instinctively he fires a missile into the bowels of
the Alien ship.

Destroying it.

Sending the remains burning to the ground not
far outside Roswell, New Mexico.

Killing all aboard—the fleshy horror, the sometime Blaine, and Blaine's companion.

It takes the air force less than seventeen minutes to
seal off three counties in eastern New Mexico. Easier
than it sounds: in the emptiness of the desert southwest it's no great chore to police what roads there
are from the air.

It takes less than twenty minutes more for the
first transport helicopters to arrive at the scene of
the crash.

But a full twelve hours roll by before anyone
stumbles across the wreck of the Alien craft.

There may be a reason for this.

The reason may have to do with the craft itself.

Which is not found till Colonel Belisarius Hightower arrives on the scene, rattled and delirious, still
shaken from his Encounter and from the hostile de-
briefing that followed his return to Davis-Monthan.

It is dusk as Hightower steps from the helicopter.
As he does intuition seizes him—an intuition that
perhaps has waited in him for hours.

The instant his foot touches ground this intuition
begins to lead Hightower. It pulls him so thoroughly,
so irresistibly that he can think of nothing else.

An airman salutes, says, "Sir! This way, sir!"

But Hightower shakes his head. Gestures toward
a hill grey and stony forbidding in the dusklight. "No,
airman," Hightower says. "This way."

As he starts toward the hill.

"Sir!" the airman calls. "Sir! You're expected at command—"

Hightower doesn't even seem to hear. He continues, toward the hill and up its slope as the airman speaks frantically into his field radio.

The airman's name is Wallace Turner. His fate and Hightower's will wrap around one another from this moment forward as long as the two of them live.

And beyond death a considerable distance.

Five minutes and Airman Wallace Turner is rushing uphill to join Hightower.

"The others will be with us in a moment, sir. I've been instructed to ask you not to disturb anything before the science types get there."

Hightower frowns, slows ever so slightly to look over his shoulder, look the airman in the eye. "Get where, airman?"

"Get wherever you're going, Colonel, sir. That is, the science people think you know—"

"They do, eh?" And he laughs.

Unpleasantly.

The airman stops talking.

He says nothing more as he follows Hightower respectfully distant up the hill and over it. Due up, straight toward the top till they are two dozen yards from the summit. Where Hightower turns, rounding the crest rather than taking it . . .

Around, around and down into the open shallow end of a ravine, and now that ravine becomes hollow, and turns . . .

As they round the bend Hightower and the airman see what's left of the Alien spacecraft.

Spectacular.

That's the only word for it: spectacular. Like some monolithic electromechanical beached whale, mirror-metal beams and struts everywhere shattered still suggest a titanic rib cage its skin gossamer silver silk torn away to reveal—

(gossamer silver silk so thin so fine so delicate how could something so fragile thunder through the

air as this wreck once thundered, unless Buck Rogers's own force field protected it?—and if it did how did Hightower's missile steal it so easily from the air. . . ?)

—to reveal vast engines, machines, turbines, apparati, and contrivances unknown to man. Now suddenly rusting as they draw near, now even the Herculean rib-beams begin to rust visibly reddening fantastic impossible anywhere on earth much less here in the dry southwest. A cartoon, Airman Turner thinks. It's like a cartoon, to see decay happen so quickly.

Hightower does not slow as he sees the spectacular whale now begun to crumble in/at their presence. Instead he hurries, sidles in between two rusting beams

(so fast the rust so fast! look how Hightower's leather jacket, brushing up against the left beam, flakes away a cloud of dust-bright scarlet powder!)

sidles in between two beams and begins now to run—to run into the belly of the whale.

The airman hesitates.

Hesitates with cause. What is there deep inside the bowels of an Alien spaceship to make a cold fish like Hightower suddenly break out into a run? What does he know—what did he see or feel up in the air above them when this wreck still could roar through the dawn?

But Airman Turner knows damn well that his orders don't allow him to back away to wait to see . . . he knows that he must follow Hightower wherever he goes, whatever he does. And he can't hesitate for no reason forever.

So he pushes into the crumbling rust-dusty wreck and runs at a dead heat to catch up to Hightower.

Too late.

By the time he reaches Hightower it's too late even to ask him to pause to think over what he does.

(An alligator, Airman Turner thinks, there's an alligator in Pogo that looks just like those two. But

*these are larger, and realer, and infinitely more
dangerous. And less alive—look how they lie bro-
ken-backed by the impact of the fall. . . .)*

As he sees them his life begins to pass before his
eyes.

Slowly, as passing lives before eyes go, and all but
unobtrusively—he still sees the reptile Aliens, sees
Hightower, sees—

The *thing* alive still alive on the floor only just
barely alive look at its abdomen burst open to show

No, not that don't look

Instead Turner sees the ichor not the color of
blood but clear some places and other places milk-
white translucent, phlegmlike but thin as water. A
wreck the abdomen is a wreck distorted distended
the skin like tripe in the butcher's case torn away to
show—

No.

*(All this while still running slow motion on the
backpanel screen inside Turner's head is* The Story
of Wallace Turner's Life *not Technicolor but low-
budget black-and-white. The production values are
so poor, the script so dull that not even Turner is
interested in watching—and it's his life! Till finally
it occurs to him.* Life passes before a man's eyes just
before he dies. *And he thinks:* A man's life: my life,
and I'm going to die. Any moment now I'll see the
end of my life, and then I'll die. *And he waits. And
though he knows that he should be scared out of his
mind, he is not afraid of dying.)*

The Alien, though—the dying broke-open Alien is
a terror. Turner looks away from the fleshy horror
inside the Alien's gut, away from his life flashing be-
fore/behind his eyes. Instead he watches the dying
Alien *thing*—and surely it is dying, for no creature
could withstand such damage and survive—watches
the dying Alien *thing* through a wide-angle lens as it
struggles to sit, as the force of the act spills up
pushes out still more of the ichor that is the creature's lifeblood—

As she sits.

As she reaches into her own bowels.

Pain, pain everywhere around them thick thick so Turner can feel it even from an Alien—in his bones carried not by sympathy but conduction from the Alien through the walls through the disintegrating floor—and he wants to cry for no reason he can name, he wants to reach out and say, *Yes, I love you, I understand and I love*—

But he does not understand.

Hightower stands before the Alien, patient and expectant.

The roof above them is gone, turned to powder drifting past them carried on the breeze like so much red snow. In a moment the walls, the beams, all of it that's left will go, disappear into the wind. All but the Aliens and Hightower and Turner and somewhere out there behind them the watchers Turner hears now—quiet murmuring maybe two dozen people trying not to draw attention. Their eyes weigh on Turner as they see . . .

See what Turner sees.

What Hightower sees.

What Hightower has come for, has waited for unmoving:

The Alien reaches into her gut and pulls forth the tiny half-digested human baby.

Human baby girl.

No.

No please no not that.

Look carefully: Turner looks carefully despite his horror and revulsion.

Watches.

Sees.

Sees first that the baby is not a thing eaten nor digested: she is an infant newborn in her mother's arms, aborning now as Turner watches, alive and breathing suddenly to scream to be heard for fear for love of the world of the universe she screams as her dying mother comforts her shows how dear she loves. . . .

Closer, Turner sees even closer now, drinking in the mystical magical miraculous phoenixlike redemption of Life from impending Death. And leaning close he sees that the baby is not so human as at first he thought, but Alien every living bit as Alien as her mother for all that the two are impossibly unlike.

It is a mystery, Turner thinks, amazing and impossible as birth itself: that mother and child could differ as much as the child differed from a human infant. It's God who creates such mysteries—only God can make a miracle.

This is how Wallace Turner gets the religion that will comfort him all his days: by seeing the Miracle of Dissimilar Birth.

Now, here and now, Hightower steps forward to take the child. That's what he's here to do, isn't it? He carries himself with confidence, doubtless that he is summoned from so far to be father/stepfather/foster to the child he could never have foreseen. . . .

Then something goes wrong.

The dying Alien mother looks up into Hightower's eyes. And look at her expression: look what she sees when she looks at Hightower. Terror! Oh what terror she sees waiting deep inside the pit that will be Hightower's soul! And now in desperation and in fear she turns, and for the first time she sees Turner.

There's a weight that comes off her as she does. Turner all but sees it rising from her shoulders.

The mother turns from Hightower in fear and in revulsion: Turner feels it just as clearly as he felt the pain. Turns from Hightower and leans forward to hand her only beloved child to Wallace Turner to love and to shelter from this day forward.

Turner hesitates only an instant before he reaches out to take the infant.

(*Touch, the cold touch of the Alien mucous slime from her bowels covers the tripe tentacles that are her hands. . . .*)

The child's crying stops. Utterly and immediately.

Turner doesn't notice—he can't hear anything but the thunder that detonates inside his ears as it settles on him that his doom is sealed forever. Nonetheless he takes Pandora from her mother's arms, lifts her to his heart to safeguard with the strength of his arms and breast.

Up: up above them as Turner looks through the rusting lacework to the sky for mercy he sees the impossible green glow engulf everything that remains of the ship.

Rust walls, struts, what paper-thin sheets remain of the bulwark and the superstructure—all of it green, green, impossible electric green.

Like strange electric fire caught hold of everything.

Oh look, look now to see what happens when the ship's generators blow, blow and vaporize exactly and precisely as they were designed: see how the ship makes lifeboats of its crew:

Look at Pandora, and see your future flash before your eyes.

Look at the dead lizards (one of whom was once and sometimes known as Blaine) look at the dead lizards and see your past.

Look at the fleshy horror and see a mother reached forward across the crest of now to comfort her babe protected in the arms of a creature alien to her—

Look how the fleshy horror shudders, sighs.

And dies.

Look at her now and see your life.

Look for the ship, the strange green light, the rust everywhere sanguine dust only a moment ago:

And find nothing. Nothing at all.

Only three dead Aliens, lying in the New Mexico dust.

A screaming unhuman child mourning for the mother that she hardly knew.

And seventeen—not one more—human Earthen people, watching in wonder terror and amazement.

Maybe it was fair and maybe wasn't, but all Pandora thought—all she *could* think—as she rose up out of the scene of birth and death was *Mommy Mommy Mommy they killed my mommy killed her killed her killed her.*

And oh but she grieved, God how she grieved for the mother who'd loved her so. She blinked and blinked away the welling wet as her eyes and her heart flooded so full of the scene that she could bear no more of it.

And so again she ran blindly undirected through place and when, and the walls of the hangar and the gates and the fences and the barricades that surrounded the base were nothing to her but flotsam fell away in time.

Oh how she ran!

As she ran the seasons seemed to wrap around her: now cold icy winter came on the summer night to echo the winter that engulfed her heart; now shift and a chill autumnal windstorm, blustery to spatter sting-cold rain against her skin, thundering and lightning so close to amplify the dread that filled all the possibilities before her.

If there'd been anything left of her heart for despair, it surely would have overtaken her. But there was no room for despair, only grief. And Pandora ran. And as she ran the seasons changed again and again and again.

Half an hour she ran as the time would have passed for her if she'd had bother to account it. Half an hour through the Ohio pinewood, sloughing through the pathless deep of the forest heedless of the ten dozen trip-trap broken branches and ruts and soggy dunes of pinestraw that didn't matter because time moved them from her as she neared.

Her wind deserted her at the edge of the forest,

where the woods met a cornfield near an infinite railroad track.

She never meant to collapse by the door of the toolshed. But she had no choice about it: she reached the door, and reflex-reached to touch the blistered green paint where it showed through to weathered-raw grey wood, and almost it seemed the wood was to her like a grounding rod.

Maybe it was.

Or maybe not: maybe the harsh touch of splintered wood distracted Pandora just long enough to let exhaustion steal her momentum.

Either way it happened: her legs fell out from under her, and she crumbled to the ground like an empty cloth sack.

I'm gone, Pandora thought. *Gone gone gone.*

She had to get up and run again, she thought. If she didn't run they'd find her. But where was she running? She thought about her mommy, about running into the waiting arms of her mommy, but Mommy was dead in the hangar, and when she thought of Mommy she wanted to cry, but she knew she couldn't let herself do that. So she closed her wide round eyes tightly as she could, drew up her gangly-long arms and legs, and curled herself into the tightest roundest ball she could possibly be.

And held tight as she could. And still as she could.

And she thought: *My mommy is dead. But what about my daddy?* Everything had a mommy and a daddy, and that had to include a Pandora, didn't it? *If I run far and fast,* Pandora thought, *maybe he'll see me.* He'd see her, she thought, and ride down on his magically shining spaceship to save her forever from horrible people like the General and the Scientists and the hateful Air Policemen who only paid attention to what the General told them.

All she had to do was run hard and for a long time. And make so much fuss that her daddy would see on the news from his spaceship ten quintillion miles away.

He'd have to, wouldn't he?

Wouldn't he?

She looked up from her gloom to see an eastbound train rolling slowly over the tracks at the edge of the cornfield.

Pandora looked into the distance, trying to see the end of the train. But couldn't; for all she could tell that eastbound train went on forever in both directions.

If I could ride that train, she thought, *would it carry me into forever?*

Slow now almost to a stop, and before her was an open empty boxcar with the words GULF+WESTERN stenciled on its side.

It wants me to get on, she thought. Which was dead wrong and she knew it because trains don't want people to do anything—they don't have it in them to feel *want,* or anything else. *Fate wants me to get on that train.*

And who was Pandora to question fate? She ran to catch the stalled train, and climbed aboard just as it lurched back into motion.

TWO

The essence of the modern myth is truth.

Oh, yes, there are those who will tell you that falsehood distinguishes Urban Legend from the ordinary tale passed by word of mouth—but those who say such things miss the underlying point. Unwritten lore is not two different things (one true, one false), but one: a single conduit for information, one most apt to carry color and fable, wonder and myth—and fundamental truth.

For despite the way a tale passed from one to another to another carries factual detail so badly, it carries essential truth very well indeed.

The tales that surround the Canaan, Pennsylvania, shopping mall make very good examples: the mall's maintenance men (it's said) tell of meeting the devil again and again deep down inside the mall's farthest basement.

The story is a lie, plain and simple—anyone could tell you that. Whether they'd been to the mall, whether they'd examined its basement, whether they'd spoken to the maintenance men or not.

But look at the truth beneath that: look how the story tells of deep basements that grow so thoroughly forgotten that their contents are mystery even to those who filled them. And who among us has not known a just such a basement. . . ?

Macdonald.

James Douglas Ignatius Macdonald was born and raised in Westchester County, New York—back in the days before the whole place collapsed on itself and became a simple extension of the Bronx. When he lived there the place was America—Middle America. Middle-class, middlebrow, Middle Atlantic: it was a place of houses and apartments and shopping malls like ten thousand other places across the face of the country, but greener and hillier and more beautiful than most.

Westchester County is a long way behind Macdonald as he sits in the helicopter, engages the quick-release hook of his wide leather safety belt. And still it haunts him—look, look out at the distance as his helicopter rises above Wright-Patterson Air Force Base. Look at the houses there in the north, visible under the streetlights that surround them—are they part of the base or a part of some suburban development? It doesn't matter. Most on-base housing at U.S. bases around the world looks like suburban America.

If America haunts Macdonald, the problem at hand looms over him like a hammer of doom. Something serious is wrong—something very, very serious. Something Macdonald never heard of. Something he never imagined.

All by itself that fact is a terror. There shouldn't

be anything this important that Macdonald doesn't know—it's his job to know things like this. His only function: to be down and inside the bowels of the government's most terrible secrets, and to know them, to have and to hold them, for better or for worse.

Of all these secrets, Macdonald himself may be the most terrible. He is repository to all of our most fearful sins: there are things he knows that could destroy the nation.

Things that could destroy the world.

Two hours ago Macdonald learned the truth about the Urban Legend concerning Space Aliens and Roswell, New Mexico. Learned that—well, not that the legend is true, because it isn't, not exactly. Not down to the last detail. It isn't even substantially correct—not the versions that Macdonald has heard. But what Macdonald learned two hours ago tells him that the legend grew from real events and honest facts. And that the events that gave it rise persist in their effect to this very day.

Quietly, quietly. Till this evening hidden deep in the bowels of the air force.

Events are already seriously out of hand. Macdonald learned the facts only moments before the vice-chair of the House Military Oversight Committee. Too many people already know what's happened—it's an odds-on bet that someone calls CNN before dawn. And once this story hits the news . . . Macdonald shudders, imagining angry millennialist mobs rioting in the streets.

The image terrifies him.

There. A floodlit streak of whiteness cutting through the woods at the south edge of the base.

Macdonald leans forward, taps the helicopter pilot on the shoulder. Points at the whiteness when he has her attention.

"There," he says. "Get me down as close to the white as you can." He isn't sure if the pilot can understand him over the rotor's din, but she seems to get the message; they ease down toward the woods. Land just inside the fence that surrounds the base.

The white is frost and snow, now melting in the warm June night. There are traces of it on this side of the fence, mostly glistening bits of frost melted into dew.

But the bulk is on the far side, in the pines.

High spring in Ohio—spring, hell; it's June, and in a few days this will be summer—high spring in Ohio and the forest is covered with snow. It's amazing. Full-winter snow, thick snow covering the pine boughs, thicker on the forest floor. Eighteen inches deep? At least that. Some of the drifts lay piled considerably higher.

The helicopter settles to the ground, settles through the snow. Its rotor slows, quiets. Macdonald takes a last look around him through the windows— looks carefully all around him through the helicopter's wide windows—pulls the door open and steps out into the snow.

It's melting, he thinks. He can feel it through his boots as he steps into the snow: cold and wet, soggy. The surface may *look* white, fresh, and pristine, but down inside the snow is slushy as an hour-old Sno-Kone.

He blinks, blinks again. Why should it surprise him that the snow is melting? The night air all around is warm and summery. *Of course* it's melting; the wonder would be if it weren't.

Still. Strange, strange. This snow is real; the winter *did* rip though here not more than two hours ago.

Macdonald steps through the wreckage of the fence. The sentries that stand on either side of it do not challenge him. Do not so much as look him in the eye. Why are they afraid. . . ? Someone has warned them. About Macdonald. Made him sound like the bogeyman.

It isn't good that they let him pass entirely unchallenged. It would be all too easy for a well-informed nut to pretend to be Macdonald.

"Airmen!" Macdonald says. "Look sharp!" There isn't time for more than that. If there were he might let into them, let them know that standing sentry means *standing sentry*.

But there is no time. Macdonald hurries into the melting snow, already trampled through and through with tracks that show the passage of at least three dozen airmen, APs, officers, Lord only knew what security personnel. Scientists, too, most likely. Macdonald has a dozen of his own on their way here. And there are those attached to the project, and almost certainly others sent in by people panicking up along the chain of command.

Yolen waits for him fifty yards from the fence, near a thicket of holly. She stands watching over the shoulders of a half-dozen technicians who probe, poke, prod, and clip away at the nearer holly bush.

When she sees Macdonald she nods to him, gestures at the techs with her clipboard. Explains. "She must've run into the holly," she says. "There's blood on the leaves, and it isn't human. Isn't—almost isn't *blood*. If we didn't know about her, didn't know what to look for, I don't think we'd have called it blood."

Macdonald nods. "Much blood? Is she hurt?"

Yolen shakes her head. "Hardly scratched, I'd say."

Yolen.

Yolen is perhaps the most important person Macdonald has in his employ. She has a sharp wit, a sharp tongue—and a sharp eye for things out of kilter. She can spot the *little* things that tell when something larger is gone awry. She is the one who noticed Airman Kenneth Estes suddenly disappear from the record files. She is the one who nearly managed to trace his disappearance to its root before. . . .

Before Pandora made her break, and turned the world on its ear.

· · ·

Pandora stared all night out the open boxcar door, marveling at the wonder of countryside that rolled past her. All her life she'd read and listened and watched TV, but that didn't—*couldn't*—show her what she saw with her own eyes. The wheat fields and the forests and the rivers and the nighttime cities were wonders she couldn't have imagined before she'd seen them in the flesh. What camera could tell her how even in the dark there were hints of color and hue in the sphere of passing night lamps? Who could ever explain the subtle texture of the leaf that blew in on the wind and settled near her hand? Amazing! Incredible! Sensual as the air rushing through the open door, pressing on her skin; luxurious as the scent of grass that filled her breathing; rich as the taste of pollen on her tongue.

All those things and more—so much new experience that it overwhelmed her. After an hour and a half she grew so tired that she slumped to the boxcar floor.

And lay there, exhausted, long into the night.

Sometime after sunrise the gentle steady rocking of the train lulled her to dreamless sleep.

It's the pounding on the door that wakes Ken Estes from the dead—

No. Not dead. He never died. He took a beating that should've killed him, but he survived it. He is alive and breathing, and if he hurts like death warmed over—well, what does it matter so long as he is alive?

Alive! *Alive* Sweet Jesus he's *alive!*

He's alive and sleeping—deep, deep asleep—in the infirmary when the MI types come for him.

The infirmary. Dark and quiet in the middle of the night, and then come the military intelligence officers, MIs banging on the door and kicking it in when no one answers, and right away they start in with the questions. . . .

And they ask them, and ask them, and ask them

over again. Ken answers as best he can, but what does he know about any of this? Two days ago he was a no-account airman on a base two thousand miles away.

He doesn't know a goddamn thing.

And still they ask: two hours they ask.

Two hours and more than once in the course of that time the biggest of them looks like he's going to start rearranging Ken's face—and then there comes a knock at the door.

The MIs look from one to another to another, and back again at Ken. For half an instant Ken is afraid they'll kill him or something—look how the eyes of the tall one get wide and desperate as he glances at the door—but then the knock comes again, and the one in charge (short, dark-haired, large hooked nose) shakes his head. "There's no time. Don't even think about it."

And he turns, and answers the door.

In a moment all five of the MIs leave the room.

The last of them (ever courteous) turns off the light as he closes the door behind him.

And Ken is alone again. Alone and in the dark—but that's nothing new, is it?

In the dark Ken hears muffled shouting from the next room over. It's Hightower shouting, isn't it? Yes, of course it is. Ken would recognize it anywhere: he could never forget anything about that terrible pig-like man.

Get away from me, Hightower shouts. *Haven't you done enough already?* And then he screams. *Be careful where you stick me with that thing, or I'll tear your balls off. I swear to God I will.*

Then Hightower is silent for a good long while. When he starts shouting again, his tone is very different. Defensive, almost. *I told you,* he shouts. *That goddamned Alien bitch beat me to within an inch of my life. What else do you want to know?*

More silence. And then Hightower roars like a vast and malign blubbery predator issuing a challenge. *I'm going to kill her, you hear me? I'm going to tear that little bitch limb from limb!*

Then there's another knock on the door of the dark room, and this time there's no waiting for an answer: the door opens slightly, and Ken sees a figure silhouetted in the hallway light.

He hears a woman's voice, low, quiet. But there's nothing soft about this quiet voice.

"Macdonald wants to talk to you," the woman says.

And she closes the door.

Pandora.

The very fact of her still amazes Macdonald. He lives in a harsh, unkind world where right is a thing a body has to cut out of events and shape for himself; a world where horrible people do horrible things and decent folk have to work hard to put a stop to them. But it is a rational world, no matter how harsh. It certainly isn't a place where bizarre UFO Alien Urban Legends come to life, escape their keepers, and set off to see the world. God forbid! But He has not forbade. Pandora is real, and she is loose, and Macdonald has an awful awful headache.

A big part of him hopes that this is just a dream; that he'll roll over and wake up in a moment and discover that last night's beer and pizza at Mario's have given him bad dreams. And go back to his life, and his world, and the equilibrium that stood instead of peace for him. But hard as he hopes it'll all just go away, he knows that it won't.

"Do we know where she is?"

Yolen looks up from her clipboard. Shakes her head. "The snow ends on the far side of the hill. No trace of her after that. Nothing the dogs can find, either—here or there. If Pandora has a scent, the dogs can't find it."

"Are we sure she came this way? Did she leave tracks in the snow?" As soon as he hears himself ask that question Macdonald thinks it's stupid. How

could she *not* have come this way? How else could
the snow have got here?

But Yolen answers politely. If it occurs to her to
scoff at the question she keeps that to herself. "Yes,
she left clear tracks in the snow. It wasn't hard to
follow her track by eye before, so many of them
trampled through the snow."

"We'll need a lot more people, then. Enough to
search this county end to end, if that's what it takes.
We need to get her back in custody before anyone
sees her."

Yolen nods, and Macdonald knows she'll do exactly as he asks—and more, if that is what it takes to
do the job. But even as she does Macdonald has an
awful feeling.

A terrible, terrible intuition.

That Pandora had already escaped from them entirely, and that nothing he or Yolen or anyone else
could do could ever contain her again.

Macdonald doesn't show up right away. It takes him
a long time to get to Ken, in fact—so long that Ken
dozes away on the examination cot, and wakes with
a sudden start when he hears voices in the hall.
Alive! he thinks. *Dear God, I'm alive!* This is at least
the third time in the last ten hours that Ken Estes
wakes to the sudden joyous realization of life. Last
night, in his room with the APs—he wrote himself off
last night. And now every time he stirs in his sleep it
amazes him that he is alive to wake to stir.

The door opens again, flooding the room with
light. "Airman Estes?"

A nurse! Oh my, not just a nurse, but a gorgeous
tall fair-haired Valkyrie of a nurse who makes Ken
Estes think—

—think—

No, he doesn't want to think of Anna.

Or his daughter.

His son?

He isn't sure about the baby, and hell, the baby

isn't even born yet. Anna's only four months' pregnant, and does it matter whether a baby is a boy or a girl when it's still a fetus?

Ken isn't sure.

And he doesn't want to think about the question anyway. Or about Anna. And he especially doesn't want to think about Anna's father, General McNamee. The goddamn fucking asshole bastard who tossed Ken into the Pandora Project and erased all sign that he'd ever lived from the face of the earth.

—except maybe dead. It would be nice to think about General McNamee dead. Reassuring, even.

Pleasant.

"Time for your medication, Airman Estes."

"Oh. Sorry. Not more painkillers, I hope? I'm woozy as it is."

"Just antibiotics. They want you clearheaded when you talk to the congressmen."

Congressmen?

"Say what?" This is a bad time to interrupt the nurse, as it happens. The syringe in her left hand is very very large, and frighteningly sharp. "I thought the Congress didn't know about Pandora."

"Ha!"

Jab!

Twist!

"Ouch!"

"Sorry. No, everybody knows about Pandora now. Almost everyone. The project broke open last night. Pandora is gone. There's no way it'll ever get back under security. If they don't find her soon the whole damn world will know what Hightower was up to."

Hightower?

Pandora?

"I don't understand," Ken says. "What happened last night?"

The nurse doesn't answer, but that doesn't make much difference: even the little bit she's told him is enough to change every fact that shapes Ken Estes's life, utterly and irreversibly.

For the second time in less than a week.

Then, just to twist him a little farther out of context, the world throws another curveball at him. He looks up, to read the nurse's badge, so that he can remember her by name.

And the badge says DR. SHERWOOD SMITH.

Macdonald keeps thinking of the old one-line putdown—*Who died and left* you *in charge?* The whole thing is such a stupid joke, exactly because in so many ways it *is* a joke.

Because somewhere in the late sixties someone *did* die, leaving Hightower in charge. Hightower and McNamee.

And the two of them had taken it on themselves to run the whole damned Pandora Project as a classified personal fiefdom.

Oh, there'd been regular reports from the both of them—thorough reports, too. They'd gone into the files in Washington, just as they ought to.

And no one had read a one of them. Not since Chris Imershein and both of his closest aides died in that helicopter crash in '67. Far as Macdonald can tell the more senior of Imershein's aides—Mitchell— was the one who'd had the billet of reading Hightower and McNamee's reports. And Imershein was the one who'd assigned it to him.

And somehow in the confusion after the crash, well, quite a few projects had slipped out of oversight.

Most of them had run their course by '72. By '76 the Pandora Project was the only one still active. That's the trouble: Pandora is a project to last lifetimes. Longer! Three soldiers have *died* inside that barracks here on Wright-Pat—not from hazard or mischance or disease.

They died of old age.

Macdonald shudders at the thought of living out the rest of his days inside a classified barracks. He doesn't like it, not one whit. Who the hell do Hightower and McNamee think they are, tossing people into that barracks and throwing away the keys? If Macdonald has anything to say about it they'll both spend the rest of their lives in Leavenworth.

Macdonald still isn't sure how they wiped Estes's records, the records of a dozen others. But Yolen is on that bead; they'll know soon enough. And when they know there'll be hell to pay.

They turn a corner, and suddenly they're in somebody's living room.

No, no, they're in the barracks. But this room looks for all the world like someone's living room, even though it's only the TV room of an air-force barracks.

"This way, sir."

There really *is* something homey about the inside of this barracks. Macdonald wonders just how deep that homeyness goes—how closely have these people knit? Are they bound together like family—and if they are can Macdonald trust them to obey orders, even if those orders might not be in Pandora's best interest?

Macdonald is pretty sure he can't.

Across the living room, down a long corridor lined with offices.

Pandora dreamed a prescient dream as she slept inside the boxcar.

She dreamed that she stood high on a mountain, watching the sky as a vast Space Alien armada spun down from the stars to rescue her.

So beautiful, those Space Alien UFOs—like a meteor shower raining down from the sky, and all for her, all for her and no one else . . .

Now fighter jets shot up from the earth to ward the armada away. But it was no use; the UFOs cut them from the sky, cut every last one of them from the sky as the Aliens sailed down to greet her—

And then her dream became a nightmare as the armada sailed right past her, left her standing on the mountain as they soared low over the earth to bomb and shoot and blast until they tore her world asunder.

Macdonald comes for Ken Estes before the congressmen can get him.

Macdonald.

Macdonald is a scary, scary man. Ken Estes knows that the moment he sets eyes on him: there are secrets inside that man. Things more terrible than most folks can imagine.

It does not please Ken that he's lived to draw this man's attention.

"Hightower says you hit him, Estes. He says you threatened to kill him. Is that true?"

That's how Macdonald introduces himself: with a question. As if to say, *Never mind who I am. I'm no concern of yours. Tell me what I want to know quickly and you may live long enough to see the sun rise.*

Ken wants to lie. He wants to deny that he did anything at all; wants to holler for a lawyer and close up like a clam. But he has an intuition that he'd live to regret even more than he regrets now if he does any of those things.

"I hit him, sir." He tries to recall what he said when he hit him, but he can't remember a word. "I'm not sure what I said when I did it."

Macdonald scowls. "Hit him? That's all?"

"I hit him more than once, sir. And I spat at him."

"I don't believe you, Estes."

Ken's heart begins to race. This is going to be the end of him—real soon now it's all going to be over. Hightower only *thought* he could get away with murder; Macdonald could do it in a moment.

"Estes," Macdonald says. "I want to show you something."

And he turns and starts toward the door. Opens

it, turns back to look Ken in the eye. Waits for Ken to realize he's supposed to follow.

Which takes a moment, mostly because Ken *really* doesn't want to go anywhere with Macdonald. Not at all.

But he knows he has no choice. He follows Macdonald out of the infirmary, through the barracks, most of the way back to his bunk.

Not good.

Because long before they get near it Ken knows damn well where they're going, and of all the places he'd rather not go with Macdonald this is the one he'd rather not go to most of all. Because he knows goddamn well what Macdonald is taking him to see.

The blood on the walls.

Ken doesn't want to see the blood on the walls. Last night as Turner and Simmons helped him to the infirmary, they led him through this hall, and he saw the blood—everywhere, back and forth across the walls, spattered like spray paint; all over the floor in thick crusting puddles; drippy clots of it congealing on the ceiling . . .

They're here.

Joy.

Macdonald stops. "Look at it," he says.

Ken Estes wishes he were someplace else. He doesn't want to see this. He didn't want to see it last night, he doesn't want to see it now, he doesn't want to see it in his dreams for the rest of his life, but he knows he will.

But an order is an order, and Macdonald is not a man Ken wants to disobey.

Ugly.

The blood has dried since last night, but otherwise the hall has changed very little. No one has tried to clean the mess; there's a narrow path of footprints down the center of the hall, but otherwise the mess in undisturbed.

"What did you do to him?"

Do to him?

Ken looks at the smeared patterns in the blood on the floor—he's seen a pattern like that before. But where?

Like the outline of a body, he thinks. A slight, thin body, gangly and just a little bit out of proportion. *And footprints—straddling the hips.* He tries not to think about what this means, but he can't help himself. And what he thinks disgusts him.

Horrible.

Repugnant.

Hightower is a loathsome pig. *I'm going to kill that pig if I ever get the chance,* Ken thinks. *I swear to God I am.*

"You're telling me you didn't do that, Estes?"

What?!

Ken looks Macdonald in the eye. The question makes him furious. He's losing control of himself again; he can feel it. He wants to, wants to—

"Sir," Ken says, "if you think I had anything to do with that," he says, pointing at the all-too-obvious pattern on the floor, "if you think I had anything to do with that, sir, you're out of your mind. Sir."

For the longest moment Macdonald stands there eyeing him coldly. He's going to come down on Ken like a load of bricks—Ken knows damn well he is. Ken's ears roar as he waits for Macdonald to respond.

And then something changes. Macdonald's expression shifts, his mood swings. He laughs—ruefully.

Slaps Ken on the back.

"Come on, son," he says. "Let's get the hell out of here."

Pandora woke in a wasteland.

That's what she thought of when she looked out to see the place: *The Wasteland,* by T. S. Eliot. Had he been here, years and years ago, to see these grit-smudged factories planted in this barren soil? Look how the tall stacks billow green-grey smoke: had he seen that, too? Seen the desperate ugly weeds that

struggle to thrive in every sheltered spot? It must be,
Pandora thought. Surely this place was the Wasteland, and its secret name was inspiration.

Inspiration to get her off the still train and *out* of
there, quickly as she could. She climbed down out of
the boxcar, saw the filthy trash-cluttered railroad
yard off to the right, and in every other direction
factories uglier and uglier as she looked from one to
the another.

Every direction but one.

Off in the left distance there was a horizon band
of green.

Pandora knew that strip of green. How could she
not know it? Even if she'd only known the world only
through picture-book encyclopedias and *National
Geographic* and *Mutual of Omaha's Wild Kingdom,*
the place on the horizon nestled near her heart—just
as it nestles near the heart of every living thing
across the face of the world.

It was the forest.

The beautiful forest.

The Emerald Forest at the far edge of the Wasteland.

When Pandora saw that Emerald Forest in the
distance, she knew that was where she had to go.
Some choices are like that for everybody, aren't
they? You come to them and you make them because you have to, because there's no way to deny a
thing as beautiful as an Emerald Forest once you've
seen it.

But even as Pandora started toward it she knew
she was making a terrible mistake.

And she was right.

Macdonald leads Ken into a dark room, and just inside the door he stops and whispers. "Wait here," he
says.

Ken does as he says.

There is only one light in the room—an interrogation light, a spotlight that shines into the face of General Belisarius Hightower.

Ken flinches when he sees Hightower. Something terrible has happened to the General; something unimaginable and grotesque. The skin of his face is stitched and swollen, crusted with bits of scab and ichor, tinted grey blue. Deep in the crevices of his sunken pig eyes the blood has gone black and necrotic—his eyes look like the eyes of a corpse.

A corpse.

But Hightower isn't a corpse: he's quite alive. He glares belligerently when he hears Macdonald enter the room. "Jake," he says. "That's you again, isn't it?"

Macdonald doesn't answer right away.

Ken is still gaping at Hightower. Somebody broke his nose, didn't they? Look, look there at the stitches up the left side of it—as though someone hit him hard enough to rip it halfway off his face.

There's a splint on his left arm, and inside the splint there are bandages soaked bright red with blood. More bandages on his ribs; an IV feeds into the crook of his right arm.

They thought I did that? Ken tries to imagine himself pounding and pounding Hightower until his nose slides away from his face—but he can't. Can't even begin to imagine.

"Tell me about Estes, Hightower," Macdonald says. "Did he do this to you? Why did he do it?"

"He hit me," Hightower says. "I told you that already."

"Why did he hit you?"

Hightower shrugs—or tries to. He winces as his arms moves inside its splint. "Search me," he says. "I never could figure why boys like that do anything." He gives a little laugh, *heh heh heh heh,* as he says that.

Ken wants to hit him. Never mind how beat up the bloated pig of a man already is; Ken wants to grab him by the throat and start pounding—

"Why did he hit you?"

"*I don't know,* Jake. Why don't you ask me a question I can answer?"

Goddamn liar, Ken thinks. *I'm going to kill him.*

"Okay," Macdonald says, "Pandora. Where is she?"

Hightower snorts derisively. "Who?"

"Pandora," Macdonald says. "Who the hell do you think I mean?"

What's left of Hightower's uniform is an awful mess. His shirt is torn and bloodstained; his belt is twisted; his fly isn't all the way up.

"Alien bitch," Hightower says. "I don't know where the hell she is."

"What did you do to her, Hightower?"

Hightower looks away from the light. He lies. All three of them know he's lying; there's no way anyone could hear him and help but know he's lying. "She was running away," he lies. "I tried to stop her. She got away." He shudders. "Then she came back. And hit me. She's strong, you know that, don't you, Jake? She acts like she's a little girl, but she's powerful— stronger than ten men. And she's a killer. Ask the scientists; they know how strong she is. She's a bloodthirsty killer, Jake. She's going to kill someone if we don't stop her."

Macdonald doesn't say a word.

"She damn near killed me, Jake."

Hightower's on the verge of crying, isn't he? Ken is amazed. An hour ago he couldn't have imagined what he's seeing now, but here it is, and he's seeing it: ruthless bloodthirsty hard-hearted Belisarius Hightower, blubbering like a baby.

Ken wants to laugh, but he knows he doesn't dare.

"What did you do to her, Hightower? I'm going to find out, one way or another. Why don't you tell me now—that'll make it easier on both of us."

Hightower sobs. "I didn't touch her," he says. "I swear to God I didn't." The room gets so quiet when he says that, and that's only right, isn't it? No one should ever take an oath like that in vain, and all three of them know it perfectly well. "I'm going to get that little bitch, Jake, I swear to God I am."

Macdonald laughs in spite of himself. "The hell you say," he says. He sounds furious. "You aren't going to get anything. You're going to wait right here, and when this is over you're going to a court-martial."

And he turns to leave the room, and Ken follows him out into the hall. Outside, Macdonald locks and bolts the door behind them.

When he's done he turns to face Ken.

"Do you believe that, about Pandora?" he asks. His eyes measure Ken as he speaks, watching his reaction to the question. "Do you think she beat him?"

Ken hesitates. He wants to say no, she couldn't've, she's just a girl, just a nice little kid who watches *I Love Lucy* and *The Little Rascals*—but when he starts to say those things he knows they aren't true. No, they're true, but they aren't right.

"I don't think she would," Ken says. "But Hightower . . ." And he keeps trying to find the words, but he can't make sense of them. Hightower is a snot-sucking pig. There's something *right* about beating him half to death; Ken would like to do it himself. "I don't know. Look at that pig," Ken says, forgetting all about the fact that he's talking about an officer to a man who, while he wears civilian clothes, carries himself with an officer's authority. "Can you look at that pig without wanting to kill him? Can anybody? Maybe she could. Maybe she did."

That's when Yolen comes running down the hall toward them, looking agitated and—scared? Scared out of her mind.

Fear is a strange thing to see on Yolen's face. It's almost as though fear doesn't belong there, as though events so rarely frightened her that the whole emotion was unaccustomed.

"Macdonald!" Yolen shouts. "I've been looking for

you everywhere. Satellite report—they've spotted
her. The train that rolled past here last night just
stopped in a railroad yard in Pennsylvania. The eye
spotted someone getting off the train in the rail
yard."

The Emerald Forest was even farther away than it
looked, and it looked *very* far away. Partly that was
because Pandora didn't have any experience with
distance—she'd spent all her life inside a barracks.
She'd seen the sun from the walled courtyard that
was partly her playground and partly Cookie's garden. But there was no distance in the courtyard. No
way anyone could see in, no way Pandora could see
out.

Except for straight up at the sun.

But it wasn't *just* inexperience that made the distance hard to judge. Anyone would have got it a little
wrong. Because the distance between Pandora and
the Emerald Forest was so empty, so blighted by industrial pollution, that it seemed less than it truly
was.

And it was a lot, too. Pandora walked miles and
hours and still seemed to get nowhere. Walked until
her heavy boots grew hot enough to bake her feet; till
her back ached so bad she wanted to lie down in the
dirt and moan. But how could she? The dirt was disgusting stuff. Not just soil but black factory dust and
something worse—something sticky gungy as bacon
grease left out to spoil for days. And trash, too—trash
all sifted through the dirt and nestled in the weeds.
Some of it rotting, some of it rusting.

The Wasteland wasn't any place to rest. It was a
place where if you lay down you lay down to die, and
God have mercy on your soul.

After a while the stark dead-empty landscape began to smother Pandora's spirit. And still she kept
going. Partly because she was Pandora, and it wasn't
in her to be a quitter—but partly, too, because she
could see the Emerald Forest out ahead of her, and

she knew that as long as there was a place that beautiful on the horizon there had to be a reason to keep going.

All through the dismal day; far into the afternoon.

Till finally at four-thirty she reached the edge of the Emerald Forest.

Which was an awful disappointment. Because it was skin thin, insubstantial as a Cookie's checkered curtains. Well, almost. Ten yards thick, maybe—but ten yards of trees weren't any forest. Just a windbreak of trees marking off the Wasteland's border.

There were cars on the far side of the trees—a whole new wasteland made of cars and pavement and tall-tall lampposts—and there in the center of it all, nearly as stark as a factory, was a shopping mall.

The Emerald Forest wasn't even a windbreak. Just a façade to hide the Wasteland from a shopping mall.

They're in a helicopter, Macdonald and Estes.

A very fast helicopter. Ken has never seen anything exactly like it before. A midsize transport helicopter with a jet engine back on the tail, and it's moving them cross-country at an amazing clip.

That's what it means to be Macdonald: if the military has it, it's his to use. And he does use, whenever he needs to. Which is often.

Macdonald nudges Ken's shoulder with the back of his hand—he wants Ken's attention. He motions Ken closer, points at his ear. Because of the noise from the engines? Yes, that's it. Ken leans forward to hear Macdonald ask his question.

"The girl," Macdonald asks, "the Alien. You think she did that to Hightower?"

For a moment it's as though Ken is considering the question for the first time—and it's absurd. Pandora? Beat *High*tower? The whole notion is funny. Pandora is just a little girl, even if she is an Alien. It is a monster that damn near killed the General, and Pandora isn't any monster.

Ken shakes his head.

"No. It can't be."

But the moment he says it the words come back to bite him, and he isn't sure anymore.

Macdonald is frowning.

"You saw the door?" he asks Ken.

Ken doesn't know which door Macdonald's asking about. He says so.

"The steel door at the far end of that wing of the barracks. Chained shut the day it was installed." Macdonald is quiet for a moment. Ken imagines him visualizing the door. Seeing—what? "Something tore it from its hinges."

Tore it from its hinges.

Ken doesn't want to imagine what could tear a chained steel door from its hinges. He tries not to.

Tries hard.

Something beat Hightower—damn near tore him limb from limb.

Something ripped the barracks door from its hinges.

Pandora was missing.

On their way to the helicopter Macdonald had pointed out tracks; she'd left alone in a storm of impossible snow. But what if—what if something took Pandora? What if she'd been kidnapped by something big and terrible. . . ?

It couldn't be. Of course. How could it?

And still. It was a different world Ken Estes lived in than he'd lived in till the day before: it was a world with Space Aliens walking upon it. And if there were Space Aliens, then what else?

What else indeed.

"What if something stole her?" Ken asked Macdonald. "Something big and *awful.*"

Macdonald shook his head.

"No chance."

Ken blinked. "Why not?"

"Look at the satellite photos—" He opens a folder, takes out half a dozen glossy-slick photo faxes. A train in a barren rail yard; a single figure climbing from the train. "She isn't kidnapped—she's loose. Spotted her getting off the train just a little while ago. She's wandering around a deserted industrial park in Canaan, Pennsylvania. On our way there now."

"How can you be sure that's her?" Ken asks.

Macdonald shrugs. "We can't," he says. "We're guessing. That train passed Wright-Pat about the time she made her break; when it came to a stop one person climbed out of a boxcar. We could be wrong. It could be an ordinary vagrant. But I don't think so."

There are people who are no friends of Macdonald's, but know him very well. These people call him Jake.

An enormous shopping mall.

Tall and broad. Ominous as a monolith.

Frightening.

For half a moment Pandora felt terrified of the thing, afraid that if she walked a step nearer to it the shopping monolith would devour her—take her and change her and make her into something that she never meant to be.

She wasn't wrong to think that—not by half.

But she set her fear aside, because she was Pandora, and she was a brave little Space Alien girl. It wasn't in her to run terrorized away from a shopping mall—no matter what it meant to do to her.

Three boys and a fat shopping lady gawked at her as she walked across the parking lot, but Pandora didn't let them frighten her away. Not for a moment. Stood her ground when the late-model Buick with the wild-eyed driver nearly ran her down, and no matter how scared she got, she didn't let it show.

Not for a moment.

When she reached the door she pulled it open without hesitating, and felt the air-conditioned breeze she'd never felt before, and of course she loved it. It was like spring from a machine, beautiful and cool. Inside there were high white walls and row

on row of shelves nigh up to the ceiling piled with
tools and toys and cans and a million amazing
things. . . !

A tile pathway led from the doorway into the
heart of the store. Pandora followed, it mystified, enchanted, gaping at the wonders that surrounded her.

She rounded a corner and saw a sign that said
LADIES' APPAREL.

The moment she saw that, it was like destiny
touched her. One moment she was Pandora, the nice
little Space Alien girl raised by a bunch of airmen in
a classified corner of Wright-Patterson Air Force
Base; the next moment she looked up and saw LADIES'
APPAREL, and she was someone else—she was someone with a grail, a purpose, a *destiny*.

Which was shopping!

Shopping glorious shopping at the miracles and
wonders piled high everywhere before her, inviting
her, begging her to *BUY! BUY! BUY!* (Those were exactly the words on the sign high above the bin
marked CLEARANCE.)

Pandora wandered toward the bin, curious at
what should warrant such a surplus of exclamation
marks. And found a crazy-quilt assortment of ward-
robe debris—last year's fashions; costume jewelry; a
hundred battered gewgaws in battered packages. Part
of her gaped wide-eyed and amazed at so many inex-
pensive treasures. But another part—the part not
taken in by the sudden glamour of the department
store—thought, *No, these aren't anything. Look at
them so beat-up, discarded. No one wants these
things. It's as though the store were trying to sell its
garbage.*

She looked up from the bin, sobered and made
sad. Sooner or later all the miraculous wondrous
clothes crowding against one another to sing *BUY!
BUY! BUY!*—sooner or later they'd all be trash.

Someone coughed.

Behind her. Close behind, almost close enough to

touch. Startled Pandora near enough to make her jump out of her skin.

"Can I help you?"

They're here for me, they've come to take me back—

But that was silly. *Can I help you?* wasn't what they said when they came to arrest you; it was what salesclerks said when they thought they might be able to talk you into buying more than you really needed. The right answer was *Oh, no thank you— I'm just browsing,* unless you really needed help finding what you were looking for.

Pandora sure didn't need any help.

She stood still as she could, hoping that the clerk could only see the back of her head, hoping that her ears weren't poking through her curly brown hair.

"Oh, no thank you—I'm just browsing," she said. She didn't get the inflection exactly right; the way it came out she sounded like she was refusing a blindfold on her way to the firing squad. But the clerk got the message anyhow.

"All right, then. Let me know if there's anything you need."

"I will."

This is about when Pandora realized she'd begun to draw attention in spite of averting her eyes whenever she thought someone might see her face, in spite of standing still, in spite of hoping that her ears didn't show.

What she felt—it wasn't the loud, icky-greasy goopy-all-over kind of attention she'd got from the woman and the boys in the parking lot. It was quieter. More curious, less demanding.

Half a dozen people scattered through the Sports Recreation and Leisure aisles, looking here and there uncomfortably, never directly at her—but Pandora could see by the way they held themselves that they were watching her from the corners of their eyes.

They don't want me to know they're watching. . . ?

And for the longest moment she couldn't imagine why.

And then it came back to her, what Uncle Wally said when she'd watch someone really close just because she was curious: *Stop it, Pandora. It's rude to stare.* It was a thing Pandora tended to forget, on account of the way people tended to stare at her sometimes like it was perfectly reasonable behavior. Which maybe it was, and certainly it was normal because they all did it and normal is what everyone does. But that doesn't stop it from being impolite.

They're trying not to be rude, Pandora thought. *How very nice of them.* And she smiled to herself and brightened up inside, and turned to walk deeper into the department store.

Three of the folks watching her turned to follow Pandora. They were pretty discreet about it, but not discreet enough to keep Pandora from seeing.

Through a tall archway into a new segment of the store—which turned out to be the most amazing, wondrous, splendificent place she'd ever seen in her life!

WOMEN'S FASHIONS!

Look, look—there against that wall. Blouses! So pretty bright after all her years in air-force drab. To wear such a blouse. . . ! Rack on rack on row on row on aisle on aisle of the most incredibly stylish trendy *so* chic blouses, dresses, coats, hats, undergarments!—sweaters, scarves, and miscellaneous accessories!

O to be young to be pretty to be a little girl Space Alien and to *shop!*

Especially to *shop!*

Into the thick of the dress racks, trying all the while she went to figure out her size. Pandora didn't know from *size;* all her life whenever she needed clothes her uncle Wally would requisition the smallest airman's uniforms he could get and then alter them to fit. He was pretty bad at it when she was little, but as the years went on he got better and better. Pandora's clothes these days were air-force drab, but they fit her well and wore better.

But whatever good you could say about her clothes, they sure weren't dresses like these!

Gingham, calico, paisley, parti-colors, plaid. Amazing patterns! Amazing colors! Amazing cuts! Amazing frills!

O to dress in a dress like this, so beautiful so bright! To be fashionable! To be *in!*

A beautiful green-yellow-lavender-cream paisley sundress! Only in her richest dreams had Pandora ever seen such a dress!

And this, look look all red pure red impossible-bright red a jumpsuit more beautiful than anything she'd ever wished for!

She'd need a blouse to go with it, wouldn't she? Pink! It would have to be pink and feel silky as silk—whatever silk felt like. (Pandora knew silk only by reputation. But what a reputation!) She threw the second dress over the arm that held the first, turned to find that display rack of pastel blouses she'd noticed. There—against the wall. Just as she remembered.

This is about when Pandora noticed that she'd drawn a crowd.

Not a really big crowd, as crowds go. Pandora had seen crowd scenes in *The Ten Commandments* and *Ben-Hur* much bigger than this one. Thirty people, maybe? About that—it was hard for Pandora to judge without actually counting heads, because she had so little experience with crowds of strangers. Like the first ones who'd noticed her, most of these people were trying to make cool and nonchalant like they weren't really watching her like a bunch of hawks.

It wasn't working. Even if they could be casual as they pleased, their numbers would've given them away. And most of them were nowhere near as casual as all that.

Well, never mind them, Pandora thought. *Why should I care if they like to watch?*

Over to the display of blouses, and there-right-
there was just the electric-pink pastel blouse she'd
always dreamed she'd wear someday. She held it up
to her breast to make certain it would fit. Glanced
into the mirror. Yes, of course it would fit. As well as
though it were made with Pandora and no one else in
mind.

What else?

She needed shoes. Oh, not that her boots were
wearing out or anything. But she needed real shoes,
ladies' shoes—how could a little girl Space Alien bear
to be seen in public wearing air-force-issue work
boots? Well, she couldn't, and that was that. She
needed shoes. Like some ladies' *Just do it!* Nike running shoes! Yes, running shoes were exactly what she
needed for running away from home.

And there on the far wall was a great big logo sign:
Nike!. Just what she needed.

That part was easy enough: the shoe department
was no trouble to find. But Pandora didn't know anything about sizing shoes—only that the double-small
work boots that Uncle Wally always requisitioned for
her always fit real funny and gave her blisters till she
broke them in. Did they make that double-small size
in ladies' running shoes? Or better still did they
make something closer to Pandora's own foot—
something that wouldn't give her blisters while she
broke them in?

There wasn't much help for those questions over
at the *Nike!* display. It was hard for her to tell which
running shoes were for women and which ones were
for men. And the sizes—the sizes were numbered on
some scheme that made no sense to Pandora, and
when she tried holding them up side by side, com-
paring one with another, the differences from size to
size were so slight that they seemed no difference at
all.

All of them looked a little on the big side. Could
she really wear shoes like these? Or would she have

to wear extra pairs of socks to bulk up her feet to fit them?

Then she turned one of the shoes over and noticed the price tag.

How could they charge so much for a pair of shoes? Airmen didn't make that much working three days, some of them. Where would *anyone* get the money to buy such shoes?

She had a bad feeling all of a sudden.

Looked at the dresses, the blouse draped over her arm.

And found prices that made the cost of the shoes look like pocket change.

So much money! Where was she going to get so much money?

Then it finally dawned on her: she didn't have any money at all.

There was no way she could buy any of the clothes she'd shopped for.

Pandora wanted to cry.

But I want *them!* she thought. Even just hearing the words in her head was enough to let her hear how silly they sounded.

She was going to cry. Any moment now she was going to lose hold of herself and start crying. She couldn't get clothes—she didn't have money, she wasn't worth money, she was no better than a beggar a bum a derelict. Worthless and poor as yesterday's trash.

She had to get out of here before she started crying with all these people watching. She couldn't bear the thought that so many would see her lose her dignity. Couldn't bear so many seeing her so washed up and worthless and poor as she was.

She turned, set her dresses and blouse on a display of patent-leather shoes. Started to head back the way she came.

"What's the matter?" someone asked. Pandora didn't recognize the voice, but it sounded friendly. "You suddenly look so sad."

Pandora frowned, turned to see a mild brown-haired woman wearing a cream-white dress with black buttons.

"I'm poor," Pandora said. "I forgot I don't have any money till I started reading prices."

"Don't be blue," the woman said. "None of us has much." Pandora tried to picture herself dressed up in blue and with her skin that color, too. She couldn't quite imagine it. "Come on," the woman said, "I'll buy you lunch. Then you'll feel better."

Pandora hesitated just a moment—half-afraid she was about the entangle herself in another snare—but no there was nothing of ensnarement or meanness about the woman, only friendliness and goodwill. She meant Pandora well. "Would you?" Pandora asked. The woman nodded. "Oh, thank you. I was so . . ." So what? She hadn't meant to start that sentence. She didn't know what the other half of it was supposed to be, and she wasn't sure she wanted to. ". . . so afraid. It's . . . scary here."

Till she said that Pandora had forgotten all about the scariness—but there it was. When she thought about that feeling she realized it'd been with her all along, hidden in the wonder of shopping: she was scared out of her mind. The mall was strange and cold and full of people she didn't trust and couldn't trust, and what she really ought to do was get the hell out of here, run for her life while she could still *go go go*—

"It's okay," the woman said. "We're all afraid sometimes."

"I'm not supposed to be afraid," Pandora said. "I'm a Space Alien."

The woman smiled. "I thought you were." She looked around her, taking in the unsubtle crowd that surrounded them. "Even Space Aliens get to be afraid, I guess. C'mon, the coffee shop's this way. You look famished."

Pandora nodded, followed. She *was* famished. She hadn't eaten since dinner last night.

So she followed the woman shyly, watching her feet as they navigated through the crowd in the shoe department. Even out in the aisle it was crowded—so many people! Wasn't there anything for them to do? *They* had money—why weren't they shopping, instead of watching her? Shopping was *important*, in a way that watching Space Aliens couldn't ever be.

Someone coughed, and Pandora looked up to see the people—so many people. Watching her because she was a Space Alien. A real flesh-and-blood Space Alien walking among them. Pandora looked back down at the floor—and kept looking at it. The attention embarrassed her. Terrified her! She knew that if she looked up to meet their stares they'd see themselves in her eyes, and run screaming through the aisles. Or they'd lose their minds and try to kill her, try to *do* things to her the way the General did, and she felt herself tremble as the memory gripped her, and she wanted to run for her life or kill him or both—

Pandora closed and opened and closed and opened her eyes. Tried to be calm. She didn't want to be hysterical, not with so many people watching. It wasn't dignified.

"Excuse me," someone said—a man's voice, awkward and pushy and full of feigned friendliness. "Could you direct me to the sporting-goods department?"

Pandora only barely managed to keep herself from looking up in puzzlement. How was she supposed to know. . . ?

He was very close. Walking beside her, trying to get her attention. She could feel his breath all warm and damp against her arm, and she wished with all her heart that she didn't have to feel it.

"I don't know where it is," she said, still not looking up.

She sidled away, but he only hurried closer to fill the empty space that made between them.

"You don't. . . ?"

"I'm not from anyplace around here. You'd have to ask someone else."

That wasn't the right thing to say, either, because if it were it'd make him go away, make him stop breathing so warm and damp and near and making her want to scream for fear of things closed in around her—

She hurried faster, began to move so quickly that she nearly left the friendly woman behind—but it didn't help a bit.

The breathing man matched her pace exactly.

Which was when Pandora realized that there wasn't going to be any getting away from him.

And then an angry male voice spoke up from somewhere behind them: "Give the lady a break, huh, buddy? No call to crowd her like that. You want sporting goods, look behind you. Second aisle on your left."

They turned back to face the one who'd spoken to him. "Who do you think you *are,* talking to me like—"

And he made a choking sound like someone had stuffed something down his throat, like maybe a fist. Pandora didn't see because she didn't look—she was too busy moving in the other direction as quickly as she could.

When she got to the TV-set display she stopped and waited for the gentle woman to catch up.

"I'm sorry," Pandora said. "He scared me."

The breathing man was nowhere in sight.

The gentle woman frowned. "I understand," she said.

And she held out a hand to take Pandora's. To protect her.

For half a moment Pandora was as afraid of her touch as she'd been of the breathing man's. But the gentle woman meant her no harm, and Pandora knew the hand she extended was an offer, not a demand. Pandora reached out, took the hand. Held it. Squeezed it.

They walked arm in arm through the department store's wide main entrance—out into the mall, where a thousand shops glittered and shone to offer them uncountable wonders for the easy price of money.

Easy if you *have* money, anyhow. But Pandora didn't.

I need to get a job, she thought. *If I had a job I'd have money and I could shop.*

Were there jobs for Space Aliens? And if there were, was it possible for her to do a job like that without drawing such a crowd that she wouldn't be able to get any work done?

If I had a job I could buy my own lunch—I could buy lunch for both of us!

And was she old enough to work, anyway?

Pandora was real vague on old and age. She wasn't sure she aged the way regular people did. Wasn't sure she even passed through time the way regular people did.

The crowd was behind them now. Mostly. Folks out in the mall were just beginning to notice Pandora, and only a few of the watchers from the department store had followed them through the door.

"This way," the gentle woman said. "The coffee shop's right here on the corner."

Pandora didn't hear at first. She'd just now looked up to see that there were whole levels of mall stacked into the sky above them.

It's beautiful, she thought. *So beautiful.*

Somewhere in the distance she could hear the strange soft roar of a fountain.

"Coffee shop," Pandora said. "Coffee shop. Sorry. It's just so—amazing. This place. Like a different world." If she'd thought about that it probably would have occurred to Pandora that the woman wouldn't likely take that exactly the way it was said. But she was too caught up in wonderment and hunger to hear her own words.

"Is it really?" the woman asked. "I've been shop-

ping in malls like this—all my life. I can't remember
the first time I saw one."

Pandora nodded. "I wish I'd lived here all my
life," she said. And sighed.

The woman coughed. "You speak American like
you were born here."

Pandora was about to say, *I was,* when it occurred to her that saying so would lead to a hundred
other questions she didn't want to answer.

"It's very kind of you to say so," she said instead.
"I studied very hard." Which was sort of a fib. Pandora studied very hard when it came to most subjects, but she hated the English textbooks and did
her best to avoid those lessons.

Not that it affected her speech in any special way.

"It shows."

"Thank you."

People were beginning to notice Pandora again.

The woman realized it before Pandora did. "We
should head in and order lunch. If we stand here
much longer there won't be any peace."

Pandora glanced around, took in the odd people
in the odd corners so obviously watching-without-
watching.

"You're right," she said, and followed the woman
to the coffee-shop entrance, where a sign told them
to PLEASE WAIT TO BE SEATED.

Pandora looked at the tables, the counter, the pa-
trons—the place looked at once alien and familiar.
Like the canteen where she'd eaten meals all her life
—and different, too, because the canteen was a great
spartan room laced with odd homey touches and
this . . . there were just as many tables, here.
Maybe more. But look at all the houseplants everywhere, and look at how everything was made up in
wood paneling, or painted to look like wood paneling,
and none of it looked all that much like wood when
you looked at it carefully.

"A table for two, please," the woman said to the
round-faced middle-aged lady who now stood before

them. The middle-aged lady had on a funny costume or maybe it was a uniform—yes, that was it, the woman was a waitress and that funny costume was her uniform. Only her uniform looked silly, where real uniforms (like Uncle Wally's) made you look like important like Pandora's uncles.

The waitress took them to a table on the mall-ward side of the restaurant, which wasn't good, because this side of the restaurant was pretty much open to the mall. All the barrier between their table and the outside was a waist-high sort-of wall, and the moment they sat down they were on display. Pandora started to ask the waitress if they could have a different table, but the woman didn't seem to hear her.

"I'll get her attention," the gentle woman said, turning to follow after the waitress. "It'll only take a moment."

Pandora touched her shoulder as she passed. "No," she said. She nodded to their watchers, gathered out in the mall. "It's all right. I'll watch them, too."

The woman smiled and sat down.

"Any idea what you'd like to eat?"

Pandora opened her menu, which was full of dishes like Mexicana Omelettes and Patty de Luxxe burgers and Turkey Club sandwiches. "I don't know," she said. "What's good?"

The quiet lady started to answer, and then stopped abruptly. Started and stopped like that three times in a row. She looked flustered. "I—that is. Are you Space Aliens vegetarians? Or, I don't know—do you eat your food alive? I mean, I know a man who keeps snakes that won't eat unless they can kill—oh. No, I don't mean you're a snake or anything, just that maybe you like food alive? If you do they don't have that here."

Pandora fell into giggle fit about two seconds into the first question. Which was so mean, with the nice lady so uncomfortable! But how could Pandora *not* laugh? Live food! Imagine that: a cheeseburger that was alive! How silly!

She's been reading science fiction, Pandora thought. She put on her best serious face and made a growling sound like one of those African carnivores on *Mutual of Omaha's Wild Kingdom.* And the poor woman jumped! For an instant Pandora thought she'd sail clear out of her skin!

And then the woman looked seriously scared.

Sobered, Pandora almost immediately. "I'm sorry," she said, "but you were *so funny!*"

The woman's breathing slowed a little, seemed to steady. She still looked a little uneasy.

"I eat just like anybody else. I like french fries and pizza and hot dogs with mustard. Honest!"

The woman looked confused. "You Space Aliens *have* that stuff out in outer space?"

And suddenly Pandora realized she'd walked into a question she didn't want to answer. About how she'd never ever been out in outer space in all her life since she was born but she was a Space Alien anyway because her Mommy was one, too.

She wasn't ready to talk about any of those things. Not yet. Wasn't even ready to think about them.

So she lied.

"Of course we do! How could we have spaceships and not have the comforts of civilization?"

The woman's eyes went wide.

"Junk food?"

"Uh-huh."

"In outer space?"

"Uh-huh."

She looked up toward the ceiling. "I don't believe it."

She knows I'm lying!

Pandora's heart like to burst out of her chest. "You don't?"

She'd never been caught in a lie before. Partly

because she hadn't told more than half a dozen of them in her life.

"Oh, no, I don't mean to say that I don't believe you. You wouldn't lie to me. I just meant—it's so outrageous. Space Aliens? Junk food? Space-food snacks? It's like a joke somebody might make up. And so outrageous that it *has* to be true." She reached out, patted Pandora's hand where it rested on the table. "I didn't mean to insult you."

Pandora felt all greasy inside—telling bold-faced lies like that to this nice lady who was buying her lunch! What a disgrace! She wanted to bury her face in her hands and hide, but she was too proud to let herself do anything like that.

"I'm okay," she said. "It's okay." It wasn't okay at all, of course. But what was one more lie, considering the circumstances?

The woman nodded. She glanced at her menu. "The patty melt is good here," she said. "My favorite."

"Okay." Pandora liked patty melts—Cookie made them every once in a while.

A waitress showed up a minute or two after they closed their menus. Took their orders, took away their menus.

When she was gone Pandora looked out into the mall—and saw the breathing man. He stared at her with wide, hungry eyes.

No!

She didn't want to see him again. He frightened her so bad! So she looked down to hide her eyes from him.

Saw the quiet woman's pretty, comfortable low-heel shoes, cool green with brassy ornaments where the laces ought to have been.

"Your shoes are pretty," Pandora said. She looked up slowly, careful not to look out into the crowd. Let that breathing man stare if he wanted to! Pandora just wouldn't see him.

"Why, thank you," the woman said. She craned

her neck to glance under the table at Pandora's feet. "Yours are interesting, too—I must say. They look like . . ." And then the woman looked puzzled. Did she realize they were air-force boots? Or was she having trouble making the connection? Pandora wasn't about to draw it for her.

But it wasn't a hard connection to make: all of Pandora's clothes were the same air-force-drab colors, and even though Uncle Wally spent hours altering them, the cut was still mighty close to regulation.

"Those aren't Space Alien boots, are they?"

Pandora shook her head.

"Can you tell me how you came by them?"

Pandora hesitated.

She didn't want to tell any more lies.

"Can you tell me your story?"

Not all of it.

"I'm trying to find my daddy," Pandora said. "He's a Space Alien, too."

"Like you?"

Pandora thought about that question before she answered it. Her mommy looked so different from her . . . she was pretty sure her daddy would be at least that different, or maybe differenter.

"I don't know," she said. "I haven't never seen him."

But I saw my mommy!

"You poor dear," the woman said. "You've never met your father?"

"No." Pandora felt dejected when she said it. "But if I'm lucky, and if I run far enough and fast enough, maybe he'll see me! If I make enough commotion, anyway. And I'm bound to make a commotion, running away. After all, I'm a Space Alien."

The woman pursed her lips as she considered the idea.

"Do you really think he'll hear? I mean, even if you make the evening news—do Space Aliens watch TV?"

I watch TV! Pandora wanted to say. But she held

her tongue; saying that would only bring on another bunch of questions.

"I hope so."

The woman frowned. She shook her head.

"You poor, poor dear." And she looked down into the glimmery surface of the coffee in the cup beside her plate. And she seemed very sad.

"I'll be okay," Pandora said. "My daddy will find me."

Those were the last words either one of them spoke for a good twenty, thirty minutes. When the waitress brought their food they ate in silence—Pandora picked at hers slowly, careful to savor each bite of cheeseburger, every french fry, every precious sip of Coca-Cola. She wanted to remember this meal forever.

She had to remember it, she knew. It was her first taste of freedom.

As she ate she watched the ones who watched her from outside. And bit by bit got used to them. Even the breathing man. *They aren't monsters*, she thought. *They aren't watching me before they pounce. They're just ordinary people.*

The quiet woman seemed somehow to have lost her appetite—she poked and prodded her lunch with the tines of her fork, but she didn't eat much of it.

"Are you okay?" Pandora asked.

"Just sad, is all. I feel bad for you."

"Oh, don't worry," Pandora said. "I'll be okay."

She didn't say it with an awful lot of confidence.

"You will?" A man's voice, pushy and aggressive. From—where? Outside! Out in the mall! "Are you certain?"

Pandora looked out over the waist-high wall that shielded them from the mall—

And saw the crowd suddenly pressed close in around them, and the cameras, and a dozen reporters, maybe more, all trying to get a look at her. Where had they come from? How had them managed to get so close so suddenly?

Someone swung a microphone on a boom over the barrier and down till it hung a few inches above Pandora's face, so close that she could read the letters CNN stenciled on its collar.

"That isn't a costume, is it?" the pushy man asked her. No, he didn't ask. That wasn't a question. It was a statement he wanted confirmed, and he sounded as though he were afraid of the answer.

But what was he asking *about?* Her clothes? They were a little odd, but not *that* odd.

"What. . . ?" Pandora asked. "I don't understand."

For a moment the man from CNN looked almost as confused as Pandora felt. "Your eyes," he said. "Your skin. Your ears. The way your head is so thin."

"He wants to know if you're really a Space Alien," the woman said. "He's asking if you're an Alien or just made up to look like one."

Pandora laughed.

"How could my eyes be a costume?" she asked. "How could I see you if they weren't real?"

For an instant the pushy man looked agitated, like he was upset and about to say something mean. Then, abruptly, something in his expression shifted —almost seemed to slip—and he laughed with her.

Imagine that: Pandora a costume. What a silly thing to think.

It only took the CNN man a moment to get his composure back.

"Then you really are. . . ?"

"Uh-huh. A Space Alien."

He waited for her to go on. But Pandora didn't see any reason to do that.

They're in the *fast* helicopter, on their way to pick up Pandora—only it doesn't quite work out that way.

The trouble starts when Yolen comes out the cockpit with an uneasy look on her face.

"Bad news, twice over," she says. "She's gone into the shopping mall next to the industrial park."

Macdonald blanches. He doesn't say a word.

"Local CNN affiliate found her before we realized what was going on. They're interviewing her—live. Already going out over the network."

Macdonald looks very, very ill. He reaches for his cell phone, starts to dial.

"Wait, Macdonald," Yolen says, "there's more. I just got a report from Wright-Pat—something big is up. It sounds like a mutiny. Hightower is gone."

The man beside the TV camera had questions that went on and on and on. After a while Pandora began to wonder if they were ever going to leave her alone. But she didn't say so—that would have been rude. Instead she answered the questions as politely and honestly as she could without telling things she didn't want to say.

"Can you tell us why you've come to our planet?"

Really! Why *shouldn't* she be here? Did the man have something against having a Space Alien in his neighborhood?

"I came *here* to go shopping," Pandora said. "But I forgot to bring any money."

"I see," the man said. (Pandora didn't think he did.) "Can you tell us what plans you have for the rest of your stay on Earth?"

"I'm trying to find my daddy," she told him. "He's a Space Alien, just like me. I miss him very much."

The reporter's eyebrows went up. "Your daddy? What can you tell us about him?"

Pandora sighed. "I've just been trying to find him, that's all. He's my daddy and I miss him very much. *Daddy!* Daddy Space Alien, if you're watching TV, I'm trying to find you, Daddy! Come get me. Please! I need rescuing!"

The reporter sputtered, stuttered, started to ask another question—and then suddenly there wasn't any chance for him to say anything, because there were police all over the place, police men and women in uniforms and Pandora knew right away

that they were here to get her and take her away for
the air force.

It goes from bad to worse to worst of all in no time at
all.

They're in the helicopter on the ground in the
industrial park behind the mall where Pandora en-
lightens the world, and Ken sits in his seat. He's trying hard to decide if he should try to hear or try not
to hear Macdonald, who's talking on the secure red
telephone at the far end of the cabin. Twice in the
last few moments Ken distinctly heard Macdonald
say the words *Mr. President,* and knowing Macdonald that means he's talking to *the* President. And that
makes Ken curious as hell, the idea that *the* President is right over there on the telephone talking to
somebody Ken knows.

The *President* himself!

On the other hand.

On the other hand if it is the President talking to
somebody like Macdonald over a secure phone, then
it's a classified conversation, and Ken doesn't like
getting any nearer to classified stuff than he has to.
Because classified means nothing but trouble to an
airman like Ken Estes.

Nothing but trouble and grief.

And then Yolen throws open the cockpit door
again.

"Macdonald," she says, not even minding how
he's on the telephone with the President. "Macdonald, listen to me, it's important. Some asshole's
called out the National Guard."

And Ken looks out the helicopter's portal, the
portal right across from him. And he sees how it's
true, what Yolen says. Because military helicopters
crowd the skies above them.

Those mean old police weren't going to get Pandora!
Not her, no sir!

She looked at the woman who'd bought her

lunch. "I got to go," she said. "I'm sorry to run off on you like this. I really appreciated lunch. It was good. You were right about the patty melt." She said it kind of quiet, not really whispering but soft enough that only the two of them could hear.

The two of them and maybe the microphone right over Pandora's head.

The woman was too confused to figure out what was going on and respond. Pandora wanted to be mannerly, but a body has to draw the line someplace. If she spent five minutes explaining how she was about to get kidnapped by evil agents of the government, the police would have her in handcuffs before she got halfway finished.

She waved good-bye and made a beeline through the restaurant, between tables and around the big flower display in the center; past a line of booths and behind the counter. She knew customers weren't supposed to go behind the counter and into the kitchen like this and all, but there wasn't anyplace else to go—there were already police there by the register, coming over the half-high wall, coming from every direction she could see, and they would've been in the kitchen, too, if they could've found a way to be there, but they weren't, and Pandora ran through it for all she was worth, past the steam table full of big trays with meat loaf, past the grill where two fry cooks stood flipping burgers, full tilt into the back door, pushing against the spring-bar-hinge door handle with all her weight and momentum, and thank God it wasn't locked or she'd've broke something for sure.

Out into a hall that wasn't a hall at all, but a walkway out in the open except that it had another half-high wall like inside the mall. Sort of like a balcony, but different because there were the back doors to different businesses along the inside wall.

At the far end of the walkway there was an elevator.

Pandora thought about trying to climb over the

half wall and make a run for it across the parking lot, but that was crazy—it was a long way down over the edge of that wall. One story up from the parking lot out there, but directly below the low wall was a drainage way and some kind of a loading access. Two storeys down from here, at least. Maybe three.

And anyhow, even if it weren't for the wall and the long tall drop over the side of it, out there wasn't anywhere Pandora wanted to go anyway. Because the parking lot was solid with police cars and fire trucks and all sorts of things, and the sky above it was wild with helicopters.

She moved along the walkway, trying the doors as she went. They were all locked.

That left the elevator.

Dusk.

Ken Estes stands in a thicket that separates an industrial park from the parking lot of a west-central Pennsylvania shopping mall. He isn't sure what town he's in. Macdonald mentioned the town's name, back in the helicopter, but Ken didn't recognize it. Now he remembers nothing.

Ken has stepped away from Macdonald's helicopter, afraid that he might hear some precious national secret as Macdonald shouts and screams first into one telephone line and then into another. There is no use for him in there. Better not to make a nuisance of himself.

He gets fifty yards from the helicopter, and keeps walking. If he were thinking about what he's doing, he'd stop, wait, listen for Macdonald or Yolen to call for him. But he isn't thinking, just wandering.

He reaches the edge of the parking lot, and keeps going.

The lot is solid with police cruisers, humvees, military transport trucks. Civilian cars, too—some of them moving in an awful panic.

He thinks of Pandora.

She's just a girl, Ken thinks. *Just a poor little girl*

who doesn't want to be locked away anymore. Why can't they let her go? He knows the answer to that question. He's seen the way time warps around Pandora when she gets upset. There really are questions of national security caught up inside her.

But knowing doesn't make Ken Estes like it. Not one bit.

He looks up at the helicopters that crowd the sky. So many of them! Shining their lights over and over and over the lot. Ken wonders how any of them will tell Pandora from an ordinary shopper from that height; and if there is no way to tell then why the hell do they bother?

Why?

He scans the sky, looking for a reason, knowing that he'll find none. And then as he looks at the corner of the sky closest to the shopping mall, something snags in his gut.

Hightower!

Ken Estes wants to scream.

Hightower is up there someplace. I swear to God he is.

Pandora hit the elevator button and waited for the door to open.

Waited forever! Why did elevators always take so long? Even longer when you had to run away, so long . . . any moment now the police would burst out the kitchen door she'd come through! Was that elevator broken?! No, no, listen, listen to the machinery whirring somewhere deep inside the elevator shaft, the elevator was rising toward her oh so slow, it'd come for her eventually but not before, before—where were the police? Pandora was sure they'd be on her already, but they weren't, not yet, like waiting for the other shoe to drop forever Pandora waited, maybe they were stuck in the crowd back in the restaurant. . . . Pandora imagined the crowd surging forward to block the police, to protect her.

Maybe. Maybe they'd do that, if they loved her. But how could they? She hardly even knew them.

And suddenly the police and the door and the crowd didn't matter, because one of the helicopters shone its light on her, and swerved through the air toward her like a hawk descending on a mouse.

No no no please no!

Pandora ducked against the elevator door, tried to hide in the thin recess it provided—but it wasn't any use. None! The helicopter *knew* she was here.

And whoever was inside it was coming to get her.

Closer, now, closer and closer, and the light narrowed on her, focused on her, on her face in her eyes blinded her—

Go away, Pandora thought. *Please go away.*

The helicopter drew closer, closer still. Close enough that if she leaned out over the wall she could've touched it.

Why are you chasing me? What do you want from me?

But Pandora knew damn well what they wanted. They wanted to own her.

A voice on a megaphone, from the helicopter:

"PANDORA!"

She knew that voice!

"PANDORA, YOU'VE GOT TO CALM DOWN. YOU'VE GOT TO COME HOME."

Uncle Wally!

The helicopter turned, now, turned sideways so that she could see in its door despite the light in her eyes. And sure enough, there was Uncle Wally sitting in a helicopter.

She wanted to cry when she saw Uncle Wally. Pandora saw him there, smiling and waving at her, and she knew an awful truth about herself—she saw him and she loved him and she wanted to go home, and she knew when she saw him that she was just another runaway little girl who'd gotten into the worst sort of trouble she could ever imagine.

She started to answer the words he'd shouted to her over the megaphone.

Uncle Wally, she started to say. *Uncle Wally I love you I missed you take me home Uncle Wally I'm so scared.*

Until she saw the horror.

Over Uncle Wally's shoulder, in the darkness deep inside the helicopter: the bulbous face; the beady, deep-set eyes—

The General!

General Belisarius Hightower watching her hungrily angrily full of terrible malevolence, waiting to get his hands around her throat and do the things to her he'd only tried to do before, and Pandora screamed.

And the elevator door finally slid open behind her, and Pandora stepped inside.

As someone in the parking lot fired a gun.

As the police, mobbed and burdened by a crowd intent to stop them, finally burst through the kitchen door.

And the elevator lowered her to hell.

Ken hears Lieutenant Turner on the megaphone up by the mall. And right away he knows what Turner is doing here. He knows who brought him from Wright-Pat, too.

Hightower.

The elevator opened and Pandora stepped out into the mall basement—and before she could reconsider, the elevator door had closed behind her.

And she knew she'd made a terrible mistake.

The basement was a dim grey place that went on as far as she could see. It was vast, cluttered, terrible, and abandoned.

Oh, no one had ever closed it off. And the blueprints in the mall office still showed it as an enormous unfinished parking garage, bigger than the mall, bigger than the aboveground lot. The developers who'd built the mall left the underground half-finished for future expansion. But the future that they planned never came, and year by year the maintenance crew hauled more and more junk down into the underground for storage, and every year they forgot a little more of what they'd put there; till now the basement was a darkly hellish place so creepy and so grimy that even the mall's maintenance men avoided it.

Pandora didn't think about the darkness or the dirt or the hellishness. She hurried into it because she had to, because the General was up there in the air, hunting for her, and she knew what he'd do if he found her.

Pandora ran so hard.

Deep, deep into the dim grime running so fast in the half dark that she could hardly see her way, and she ran, and ran, and every time she stopped she knew the General was right behind her waiting to ravish her.

He'll find me soon, she thought. How long did she have before they found their way down here? Not long. No time at all.

I have to hide.

Hide.

And then she saw it, over there by the wall, among the boxes on their storage pallets—a crevice even darker than the darkness of the basement.

Pandora hurried across the open floor and ducked into the crevice, crawled inside—deep, deep inside. The rift was even, steady—it went farther back into the dark than Pandora could have imagined, then finally began to narrow and narrow farther until the only way she could move any farther was to squeeze her shoulders and ease back one leg at a time. Here the space was so close that she could hardly look back to see where she was going, but that didn't matter, because it was too dark to see back there no matter how she looked.

She twisted sideways and eased back farther still,

and now her knee found a ledge—no, not a ledge. It was a step-down, a stairstep almost. Or maybe like a curb.

Ken knows he shouldn't wander into the search.

But he keeps thinking: *I can help her. I can help her find her way out of the mall, out of the crowd, out of the circus; I can help her home and everything will be fine.*

And he wanders into the circus.

Across the now dark parking lot flashing bright and again with the searchlights hung from helicopters; into the wide-open loading bay that accesses the mall's basement. None of the sentries challenge him; he (like so many others) is in uniform, and few here know one another.

Down into the basement.

After a while Pandora got used to being terrified in the dark, and her terror turned to depression. And the depression made her feel so tired!

So tired that she fell asleep hiding in the dark crevice.

And as she slept she had a nightmare.

In her dream she felt the basement air tingling with static electricity, felt every hair on her body prickle as it tried to stand on end. She was in a room like a cave, but where caves have walls of rock and dirt, this room's walls were made of mall garbage pressed against itself. There was a fire in the center of the cave, and the fire rippled tongues of flame as she stepped toward it.

I've got to look into the fire, Pandora thought. She was afraid to look, but she knew she had to. She was afraid she'd see, see—she didn't know what. But she knew that the fire was the reason for her nightmare, and she was terrified to see it.

She was right to be scared, too.

Because the fire spoke to her.

"*Closer,*" the fire said, "*come closer, girl.*"

Pandora knew that voice. She knew it and she hated it.

"No," she said, "I won't."

The fire laughed at her. The laugh was as familiar as the voice, and frightening—the sound of it made Pandora feel cold and lonely and abused, and she wanted to wake out of her dream, but when she tried to open her eyes nothing happened, and her nightmare dream became a trap she couldn't spring. . . .

"I hate you!" Pandora shouted. "You aren't any dream of mine! Go burn someplace else!"

The fire laughed again.

Pandora kicked dirt into it, trying to put the fire out, but the flames did not subside.

"Come to me, Pandora," the fire said. *"I want to hold you in my arms."*

"No!"

The fire roiled, boiled, faded then burst to fill the air. Pandora blinked away the sooty brightness. When she could see again she saw the flames parting like a wave rolling away from a stone. In the center of the brightness there was a face—

The General!

That was the voice! It was General Hightower rising out of the fire—look at him, look at the bulbous bloated pig face leering at her terrible unpretty unhuman *Hightower* with devil horns growing out of his head, Hightower with skin as red as blood, he was a demon damned to hell and now he came to get Pandora, to take her, to ravish her, she was going to kill him if he tried it kill him or die trying, she was.

Pandora screamed.

"Pandora"—rising now, Hightower the devil rising out of the fire like Venus from the sea; watching her with wide, ravenous eyes—*"you are extraordinary. Come to me, Pandora—let me hold you."*

Pandora eased away from the devil, slowly, slowly eased back against the wall and slid along it, rubbed her back against the crusty sticky greasy mall garbage that the wall was made from.

"What do you want from me?"

The Hightower devil laughed.

"What do I want from you? *But it's you who've dreamed of me."*

"I never meant to!"

The devil stepped away from his fire and walked closer, closer—

"Leave me be! I don't like you! I don't want anything to do with you!"

"Do you think I care?"

Pandora bit her lip. "You can't take me to hell," she said. "I never did nothing wrong!"

The devil Hightower laughed again.

"You killed a man," he said. *"You never even cried."*

That was a plain, bold-faced lie, and Pandora knew it. "I never killed nobody! I never did!"

The devil laughed and laughed.

"Stop that! Stop picking on me, you awful—"

Then something came over Pandora. Something like courage, in a way, and in other ways like foolishness. But mostly it was anger so powerful it consumed her, boiling her blood until she just couldn't think anymore, and she started doing things when she knew they were insane.

Crazy even in a dream.

Like punching the Hightower devil upside the head. She got mad and she balled her fist and she popped him one, just like Uncle Wally taught her when he was showing hand-to-hand combat, and when her fist hit home she felt the strangest thing.

Because the devil's head wasn't hard the way people's heads are.

It was soft like clay, and when she hit his flat left temple his whole head mooshed sideways, and one of his eyes popped out. Pandora was so mad she didn't even care. She hit him and hit him again, till now the top of his skull ripped clean and brains went flying in every direction.

Brains and ichor, purplish reddish glowy stuff. Everywhere. All over the trashy walls; sputtering in the fire; like pasty red-grey glue all over Pandora's hands.

The devil didn't care. He kept on screaming at her even though his head was broke, taunted and berated her even while she pounded him until he fell into the fire and sank into the flames.

Later, when she was awake, it occurred to Pandora to wonder why the devil let himself take such a beating, or if it was that being a devil made him nasty and scary and fiery but not especially strong, or what. But while she was doing it, beating up the devil seemed like the most natural thing to do, and Pandora felt real good about it.

Before the fire drowned him, the devil looked Pandora in the eye. And he spoke to her.

"Hit me all you want," the devil said. *"Pain is only pain. But you, little girl—you're empty and small and alone, and everyone who loves you hates you. Nothing ever changes that. And nothing could protect you from your fate."*

A curse. A great and terrible curse that she'd never ever live away no matter what.

"What do you mean?" Pandora all but shouted at him.

"You'll see."

The devil Hightower smiled.

And Pandora knew by the self-satisfied light in his devil eye that he was about to tell her all the worst secrets of her fate, to sap her will and break her purpose.

"No!" she said. "I won't listen! I won't!" She hit him and hit him, till finally the devil's fiery arm shot out of the flames to grab her fist and hold it.

And Pandora listened, no matter how hard she wanted not to.

"You're looking for your father," Hightower the devil told her. His hand was made of fire and as he held her fist her hand was burning. *"You're going to find him—in a place you won't expect or accept."* She struggled to pull her hand away from him, but no

matter how she tried, she could not loosen his grip. Now the burning worked its way down through her skin, into her nerves—she felt like, like the flesh of her hand was cooking and then she could smell it like meat on a grill. And the smell and the pain brought last Christmas back to her, and she remembered the skin of her hand boiling in oil, all but boiling away, and the smell and the pain and the oil and the days of pain and salves and bandages as the scientists prodded and cajoled her with their eagerness to record every moment that she writhed and screamed, and now in her dread she screamed again, and she tried to beg release but she couldn't find the words, all words were lost to her. The devil saw, and he smiled. *"When you find him you're going to deny him to his face—and then you'll run away."*

Then the fire died to embers, and the devil was gone, and Pandora woke covered with sweat, shivering with fear, alone in a place she never meant to go. Her hand still throbbed where the devil burned it.

She probed the skin of her scarred hand carefully with the fingers of her good one. And found new welts and blisters that described the devil's fingers.

The first thing Pandora heard as she woke was the voice on the megaphone.

"PANDORA," the voice said. "IT'S TIME TO COME HOME, PANDORA. WE'RE SORRY YOU WERE SCARED. WE'LL NEVER LET ANYONE SCARE YOU AGAIN. WE PROMISE." Uncle Wally! It was Uncle Wally's voice! Again!

Oh, Uncle Wally—why do you have to betray me like this—over and over?

Pandora wanted to cry.

It was the General who made Uncle Wally lie, Pandora knew it was. And oh, how it hurt to have her uncle Wally lie to her! Anybody, *anybody* but Uncle Wally!

It was bright light outside in the basement— someone had found a light switch and turned on the basement lights, or the army had brought down floodlights, or something. It was still dark here in Pandora's hidey-hole, but outside was so bright it hurt Pandora's eyes to look at it.

"PANDORA—WE'RE WORRIED ABOUT YOU, PANDORA. PLEASE COME HOME. *PLEASE.*"

Pandora bit her lip.

"Go away, Uncle Wally! I hate you I hate you I hate you!"

So upset she didn't even realize she actually *said* those words, instead of thinking them. Even so, she said it quiet quiet under her breath so quiet no one else could hear not even if they stood right there two feet from Pandora in the crevice. Of course she said them quiet! Those words hurt her throat when she said them quiet. If she'd said them loud they would have killed her.

Because she didn't hate him. She couldn't hate her uncle Wally. She just hurt, was all. And *God* how she wanted to go home. But she knew she never could, because after everything that happened, home just couldn't exist anymore.

"COME HOME, PANDORA. IT'S TIME TO COME HOME."

No it isn't not never it won't be!

And she knew it was the end about to happen to her. Knew it sure as she knew she was a Space Alien, through and through.

Footsteps. Somewhere close by—out there by the front edge of the boxes. Coming toward her. Quiet, quiet footsteps.

Steady. Careful. One set—there was someone out there looking for her very deliberately. Intently.

"Pandora . . . ?"

The voice of Airman Ken Estes.

Uncle Ken!

"But you died!" Pandora said. "You're dead, I saw—"

And there, right there, she'd given herself away.

No!

She backed farther, farther into the crevice—over the ledge and into gritty pebbly dirt.

"Pandora? Is that you, Pandora? No, I'm not dead. I'm fine."

There he was. Alive and well; dressed and tidy. Pretty. Not even rumpled—the creases on his uniform slacks were sharp as though they'd just been pressed.

She backed farther into the dark.

The dirt was moist and rocky here, and now her shoulders pressed through a battered ventilator frame. There were the nubs where there used to be slats, and the slats were torn away.

"Everyone's really worried for you, Pandora. We know what the General did to you, and Macdonald's going to court-martial him for it. Everybody's sorry."

Pandora didn't say a word. She just kept backing away.

"The General got loose, but Macdonald's going to arrest him again—you can bet on that, Macdonald is a sharp guy. You don't have to worry about him."

But Pandora had seen the General already. She'd seen him on the helicopter, and she'd seen him in her dream, and she knew that if she went with Uncle Ken the General would find her again, and she knew what he'd do to her.

Pandora hated that General so much. She held her tongue and kept herself hidden.

"Pandora? You're there, aren't you?" Now Uncle Ken was looking right in at her. Pandora didn't think he could see her, this far into the dark as she was. But it was hard to be sure. It certainly *seemed* like he was staring right at her. "Why are you hiding from me? I promise I won't tell people where you are if you don't want to come back. I can see why you'd be afraid."

She kept her quiet.

"Everybody loves you, Pandora. Remember that." Maybe that was true, and maybe it wasn't. But

Pandora knew she couldn't trust it. She backed deep into the ventilator shaft.

"You want me to go away, Pandora?"

He was still staring right in at her.

"You want me to go away, pretend I never heard you?"

She had to hold herself very very still to keep from answering that question.

"If you want me to go away and pretend I never heard you, all you've got to do is stay quiet. I'll understand. If you don't want to come home, you shouldn't. It wouldn't be right to take you home against your will. Not the way I see it. Maybe others wouldn't agree—but if you don't talk to me now I won't tell them I know where you are. I won't."

Pandora didn't say a word.

"Okay, Pandora." Uncle Ken sighed. "It's okay. But you ought to know we miss you."

And he left.

Pandora got all weepy after Uncle Ken left. There was a moment when she almost pushed herself out of the ventilator shaft and went running after him, crying and wailing and wishing she was home.

But she didn't.

And that was good.

Because when Ken wasn't gone five minutes she heard the General shouting in the distance:

"*Estes!*" he shouted. "*Estes! Where is the Alien bitch, Estes? You're going to tell me or I'm going to kill you, I swear to God I am!*"

Pandora almost ran to him to save him, but she was too afraid. Later, when she remembered it, she hated herself for cowering in the ventilator shaft as the General beat on Uncle Ken, but while that nightmare happened Pandora was too scared to move at all.

THREE

Most Urban Legends sooner or later find their way into the pages of supermarket tabloids. Garish, tawdry, badly printed, and still these peculiar publications offer something of considerable value: they're motherloads of modern myth.

Cornucopias of folklore.

A few of them—*The National Interlocutor* and *The Weekly World News* in particular—seem to specialize in publishing Urban Legends whole cloth and unsubstantiated, as though they were unvarnished fact. Witness the following, excerpted directly from the pages of a recent *Interlocutor:*

DEAD BABY

TALKS LIKE LIVING CHILD!

Emma Henderson didn't take it lying down last summer when her daughter died of cancer, no sirree! Where most parents spend days weeping and grieving, Emma got off her duff and got going—she called a voodoo lady to bring her baby back from the dead!

''At first Lisa didn't like it being a zombie. She kept rotting, and that awful cancer in her tummy kept growing, just like it'd never died!'' says Henderson, an African-American woman in her mid-30s. ''After a while the rot got so bad Lisa like to have died all over again!''

But tragedy averted itself, Henderson continues, when Lisa's cancer tumbled from her crumbling remains. ''That yucky old cancer, it opened just like an egg—and there was baby Lisa alive inside it!''

These days Lisa is a happy, healthy, 15-pound baby—but she talks just like she could when she was a 8-year-old girl. ''You be careful what you say to her,'' Henderson concludes. ''She's *strong* just like she was when she was a zombie!''

When the basement was quiet again Pandora stopped shivering and began to get numb.

She hated herself, and the more she thought about Uncle Ken screaming, the more she heard the sound of his screams echo inside her, the more she hated herself.

She burrowed farther and farther into the ventilator shaft, pulling away from the world without even realizing what she was doing. After a long time she looked up and saw the grating above her—it was like a sewer grating, almost, or maybe the top end of a ventilator shaft. When she looked up at it Pandora could see the night sky and thin leafy branches—the branches of shrubs?—swaying back and forth in the wind. Cool clean air came down through the grate; moonlight shone through the iron slats. In the moonlight through the slats Pandora could see a painted iron ladder not far from her shoulder.

All I have to do is climb out of here, and I'm free.
Free?
Maybe free.
Or maybe they'd be up there waiting for her.

Pandora steeled herself and pushed through the tightness of the shaft till she was on the ladder, climbing to the top, peering through the slats. Trying to see who waited to capture her . . .

But no one did. There was no one up there. Nothing but bushes and the breeze and the night sky, and not too far away a gas station with its lit-up orange-blue-white GULF sign rotating endlessly.

Off in the distance and across a four-lane highway, the shopping mall.

Pandora blinked. Could she really have run that far underground. . . ?

She reached up to touch the dirty-gritty-greasy iron grate. It was loose—not bolted or welded down, just held in place by its own weight. She pushed it up, eased it out of the way.

Crawled out of the shaft, into the bushes that surrounded the vent access. Pushed the grate back to its place—bits of rock and dirt and twig scattered down the shaft as she moved it. Pandora bit her lip when she heard the sound it made—so loud it was sure to attract the notice of anyone as near as Uncle Ken had been.

But no one heard. Pandora crouched among the bushes for the longest time, watching the cars and trucks whiz by on the road out beyond the Gulf station; listening to the chatter of the helicopters flying 'round and 'round above her. Crouching low to hide from the folks gassing up their cars not thirty feet away.

She thought she hid herself well.

"You're the one, aren't you?"

Out of nowhere—behind her! Pandora turned to face the voice, scared half out of her skin and ready to fight—

"The one they're looking for. All these police cars, all these uniforms. Helicopters! Land's sake! What've you done, child?"

Pandora blinked. And thought: *She's so loud that the police are sure to hear her.* And held finger to her lips to motion quiet. And nodded.

When the woman responded she was quieter. "Is it true, what they said on the radio? Are you really somebody from out in space? Or escaped from a secret laboratory, someplace the government won't admit to?"

A government laboratory! Imagine that! What a thing to ask. As though Pandora was something some crazy old scientist could just dream up and pour from a test tube!

She laughed in spite of the fact that she knew she didn't dare make that much noise.

"Hey—I didn't say that! It was on the radio. It was!" There was light enough from the gas station that Pandora could see the woman clearly. She was tall and heavyset and had skin the color of black coffee. Her crew-cut hair was shorter than Uncle Ken's.

The woman knelt down, bent close into the shadows that hid Pandora, and whispered. "If you aren't a mutant laboratory freak," she said, "then how come they after you so bad?"

As she asked the question a breeze caught hold of the bushes, and for just an instant the streetlight shone on Pandora, and the woman saw her clearly for the first time. The sight made her gasp.

"You *are. . . !*"

Pandora nodded. "Yes," she said. "I'm a Space Alien."

"You poor child," the woman said.

"I'm trying to find my father," Pandora said. "That's why I was on TV—so that he could see me from outer space and rescue me."

"You were on TV?" There was awe in the woman's voice.

"Not on the movie of the week or anything. Just on the news. CNN, I think—that's what the microphone said."

The woman nodded. She still looked impressed.

"We got to get you out of here, child—this place isn't safe for you."

Pandora nodded. "I know."

"You want a ride? Me and my baby girl, we're going south. There's a special doctor down there who my baby needs to see," she said. "I'll take you far as you want to go."

A helicopter roared by overhead; its search beam only barely missed them.

"Could you?" Pandora asked. She was nervous about taking a ride with somebody she hardly knew, but the helicopters scared her worse than that. "Please?"

"I surely will," the woman said, nodding, watching Pandora through the dark with a stare that seemed to measure her.

"My baby girl is in the car," the woman said. "Her name is Lisa." She paused after saying the name, as though there were something in it Pandora was supposed to understand—and beware. "Lisa is *special.*"

"Special?"

"She's a tiny baby. But she speaks as though she was an older child."

When Pandora heard the woman say those words, a little red warning light went on deep inside her skull. Like—like she knew right then all about the terrifying child, but didn't yet understand enough to put what she knew to words.

"I understand," Pandora said. But she hardly did.

"Wait here," the woman said. "I'll move my car so that the door is there beside the bushes."

Another helicopter flew high and straight above them. Its searchlight scanned the ground around Pandora, but it didn't touch her.

The woman brought her car around, parked beside the bushes, reached back to open the rear door. Pandora slipped in quietly as she could, staying low, praying no one saw her. . . .

"Lie flat," the woman said. "Hide yourself under these blankets."

Pandora covered herself with the blankets, head to toe. She left a tiny gap between the two folds over her head—a gap just wide enough to see through.

"Who is it, Mama?" a tiny voice asked from the front seat. That was the woman's daughter, wasn't it? There was something about her voice that terrified Pandora. She wasn't sure why.

"She's our friend, Lisa. She's special. We're helping her."

"My name is Pandora," Pandora said.

"Pleased to meet you, Pandora," the woman said. "I'm Emma Henderson. This is my daughter, Lisa."

"Who are you, Pandora?" the girl asked.

Pandora didn't want to answer. She didn't want to *talk* to that baby. But there wasn't any avoiding her if they were going to be in the car driving across the country. "I'm a Space Alien," she said. "I'm running away from the government."

The baby's head poked up over the top of the front seat. She tried to peer at Pandora through the gap in the blankets. Pandora didn't think she could see much—but Pandora could see her. The baby looked like a one-year-old, but she held herself like a grown-up. Her eyes were soft round baby eyes, but they focused keenly as the eyes of an adult.

Something *weird* about that child.

"You look strange," Pandora said. "There's something about you, isn't there?"

The tiny girl's eyes went wide.

"You really are a Space Alien, aren't you? That's how you know, isn't it? Because Space Aliens know everything?" She blinked again. "I read that in the newspaper at the grocery store. Is it really true?"

Were Space Aliens supposed to know everything? Pandora couldn't remember.

"I'm a Space Alien," Pandora said. Which was a non sequitur and she knew it, but so what? All-Knowing Space Aliens are supposed to talk in non sequiturs, aren't they?

"I know."

Emma reached over to pat her daughter's head. "You get in your car seat, Lisa. You know it isn't safe for you to ride around in the car standing up like that."

"*Mama!* I want to see the Space Alien. She's still hiding from me."

"Hush, child. She isn't hiding from you. She's hiding from the government. You keep staring at her that way you're going to show them exactly where she is. Now sit in your seat—you can see Pandora later."

And she turned on the radio. And from the radio came the voice of a man with a beautiful drawl, and he said the strangest things.

It was a bastard with a real warped sense of humor who named Pandora. Afterward no one was ever sure who it was who'd first made the stupid joke ("Call her *Pandora*—she gets out of here it's *all* out of the box! Heh heh heh!") but it happened somewhere on the long transport flight to Ohio from the southwest. When it was over the only thing anybody knew for certain was that it couldn't—no way in hell—have been Lieutenant Colonel Hightower or Airman Wallace Turner who made the joke. Hightower spent the whole flight glowering, staring out his window. Cursing under his breath. Didn't say a civil word to anybody. If he'd made that joke that day—well, there wouldn't have ever been an end to that story.

Turner didn't talk much to much of anyone, either—but for a very different reason.

Turner and the strange infant . . . something was happening between them. Tying them together somehow. Everyone who saw the two of them together couldn't help but think *They look like a mama and her babe,* which is about as strange a thing as you can possibly think about a nineteen-year-old male airman first class. It made Turner remarkable, and probably a little weird. If he'd told the joke that gave Pandora her name—if he'd *heard* it where anyone could see the way he reacted to it— someone would have told the tale, and it would have been as much a part of the legend as Pandora's dead Alien mother lying at rest invisible to entropy in hangar seventeen.

Silence on the line.

"I saw her, Barry. She was—amazing!"

"Saw who, friend? Who did you see?"

Again, silence.

"The Space Alien. The girl Space Alien who's loose in Pennsylvania."

Now was Barry Farber's turn for speechlessness.

"Tell me—tell me everything. Tell me exactly what you saw."

"I was in the mall. In McCrory's. Looking for place mats and a tablecloth—my youngest and our Labrador shredded the old ones this morning before I woke up. Heh. The darlings! I stood in the aisle at McCrory's, third aisle from the left, and a hush came over the whole place, so strange and quiet that I almost thought it was the Second Coming!"

Quiet. Quiet. More quiet.

"Yes? Go on, go on—don't stop there!"

"I look up to see what was the matter, and there she was! So strange, so beautiful. Barry, I tell you, I saw her, and how could I help but love her? She's like that, Barry. Your heart goes out to her the moment you see her.

"And then it got even stranger, because she turned to look me in the eye, with those big big so big eyes of hers, like the big teacup-and-saucer eyes of an elf in a Disney cartoon movie, only not like that, more like a flying-saucer Alien in *Close Encounters*, beautiful, beautiful, so beautiful. I felt my life pass before my eyes! She was a Space Alien, Barry, and I loved her so much. I saw her and my future flashed before my eyes, and I knew that I'd be calling you and telling you all about this right here right now over the airwaves. And I hope that maybe somewhere someplace she can hear me on the radio, and I hope that she knows that we love her, even though the army tried to walk right into the mall and kidnap her."

Pandora hardly heard what Barry Farber said after that.

"I'm sure she knows how you feel, wherever she is." Barry Farber cleared his throat. "You know, even after all the reports on the news, you're the first witness to call us. What else can you tell us. . . ?"

Emma glanced back at Pandora, lying on the backseat, hiding among the blankets. "It bothers you, doesn't it, child?"

She switched the radio off before Pandora could tell her that it did.

They're in Macdonald's office—Ken, Macdonald, Yolen, and Dvorkin. Yolen and Macdonald are talking; Dvorkin stands quietly by the door.

Ken isn't sure why he's here, except that Macdonald hasn't dismissed him yet, and his billet has disappeared, and he isn't sure who he's supposed to talk to about getting a new one. Ken asked Macdonald if he wanted him to report back to Wright-Patterson as Macdonald was ordering him back onto the fast helicopter in Pennsylvania, and Macdonald had said, *No, Estes, I'm not done with you yet,* which scared the hell out of Ken but there wasn't a whole damn lot he could do about it.

He wants to go home, but there is no home. He wants to curl up in a bunk and sleep for a week, but there's no damn way he's getting that billet, and he knows it.

So Ken sits in the deep soft leather armchair in the far left corner of Macdonald's office, and he listens to all kinds of classified stuff he doesn't want to hear.

Yolen hangs up the scrambled phone. "They've found Lieutenant Turner," she says, "in a field not far from the New Canaan mall. He's been shot—firing-squad style, bound and blindfolded, shot with a single bullet. Someone botched his execution—he's lost a lot of blood, but he's still alive."

"Where is he?"

"Local hospital. He barely made it there."

"Can we move him?"

"Not yet."

Macdonald nods. "When he's well enough to move, move him back to the Pandora Project's infirmary on Wright-Pat. Seal that whole damn place drum tight." He frowns. "Have them do that now, before Turner gets there. I want the Pandora Project locked up even tighter than it was before security broke. Nobody in, nobody out, all communication goes through this office. Anybody even *asks* for access to the project, I want to know who and I want to know why."

Yolen nods.

"You think Hightower is responsible for this?"

Yolen laughs. "Who else?"

Ken tries to clear his throat, but no one hears him.

"What do you think he's up to?"

"Pandora," Yolen says, "what else? He's obsessed with her. He says she nearly beat him to death."

"You think she did?"

Yolen rolls her eyes. "No," she says. "Something

beat him—very, very badly. But Hightower is a nut. Remember, they tried to drum him out of the air force twice in the fifties."

Ken clears his throat again. "Ah—sir," he says.

Yolen turns to face him. She looks angry and annoyed, and Ken is very very sorry he's brought her attention down on him. "What is it, Airman Estes?"

"I saw Hightower, ma'am," Ken says. "In the shopping-mall basement. I was down there looking to see if I could find Pandora while you all were on the phone."

Yolen looks annoyed. Macdonald looks curious.

"Go on, airman."

"I came around a corner and there was Hightower —half a dozen of his goons were with him."

Macdonald is suddenly very focused. *"Goons?"*

"His air policemen, sir."

Macdonald looks at Yolen. "What is he talking about? What kind of air police has Hightower got working for him?"

Yolen looks—unsettled. "I'm not sure yet," she says. "But I've found forty or fifty people who've disappeared over the years. Ugly customers. Heading into court-martial, sometimes, others in the middle of dishonorable discharge. Killers; thugs; drug runners. People from Vietnam caught red-handed in the middle of a scragging. They disappear in the middle of proceedings, and no one asks why."

"What's the connection to Hightower?"

"I haven't found one. But Hightower had forty-five APs assigned to him, and none of them have paper trails back home. No school records, no driver licenses, nothing. I don't think they're real people."

It's quiet for a while as Macdonald digests this. He looks very unhappy.

"What did Hightower do when he found you?"

"He asked me where Pandora was. I told him I didn't know. He started shouting, screaming in my face. He roughed me up a little. Took out his pistol and hit me with it a few times."

"Is that all?"

"I think he would have killed me, but a squad of National Guards came around the corner at the far end of the basement. When he saw them he and the APs let go of me and took off."

Macdonald's eyes narrow, and suddenly Ken knows the other man hears the part of the story he isn't telling.

"You told Hightower you didn't know where Pandora was," he says. "That wasn't true, was it?"

Ken wants to lie. He wants to say no, no sir, not me, no way in hell, but he knows damn well Macdonald will see through him. He considers telling the truth—and that scares him even worse.

"Ah, sir," Ken Estes says. And then nothing.

"Tell me, damn it. Tell me now, Estes, or I'll find out for myself."

Ken feels the blood rush out of him all at once, and suddenly he's too weak to hold himself upright in the plush leather chair, too weak to do anything but tell Macdonald what he wants to know—every last word of it. All about the far corner of the basement, and the little sounds, and the feeling in his gut like he knew where Pandora was, and how he heard her answer so faintly he almost thought it wasn't her.

And how he let her go because she didn't want to come with him.

He knows this is going to get him court-martialed. He's in deep deep shit and he should have gotten himself a lawyer before he said a word, but he didn't, and now he's fucked but good.

But when he's done Macdonald is laughing. "I like your instincts, Estes," he says. "I don't think you could have played that better if I'd given you a script."

Ken is stunned.

"I'm serious, Estes." Even Yolen looks skeptical. "You know something?" Macdonald asks. "I think Pandora wants to go home. Underneath the weird and the Space Alien and everything bizarre she's just a little girl run away from something horrible. And if she could find a way to go home safely, she would."

Ken laughs. "I thought that, too," he says. "I did! —But I couldn't find a way to say it."

"We need to follow her," Macdonald says. "We need to be there when she decides she wants to come home."

Yolen thinks they're both out of their minds— that's plain from the look on her face.

Then suddenly the whole question is irrelevant, because the secure fax is going off. Dvorkin steps away from the door to stand above the fax and read as the print comes away from the transfer head.

"No," he says. "No no no *no*."

He takes the paper from the fax and hands it to Macdonald, takes a phone from the cradle beside the fax. As Macdonald reads Dvorkin is asking questions.

As he hangs up the phone Macdonald speaks four unprintable words. "*What the hell is this?*" He holds the paper high for everyone to see, waves it back and forth above his head.

Dvorkin turns bright red.

"Macdonald, sir," he says. "Sir. We don't *know* what the hell that is. We don't know how it got into the AP feed. We don't know how anyone got a legitimate Pentagon exchange to list as the contact; we don't know why the exchange disconnected this morning at five A.M. We think it's connected to the untraceable orders that keep coming out of the Pentagon—but we aren't even sure of that. Sir."

"Hightower," Macdonald says. "Goddamn Hightower."

Yolen shakes her head. "You're forgetting about McNamee," she says.

Exact text of the peculiar notice that appeared on Wednesday's AP Newsfeed:

The following appeared on Tuesday's AP news-wire without the knowledge or consent of AP. AP denies all knowledge of the story, and points out

*that calls to the contact number—asking for ex-
planation of the swarm of helicopters and military vehicles that appeared on live CNN video
feed—are answered by a message indicating that
the number has been disconnected.*

WASHINGTON (AP)—Highly placed Pentagon
sources today asserted that yesterday's events at
the Canaan, Pennsylvania, shopping mall were
nothing but a monumental hoax. Interviews available. Contact: (202) 555-8956.

Voice-over: *A real Space Alien—or a real hoax?*
Bold white letters centered on the screen:
CROSSFIRE
From Washington, Crossfire. *On the left Thomas*
Wine. On the right, William Cannon.
Space Aliens in the shopping mall?—Tonight
William Cannon (sitting in for John Sununu) and
our own Thomas Wine discuss this afternoon's
sensational interview with the Alien in the
Canaan, Pennsylvania, shopping mall.
And in the Crossfire: Sarah Collier, Professor of
Anthropology at the University of Northeast Texas,
and Dr. Janice Eisen, author of the best-selling
Modern Man and Immoderate Myth: Three Views of
the Human Body in the Shape of the Human Mind.
Cannon: *Dr. Eisen, in your controversial book you*
posit that the human body takes its form
not because of our evolution from apes,
but because the human mind demands
our physical nature. Do you think this
would explain the rough similarities
between us and shopping-mall Aliens
like—
Wine: *Now, come on, Bill. Pandora looks nothing*
like a human being and anyone could see—
Eisen: *Yes, Bill, that's exactly what I'd say. Two*

*arms, two legs, a head. Hair. Eyes, mouth.
Any intelligent species needs—*

Wine: *Janice, that's about the silliest thing I've
heard all year—*

Collier: *I'm with Bill. It is a silly idea. But I can't
agree that Pandora is so obviously Alien.
The things that mark her as an Alien—
eyes as big as saucers, translucent skin,
long, pointed ears—how different are
they? Ever seen a wild bull? The
differences between wild oxen and dairy
cows are more pronounced than the
things that separate Pandora and the
woman who shared lunch with her—*

Cannon: *Well, if she isn't an Alien, then why the
hell is the Pentagon willing to use every
bit of hardware it has to try to get her
back?*

Macdonald shuts off the video feed. "Get them for
me," he says to Dvorkin. "I want both of those
women on the team for this project."

After a long while Pandora fell asleep.

When she woke it was pitch-dark night, and they
were alone on the road a long way from everywhere.

She pushed aside the blankets that covered her.
Sat up and stretched. Yawned. "Where are we?" she
asked.

She wasn't sure she wanted to know.

"Interstate Highway 81. Deep inside Virginia."

The baby stirred in her safety seat.

"Oh." She knew Virginia from maps and stories,
but that was all. She didn't see much more than that
looking out at the dark highway—just the road out
ahead of them, hints of the grassy median, and away
at the right edge now and then the specters of pine
trees.

"Do you know where you're going, child?"

Pandora thought: *I'm going to find my daddy.*

That's where I'm going. It felt purposeful and direct;
she felt like every step she took brought her closer to
him. Like—like something deep down inside her had
slipped forward in time to see her future, and knew
which way to turn, which step to take, which way to
look. Like destiny or something.

She was sure she was going the right way, but
that was all she knew.

"I'll know when I get there," Pandora said. She
wasn't sure that was right, but she hoped it was.

"Just say the word, I'll drop you off. We're going
all the way to the delta."

Pandora thanked her. "That's nice of you," she
said, "but I think—I think we're getting close."

Emma nodded.

"You Space Aliens," Emma said. "You always
think you know it all." And she laughed, as though
this were the most outrageous joke she'd ever heard.
After a while Pandora laughed, too, mostly just to be
polite.

"Mama? Is the Space Alien leaving already?" In
the dark the baby sounded—like an old woman. Pandora wasn't sure why. "Don't let her go before I get a
chance to see her, Mama. I want to see the Space
Alien for myself."

"I'm here," Pandora said. "You can look at me if
you want."

Pandora leaned forward to look over the seat. She
could see the woman and the baby faintly by the
glow from the dashboard.

The baby looked up.

"I can't hardly see you in the dark," the baby
said. She stared at Pandora anyway, scrutinizing her.
After a moment she leaned forward to release the
restraining buckle on her safety seat.

"Lisa, child, you know . . ." Emma started. But
she never finished the sentence. Just let it hang
there, like a cloud promising to rain.

"Yes, Mama. I know." But she still pulled off the

restraining straps, climbed out of the seat. Stood in the space between Emma and the safety seat.

Stared at Pandora.

"You're strange," Lisa said. "But—are you really a Space Alien? I thought Space Aliens looked—different. Yucky or something. You know what I mean?"

Pandora shook her head.

The little girl reached out, touched Pandora's face. Probed carefully. Not rough or anything, but firm, and strong—Pandora was amazed that a baby's hands could be so strong. Was she trying to see if Pandora's face was a mask? Was she trying to feel deep down on Pandora's face, to see how the bones underneath the flesh were different from a regular person's? (And they *were* different. Pandora could still remember the day when she was tiny when she touched Uncle Wally's face and found no bones where bones should have been, and other bones in places where Pandora had none.)

"Your eyes are very big," Lisa said. "Have they always been so big?"

Pandora frowned. "Not when I was little," she said. "Everything was smaller then."

"I know. But not like that. Were they always bigger than your cheeks like that? It looks so strange."

"They always were." Pandora pursed her lips. "They don't seem strange to me."

The talking baby nodded. "They wouldn't, would they?"

There was a sign up ahead.

WYTHEVILLE	3
BRISTOL	75

Pandora didn't know anything about Bristol or Wytheville, but when she saw that sign, read the word BRISTOL and the distance, she felt an awful chill. And she knew that Bristol was close to where she had to go.

. . .

It's six hours since the helicopter set them down on the roof above Macdonald's office, and they're back in that office after two hours' sleep and a trip to commissary—mostly for coffee.

Macdonald, Yolen, Estes.

Macdonald is still trying to figure out how Hightower mobilized so many people so fast. How he got them all coordinated on the ground in Canaan without leaving an enormous paper trail. And there isn't any trail—none at all. The orders came somewhere in the Pentagon, and they look serious and secure, but they come from no apparent source—there's no one but no one who admits to them. Oh, the grunts in the field know the NCOs who gave them their orders, and the NCOs know their lieutenants. And so on. But somewhere in Washington there's a false command that Yolen should've spotted the moment they set up shop, only she didn't because it wasn't even *there* yesterday. Macdonald has Dvorkin working his way through that wing of the Pentagon, one office at a time: if he can't buttonhole a command, at least they can buttonhole a desk. If they're lucky he'll hit pay dirt sometime tomorrow afternoon.

If they're lucky.

Macdonald has a feeling they won't be.

Macdonald has a feeling that someone way deep in the Pentagon is running a sleeper of a contingency plan, a plan buried deeper, forgotten more thoroughly than Pandora ever was. It could take him all year to find someone like that. Weeks at least.

Meanwhile everyone—*everyone*—has orders to verify mobilization orders.

This isn't going to happen again. Or if it does it'll be over Macdonald's dead body.

Estes is on the couch on the far side of the room, looking appropriately uneasy. He doesn't belong here. He knows it; Macdonald knows it. But Macdonald's been keeping him on a real short leash. Keeping him right where he can watch him with his own eyes. Macdonald isn't sure why. An intuition? Something like one. There's a use for Estes somewhere in this nightmare, and Macdonald wants him handy when the need arises.

The fax decrypter beeps and whirs and begins to print. Yolen turns to take the paper.

And when she sees what's coming out her eyes go wide as saucers.

"Jesus, Mary, and Joseph," Yolen says as she reads the decoded sheets inching into its tray.

This is a peculiar thing for Yolen—born Jewish, spent most of her life a practicing Quaker—this is a very odd thing for Yolen to say. But she says it nonetheless. Perhaps it's the strain of the circumstances that has her borrowing someone else's expletives.

"What?" Macdonald reaches to take the paper from her, but Yolen's too absorbed; she doesn't even notice. "What is it?"

"Aliens." She finished reading, half-unconsciously passes the first sheet to Macdonald as she takes the second from the printer's output tray. "Spaceships. Thousands of them."

It's a joke, Macdonald thinks. *This has to be a practical joke.* But he's never known Yolen to play a practical joke in all the years they've worked together.

Still, he scowls, grunts, asks her what she's talking about.

She looks up, looks Macdonald in the eye. "The big telescope out in Arizona—it found something among the asteroids."

"What are you talking about?"

She takes the second sheet that comes from the fax, hands it to Macdonald. "See for yourself."

And there's the picture from the telescope. And it's an armada—thousands and thousands of them. Thousands of Space Aliens coming to destroy the world.

They went through Bristol so fast Pandora almost didn't realize that they'd been there. Forty minutes

later they were in Tennessee. A few miles south of
the Tennessee border they were deep in pinewoods
again—woods as deep and mysterious as the night.

Why aren't we there yet? Thirty miles ago Pandora was sure her destination was someplace just
around the next corner—and now she felt exactly
the same.

Thirty more miles.

Fifty.

And up ahead, at the top of a long, long hill—that
was the place. That rest area, right there.

Pandora leaned forward to touch Emma's shoulder.

"This is the place," she said. "This rest area is
where I've got to go."

Emma grunted, surprised. "You're sure?" Which
meant *Are you sure? Out in the middle of nowhere?*
And also *So soon?* and *Couldn't you have warned
me?*

"Yes, I am."

Emma shrugged, switched on her right-turn
blinker. In a moment they were coasting into the rest
area.

It was about as ugly as a rest stop could be—
deep-down ugly, dying trees, overflowing rest rooms,
litter scattered everywhere in the overgrown grass.

"If you're hungry," Emma said, "we've got sandwiches in the cooler. In the trunk. Nothing fit for
breakfast, but better than no breakfast at all."

Pandora hadn't eaten since yesterday at the
greasy hamburger coffee shop with all those people
and television cameras watching. She was starving,
but she wasn't sure she wanted to eat in a place as
filthy as that rest stop.

But she knew it might be a long time before she
could eat again, so she tried to sound like she appreciated the offer. "I'm very hungry," Pandora said. "I'd
like that very much."

"I'll get the cooler out of the trunk. Why don't you

find one of the picnic tables over there—" she pointed "—and brush it clear of leaves?"

"Sure, if you'd like."

She was almost done brushing away the pine needles when Emma set the ice chest on the table.

"Just a minute," Emma said. "I'll go get Lisa."

Pandora would just as soon have let Lisa sleep. She had a serious bad feeling about her. It was like— like she was dangerous, somehow. Which was silly! How could a baby be dangerous? What could a baby do to a Space Alien?

Nothing, that's what.

But Pandora dreaded the sight of her. She almost ran away when she saw Emma reach into the car and lift the girl from the car seat. Almost screamed when the baby opened her drowsy eyes to stare at Pandora.

Run!

So silly. Such a silly silly thing to feel.

Pandora was too brave to run. She wasn't about to let a baby scare her.

Emma dished out the food, that was almost as gross as their surroundings. Soggy salami sandwiches wrapped in worn wax paper. The salami part was stiff and greasy slick around the edges, as though it had spent a long time drying out and getting putrid before anyone remembered to put it into a sandwich. The bread was mushy from the cooler ice melted into it.

And the taste—it made Pandora think of dead things rotting in the ground.

She ate it anyway because she was too hungry to fuss. When she was done the flavor stayed with her, cloying, no matter much water she drank from the fountain, trying to wash it down.

Baby Lisa sat on the far side of the picnic table staring at Pandora the whole time. Not eating, even though her mama had set food out for her. Not even blinking. Just staring, staring, like a snake trying to hypnotize the animal it's about to eat.

The woman brushed her hands against one another. "Can I ask you to watch my Lisa?—I've got to use the rest room."

Pandora wanted to say, *No, no, please don't ask your daughter scares me,* but there was no way she could. She owed the woman too much.

"Sure," Pandora said.

Emma smiled. "You're very gracious," she said. And wandered toward the concrete cubicle at the far end of the rest stop.

Lisa smiled frightfully as her mother walked away. She kept smiling, staring and smiling that terrible smile the whole time her mother was gone.

When her mother was almost back with them the baby leaned across the table and whispered to Pandora. "You aren't any Space Alien," she said. The words hit Pandora like a hammer, so hard she wanted to *scream.*

But she knew she didn't dare.

But the worst part wasn't the words. The worst part was something in the baby's voice that told Pandora she knew a terrible secret about her, something big and hideous and true, but there was no time to ask because now the lady was back with them, back and here and listening and there was no way Pandora could bear to have the baby say those words again where anyone else could hear them.

"I know what you are," Lisa said. "But I'll never tell."

Any minute now Pandora would be crying like she was the baby and the baby was her, and it was awful, awful, she was falling to pieces, and when she tried to keep from crying as she looked up to say good-bye to the lady who'd been so nice, it wasn't any use; she heard herself sobbing weep weep weep in between her words, and the lady said, *Are you okay?* and Pandora lied to say she was fine.

But she wasn't fine. She was awful. She didn't say it, and she couldn't say it, but she felt almost as bad as when she saw her mommy dead in the airplane hangar, and all she could say was thank you and good-bye, and she never looked back until it was too late.

When she was alone—out by what had once been a barbed-wire fence, but now was just a curved line of rotten posts and a few wild rusted strands of metal that'd once been strings of wire—when Pandora was alone, she howled and wailed at the setting moon, but the moon ignored her.

Macdonald rubs his eyes. "How fast are they moving? How long before this gets out? How long before every kid with a hobby-shop telescope can see exactly what's out there waiting for us?"

"A day. Two days? Maybe not even that long."

FOUR

The Unidentified Flying Object may well be the most fabulous artifact in all of contemporary folklore. And commonest, as well—for few children of the city can see a falling star paint its crayon mark of light across the rural sky without knowing in their hearts that they've seen a spaceship come to Earth. Oh, most of them—driving cross-country late at night, say, or camping in the wilderness—most of them realize they've seen nothing but a bit of interplanetary debris come to earth. But there are plenty enough ignorant of even that small cosmology, and week by week the tellings and retellings grow. One recent poll found that twice as many Americans believed in Space Aliens as credited the existence of a Supreme Being—though the fault here may lie in the couching of the question, and not only in those answering.

Here, for instance, a particularly telling example of the UFO legend in its common form, recounted so colorfully in this transcript from the oral history archives at the University of Southwest Virginia:

Billy Wildman: *Just like you say we 'uz driving 81 out of Bristol, must've been like to 4 A.M., and we look up and there's this light! In the sky, a light! And we say, I say to Benny-Joe, I say, Benny, that's one of them a steroids, we ought to get it for ourself, they's worth money. I read about that. So we drive on out yonder and of'n the highway, and we drive a ways. And there it is! Only it ain't no asteroid. It's a spaceship, and this old man gets out of it—plain old man, could've been you or me but older—gets out of it and goes into his cabin right next to where he's parked the spaceship. And that's all! We tried to go in and talk to him, but there was this wall we couldn't see between us and him.*

So anyhow we go back the next day, to show everybody this spaceship and this cabin with the old man, but we couldn't find where it was no more. Or maybe it wasn't there? Ain't no way to say. First we saw it was in the dark, and who knows where the hell they been in the dark?

Notice the peculiarly American turnings on the myth—the old man; the way that the meteorite be-

comes a spacecraft, where the reverse is ordinarily
true. What does it say about our society that we produce such myths as this? What does it say about
Wildman that he turns his tale in this ingenuous direction?

"We found her," Dvorkin says as he barges into the
Macdonald's office—unannounced and without warning. He carries a thick folder of photographs under
his arm. "She's at a rest stop on I-81 in Tennessee,
eating at one of the picnic tables."

It never ceases to amaze Macdonald, the things
they can track with satellite photographs. They can
(quite literally) watch anyone anywhere in the entire
world, so long as that person is outdoors. Even follow
the subject inside certain types of buildings.

"I thought you were tracking down the rogue contingency plan, David," Yolen says. She looks unhappy. She's always been hard on Dvorkin;
Macdonald has never been certain why. Perhaps he
reminds her of someone. . . ? But it's hard for Macdonald to imagine who that might be. Dvorkin is a
red-haired man with milk-white skin—ruddy in the
summer—middling height, the slightest South African accent; Macdonald has rarely seen anyone re-
motely like him.

Dvorkin coughs. "I am, ma'am," he says. Macdonald thinks he's very wise to speak to Yolen this way.
Yolen is a tough customer. "It's at a dead end—we
traced it back to two of McNamee's cronies in the
Pentagon. Can't find either one of them, though—it's
as though they've vanished from the face of the
earth."

Macdonald scowls; he knows all this. What he
wants to hear about is Pandora. He clears his throat,
looks Dvorkin in the eye.

"How did she manage to get out of the shopping
mall without bringing the mob down on herself?"

Macdonald is very glad she managed it, all things
considered. He wants her to come back on her own

terms, in a sane place, at a sane time. If those fools had got hold of her in the mall there'd have been no end of grief over it.

"Telephone access hatch for the mall," Dvorkin says. "All the way across the street—by the gas station. We've got her talking to a woman at the gas station—a customer—and got her getting into the woman's late-model station wagon. And we've got the station wagon driving across Pennsylvania, down through Maryland and Virginia. Into Tennessee."

Macdonald nods.

"Good work, David. Get a team down there—I've got a feeling she's going to want to come home soon. I want to be there for her when she does."

That's when Dvorkin's beeper goes off.

Macdonald *hates* beepers. He'd just as soon see Dvorkin stop wearing the damn thing—in Macdonald's book the crisis hasn't happened that was so urgent it was worth hearing that shrieking noise even one more time. But Dvorkin isn't comfortable without the damn thing, and Macdonald doesn't micromanage.

Dvorkin reads the beeper, turns it off. Reaches for Macdonald's phone, dials, speaks. He's only on the phone a moment before he hangs up, shaking his head.

"She's gone into the forest," he says. "Dense pinewoods in that part of Tennessee. No way for the satellite to track her."

Maybe Dvorkin thinks this is a problem; Macdonald certainly doesn't.

"It's all right," he says. "We send down a couple teams, keep the eyes watching the edge of the forest. When she comes out, we'll be ready for her."

A MESSAGE FROM PASTOR DON
OF THE RELIGION TELEVISION NETWORK

Brothers and sisters, strange events roam our land. That some tumult or upheaval augurs is no secret to those who've followed the news reports of recent hours. But the significance of these events is still very much in question.

There are some among us who say, *"Listen, listen, listen, the end is near: gather in the Ruins at Megiddo."* I have heard them give this counsel publicly and to all who'll listen.

I have heard them preach these words this very hour.

I would tell you that it is likely not *that* time.

I tell you: Wait. Listen, watch. Tumult does hang above us, but this is not the apocalypse we've waited for so long. If an end is near—and what thinking, hearing soul cannot know we approach some terrible ending?—if an end is near it is only *an* end, and not *the* end. Go to your basements, go to your shelters: prepare for the war that may well be upon us. But gather not in the ruins; for that battle lies ahead of us.

As Pandora hiked through the Tennessee woods she felt as though she were walking through her own heart. It was as though the trees and the brush were the road marks of her life, and the path she followed was her destiny.

And maybe it was.

HEARD ON WABC
NEWS TALK RADIO SEVENTY-SEVEN

Voice #1: Dittos, Rush! From Tylerville, Tennessee! Want to thank you for finally bringing some common sense to the airwaves around here.

Voice #2: Thank *you*. (Clears throat.) Now what's this about your seeing a girl?

Voice #1: I saw her, Rush! The girl on TV, I saw her in person and she's real, she's amazing, she's incredible!

Voice #2: What?

Voice #1: The girl on CNN, Rush. I saw her!

Voice #2: (coughs; growls) I don't *care* what you

saw on CNN. We don't talk about UFOs
on this show. And we sure don't talk
about little Space Alien girls running
amok in Tennessee!

Two hours Pandora hiked through those woods. Long
hours when she hadn't slept since way up in the
north part of Virginia the night before—and after a
while she just wanted to find a dry, soft, comfortable
bed of pine needles and sleep for a million years.

Sleep for a million years.

But she didn't stop. Didn't sleep. She kept going
deeper and deeper into the forest, high up into the
hills that overlooked the interstate, and past those so
far that she couldn't see the highway or anything
anymore—just woods, woods, and more woods. Near
the stump of a broken pine she stopped to wonder if
she was lost. She didn't think she could find her way
back. More than once she'd had to turn to follow the
contour of a hill, and now there was no way she
could remember which turn, which hill, which direction.

But even if she was lost she still had her sense of
where she had to go. Which was up, up ahead over
this hill, and beyond that into . . .

After a long time there was a change in the look
of the woods, a weird change she couldn't figure for
the longest time—until she realized it was the trees.
The trees were no longer pines, but some strange
unknowable broadleaf species, bizarre as bonsai re-
produced to scale—

And then the path that was her destiny took a
bend, and Pandora saw the house she'd known would
be there. And she had known, too—*known* it. She'd
seen it in her mind for a long way away, and here it
was, just as she'd pictured it.

Down to the tiniest detail on the intricately
carved doors.

This is where I've been going all this time.

But what was here? Why was she here?

My daddy.

And felt a chill of dread, and for the longest moment could not understand why.

Until she thought of the devil, back in the nightmare she'd had in the mall basement. *You are looking for your father,* he'd said. *Very soon you'll find him—in a place and time you won't expect. Won't accept. When you find him you will deny him to his face. And run from him.*

I won't run, Pandora thought. *I won't deny.*

But she hadn't seen him yet. And there was no way she could be sure.

Besides, what did the devil know? This old house wasn't anyplace where she was supposed to meet her daddy. It was just a house along the way, and now that she'd seen it she'd move on.

In a minute or two.

But first she had to get a better look at the house. She had to see—those shutters. The windows. Why did this house look like someplace out of a storybook? Why were there flowers all around—at the base of the house, in little pots there by the windowsills? And there, over there—that was a garden in among the trees. A rock garden—it was a rock garden if it was organized around rocks that way, wasn't it? Pandora thought so.

Beautiful trees surrounded the rock garden.

These trees were like no others Pandora had seen. Small broad waxy leaves; bark etched deep with crevices and ridges; and there at every crux of major branches jellied tufts of oozed-out sap. Look how they grew low to the ground, look how their branches weighed down and wide, where the branches of most trees soar toward the sun. Were they fruit trees? Pandora could imagine how fruit trees might be bred to grow low for easy picking, or how the weight of fruit could pull the branches toward the ground.

Whatever these trees were, they were nothing

like the sharp-needled pines that crowded the edge
of the forest where she'd started.

The dirt here was different, too—it was dark
black brown where the soil everywhere else for a
hundred miles was palish bright red.

"I thought I'd see you today."

Pandora nearly jumped out of her skin. She
whirled around, ready to fight—and saw a tall, very
old man standing almost close enough to touch.
Eighty years old? Ninety? From the look of him Pandora thought he could've been a million.

"What?" Pandora tried to stop the question from
sounding like a threat. But it came out that way anyhow, and once she'd said it there wasn't a whole lot
else she could do. The old man was dangerous—frail,
yes; old, yes; dangerous, too. It wasn't even safe to
apologize to a man as dangerous as him. "What do
you want from me?"

The old man blinked.

He looked surprised. He didn't look angry, or
threatening, nor even especially scary. But Pandora
knew better; she knew he was a threat.

It didn't occur to her to wonder how she could
have so developed an opinion of an old man she'd
never seen before. Some things you just *knew* if you
were a Space Alien, that was all. And when you knew
them you didn't have to question them.

Except maybe sometimes when it turned out you
were wrong, like when—but times like that weren't
important. Not to a Space Alien.

"Nothing, Pandora," the old man said. He looked
defeated. "I'm here to do whatever I can."

Liar!

"Why? Why would you want to help me? Why
would you be—waiting for me here?"

That was it exactly, that was the thing that made
her so afraid—she couldn't figure why he'd be waiting here in the place her heart found for her.

And how did he know her name?

"It's an old debt," the old man said. "One I could

never repay or repair. I'm here because I know in my heart that I have to try."

Pandora shook her head, but even as she did it she wasn't sure what it was she wanted to deny. "I'm here to find my daddy. He's a Space Alien, just like me. Is my daddy here?"

The old man frowned. He looked as though he were about to cry.

And how could Pandora be harsh with him when he was about to cry? Even if he was the devil from her dream, how could she be mean to him?

She couldn't.

"I had a dream," Pandora said. "In my dream I saw the devil, and he told me that I'd find my daddy. Is my daddy here?"

Now the old man *was* crying.

It made her very uncomfortable to see him crying, all weird and wounded looking like that. It wasn't good to cry like that in front of strangers, and Pandora knew she was as strange to him as he was to her.

"I don't think I could ever tell you."

Pandora didn't understand. But the sight of the old man was enough to break her heart. Despite the fact that she didn't trust him and disliked him instinctively, she reached out to touch his arm.

"Don't cry," she said. "I didn't mean to hurt you. I didn't."

The old man nodded. "You didn't hurt me. I hurt myself, a long time ago."

Whatever *that* meant.

She didn't want to ask the next question. She didn't want to know the answer. But found herself asking anyway, despite caution and good sense:

"How. . . ?"

The old man shook his head. He didn't say a word.

And what could Pandora say to that?

Nothing.

Not a damned thing.

After a while she pointed at the trees. "They're beautiful," she said.

That made the old man smile.

"Thank you. I thought a long time before I planted those trees. They've served me well, I think." He frowned. "I haven't invited you in. For coffee? Or tea? I have peaches and more peaches if you have a taste for fruit."

Coffee. Uncle Wally never let her drink coffee. Though he sometimes let her have thin tea.

"Yes," Pandora said.

"Okay, then," the old man said. He turned and started toward the door. "What did you want—coffee, tea, fruit? I can make lunch, if you like."

"All of them, please." And realized why the old man had chuckled at the answer: she was supposed to choose something, not just accept it. But she was *starving!* All she'd had to eat all day was Emma's gross-out salami. "I'm very hungry," she said.

"If you say so. But coffee and tea don't usually go together well."

"They don't? Oh. Just the coffee, then. My—" She was about to say, *My uncle Wally never lets me have coffee and I want to try it.* But that wouldn't do. "Just the coffee."

He led her into the house that was warm and cozy as a rich lady's private library in an old-time movie. Tidy, too, which was pretty amazing to Pandora, who'd lived all her life with bachelor soldiers and *knew* how they all had messy quarters. Except when somebody was on them about having an inspection.

The old man pointed her at an old wooden table and told her to help herself to the peaches in the bowl at its center. Pandora took one, bit into it, tasted the savory-sweet sharpness of the fruit, felt the fuzziness against her tongue as the skin burst against her teeth. Cookie never got peaches like this.

Cookie tried hard, he really did, but there was only so much he could do with air-force rations. Sometimes not much at all, in fact.

As she ate, Pandora wondered what was happening back home, in the barracks. She worried for Cookie and her uncle Wally, worried for all her uncles.

Till now she found herself thinking of the General.

She didn't want to think about him. But she did.

She got so angry when she thought about the General. She wanted to kill him. She wanted to be enormous like *The Attack of the Fifty-Foot Woman* and lift him up by the scruff of the neck and beat him to a pulp.

She imagined the General tiny as a rag doll, imagined herself picking him up and pulling his limbs from his torso, one by one by one. There was blood everywhere in her imagining, jetting from the ragged stumps of his arms as the General screamed—

Pandora shuddered. What a terrible thing to imagine! Almost like—like it made her as bad as he was.

But the vision didn't go away, and even if it shamed her Pandora still wanted to kill that awful man. She wanted to kill him as horribly as she could. And Pandora knew it maybe made her just as bad as he was, but she didn't care.

"We need to get Pandora home before that armada out there gets close enough for anyone to notice," Macdonald says. "Get a team ready to search the woods—if she's lost in there, we may have to help her out. And keep an eye out for cameras—I don't want her on TV again. There's going to be enough hysteria as it is."

"Got it," Dvorkin says.

"Any sign of Hightower yet? What about Mc-Namee?"

Dvorkin shakes his head. "No sign of either of them."

Macdonald grimaces. "This smells bad—real, real bad. I don't like it at all."

. . .

"Sandwiches?" the old man asked as he reentered the room carrying a big plate piled high with triangle-cut sandwiches. "Ham and turkey, here. I've got provolone on the cupboard if you'd rather. . . ."

They smelled wonderful.

Wonderful.

In his other hand he carried a wide bowl filled with chips—corn chips, they looked like. Nestled among the chips was a smaller bowl filled with something like spaghetti sauce but different because it was thinner and there were chunky bits of vegetable stuff in it. . . .

"Salsa," the old man said. "You look as though you'd never seen it before."

Pandora looked up at him. She felt confused. "I haven't. What's it for?"

"It's a dip. For the chips. Like sour cream and onion, but spicy. And it doesn't give you indigestion." He frowned. "Or do you. . . ?"

Pandora shook her head. "Not me. Never."

"That must be nice. My stomach gives me awful trouble sometimes."

Pandora nodded. "It is."

The old man set the bowl and platter down, turned, walked back into the kitchen. He came back a moment later with plates, glasses. A tall pitcher of icy-clear water that had big beads of dew growing on its surface.

Pandora was ravenous.

"Help yourself," the old man said.

Pandora did.

The food was delicious as it looked. As it smelled! Pandora ate so many chips, so much of the strange salty-spicy-oniony salsa dip, so many sandwich halves that in no time at all she'd lost track of how much and how many, and after that she kept on eating for a good while longer because she was still hungry.

Not full yet, anyway.

She wanted to be full; God only knew when she'd get the chance to eat again.

When her stomach was almost full as it could be she finally thought to ask about her daddy.

"Say, mister," she said, "is my daddy around here? I'm looking for him. Something made me think he was here from halfway across the country, and I think that maybe he might be."

The old man stumbled over his own tongue.

"You'd know him if you saw him," she said. "He's a Space Alien. Just like me!"

"I—" the old man said. And then he just stopped.

Like he knew something he couldn't never say for nothing no matter what.

Because it hurt, maybe?

Or because. . . ?

Because what?

"What's the matter?" Pandora asked him. "You seen my daddy or haven't you?" And then a scary thought came over her. "He's okay, isn't he? He isn't hurt or something, is he?"

"Your father's fine," the old man said.

Pandora nodded.

"But have you seen him? I never met him—not yet. Is he as strange and wonderful as I know he is? As good and generous and great?"

The old man shook his head. "I'm not the one to tell you that."

Pandora nodded.

Spent a moment thinking about what the old man meant. And said the first thing that went through her head, which maybe she shouldn't have, but she felt so logy and comfortable with the fullness in her stomach that it was hard to worry about what she did or didn't say. "Are you his enemy? Is that what you mean? Are you my daddy's bitter enemy out in outer space, and are you here to capture me to hold me ransom till he gives up?"

The old man laughed.

"It won't work, if that's what you're doing. I won't

be a hostage. I *can't* be! I'm a Space Alien. Nobody can capture me. I wouldn't let them!"

He just kept laughing and laughing and laughing. If Pandora didn't know that mean old man was an underhanded earthling, she might've took it personal.

"No, Pandora. I like your daddy fine. We're close, he and I. Certainly there's no enmity between us."

Pandora nodded. *I bet,* she thought. But she didn't say it. She didn't believe a word the old man said. Not for a minute.

"Then how come you get so shaky when I ask you about him?"

The old man shook his head. "Your question doesn't make me uneasy."

Which was a straightforward lie. An obvious one, too: even if Pandora had been in a mind to trust him she would have seen how he wasn't telling the truth.

No.

"Every time I ask you about my daddy, old man, you get weird as a mess cook serving ptomaine. I ask you why, and you tell me you don't do it. How come you think I'm blind? How come you think I'm stupid?"

He didn't answer right away.

Didn't answer after Pandora waited for a while, neither.

"Well?"

The old man snorted. " 'Well' what, Pandora?"

" 'Well,' when are you going to tell me about my daddy?"

"My name is Walt," he said. "Walter Fulton."

It wasn't an answer, and both of them knew it.

"When are you going to tell me?"

Old Walt Fulton, ancient as time, looked away. Got out of his seat. Went to the dining-room window and stood beside it, staring out into his strange woods.

"I'm not," he said. "I can't."

I bet you can't.

"Why not?"

"Because if I told you, you wouldn't believe me. You'd hear me say words I never said, and not hear those I did say. And you'd get mad, and—I don't know what else. But I know that I'm not the one to tell you. I shouldn't be. Can't."

She believed *that*, all right. In a pig's eye! Ha!

"Tell me anyway. Tell me what you know."

"I won't."

Before she could protest he was moving across the room, first toward her, and Pandora was afraid he was going to *do* something—touch her, hit her, breathe at her, something. Maybe just look at her. But no; before he got to Pandora he turned toward the foyer and walked to the door they'd come in through.

"Come with me," he said. "I can't tell you anything. But I can show you. And if you see maybe you can know for yourself."

And he opened the door.

And stood there.

Waiting for her.

Now it was Pandora's turn to fall all off balance. He wanted her to *what*? Where was he going? And why. . . ?

She got up from the table, started toward the door uneasily.

"I don't understand," she said as she walked through the door. "Where are we going?"

"Not far," old Walt Fulton said. "Just past the rise."

He nodded uphill—away from the direction Pandora had come by. And started off in that direction without bothering to look to see if Pandora came along.

Old Walt Fulton was a weird one, Pandora decided. But she didn't know the half of it.

"This way," old Walt called back to her when he reached a knot of trees so dense she could hardly see him waving to her.

"Wait," she called to him. "I can't walk so fast."

He waited while Pandora took her own sweet time climbing uphill to meet him. Of course she did! It served him right, the way he treated her—talking weird, refusing to answer questions, dragging her off to see God knew what, and while he ran off so far ahead that she got winded trying to keep up. He had a lot of nerve for a bent old earthling man.

But it didn't seem to bother old Walt Fulton, no matter how she dawdled. He never got impatient, never got annoyed. Just the opposite, in fact: he looked amused and enchanted.

Like—it was like . . . *He acts like he loves me. Like he loves me too much to mind what I do to annoy him.*

Pandora wasn't sure she liked that. She decided to ignore him.

"That was a performance," Walt Fulton said as she drew close to him. "You're quite the little princess."

Pandora smiled. Sighed. "Yes," she said, "I am, aren't I?"

It's not entirely to Pandora's credit that she said those words deadpan and entirely serious.

Nor to Walter Fulton's that he wasn't able to keep himself from laughing when he saw the ingenuously haughty look on her face. Not that any sensible arbiter could blame him: that imperious expression on Pandora's beautiful and strange face—it *was* a sight. She *did* look remarkably silly.

But she didn't know that.

And when Walt Fulton laughed to see her the laughter was a spear that found her heart through every armor, bone, and breast Pandora had to ward away the world.

And *hurt.*

In her imagination Pandora crumpled up and died. Her knees, her arms, her neck—all of them went slack, and she fell like a rag doll off the hillside. Went tumbling down among the trees.

And down in her heart she felt a stone-hard coldness that was frigid as the deepest coldest rock on earth.

"Oh," the old man said, because he saw right away what he'd done. "Pandora—I'm sorry. I didn't mean—"

Pandora didn't listen to him. She just sat on the ground all covered with thick crinkly leaves and waited for the trees to wither, break, and rustle away in the wind; for the sky to close in around her. For the world to end.

Old Walt knelt beside her. Took her hand. (Which was yechy but how could she complain how could she protest when the world was folding up? There was no time.)

"I'm sorry, Pandora," the old man said. "I didn't mean to laugh. You're my princess. You'll always be my princess."

Like that mattered! And what business did he have making her his princess?

And why did it matter if mean yechy old Walt Fulton laughed when she acted like a princess? Why should it matter at all about *him?*

But it did matter. It mattered a whole lot.

Mattered so much it hurt.

But it shouldn't!

And Pandora wouldn't let it! She wouldn't! Faugh on old Walt Fulton! She wouldn't *let* it matter what he thought!

"Let go of my hand," Pandora said. "I'm fine. And I'm *not* your princess, now or ever."

Cold wind rushed around in the air. Or maybe Pandora just imagined that it did.

The old man let go of her hand. Stepped away. "I'm sorry," he said. "I didn't mean to hurt you."

Pandora shook her head imperiously. "Don't worry. *You* couldn't." As if to say: *Old man, you're too far beneath me to be a threat—you're nothing that I fear.* And she meant it, too, even if it was as big a lie as any the old man could tell.

The old man nodded, but it was plain he didn't believe any more than Pandora did herself. "This way," he said. And started into the thick woods at the crest of the hill.

Pandora followed directly, and quickly; she didn't want to be left behind again.

Not that there was time for her to fall behind. It wasn't more than half a dozen yards from the spot where they'd stood talking to the place where the old man pressed an opening in the vines and weeds to lead her out—

—out into the most beautiful place in the world.

A narrow plateau close in by the foot of a so-tall mountain that reached so far into the sky that its peak stood obscured by clouds, and all along the inmost edge of the plateau a river ran ribbon pretty along the mountain. Apple trees lined the riverbank unevenly; bright ankle-high grass filled the space between the trees.

"It's beautiful," Pandora said.

Old Walt Fulton grunted, nodded. He didn't bother to turn around.

Pandora hardly noticed. She hardly even realized she was walking, following old Walt Fulton across the plateau, halfway across the plateau now, and moving crosswise and upstream. The old man led her toward the water, then upstream along the brook. When she looked in the water she thought of the old man, but she didn't know why.

They walked a quarter mile before he paused under the shade of an apple tree. And sat down on the ground. And rested his back against the tree trunk.

"You might as well sit down," he said. "This takes a while."

Pandora pretended to ignore him. She kept walking. Not very far—instead of going anyplace she wandered around, looking close into the grass at the ants and crickets and bugs that lived down inside it. At the apple trees where caterpillars crawled around on some of the hanging fruit, and one of them eating,

nibbling one tiny corner through the bright green
skin of a tiny apple. (She wondered: were those
worms?—Worms like when people talked about
wormy apples? They didn't look anywhere near as
gross as she'd always imagined. When she thought of
worms she thought of slimy stretchy gross-out
things, but these were fuzzy and beige and almost
pretty, and look at the roundness of the tiny eyes
and the motion of all its pinpoint legs. . . . Like a
stuffed toy, almost. But smaller and alive.)

Pandora wandered toward the bank of the stream
and stared down into the water. Inside there were a
thousand little things swimming, and for a moment
she thought they were fish, maybe guppies or gold-
fish like Uncle Simon liked to keep, but when she
looked close she saw they weren't fish at all—tadpoles? Were those tadpoles, like the drawings in her
picture book *All God's Creatures*?

They had to be. Nothing else in *All God's Creatures* was round and lumpy like that, with green-
grey-green skin just the dirty color of the algae that
grew where water lapped against the stones on the
bank. And look at those teeny-tiny feet, and the tail
even bigger than the lumplike abdomen. What did
they feel like, to touch them? Pandora was about to
reach into the water to try to catch one when the
stream went crazy with a wave larger than the current, and Pandora heard the sound of something
enormous roiling up out of the deep center of the
stream, and look, look over there by the tree where
the old man sat dozing: shiny metal, bright glass, and
something Pandora couldn't begin to name—

—to name—

—look! Rising, rising magnificent out of the water
and the old man too fast asleep to see! She wanted to
go to him to wake him to show him the wonder the
spectacle but there wasn't any time, no time to take
her eyes from the spaceship—

—*spaceship!*—

It was beautiful. Beautiful. A million times more

beautiful than the wondrous ship she'd seen in the vision of her birth of her mother's death of the spaceship bursting from the sky as the General who wasn't then a general shot her mother down . . .

Smaller than that ship. Lots smaller; where that ship was enormous, like a triple tractor trailer, this was like a pickup truck. With a camper shell on back? About that big. Maybe a little bit larger, but not by much.

Pandora wasn't sure how big that meant on the inside.

And where that greater ship had flown pretty through this sky, this smaller one looked like a sculpture. Like someone had made it carefully, consideredly. It looked designed not just to sail through outer space, but—to *live* in.

To *live* with.

Was this why the old man had brought her here? To see this? But how could *he* know about. . . ?

He couldn't. It just wasn't possible. He was an earthling. A dumb old mean old stupid old earthling, even if he did know something about her daddy that he wouldn't tell her.

Even if he did know her name.

Earthlings didn't have spaceships.

They didn't even *know* about spaceships.

(But the old man knew about this one, didn't he? He'd brought her here to see it, and he'd summoned it up out of the water, and, and—)

Something was very wrong.

The world was tilted on its ear.

Everything, outer space, the universe, all the planets and stars and stuff everywhere—*everything* was turned on its ear.

So strange.

So impossible.

The ship, so beautiful.

High overhead, the rumbling of a jet.

An air-force reconnaissance jet. One of the really expensive ones.

Pandora thought: *Oh no it's seen me it's seen the ship the river everything it's looking for me and now it's found me no no no!*

And she turned to run for her life.

Never mind the old man. Never mind the spaceship, the river; just run—

—run—

A hand! A hand on her arm!

And Pandora whirled to turn to face her attacker—

Who was no attacker at all.

Just the old man, old Walt Fulton, touching her arm to get her attention to—

To what?

"It's okay," Walt Fulton said. "He can't see us from there. The river is protected."

Protected?

"Don't touch me," she said. She yanked her arm away from him before he could respond. "What do you mean, *protected?*"

The old man stepped back. He looked—as though he'd touched a fire, and had to hold himself to keep from swearing over burned fingers. Or maybe he didn't look that way at all; maybe that was only what Pandora wanted to see in him. Either way, he pulled back. And he told her about the river.

"There's a sky screen here. Over the hill. Has to be. If there weren't, they could see my ship from up above—on days when the stream runs clear. Which come more often than I like."

Pandora looked at him confused and surprised. What did he mean, *my ship?* He couldn't have a spaceship. He was just an earthling.

Unless he was from the future or something. "Are you from the future? How. . . ?"

The old man shook his head. "You'll know that soon enough," he said. "I've already shown you more than I ought to've."

"You haven't shown me inside the spaceship," she

said. "You have to. Have to!" She looked at him very hard. "I'll be mad if you don't."

At first her threat seemed to confuse the old man. Then he laughed and shrugged. "No more harm than I've done already," he said.

As the ship opened wide.

Like a flower, blossoming; that was what Pandora thought when she saw it. Exactly like that flower on the nature show, the one in the time-lapse photography picture where it bloomed all at once in just a moment even though in real life it'd took days to bloom. Where a moment before had stood sleek walls impervious to wind and rain and flood, now great wisps of gossamer knit foil furled themselves out and open, and here before them was a door, and a ramp led up to it.

Inviting them.

The old man had never pushed a button to operate the thing; had not gestured; nor ever said a word that some mechanical intelligence aboard the ship might take as a command. The ship simply opened to invite them, and did so because the old man had said it might as well.

Pandora's eyes went wide with awe.

"Can I go inside?" she asked. "Can I really?"

"Of course you can," the old man told her. "You always could."

He said that. He really did. But when Pandora asked him what he meant by it—much later in that day—he refused to explain. Worse: he pretended not to hear the question.

That bothered her for a long time.

But it didn't bother her as she stepped up the ramp, as she got her first glance ever in her life inside that spaceship's door. Then and there, at the door of what she knew in her heart was the most incredible spaceship in the world/in outer space/in the entire universe—how could she think about hard questions? How could she think about what the old man meant, and what he knew, and what awful plan he had a working?

All of that was—immaterial. Meaningless.

Then. And there.

Inside the ship was amazingly larger than without. So large, in fact, that it defied the principles of geometry. As Pandora understood them, anyhow. The contradiction struck her the moment she saw inside. How could a spaceship no taller than an ordinary house have this living room (or was it a foyer?) with a cathedral ceiling two stories high?

And never mind geometry, what about physics: this furniture—Nordic modern, like you saw on TV shows from the late sixties—this furniture with its throw pillows and light construction, all of it so obviously unattached—how could furniture like this suit a place meant to rise up and soar through the skies, beyond the skies and space the universe the suns—?

But it was beautiful, even still.

"You'll want to see the bridge," Walt Fulton said. "The hall in the back on the left is the one that leads there."

Pandora didn't pay any attention. She was too busy wondering why it was that the inside of a spaceship would look like a picture of a Frank Lloyd Wright house in *Better Homes & Gardens*.

Which was exactly what this looked like, now that she thought about it.

The old man walked around her, past her. Stepped through the doorless doorway at the far end of the room. Just before he disappeared he turned back to face Pandora, waved to get her attention.

"You coming? The bridge is this way."

Pandora grunted.

Sighed.

Shrugged.

Followed.

The old man was full of mysteries and mystery; it was almost as though—

As though he were a Space Alien.

After all, how could an earthling-normal old man be full of spaceships and mystery and time out of sync? He couldn't, and that was that.

But he was.

And old Walt Fulton was human as could be.

Mystery.

The hall had a peculiar curve to it that Pandora couldn't quite figure—a tilt, almost, but with roundness to it, and so long and slow that it was hard to see what way it went because there was only a tiny bit of it Pandora could see at any one time.

A line of doors strung along the right side, spaced wide—thirty feet apart, at least. The hall went like that on and on long and far. So long that there was no way the ship's outside size could ever contain it.

After the foyer Pandora had almost expected this hall to be this way. This was a spaceship, after all; and if it could fly through space and time and everything, there was no reason it couldn't be like a ten-gallon hat with a hundred gallons of water in it.

"Why is it so far?" Pandora asked. But she knew the answer.

"Because it is," the old man said. "Bridge is at one end of the ship; stern is at the other."

That wasn't the real answer, of course. The real answer was *Because it's a spaceship*. Why else? What other reason was necessary?

"Will we be there soon?"

The old man nodded. Which Pandora only barely saw him do, since he was ahead of her a ways and walking with his back to her.

"This is it," he said. "This door."

It opened before he could touch the handle.

Which was when it finally occurred to her to wonder: was the ship smart or something? Did it have a computer brain like Hal on *2001*? And if it did, would it try to hijack them once it had them in its clutches? Pandora didn't like that one bit. Computers were one thing when they sat on your desk with the little cursor on the screen going blink blink

blink, but the whole idea of a computer run amok
taking over a spaceship no not even taking over because there it was in control like it was *supposed* to
be that way. . . ! Opening doors, dragging spaceships out of creeks, doing God knew what else with
nobody telling it! No thank you very much, please.

"Is the ship going to take off on its own? Fly into
outer space with us in here, before I even find my
daddy?"

The old man stood in the doorway, waiting for
her.

"No," he said, "why would it do a thing like that?"

Pandora rolled her eyes.

"Because there's a computer inside. Like Hal? On
2001?" The old man looked puzzled. "You know, the
movie?"

He shook his head. "I never saw it. What happened?"

"The computer was in charge, and it went crazy
just like all computers do sooner or later. And it tried
to kill everybody. I'm not sure—maybe it did kill
them. I didn't understand the way it ended, except
that there was a picture of a big baby at the end."

"Huh." The old man frowned. "I never had any
problem with the computer here. But I wouldn't—
there really isn't enough brain inside it for the thing
to go crazy. Just a lot of reflexes, is all."

"Reflexes?"

It didn't make any sense. Reflexes were people
things, things that made you jump when somebody
said *boo,* or flinch when you touched something hot,
or—well, physical stuff. Computers weren't like that.
Were they?

"Yeah, reflexes. The computer here doesn't think
about things. Just sees them and reacts. Or hears
them, smells them. Whatever."

Pandora nodded sagely.

*Space Alien technology. Of course. A computer
so smart it doesn't have to think.*

Past the door. Inside the bridge.

Like the cockpit of an airplane. Steering controls here in the pilot's seat. An identical set of wheels and levers in front of the seat to the right. A few odd dials and gauges high up on the dash—not that many considering how these were controls for flying into outer space past the planets beyond the stars and all. There were plenty more on the wall behind the pilot's seat. A whole damn wall covered top to bottom left to right with screens and dials and stuff. Maybe those were the ones the pilot didn't need to be able to see all the time? Either that or the ship was designed for Aliens who were *really* different, different like Pandora's mommy, who could look both ways at the same time.

No telling.

Beyond the dash the windshield stretched up to the ceiling, staring out at the blue sky everywhere before them—

Sky.

How could she be looking at so much sky all at once unless she was looking *up*? But she wasn't looking up, she was looking *out*, and, and—

There. At the top edge of the windshield.

The tops of apple trees.

Upside down.

Pandora felt dizzy. Even a little woozy.

She eased herself into the pilot's seat, because if she didn't sit down right away she was going to be ill.

That was about when the old man noticed how she'd turned green. For a moment it sounded like he was going to laugh at her again but then he stopped and it was a damn good thing he did because Pandora was going to hit him but good if he so much as snickered.

"Oh," the old man said. "Artificial gravity. I should've warned you. But you—I mean—"

He didn't finish saying whatever it was he was going to say. Maybe because Pandora glared at him. She was going to hit him. She really was going to hit him if he made a joke about a Space Alien getting spacesick. She was!

"I didn't think it would be a problem for you; it was never a problem for your mother. The ship keeps every room at the right *up*—all the time."

Her balance was coming back. There wasn't *really* anything to be woozy about, was there? Up and down were perfectly sensible. The way they felt was perfectly sensible, anyhow. Wasn't it? It wasn't like she could feel herself hanging upside down walking on her head or anything. All she had to do was pretend everything was normal, and it'd *be* normal. Wouldn't it?

Fine. She was fine now. She just had to keep telling herself that.

It'd be better if she didn't have to look out the wide spaceship window. Much better. And after all, she'd already seen the bridge, hadn't she? Might as well get out of here.

Get away from the sight of up and down gone wrong.

Out of the space-pilot seat. Stumbling into the hall. Leaning against the wall; breathing deep, deep . . .

A little better now. Vertigo receding; her pulse slowing, growing steadier.

"Are you okay, Pandora?" The old man sounded genuinely worried. More concerned than he had any right to be.

"I'm *fine*," she said. As if it was any of his business! She pushed away from the wall, started down the hall. . . .

"That's the wrong way," the old man said. "You don't want—"

The hell she didn't!

"I know where I'm going, damn it!"

Halfway down the hall there were doors, two of them, facing one another from opposite walls of the corridor. One of them was heavy and secure, made of metal like the door of a vault. The other was a simple wooden door, almost exactly like the door to Uncle Wally's office. It was an earthling door, and it looked out of place here in the spaceship where all the fixtures were quietly exotic. Pandora should have paid attention to that door. Its strangeness was important. But she hardly even noticed it. Instead she stood staring at the vault for the longest time, trying to understand why someone would put a safe in the middle of a hallway.

Until her shoulder brushed against the earthling door, easing it open. And Pandora turned to see the strangest room.

Strangest, strangest, *strangest* room.

So strange that in a moment Pandora had forgot all about being mad and dizzy and woozy.

What was strange about it was nothing strange at all.

Nothing.

The room at the end of the hall was something from *Leave it to Beaver.*

Not Beaver's bedroom—it belonged to an older boy. Five years older? Six? It could've been the bedroom of Beaver's older brother. What was his name? Wally? Pandora wasn't sure. All she remembered about the show for sure was the name of the brother's nasty friend—Eddie Haskel?

Maybe she wasn't even so sure about that.

No question about sure or unsure where it came to this room, though. There was nothing *spaceship* or *outer space* or *UFO* about this place. Nothing *Alien!* Nothing, nothing, not a damned thing at all.

But here it was. The last room at the end of the spaceship hall.

Pretty blue curtains. Not too pretty—just rough and homey enough that they said *boy* instead of *girl.* Big framed football team photos—three of them. One on each wall except the wall with the curtained windows. *(Curtained windows? How could there be curtained windows on a spaceship? Spaceships didn't have big wide bedroom windows with sun streaming in so bright you could see it through the curtain, did they? It was—bad design, wasn't it? Didn't windows have to be small and strong to stand hard against the infinite vacuum night? Didn't spaceships have ports, little bitty round windows like on an ocean ship? Didn't they?)*

A football trophy on top of the bookcase.

Three stuffed animals piled at odd angles in the back corner beside the closet.

Beside the bed a dresser, almost as tall as Pandora. Calico bedspread. And there on the far side of the bed a nightstand with a lamp and a telephone—

And a photo.

A photo.

A photo of Pandora.

But how? How could there be a photo of Pandora from back when she was little—how could that photograph be here? And why?

She recognized the photo. It was one of the ones the scientists took back when she was just a baby. She'd seen it lots of times—it was on top of the file of photos of her at different ages.

The weird part was the way the photo had gotten all yellow. Pandora had seen that photo just last month, and it wasn't yellow at all back then.

"Where did you get that picture?" Pandora asked, looking over her shoulder at the old man. He was more than a few steps behind her. "Why is it here, beside the bed?"

She thought: *My daddy would have a picture of me beside his bed. —But my daddy wouldn't have a room like this.*

And: *Maybe my daddy stayed here once?*

That was wrong, too. Her daddy was too Alien to sleep in a room like this one. Ever. Even if it was on a spaceship.

The old man looked puzzled. Worried? Alarmed? All those things. Pandora couldn't figure why he'd get all weird just because she asked a question. But he did—look at him.

"Is this your room? It looks like a boy's room."

The old man nodded. "The first time I saw this room," he said, "someone I loved told me that this room is in my heart. Maybe that's right. I don't know. . . . Sometimes I think there's nothing anyone can do to change the past." He looked away at his window. And muttered under his breath: "I ought to know by now, but damn me if I do."

Later—much later when she was admitting to herself obvious things that she'd long refused to accept—Pandora understood exactly what the old man meant. And even felt bad for him, in spite of everything. But there and then in the boy's room in the spaceship, the old man and the photo and everything else were all mysteries.

Impenetrable.

Inscrutable.

Unknowable.

She looked at the old man now turned back to face her—looked him square in the eye; wore her expression wise as she could.

And she nodded, as if to say she understood and sympathized.

Not that she did.

"You aren't going to tell me why my picture's here, are you?"

The old man shook his head.

Pandora eyed him carefully.

"You aren't very nice sometimes, old man." And she knew damn well that she wasn't being nice herself, the way she'd said it.

The old man sighed; he looked defeated. "No," he said. "I'm not."

Whatever *that* meant.

Pandora stepped farther into the room; looked carefully at every little thing. The bedspread. The rug, which was a thick coarse olive-green shag. The tall dresser with its white-and-red Formica surface.

The window covered with a pretty blue curtain—opaque but translucent. And she thought: *Why is the curtain drawn? What's on the far side of that window. . . ?* But the answer to that was obvious, wasn't it? Outside the window were the stream, the plateau, the mountain looming high above them. The sky. All the same things Pandora had seen outside the spaceship's other windows.

What else *could* there be outside the window?

Pandora had an awful feeling. An awful, awful feeling. It told her that she ought to leave that curtain hanging as it was; to turn away and get on with her life. But how could she do that? How could she look away when she knew damn well there was something important waiting just beyond the curtain?

She couldn't. It wasn't in her not to look.

She reached forward, pulled the drape aside—

"Pandora?" The old man. "Please, please don't—"

She ignored him. *Of course* she ignored him.

At first the scene before her looked—well, like nothing special. What was so weird about a tiny graveyard deep in the woods? Most all the stones looked old and worn; and look how the trees grew close to cover at the edges of the field.

It was pretty, in its way.

Odd only that it was there at all—and it was there, somehow; Pandora could see it wasn't any picture. And she could feel how the window was a gate in time and space because she was a gate like that herself, and knew what it felt like when there was a rift in time and space not far from her. She didn't understand why any boy would want a cemetery view outside his bedroom—couldn't begin to guess—but other than that . . .

Then she saw the names.

Especially the name on the grave in the foreground. It wasn't easy to read that name. Not with the spray paint all over it. Old and flaking-away paint, but it was there, wordless letterless graffiti obscuring the letters carved into the stone:

WALTER FULTON
AGE 8

No dates. Only an age.

Beneath the headstone was a great oblong depression—this where every other grave in the clearing bore the slightest bulge of earth settling around a coffin.

He's dead, Pandora thought. *He died when he was eight.*

And then he was alive again. Somehow.

She turned to look at the old man, to see if she could tell how the grave still marked him, now that she knew to look for its traces. And saw him, apprehensive, tense; but otherwise only an old man like any old man.

"Now you know my other secret," the old man said. "It isn't anything I like to share."

"How. . . ?" Pandora asked him. "How come. . . ?"

"Space Aliens. What else?" The old man sighed. "You ought to know about that."

Pandora nodded. *He's right. I should have known.* "Did it hurt?" she asked. "Dying like that—did it hurt? Sometimes I'm afraid to die."

The old man shrugged. "I guess. The car hit me so fast I didn't feel it much."

Pandora winced. Turned to look back at the grave, because looking at it was easier than thinking about an eight-year-old boy pasted across the bumper of a late-model Buick.

Beside Walt Fulton's gravestone was another—this one looked a few years less old than the first.

JANET FULTON

"Whose grave is that beside yours? A relative's?"

"Uh," the old man said. He hesitated. "That's my mother."

Pandora felt an unsettling chill; she didn't understand it. But she had a notion that it meant she'd stumbled over something very important.

"Was it nice—being buried next to your mommy like that?"

The old man coughed. "I was gone when they put her there."

Back behind Walt's grave, behind his mother's, there was a great large stone with two inscriptions:

WILLIAM FISCHER VICTORIA FISCHER

No dates on this stone, either. Something about it —what? The old man would know.

"That stone, there," Pandora said. "The big one. What's weird about. . . ?"

"Old man Fischer's grave? Nothing weird about it, I don't think. Old man Fischer was a strange one, though."

Pandora nodded. She didn't think Walt Fulton was telling everything he knew, but there was something in his voice that made her think it wasn't really that important to her anyway.

"They made you alive again? And then abducted you? I know all about Space Alien abductions. I read *Communion.*" She turned to look the old man in the eye as she asked this; she wanted to see his expression when he heard her ask.

Whatever she'd expected, the old man disappointed her. Because he hardly reacted at all.

"Maybe," he said. And shrugged. "I don't know. Nobody made me go. And I was never sorry once I'd went."

Of course not! How could anyone be sorry, if they got to go out into the stars and be a space pilot? Pandora couldn't even imagine it.

"They did, then! They did abduct you!"

The old man shook his head.

"*Abduct* is a word that means—like kidnapped, almost. Nobody kidnapped me. Nobody ever took me anywhere I didn't want to go, except—" he coughed again "—never mind that. It's not the same at all. The ones who woke me up from the dead never made me do anything. They just showed me how it was better with them than anywhere else I could be. And they were right."

Pandora shrugged. "Same difference. They abducted you."

The old man sighed. Shook his head. "I won't argue with you." He looked at the door. "Are you ready to go? Anything else you want to see?"

Pandora didn't answer right away. She had a notion there was something else she needed to see before she left, but for the life of her she couldn't imagine what it might be. Couldn't figure it no matter how she tried. Whatever it was.

After a while she gave up trying.

"I guess I am."

The old man led her out of the spaceship a different way than they'd come in. Back down the corridor they'd come by—and then, five doors past the bridge, the old man opened a door on the opposite side of the corridor. Took Pandora's arm and pulled her out before she knew where she was going—

And suddenly they were outside the ship, up up in the air by the point at the top hanging suspended hanging in midair—

Pandora should've known it was okay. The spaceship was a Space Alien thing; it wouldn't ever make her hurt on purpose. But no; there was no time to think. All she could do was see where she was, and scream, and scream again, and wish to God that the old man and the spaceship and the air would let her *down*—

—*down*—

—*down* on the ground where she belonged—

—*down*—

—wished for *down* with all the wish she had, sincere to the inmost chamber of her heart—

—and suddenly she was plummeting, her arm

lurching out of the old man's grip as she shot rock heavy into the icy-cold water of the stream.

Hit the water hard, and with such momentum that she was deep down under in an instant. And Pandora couldn't swim! But she was only under for an instant; just that quickly invisible hands hands of ethereal force from the magical Space Alien spaceship wrapped around her, lifting her out of the cold and the wet, pushing the water from her lungs, pressing her heart to beat where it like to stop from shock. . . .

"Oh Pandora," the old man said. "Don't cry, Pandora. Pandora Pandora don't cry you'll be okay, you'll be okay I promise."

He sounded like he was on the verge of crying himself.

But Pandora wasn't crying! She wasn't! She was coughing, and, and, well, coughing and choking to get the water out of her wind. Cold awful slimy-muck tadpole water, and you know where those tadpoles go to the bathroom, don't you? Of course it sounded like she was crying. But she wasn't.

Still, she didn't struggle when the old man hugged her and started crying like he was relieved to see her safe; and she didn't argue when he lifted her in his arms and carried her to his cabin.

Didn't protest when he wrapped her in warm blankets in the big armchair by the fireplace in his den, built a roaring fire to help her warm her soggy bone-chilled self.

She sat there, numb and shivering, trying to get warm and feel better and most of all trying to digest everything she'd seen and heard that day.

After a while, still cold but warming, she dozed.

She woke a long time later, warmer and more well, still wrapped up in the cozy-warm comforter blanket. She opened her eyes to stare at the fire— and that was when it finally came to Pandora.

The obvious.

The obvious came to her.

He's my father. The old old old earthling man Walt Fulton, he's my father.

Immediately she chased the idea away. He wasn't her daddy! Not *no* earthling old man was *her* daddy! Her daddy was a *Space Alien!*

And still the sense of it arrested her, no matter how she hated the thought of it. All the strangeness about the old man; the fact that he knew so much; the fact that he was a spacefarer, even if he wasn't a Space Alien. The only thing that made no sense at all was the fact that he was so impossibly different from her mommy who'd borne her—*who Pandora* knew *had borne her, because she'd seen it happen, back through time!*—they were so impossibly different from one another that Pandora couldn't imagine how they could ever come close enough together to create her.

And then something snapped inside Pandora, and she found herself furious, incensed at the very idea that this, this *earthling* could even for a moment pretend to be her father. . . !

Just like that, just like that she made the devil's words come true:

Because she denied him who was her own.

The fact of what she'd done was lost on her, of course. Pandora only knew for certain in her heart that the old man was nothing to do with her, and was no one she wanted anywhere near her. He was nice enough as strangers went, but there were few who were stranger to her than he was.

Not that she snuggled any less into the blanket he had brought her. Not that she enjoyed the fire any less as its radiant warmth soaked into her, soothed her bones. Not that she refused the rich hot hearty stew the old man brought her after a while. She didn't even mind his company as he sat down in a chair on the other side of the fire from her, and ate slowly from his own stew bowl.

She had no special scruple against enjoying the company and hospitality of strangers.

Not that Pandora had any intention of taking advantage of the old man. She wasn't that kind of girl! But her chair was warm, and homey, and she was so tired. . . !

"You aren't my daddy," she said. "I know you aren't."

The old man didn't say anything. He stared at her with his eyes so full of quiet. His face looked serious but patient.

"My daddy is a Space Alien. He is!"

Silence.

"If you were my daddy you would have loved my mommy. But you don't! You don't love my mommy. You don't even like to talk about her! You never loved her. I can tell."

The old man frowned.

"You aren't wrong," he said.

It wasn't an answer.

And what could Pandora say to that? Nothing. Nothing at all. She closed her eyes, trying to understand where and why and how she was, and how come the world kept tilting on its end.

But no matter how long she held them shut, the world, the universe—none of it was any clearer to her. And after a while she snuggled deep in her blanket and opened her eyes and watched the fire burning, crackling, flickering as flames rose and settled with the shifting combusting of its embers.

In the corner of her eye she could see the old man biting his lip. Looking more and more uncomfortable as the evening wore on. It occurred to her that she ought to ask him what the trouble was, because that just might do something to rest his unease. But she couldn't bring herself to ask him, and after a long time she decided that it was probably the best thing not to.

Sooner or later he'd figure out what was eating at him, and he'd say something about it. That's what Pandora figured.

And she was right.

About when the clock on the mantel reached eleven in the evening, the old man sputtered, and made four false starts at a sentence, trying to get Pandora's attention.

She turned to see what he was about, and he told her this as he lifted himself out of his armchair:

"I could tell you," he said, "how I sailed inside a sun that blinded me, and lived to tell and saw to paint the tale. I could tell you what it's like to die murdered, butchered, eaten by cannibal space pirates who leave your soul and bones for the cavalry to suck from the black empty grave of space rescuing you after it's too late to save your life but still in time to retrieve it. I could tell you what it's like to love an Alien woman for a life that only lasted days before she metamorphosed to a creature I could never love. I could tell—a thousand things."

Pacing—the old man was pacing, now, back and forth across the room. As he strode his arms gestured wildly.

"I've told the tale of each of these in my time; I've lived them and learned them well enough to share them.

"But now for half a thousand years lived back and forth adrift through time—as all spacefarers live—I've known and loved a daughter that I never sired. A child stolen from my genes! A girl I never fathered on that creature hideous as death made live!

"I cannot tell you what it is to love a daughter you never made. I cannot tell you what it is to see her when you never knew she was. I do not understand this thing; I only live it day by day and pray God will forgive me.

"Pray *you* forgive me.

"This child . . . how can I say? I never knew her; nor knew of her till she was nearly grown. If I had known—oh, but if I could have known of her even a moment more before I first saw her. . . ! But there wasn't time nor knowledge. I learned she was my own only after we first met. And what I did when

I met her was a thing she'll never forgive. Nor will I forgive myself!—no hope of that."

He sighed. Turned to face Pandora, looking grim.

"I never met my daddy neither," Pandora said. "If I met him and he was mean—I'd be so sad. I love my daddy. I know I'll love him when I meet him."

The old man began to cry again.

"I'm sorry," he said. "So sorry." He was crouched before Pandora, staring her in the eye. As he apologized he took her arm and held it in both of his rough, gnarled hands.

Pandora still didn't understand, though she should've and would've if she hadn't blinded her heart to the possibilities she wasn't willing to accept. If she'd understood—it would have been a very different life she lived. And the world would have forgotten her soon enough, and forgetting, it would have lost the catalysis she brought upon it.

But how could she? It wasn't possible. She wasn't *meant* to understand, no more than the old man was meant to float back and forth through time to see her.

What a body will do he owns. But what he's done belongs to fate, the universe, and God; what's done is done. There can be no undoing, and there's precious little one can do to make amends where the River of Our Destiny has flowed to meet the sea: these are absolute truths about the nature of the universe. There are no special provisions in the universal laws for folk cut loose in time.

No matter that they can shoot their own fathers; if the bullet strike true it were the bullet that always was and always meant to be.

If the old man were back in time to amend what he'd done but had still to do, there yet could be no undoing the act. Nor any easing nor bending of effect —all he could ever do to what was done was help to make it happen.

And that, of course, was exactly what the old man did, speaking to Pandora.

"I'd die," she said. "If my Space Alien daddy was mean to me—I'd die." She shivered. "But he never would be! He never could be. He's my daddy. He's a Space Alien. He's good. I know."

And the old man reached out and hugged Pandora. And he cried and cried and cried.

Pandora felt so bad for him she didn't even try to fight him off. Even though he did make her uncomfortable, with all that huggy stuff and all.

"It's okay," Pandora said. "You'll be okay. She'll still love you. Maybe someday she'll even forgive you."

He got quieter after that, but he held her very tight, and he still cried—Pandora could tell that by the way his tears fell on her T-shirt, soaked in and made her back feel all yechy-wet.

Very yechy.

But what could she do? It wasn't like Pandora had the heart to push him away. To tell him to mind himself and stop trying to hold her. Just looking at him, just being near him, she knew how bad he felt. It wasn't in her to hurt someone already hurting like that.

"You'll be okay," Pandora said. But what she really thought was how he deserved to feel like he did, treating his daughter like that. People who were mean like he was *deserved* to feel bad. After all, it was only fair, what with them hurting people they loved.

The old man nodded. (Pandora felt it instead of saw it, on account of how he was still hugging her.) "I'll be okay," he said. It didn't sound like he really meant it. But it did sound like underneath the unsureness and the not-quite-truth—under that was something strong and almost healthy; like a little bit of him starting to recover already even though he was still hurting really terrible.

And Pandora thought: *How do you get better after a hurt like that?* And she didn't have an answer.

"Just keep trying," she said. "If you keep trying to

make it up to her, sooner or later she'll notice. And sooner or later it'll all be better."

"Yes," the old man said. "Yes, of course." He let Pandora loose, stumbled back into his velvet chair. Sighed—not out of frustration or exhaustion, but more like something terrible had begun to lift itself off him.

Or maybe it was exhaustion—for in a moment the old man sat unconscious in his chair, oblivious to the world. Pandora waited a long time, listening to hear him go on about his daughter who made Pandora's heart ache to think about her. But there was nothing, and after a while she heard the old man snoring.

Eventually she fell asleep herself, and dreamed all night long of warmth and security and with a sense of belonging she'd never felt before in all her life. She dreamed about Space Aliens and spaceships and human abductees turned space pirates to run amok across the universe. . . .

It was a wonderful dream. Like a movie on TV only she was the heroine and everybody she met everywhere she went all over the universe knew about her and loved her and all of them were so happy to meet her!

In the morning she woke before the old man did, and quiet as she could, quiet as an Alien mouse dancing weightless on the vacuum surface of the moon—quiet as she could Pandora stole away.

"Still no sign of Pandora, Macdonald. I'm half-afraid she's got herself lost in those woods. Lost, or hurt or something—or maybe she just moved into them for good."

"Relax," Macdonald says. "She's a tough kid. She's okay. She'll show up sooner or later."

When Pandora got outside she headed uphill— toward the plateau.

Toward the spaceship.

This time it was closer than she remembered—it only took her a few moments to reach the crest of the hill.

When she was up on the plateau she hiked upstream along the brook until she stood by the tree where the old man had called up the ship in his sleep —and stopped.

If I take his spaceship, it's stealing, she thought. She knew that was wrong. Of course it was wrong. Of course she knew!

But this was so important . . . if she could steal that spaceship she could ride out across the stars and find her daddy for herself, and all her troubles would melt away.

The more she thought about it, the more the spaceship seemed to call to her, to draw her out to tempt her—

Come up, O spaceship! Rise from the water!

But the spaceship did not rise.

Didn't even stir the water.

Pandora thought back. What exactly had the old man done? He'd slumped against the tree and said, *This takes a while.* Nothing else. Not that Pandora had seen.

I've got to be patient. It'll be here soon.

But how could she do that? Pandora had no patience. There wasn't any in her nature.

So she tried again, this time speaking aloud: "Up from the water, Spaceship! Up!"

When she heard the words they sounded so silly that they made her blush.

She stepped back. Leaned against the tree. And did her very best to wait for the spaceship patiently.

She managed all of a minute and a half before it got so bad she just couldn't wait anymore. But that was enough, wasn't it? Surely it hadn't been that long that she'd wandered along the bank watching polliwogs while the old man rested.

"Spaceship. . . ?"

She stepped forward. Peered down into the water.

And saw nothing. Nothing but the pure clear water of the mountain spring that fed that stream. And sand and rocks down underneath. Here and there a water weed. A school of tadpoles off to her left.

It's gone, Pandora thought. *My ship my ship it's left without me!*

And she began to mourn.

I loved my ship. I miss my ship. I want it.

Even though she knew it wasn't hers, and she'd only meant to steal it.

She walked out to the far end of the plateau where the flat ground sloped away into a mountainside. Sat down just past the edge, and pouted.

And every time she thought of it she thought, *My spaceship doesn't love me anymore.*

And she felt so sad.

Sadder and sadder.

If I was a real Space Alien, my spaceship would come to me.

It took Pandora a while to realize she was crying. It didn't come out in sobs, didn't come out as screaming or moaning, nothing like that. She blinked because there was something in her eye, and as she blinked fat wet beads of tear rolled out onto her cheeks.

Maybe the baby was right, Pandora thought. *Maybe I'm not a Space Alien after all.*

But she was! She *was* a Space Alien, and she was looking for her Space Alien daddy, and, and . . .

Looking for my Space Alien daddy.

The words sounded so hollow, so empty inside her head. There was nothing left in them, was there? They were empty, bankrupt, and the baby was right. Pandora wasn't any Space Alien. She was just some mutant freak who crawled out of a test tube somewhere deep in the bowels of the air force, just a freaky *thing* that no one loved and everyone wanted to own, and it was time to give it all up and go home before someone chased her too hard and too excited and someone got shot.

That's all. Time to go home. Because there wasn't any point.

I miss my uncle Wally, she thought. And that got her crying all over again. That was the worst part about running away: when you felt awful and alone and ascared and you need a hug, and you need to find your uncle Wally but you can't because of the General.

The General.

She hated him so bad.

Hated him. Look, look what he'd done—just trying to do that awful thing to her, he'd made Pandora throw away her life, her uncle Wally and Cookie and everyone, all of them lost to her forever and there was nothing she could do, she missed them so bad but the General won, didn't he? He took away her life and she couldn't have it anymore.

You can't go home again, she thought. She heard that lots of times before but she never understood it, not till now.

And finally it came to her: she had to go back to the old man in the cabin on the hill. No matter how ashamed she was, no matter how hard it was to face him. There was a reason why her heart had led her to him from so far away, and that same reason was why she had to go back to him.

And she got up, and climbed back onto the plateau, hiked downstream along the brook until she found the path that led back to his cabin.

But when she got to the place in the woods where the strange trees grew, there was no sign of the cabin. No sign of the cabin, the old man, the garden, nothing but woods and trees and a path that led back down the mountain as Pandora had come.

"It's the President, Macdonald. The French telescope in Polynesia just found the Aliens."

Macdonald winces. The French have been giving the President hell over Pandora. He doesn't want to

think about how they'll respond to a couple thousand
Alien spacecraft plummeting to earth.

Doesn't want to think, but he does, despite himself. And what he thinks as he remembers the hell
they've given the President—what he thinks is that
he isn't sure which side they'll be on.

And chases the thought away, because it's unwor-
thy. Not even the French would ally themselves with
an Alien invasion. Not even the French. . . ?

Pandora got lost on her way back down the mountain. She meant to go back the same way she'd come,
down toward the highway rest stop where the lady
and her baby had left her. But she made a wrong
turn, or took the wrong path, or something, and the
hike through the woods ran long into the afternoon,
and when she came out of them—on the side of a
long gentle mountain dotted with pine trees surrounded by blackberry brambles and fields of onion
grass . . .

She was going home.

That was the only thing left to do, wasn't it? The
Space Aliens weren't coming to rescue her. She
wasn't going to find her daddy. Whether she was a
Space Alien or not, she had a life here on Earth and
she had go back home and face it.

Even if that did mean facing the General.

She knew what he'd try to do to her the moment
that he saw her. But she told herself she'd have to
face him anyhow, sooner or later—and maybe that
was true.

Dvorkin brings the news about Pandora—the satellite
has spotted her on the side of a mountain seven
miles from the rest stop where she'd last been seen—
while Macdonald is on the phone with the President.

Macdonald is too busy; in a fit of pique he waves
Dvorkin away, covers the receiver with his hand, and
says, "Bother someone else, David. This is the President on the phone."

Serious mistake. Dvorkin is following orders; Macdonald told him to notify him immediately—*immediately,* no matter what, no matter who he had to interrupt—the moment anyone spotted Pandora.

But that is the old order, and the new one is *bother someone else, David.* And what can Dvorkin do? He nods, ignores the pique, and sets the photo fax in Macdonald's in-box.

By the time Macdonald gets off the phone, twenty-seven minutes later, Pandora is gone again. It will be a long while before they find her again.

FIVE

There are some who will tell you that demonography is dead lore. After all, they say, demons are rare in contemporary folktales, and where they do appear we see only the briefest, most sterile glimpses of their once terrible faces.

And how (these people continue) can the study live where the myth lies so nearly dead?

Here again those who would paint our mythic landscape with their colorless brush have overlooked the subtle truth: our demons have not died, but metamorphosed.

Where once Old Scratch populated a thousand fireside tales now an infinite tribe of garishly dressed devil worshipers crowd the fields, the hills; the cities and the towns. And most especially the airwaves.

Airwaves indeed.

Is there a televangelist anywhere in the land who has not at least once solicited contributions to fight the terrible spread of satanism?

And of all our tales of satanists run rampant, are there any so colorful as those surrounding the phenomena we call crop circles?

Perhaps there are. Few come to mind.

The first crop-circle reports date from the early 1960s, or perhaps a few years earlier; they first appeared in English oatfields, but soon enough there were tales of these strange circular patterns in every corner of the world.

The circles themselves are real and verifiable; there's no doubt of this. And there's no doubt that many (if not all) of the circles are the work of mischievous hoaxers. But the tales that surround them are the purest, richest modern myth.

Some tales purport that Alien UFO spaceships produce the circles, pressing their mysterious designs into the crop with the force of their landing. Others tell how the circles are some arcane legacy of lost Atlantis, only lately come to flower.

The commonest tale is none of these, but rather another from the televangelists—who tell of Satan's earthly minions drawing crop circles with wands made of cold unburning fire. The patterns (so the televangelists say) summon the Dark Lord to this world—much the way a circled star would draw him in the medieval myth.

In some tellings the ritual includes a sacrifice. Of a small animal, perhaps, or a precious keepsake. And ever so rarely the story tells of human sacrifice.

The sacrifice of a child, specifically. A girl child still before her menses.

These are chilling tales indeed—the more so because there's something disturbingly convincing in the manner of those who recount it.

But here we grow too close to the tale, and begin to mistake it for the truth. Step back a way and look carefully, and you'll see two truths hiding in the strangeness of these satanistic tales: first and most obviously that we have matured as a people to become our own demons.

And, arguably, the myth speaks of religion perverted, literally inverted. It describes a faith that warps and poisons the pious—transforms the zealot into a ruthlessly violent creature. And that, sadly, is not only the stuff of our myths: it's in our headlines, too.

When Pandora had hiked downhill through the blackberry brambles for half an hour, she saw cornfields in the distance. When she crested the last rise before the corn she caught a glimpse of a highway on the far side of the planted fields—miles and miles away.

That's where I've got to go, she thought. *Go to the highway and hitch a ride into town.*

She knew about hitchhiking from that episode on *Rod Serling's The Twilight Zone*—she could never forget it. That hitchhiker was so scary!

But he didn't scare Pandora.

Hitch a ride into town and turn myself over to the authorities.

She took her bearings on the rise and set off into the corn.

Things went wrong almost the moment she started—the corn was taller than she was, and so thick this time of year she could hardly see through to the sun. The cornrows didn't go exactly where the highway was, and field by field she jagged and zagged until she wasn't exactly sure which way the highway was—and by then there was no way to see.

So unsettling! Pandora wasn't the kind of girl who could be comfortable not knowing where she was going. And even worse, when she was in the corn for a while this awful *feeling* came over her.

A feeling like there were eyes watching her.

Following her through the corn.

She turned and called to see who it was, but there was no answer—no sign of anyone, no one, nothing at all.

"Who are you?" Pandora shouted. "Don't try to hide! I know you're there!"

But whoever it was stayed hidden.

The feeling went away for a while after that. But it came back as she reached the next cultivated rise.

Something rustled in the corn—then stopped abruptly.

It's here again.

She whirled around to face the watcher in the corn, but there was no one to confront.

No one she could see.

But even if she couldn't see, she could feel. The presence she felt was hungry and predatory, like a carnivorous animal starved and beaten for days until it goes mad. It was a presence that wanted to tear her apart and consume the pieces.

"I know you're out there!" Pandora shouted. "I know you're out there, and I'm not afraid!"

But she was afraid. She was very, very afraid.

"We've lost her again, Macdonald," Dvorkin says. "She wandered into a cornfield and the satellite lost track of her."

Macdonald is just getting off the phone with the President. He looks shaken, unnerved. He looks like a man unaccustomed to abuse who's just taken a truckload of invective.

"What?" he asks. "Lost who?"

He lifts the photo fax from his in-box, examines it.

Looks up at Dvorkin. "Lost her again. . . ?"

And then it sinks through to him. And he begins to swear.

There was a wide flat rock on top of the rise; when Pandora stood tiptoe on top of it she could almost see above the corn. She was pretty sure she could see a wooded ridge off in the distance, and it looked like the highway ran along it—but it was hard to be sure.

She could see the field below her very clearly.

There were circles in that field—three interlocking circles in the corn.

Crop circles.

Pandora gasped when she saw them.

Pandora knew all about crop circles from that special on the UHF channel. Very scary! Mysterious satanistic UFO Alien *magic* stuff, and worse. No wonder she felt so *stalked,* with crop circles in the corn!

I've got to get out of here, she thought. She had to get to the highway as quickly as she could, but the field with the circles was between here and there, so wide she'd get lost again if she tried to go around it. And she knew it was bad luck if she went through the circles, so she tried to go around.

Sideways through the field and then up again—but when she looked back from the next rise she saw that her path had somehow taken her dead center through the middle of each ring.

After that the stalking got worse. Now it was as though there were many of them, five, six, maybe a dozen, or maybe the thing that followed her was large as some monstrous beast. She heard voices, and the sound of footsteps near enough to touch, and bit by bit the stalking herded her toward some awful place she couldn't bear to see. She could feel it waiting for the right moment to attack, and she knew she didn't dare resist.

But it was just like before—every time she turned to shout, demanding to be left alone, there was no one.

No one but the breeze and the corn and the sky barely visible above her.

"We're getting glimpses of her now and then. I think she's lost—it looks like she's wandering back and forth through the cornfield."

Macdonald looks sweaty and uncomfortable. "Okay," he says. "Okay. Have the team go into the field and look for her, all right? If she's lost, she'll appreciate the help. I think she's about ready to come home anyway. Maybe it's time to give her a little help."

Pandora was lost. Seriously lost. The whispers in the corn were everywhere around her, now. She had to run to stay ahead of them, and every time she ran she got more lost. And finally she just started running, and damn the voices, damn the stalking, damn everything—Pandora ran and ran until she couldn't run anymore.

When she was too exhausted to run another step, she stumbled and collapsed into the powdery red soil.

It was over, then, and she knew it: she waited five long moments for the predator to come to her, take her in its massive jaws, and rend her limb from limb. But it didn't come for her right away: instead it left her waiting, limp and exhausted but shivering with fear.

"Haven't seen any sign of her since the satellite caught her, twenty minutes ago—standing on a rock at the top of a hill," Dvorkin says. "It's almost like she's disappeared."

"Damn," Macdonald says. "This is all wrong." He shakes his head. "I should have gone down there with the watch team. I should have gone down there the minute I got off the phone." He sighs. "Well, maybe there's still time. Get the fast helicopter ready —we're putting this show on the road."

Pandora lay terrorized and exhausted in the dirt. She could feel the stalker watching her, waiting for a moment she couldn't imagine.

It could kill me now, she thought. *I'm not afraid to die.*

But it waited. Why was it waiting? What was it planning? Something terrible—terrible, Pandora could feel it—

But the stalker never came for her. After a while Pandora realized that she had her breath back. She looked around, listened for the murmuring sound of predatory breathing—and heard nothing. Eased herself slowly back to her feet.

Hurried up another long cultivated rise, hoping to get another view of the highway, hoping to get her bearings back.

The stalker followed her up along the ridge—quietly, discreetly. Trying to remain unnoticed.

But Pandora did notice. She looked back cautiously, trying to catch a glimpse of the stalker in the corn—but there was nothing to see.

"I'm not afraid," she whispered.

But she was terrified. And every step she took she grew more and more frightened, until finally she knew it was the end. She bolted again—ran sudden and crazily, not even watching where she was going.

After half a dozen steps something pelted her from behind—something jagged and enormous, like the talons of a monstrous claw. The blow tore open the skin of her back and threw her off balance. She stumbled through three rows of corn to fall and smash her head against the rock at the end of the ridge.

After that the world went black around Pandora. She lay unconscious in the field for hours, dreaming nightmare dreams she wished she'd never seen.

They're in the fast helicopter, now, flying down to Tennessee.

Macdonald looks up at Yolen. "What's the word on Hightower? McNamee? Still no news?"

Yolen shakes her head. "None."

"How many sets of bogus orders have we had to countermand since Pandora first ran? Any idea?"

She shrugs. "Three dozen, give or take."

"I'd bet my last dollar—my last damned dollar—they've got something to do with the no-source orders that keep coming out of the Pentagon. McNamee has been around long enough; he knows how to jimmy the system if anybody does. —If, hell. Isn't any question. Look how long he kept Pandora in his pocket."

Yolen nods slowly; makes the faintest purring sound—which could mean mm-hmmm and could mean anything at all. But mostly it sounds like she's thinking—like something inside her head is making an important connection. Like maybe she can see her way through to the bottom of the problem.

When Pandora came to, her head throbbed and her back ached, and there were helicopters in the air above the cornfield—half a dozen of them, maybe more, probing the ground with searchlights. Inch by inch, foot by foot, scanning back and forth across the field.

I'm saved! she thought. *They've come to search for me!* Her heart beat like a jackhammer, pounding thrilled and terrified, and she had a terrible impulse to run away and hide. But she didn't run. She lifted herself up off the ground, stood on her tiptoes, and waved her hands above her head.

"I'm over here," Pandora shouted. "Help me! Save me! Over here!"

The lights shone past her, back and forth, but if anyone noticed her there wasn't any sign of it.

"Over here!" she shouted, forgetting about the ache and the throb and jumping as high as she could, trying to get the helicopters' attention. "Over here!"

But no one saw.

They should've seen, that was for sure. She was jumping up and down on a big flat rock on top of a rise, and now she could see by the searchlight that she was on the rock above the crop circles, the same place she'd been hours and hours ago—and look, there in the distance, that *was* the highway, Pandora could see a line of headlights glaring in the distance.

"Here! Down *here!*"

And now one of the big lights was on the hill just below her, slowly carefully searching the ground before her, heading toward her, and if it just kept moving toward her for another long moment she'd be right in the middle of the beam, and they'd have to see her then, wouldn't they? Wouldn't they?

Unless they were blind.

Unless she was invisible.

She kept waving her hands back and forth above her head, kept shouting and praying they could hear her over the thunderous noise of the rotors.

And then just before the light could touch her, the predatory presence rose up out of the corn to engulf her. Pandora felt as though she'd been tackled by some enormous beast—something powerful and hungry, enormous legs slamming against her chest to throw her off the rock and send her tumbling downhill through the corn, away from the light and salvation; and now she could feel and hear great slavering jaws clamp around her arm and *pull,* and if the sleeve of her jacket hadn't given way the monster would've ripped her arm from her shoulder, and Pandora *screamed.*

Screamed!

She rolled onto her side and over and over again as the monster's claws batted her, pounding and slamming and trying to push the wind out of her lungs, like a cat batting the life from a mouse until it cracks the creature's spine. But Pandora's spine didn't break, no matter how it pounded her, and now she was loose just a moment just free enough to get to her feet and *run*—

Run for her life.

Down the last three steps of the hill, through the hollow where searchlights wandered back and forth across the crop circles—but Pandora didn't see any of that. All she saw was the darkness and her fear, and the screaming that consumed her made a line down the center of her heart, and the line was a path she knew she had to follow. It guided her as she ran —battering through the corn, pushing stalks and rows aside where she could and stumbling sometimes, and the monster was right behind her, trailing in the dark, pushing and swiping and growling at her.

And she ran.

Blindly, almost. She didn't pay any attention to her path or the helicopters or the monster snapping at her heels, toying with her like she was a battered mouse. The only thing she watched at all was the path she knew in her heart, as it led her through the circles over hills and fields and through the corn, till now terrified exhausted she could see trees around her and an endless stream of headlights just beyond the trees.

She couldn't feel the monster anymore. Was it still somewhere in the field? Could it even follow her into the trees? For a moment she felt triumphant, joyous and exultant—it didn't matter anymore whether or not she could get the helicopters' attention. It didn't matter when she looked up to see the helicopters give up and go home. All she had to do was prance down to the edge of the highway and put out her thumb. A few cars would go by, and then a friendly stranger would pick her up and drive her away to civilization and telephones and she could call the President and give herself up.

Or maybe she'd call CNN. She sure liked CNN.

And then she saw the dog.

Once she'd found the dog what else could she do? She had to do what she could for it. Just had to.

When Macdonald gets to Tennessee he finds the advance team trying to search the whole field by air. That's crazy: it's dark already, three hours past sunset, and the corn is tall and dense enough to hide Pandora in broad daylight. They need people on the ground, not just searchlights from the air.

"David," he says as they land. "Get on the radio. Get me two dozen humvees from the depot in the Smokeys. Get them here *fast*." He frowns. "Make sure they all have spotlights."

Dvorkin nods. "Right away," he says. And he gets on the comm.

"Good. —Jane?" Yolen looks up from her console. "Have them break the search up into teams. I want them to comb the field—systematically. I want people on the ground searching every inch of the corn out there. Put the helicopters on the ground—they're wasting their time, waving their lights back and forth across the field."

She found the dog at the crest of the ridge only a moment after she found her way out of the corn. She could see him by the flickering light of headlights on the highway, and what she saw made her ache.

The dog was in pain. He was dying. Horribly. He didn't seem to cope too well with noises—the poor thing winced and shuddered every time a truck roared by.

"Doggie. . . ?" Pandora said this in a low, quiet voice, afraid that she'd startle him and make him jump and hurt himself.

He would have hurt himself if he'd jumped, too. He lay on his side, and he had a big ugly cut down the center of his tummy, and all his guts hung out of it into the dirt. Almost all of them—there were some still attached inside him. Had to be, or he'd be dead already.

He was an awful mess. He was going to be dead very soon.

"Can I help you, doggie?"

The dog opened its eyes and looked at her. Panted soft and steady and in a way that made Pandora think how brave he was to hurt so terribly and still not cry.

She was afraid to get too close. Afraid she'd slip and touch something too delicate to touch, and wouldn't that kill him? Wouldn't it hurt him? What if he was scared of her, and tried to get away if she got too close, and wouldn't that yank him away from his own entrails?

Terrible terrible terrible.

But he didn't move as she drew close; didn't even flinch. When she held her hand out to let him smell (the way she'd read about in the book about dogs, where it told how you introduce yourself to a dog you've never seen before) he sniffed at her, watched her. His eyes seemed to accept her, but it was hard to tell for sure if that was acceptance because he didn't move an inch.

There wasn't anything Pandora could do for him, no matter how she wanted to. Nothing but sit down in the dirt beside the dog and pat his head to comfort him on his way to hell.

It had to be the monster that did this to him, didn't it? Pandora imagined how it disemboweled the poor dog, and the image made her tremble.

She patted the doggie on the head, and the dog turned to look at her, shifting his guts in the powdery red dirt. It sniffed at her hand, licked her fingers.

And waited to die.

But he didn't die—not right away. The dog held on for the longest time, panting, nuzzling at the palm of Pandora's hand, whimpering every now and then when the agony got to be too much for him. When that happened she tried to talk to him until she remembered that a dog couldn't possibly talk back to her.

"Doggie. . . ?" she said. "Are you okay, doggie?" And she got so afraid he was going to die on her, and Pandora didn't think she had the heart to witness that, but how could she do otherwise? How could she leave the poor dog alone to die when it was so plain he needed company?

She just couldn't, couldn't no matter what. It wasn't in her to let down someone in need, even if that someone was only a doggie.

That's why she was still sitting on top of the ridge when the monster came for her. And why she didn't run when she heard it.

Pandora stood when she heard the rustling out in the corn, felt the looming dread that'd shadowed her all day back and forth through the field. She stood to face the monster and there in the flickering glare of the headlights she caught her first glimpse of it—not a real glimpse of some terrible reptile carnivore, but a glimpse of its shadow flickering in the dirt where the corn gave way to pinewoods.

"I'm not afraid of you," Pandora said, and that was a lie and the truth at the same time, for even though she was terrified, she was braver than she was scared. "I'm not going to let you hurt the doggie."

The monster ignored her. It braced and lunged, and now it was in the air flying at the doggie, flying at Pandora, and Pandora felt her blood run cold with fear. She could feel herself wavering through time, and in a moment she knew she'd be someplace a million years away in the land of the dinosaurs or something to leave the doggie lost and dying and alone in the jaws of the monster.

In the jaws of the monster.

And suddenly she felt her terror turn to rage, and the rage was a light that burned her like a bonfire.

As time faded back to *now* and Pandora forgot everything she ever thought about monsters, forgot she was just a little girl and the monster was deadly and carnivorous, frightful and hungry to kill her—forgot her fear and her common sense. And met the monster's lunge head-on.

It was a really stupid thing to do, and she knew that when she did it. But even in that tiny instant she had to decide, she knew in her heart that it was the only thing to do, no matter if it killed her: she had to save the doggie or die trying because it's better to die fighting than it is to stand aside and allow the murder of something that you care for, and Pandora faced the monster lunging flickering in shadows and slammed it in the snout with the ball of her fist, and the monster screamed as its lunge flew awry from the force of Pandora's blow.

Maybe she should have turned and run when that happened, but she didn't. She saw the shadow of the monster trying to find its way to its legs in the underbrush, and she went after it—grabbed the head and pulled it, pounded it into the side of a tree. Found the soft round eyes with her hands and clawed them—

—as the monster *screamed*—

And Pandora punched it, and punched it again and again and again, as all the while the monster screamed and thrashed and clawed her, raking long groves in the skin of her neck and shoulders, but she didn't stop, she didn't back away, she didn't run, she *fought,* and now the monster bellowed in fear and rage and scurried into the darkness of the corn.

At first she didn't realize what she'd done. Of course she didn't realize! Pandora was just a little girl! She wasn't a hero who went around beating up on monsters in the shadows!

But she had beaten it. Somehow she didn't understand she'd beaten the monster till it turned tail and ran.

I won! Pandora thought. *I won I won I won!*

She turned to share her jubilation with the doggie—but when she looked for him, the dog was gone.

There was no trace of him—no track, no trail, nothing. Pandora looked and looked for him all around the ridge, but she found nothing.

The monster came for Pandora again while she was searching. It was different this time: just her alone and nothing, no one she needed to protect. When she heard the monster her courage deserted her, and she ran. She didn't think about it while it was happening, but later it made a kind of sense—she was as brave as she could be when the doggie needed saving, but when it was just her she was scared to fight.

Maybe that was it.

Or maybe she ran because of the venom and the rage in the monster's scream as it came for her—the sound it made was the death scream of a doomed thing, venting the anger and resentment and the bitterness that was its life, screaming the rage that made the monster want to avenge itself, and she knew when she heard it that the thing was dying and it meant to take her with it if it could.

And Pandora ran.

Ran.

Down along the ridge till suddenly she was on the shoulder of the highway waving at the passing cars. She was sure one of them would pull over to help her, to save her from the monster, but none of them did—they honked their horns at her. Two of them swore at her as they sped by, and one shouted: "Stay off the highway, lady, what you trying to do, get yourself killed?"

Pandora could hear her blood pounding in her ears, feel fat welts of sweat inching along her collar, down her back, and she wanted to turn and face the cars and scream for help, *help!* but she didn't dare, there wasn't time, the monster was all but on top of her she could feel it so close, so close she could feel its breath on her neck, smell the stink of rotting flesh in its breath, and Pandora ran and ran along the shoulder of the road while people honked and shouted and jeered from the windows of their cars, and suddenly up ahead there was an overpass with a sheer concrete wall beside it.

And that meant there was noplace to run.

Noplace at all, unless she wanted to run out into the traffic and die.

There was a big green-with-white-writing sign above the overpass. It read:

EXIT 57 PINE JUNCTION

And below that

CLOSED INDEFINITELY FOR REPAIRS

And when she read the words *Pine Junction* Pandora felt a chill that had nothing to do with monsters or highways or being trapped with nothing to do but die and nowhere to go but straight to hell.

Pine Junction.

That was when she noticed what was beside the sign.

Which was trouble. Bad trouble: the ridge wasn't just a ridge where it met the overpass, but a sheer clifflike wall lined with broken rock where the engineers had blasted to make the highway. No way in hell Pandora could climb it—not with a monster so close she could almost taste the stink of him.

Ten steps left before she ran into the wall, full tilt.

Five.

She had to turn and face the monster again.

That was the only thing to do, wasn't it?

Turned *now*, right at the wall, and brought her left foot up to kick against the concrete wall to stop herself.

And the monster damn near ran into her. It would have, too, but at the last instant Pandora pushed herself aside and the awful thing crushed into the concrete wall instead of hitting her.

The impact left the monster dazed, reeling; Pandora watched it slump to the ground and bellow in agony—no, she didn't watch it, exactly, she felt it, she smelled it, she heard it, she saw shadows flicker around it as the awful thing writhed and moaned. And now suddenly it shook off the injury, rolled onto its ursine legs, and gathered itself up to leap—

And without even thinking about it, Pandora pushed herself off the wall with her leg that had braced her stop. Pushed herself in the only direction there was any room to go.

Which was out into the highway.

Out into traffic.

She wouldn't have gone that way if she'd thought about it. Running out in front of a Mack truck was just as sure to kill her as any monster ever could. But she didn't look at the truck until she was already in its path, and she didn't think about it until it had nearly run her over, she just ran out into the middle of the road intent to cross and get *away*, and the horn on the truck blared and the cars screeched as they tried to stop, but they couldn't, there wasn't time to stop, there were only feet away from her and moving *fast*—way up over the speed limit, close to eighty, ninety miles an hour.

And the idiot monster followed her right out into the middle of the highway. Stupid thing to do! *Very* stupid!

But the monster didn't die right away—and neither did Pandora. Pandora heard the truck's horn blaring in her ear, and she looked up to see it bearing down on her, and her Guardian Angel sent her reeling out through time. The monster somehow fell through time beside her, following her—

As Pandora kept running across the highway that now was and wasn't was and wasn't there as she moved terrified back and forth through time, kept running from the monster who was sure to kill her, sure to kill her the moment it got close enough and closer now, closer—

And then the world went red with blood.

It started like this: Pandora was back *here* and *now*, already somehow across six roaring lanes of traffic and the big ditch in the median. She stopped for a moment trying to see where she was. Stood on the highway's far shoulder, looked back—

And saw the monster.

What she saw was death in motion.

Because the monster had faded out of time right along with her—but behind her. And behind Pandora there were six roaring lanes of highway traffic.

She saw it as a shadow in the headlights of the big

Mercedes diesel truck that slammed *splat* into the monster's head and chest, breaking it open like a big sack of blood. Then *splat!* again on the bumper of the truck as the monster flew into the air. She saw its arms and legs swing wild and painted in blood, looking like the Raggedy Ann doll that Uncle Wally got Pandora when she was little . . . and now down again *bamm bamm bamm* on the hood of the truck bouncing like a ball up and down, and then the monster fell under the bumper and a big spray of blood shot up from under the truck's wheels. Brains scattered on the highway; blood went everywhere; bones snapped and ground into the pavement, shattered so forcefully that fragments of skeleton flew up out of the monster's flesh to sting Pandora's cheeks.

The truck and half a dozen other cars slowed to pull over on the shoulder of the road, and a tiny voice inside Pandora wanted to run to them and plead for them to take her home, *take me home please take me home,* and that was what she'd meant to do, wasn't it?

But the sight and the blood and the bone and the stinging on her cheeks were too much. Too much! She didn't listen to the voice—she hardly even heard it. She did the only thing she remembered how to do: she turned away from the grue and the gore and the screaming drivers shell-shocked climbing from their cars.

And she *ran.*

Macdonald made a big choice when he decided to take the fast helicopter down to Tennessee. The fast 'copter got them to Tennessee from Andrews in less than an hour. But it was a trade-off: the 'copter only carries so much gear. There's secure comm and a console for Yolen, but the secure fax with its direct connection to the intelligence culls off the wire services—they'd have to take the mobile command post to have access like that. But driving the command

post down from the nearest base—near Richmond—
would have taken twelve hours, maybe more.

That saved a lot of time. But it cost them something more: information. In a very real sense, Macdonald's office is *about* information. And without his
connections, he's crippled. And when the bulletin
describing the terrible highway accident in rural
northwest Tennessee comes through on the UPI feed,
it comes in to Yolen's console back in Washington.

Miles and miles away.

When Pandora stopped running she was at the edge
of a town. Pine Junction, population 73—there was a
sign that said so underneath the streetlight. Up
ahead there was a town square with a gazebo and
benches and everything, just like on the *Wonderful
World of Disney* movies, oh, oh, it was so lovely to
see it in real life. On the far end of the square there
was a TV station with the letters WLBO stenciled on its
side, and beside the station there were a TV tower
and a satellite dish.

On the far side of the TV tower there was a little
building with a picture of a badge on it, and beside
the badge there were the words PINE JUNCTION TOWN
POLICE.

When she saw that Pandora remembered everything she forgot watching the monster ripped to
shreds under the bumper of the big Mercedes truck.

I'm going home, she thought. *Home home home
home.*

All she had to do was go into the police station
and tell the officer on duty who she was and that she
was from a secret government project and they ought
to call the Pentagon or the President or maybe Dan
Rather or something. And they'd give her cocoa and
wrap a blanket around her and tell Pandora funny
stories till the authorities came to take care of her.

Pandora couldn't wait!

She hurried through the town square, up the
white bright-lit sidewalk that led to the police sta-

tion, and knocked three times outside the door. But before she even touched the door she knew something was wrong. The glass beside the door was black as night where it should have been radiant and inviting.

All the police station windows were dark like that —and no one answered no matter how Pandora knocked.

She knew what was wrong before she even knocked. But for three long moments she told herself, *Any second now, any second now the officer will answer and he'll be so happy to see me, he'll love me just like everybody does O O I just can't wait to see him.*

And then she saw the sign.

PINE JUNCTION TOWN POLICE
OFFICE HOURS:
MONDAY THROUGH FRIDAY 8:00 A.M. TO 5:00 P.M.
IN CASE OF EMERGENCY DIAL 911.

There was a pay telephone beside the door, but that didn't do Pandora any good—she didn't have a dime to her name.

I'll have to wait till morning, Pandora thought. She felt so sad. Everything kept being harder and harder than it should have been, and no matter how she tried nothing ever went right. She got so mad sometimes!

Maybe she ought to dial 911, she thought. Didn't phones work like that? Weren't there some numbers that worked even when you didn't have a quarter for a call? Pandora wasn't sure. She'd never had to use a phone before, and never seen a pay phone except on TV.

So she kept thinking that, kept thinking dial dial dial 911, but she hated the whole idea. And she frumped off to the bench by the gazebo thinking how it was so dumb to have a police station that was only open in the daytime. Pandora never saw anything

like that on the cop shows, and everybody knows cop
shows are just like real life.

But Pine Junction wasn't like the cop shows. It
was a weird place—weird with its police and weird a
lot of other things, and nobody in town would have
cared if they knew their police station hours made
Pandora mad.

So she sat down on the bench beside the gazebo.
And waited for the morning.

After she'd sat for a while she fell asleep on the
bench.

And as she slept she dreamed.

The first thing Pandora saw in her dream was the
spaceship. The one that carried her mommy down to
her death.

First she saw it just as she'd seen it in the hangar,
at the moment she'd first set eyes on her mommy.
The ship; the jets; terrible explosion as Hightower
shot her mommy from the sky. And on from that
until the moment where her dying mommy handed
Pandora to Uncle Wally.

Then something twisted, like a current snapped
in time. And all the circumstances changed.

Changed because now she remembered it as it
never happened. In her new dream the spaceship
was even bigger and faster than it truly had been;
and this time there weren't any planes, and there
wasn't any Hightower, and there wasn't anything but
the spaceship hurtling down through the clear bright
Mexican sky—hurtling through the sky forever as a
fiery streak building on the radiance of the day.
Burning white-hot inside where her mommy and the
lizardoid Blaine and Blaine's lover cursed at their
malfunctioning equipment; and her mommy so pregnant with Pandora, her flesh so soft, so damp and
spongy in the heat leaking through the spaceship's
hull; and her mommy stood above the spaceship's
controls spitting and trembling and trying to get the
bloody damned thing to *work!* which it wouldn't do

no how no way wouldn't work for nothing and the
ship thundered across the daylit sky above Baja, into
Arizona, all across New Mexico; burned bright white
burned hot—

And Pandora's mommy cursed one final time—

And the two lizardlike Aliens stared longingly into
one another's eyes—

And Pandora screamed in her sleep—

And the spaceship slammed hard into the side of
an Arizona mountain.

It was quiet after that. —After the ship's remains
finished settling into the mountainside.

Even before it started, Pandora was afraid to look
into the next part of the dream. Because little by
little she could see closer and deeper into the remains of the ship—and what she saw was the most
terrible thing she'd ever imagined.

She saw the bridge of the spaceship utterly broken, entirely destroyed.

Saw Blaine and his lover dead, just as they'd been
in the other vision.

Saw her mommy just as dead as she would be if
evil General Hightower shot her out of the sky.
Worse—where her mommy lived long enough to see
Pandora in the other vision, this time she was dead
long before falling machinery burst her womb and set
Pandora free.

Free.

But what is freedom to an infant?

Pandora saw her infant self small and alone and
despised by the very bedrock of the world that surrounded her; saw the baby that she might have been
abandoned because the only mommy in the whole
world who was guaranteed to love her was dead and
gone before she could call a new mommy to see after
Pandora.

Pandora thought of the moment with her mommy
and evil Hightower and Uncle Wally, and thought
how her mommy weighed the two men so carefully
and handed Pandora to Uncle Wally. —And wasn't

there something magic in the air when her mommy touched Uncle Wally? As though Mommy passed her love along when she handed him Pandora.

But there was no Uncle Wally in this terrible vision, and Pandora's mommy was already dead. Pandora the infant lay battered and bruised and alone in the rotting metal of the ship, and she screamed and screamed and screamed. Pandora the maturing Space Alien girl wailed along with her.

After a while the ship began to crumble around infant Pandora and the three dead Aliens, just as it had in the other vision when Uncle Wally took Pandora from her mommy's arms. And just as before, the three of them remained inviolable, untouched by time, wind, rain, or decay; but whatever magic the ship bestowed upon Pandora in the original vision was gone here.

Pandora didn't entirely understand this until the California condor landed beside her infant self. And it absolutely was a California condor; Pandora recognized it from the TV special called *Our Endangered American Treasures*. It was a California condor, and it was a hunting bird as well as a carrion eater.

And as Pandora marveled at the beauty and the majesty of the creature, thrilled to be in the dream presence of a creature so rare and regal, the condor struck.

Struck Pandora, who was an infant on the dusty mountainside.

Snapped down with its sharp cruel beak, plucked the left eye from screaming infant Pandora, and swallowed it.

No *out* through time; no special lifeboat from the ship that wasn't ship no more; no one and nothing in all the world to protect her.

Something in Pandora curled up and died as she saw herself eaten alive.

If she'd had any choice she surely would have run screaming from the mountain; and even if she had, the simple image of the bird swallowing her eye

would have haunted her the rest of her life. But she
couldn't; there was no release from this nightmare.
No matter how she tried to wake from it. And because there was no release Pandora saw everything
the condor did to the infant who she might have
been.

When the bird was done it picked apart her
fleshless bones.

Macdonald walks the cornfield.

They *all* walk the cornfield. In the night, in the
sweltering Tennessee summer heat that doesn't go
away some nights no matter how late it gets. All of
them, every last living body Macdonald has at his
personal disposal walks searching that godforsaken
moon-black cornfield in the middle of Nowhere, Tennessee.

What is it, a hundred of them? Two hundred?
Macdonald has a large staff, but not an enormous
one. Staff isn't the point of Macdonald. The point is
that he's the President's arms and legs, the man who
goes down into the bureaucracy and buttonholes the
bastard who thinks he's his own damn boss, gets him
to do what the President was elected to *make* him
do, that's the point of Macdonald. And he has enough
people to do whatever he damn well has to, to get his
job done, no one more, no one less, every damn one
of them personally handpicked staff, every one of
them responsible to him, no bureaucrats, no GS
grades, no bullshit—every last one of them *knows*
that Macdonald goes when the President goes. Knows
that they all go with him. Unless the new administra-
tion asks Macdonald to stay on, which isn't bloody
likely, but stranger things have happened . . .

Just this moment Macdonald wishes to hell and
back again that he had a bureaucracy the size of the
Pentagon to call up—and maybe even that wouldn't
be enough. There *just aren't enough* of them, damn
it.

Because there's no sign of the Alien girl.

But what sort of sign *should* there be? And how the hell are they supposed to see it, here in the cornfield in the moonlit dark? And if they *could* see, there wouldn't be anything *to* see. The red clay is too hard to show the passing of someone as slight as Pandora. What they need is dogs—bloodhounds for tracking. But something's wrong and the hounds they called in haven't turned up, and they *keep* not turning up, all through the night.

The heat is getting to Macdonald, and he knows it.

And then his phone rings.

Right out there in the middle of nowhere.

Well, it's not a phone, actually, it's really a field-grade comm set, what the hell else do you take out into a cornfield in the middle of nowhere? Almost one of those damnable beepers Dvorkin likes to wear, and Macdonald doesn't like it a whole lot better but what choice has he got? This is no time to be out of touch.

Not by a long sight.

So anyway he answers the phone.

And wouldn't you know? It's the President.

"Macdonald," the President says, "your girl is on CNN. She's been on CNN for most of the last hour. What the *hell* are you doing in the middle of that cornfield?"

And Macdonald faints away and dies, right there.

Pandora dreamed again, and now in her dream she sat huddled inconspicuous in the corner booth of a coffee shop, nibbling her lunch as she listened to two raucous men exchanging stories at the counter.

First one of them told a story about a woman so sad about the death of her little girl that she made her be a zombie.

And his friend said, I heard that before, it isn't true, it's just an Urban Legend.

Pandora wanted to say, *I met that girl, she's real and true and not no legend she's a monster.* But she knew that if she did the two men would realize that she was a Space Alien, and they wouldn't say anything in front of her anymore.

You want to hear a real story, the second man said? A *real* story? I'll tell you a story.

And then he told about Sasquatch wandering the woods, always hunting but never catching anything. Always right near by but just out of sight.

He's real, the man said. I saw his tracks once. They were enormous.

His friend just laughed at him. Talk about your Urban Legends! he said. That one's so old it's got a beard.

But Pandora knew Sasquatch wasn't any Urban Legend. Didn't she?

And then the first man began to tell a story about an Alien spacecraft downed over Roswell, New Mexico, in the late 1950s. And how they'd found real Aliens, dead inside the wreckage. And transported the remains to Wright-Patterson Air Force Base in southern Ohio. Where they've been on ice for all these years.

Before Pandora could stop herself she'd stood up and started shouting. *I'm not any Urban Legend,* she screamed. *And I'm not dead and there isn't any ice!*

There was one important thing about that awful dream that Pandora didn't have a clue of: the TV cameras. She didn't know (and couldn't) that the WLBO morning crew showed up only a moment after she closed her eyes; that the morning news anchor recognized Pandora the moment he saw her sitting on her park bench. How could he have *not* recognized her? He'd watched her CNN interview so carefully, so deliberately. Pandora was a wonder to him, and rightly so. He called the cameraman (who wasn't due into the studio for another twenty minutes) and hurried him so stridently that the poor fellow ended up leaving his home before he'd shaved, much less made his coffee.

But what did that matter, five minutes later? What did it matter when they finally got the camera running, finally got through to CNN (WLBO was an independent, but it had a news-sharing agreement with CNN) to let the network know what news there was? What did it matter when the morning anchor and the cameraman and CNN and Pine Junction, Tennessee, had the biggest scoop yet in a year of amazing and impossible news?

It didn't matter worth a damn, that was what.

And then Pandora began to dream.

Well, not dream, exactly. Pandora *thought* she was dreaming, all right—but what was really happening down inside her was something much more like a vision than it was a dream.

A vision.

Like a prophecy, but different, because what she saw wasn't her future but a past that might have but had not come about: and it was real. Real because Pandora *was* strung weird through time, and the lifeboat Guardian Angel that protected her had been wearing down for months, and after the battering it'd taken saving her on the highway, it'd begun to run seriously amok. Because her Guardian Angel ran amok, Pandora's nightmare bridged the gap between now and *un*when; and as she dreamed her dreaming heart projected a vision into the air around her.

And the TV camera saw it. As though projected onto glass, a ghost of all that had and had not happened.

And the camera broadcast Pandora's vision out through the airwaves to all of mountain Tennessee; and repeated its own signal into the satellite antenna to CNN. And CNN broadcast Pandora and her terrible dreaming for all the world to see.

There was a transition when the dream was over, and before the next one started. And in that dark and quiet space of time Pandora had another revelation: *That dream,* she thought. *That was what would happen if Hightower hadn't've shot my mommy out of the sky.* And that made her cry even harder, because she couldn't cope with the idea that the worst possible things can sometimes be a part of the best outcome the circumstances allow.

And then she began to dream again.

Actually Macdonald's call from the President doesn't happen exactly like that.

The way it really happens is that it isn't the President on the phone at all—that's just an imagining, a hallucination, almost, brought on by the heat and the sweat and the fact that Macdonald's been too damn long without a night of sleep.

It isn't the President on the phone; it's Yolen.

Trouble is, she's got the same bad news for him that the hallucinatory President did, and even if she says it a bit more demurely (imagine that, imagine that, Macdonald just thought of old she-tiger Yolen as *demure!*) even if she says it a bit more demurely it's still just as bad.

And Macdonald, Macdonald isn't a suicidal man, but just that moment out there in the heat and the sweat, just that moment he has this terrible urge to blow his brains out.

He doesn't do it, of course. There isn't time. He's got work to do.

There were other important things happening as Pandora dreamed her life story onto live global-satellite TV.

One of them was at the office of the local sheriff—a man in Tylerville named Mike Peterson. Till six months ago Peterson had been a deputy; now the old sheriff was retired, and Peterson found himself appointed to fill out the sheriff's term. And where all his working life he'd thought of nothing but his duty and the law and (privately) the romanticized bits of detective work—suddenly now his head was full of worry over people and politics and the possibility of standing for election.

It didn't make him a happy man.

Which may explain why he got so excited when the calls came in from the army and the FBI.

Separately, and almost simultaneously. And neither caller seemed to know about the other.

They both wanted the same thing: they wanted Mike Peterson and his department to take someone into custody. And hold that person till—

Well, that was where they wanted something separate—each of them had pretty specific instructions about who he was supposed to hand this person over to, and under what circumstances. And both of them invoked the highest authority.

Strange. Very strange.

But not nearly as strange as the fact that they were asking him to arrest an Alien.

That was exactly the word they'd used: *Alien*— and though they both used it a little differently, there was no mistaking their meaning.

She dreamed now of the General, and what he'd done to her. Five nights ago? Six? It wasn't long, but it felt like a lifetime, and Pandora had lost track of the days.

But she hadn't lost the memory.

She remembered the dark, the hall, the barracks; remembered Uncle Ken screaming in pain and terror for his life. She hated that memory. *Hated* it! The very beginning of it made her tremble in her sleep, and she wanted oh how she wanted to be *away*.

She remembered it all the instant she saw the hallway. She saw herself running, and in a moment she'd round a corner and slam into General Hightower's porcine gut, and they'd both end up falling to the ground. But not before the General saw his future looking at him from Pandora's eyes, and it got him so upset. . . . She'd get up and try to jump over him to save Uncle Ken, and he'd grab her ankle and pull her out of the air, he'd jerk down hard and make her *smack* headfirst into the terrazzo. And she'd be senseless, and he'd beat her and beat her and when she was all but unconscious he'd *touch* her—

And then it'd be too much, and even though she was stunned and blind to the world, the *touch* would reach her where she lived, and the saving thing inside her would whisk her away through time.

Only.

Only it didn't happen like that this time.

It happened worse. So much worse! —because this time there was nothing to save her, and in the dream the General did things to her that no one ought to do to anyone else ever no matter what.

And while he was doing it, Pandora screamed and screamed for her father to come down from the stars and save her.

And maybe he did.

Something did, that was for sure.

It turns out Pandora is on TV just across the freeway from where they are now—over in Pine Junction. Macdonald hollers into the comm set, and they all pack up to roll over—

And that's where trouble starts all over again.

Because the only bridge over the freeway for a dozen miles in either direction is washed out, closed, impassable. And the only ways around are overland through the woods or way out and around along unpaved roads through the Tennessee woods—an hour, easy. Maybe more.

There isn't that kind of time.

Macdonald radios the helicopter pilots—both of them, the pilot of his fast helicopter and the pilot of the big transport that brought most of the staff down from Washington—but there's a mechanical problem with his fast helicopter and the transport is going to need forty minutes to get warmed up.

They told him there would be days like this, back in OCS. He didn't believe them.

He does what he can: he calls a dozen new fast
helicopters in from Andrews, then puts a call in to
the FBI asking them to call the local police, get them
to pick Pandora up from the Pine Junction Square.
He calls CNN, putting in a polite request that they
pretty please cut the shit. Which they'll ignore just
like they ignored all the others, and the President
won't let Macdonald shut them down no matter how
bad he wants to.

Damn it.

And Macdonald waits. What else can he do? He
waits and he tries to clear his head.

And he waits.

And it's morning, damn it. And he hasn't slept.
And *damn it* he could use some rest.

The call from the FBI lady left Mike Peterson
amazed.

Oh, he'd heard people talking about the fuss on
CNN two, three days back. But he hadn't seen it for
himself, and he hadn't took it serious. And he hadn't
heard a word of the news that morning. Wouldn't
have believed a word of it if he had, either—Mike
Peterson knew about strange business firsthand, and
because he knew about such things he wasn't in-
clined to take hysterical reportage any too serious.

Which is why, when he got off the phone with the
woman from the FBI, he decided he was going out to
Pine Junction himself.

*Space Alien, my left foot. Ain't no such thing as
Space Aliens. Even if the self-important lady from
the FBI does want me to go in and arrest one.*

And the reason they wanted him to arrest her—
that was the worst thing. What kind of silliness. . . ?

"She's dreaming," the woman'd said. "And they're
catching it on television, and CNN is broadcasting it
worldwide. And they won't stop!" —Peterson wanted
to interrupt her, wanted to ask, *Well, then why the
hell don't you* make *them stop?* but he was still too
dumbfounded to get his jaw working. —"It's a secu-

rity risk. We've got to put a stop to this. We need you to go to Pine Junction and take her into custody."

The only part that made any damned sense at all was the fact that they were asking him to do it, instead of doing it themselves. It'd take them hours to get there themselves, unless they planned on going in by long-distance helicopter—the road that connected Pine Junction to the interstate was washed out and all but impassable. The only way in there was by the back road from Tylerville—not the world's toughest drive, but it wound all crazy through the hills, and if you didn't know each of the dozen or so forks intimately—well, you could spend all week trying to find the place if you took the back road.

Not a problem for Peterson. Wouldn't take him twenty minutes to get there. And (he decided, staring at the phone) he might as well get on with it. If he spent another five minutes here, trying to figure out what the hell was up the way he had after that first call—the one from the army—the phone would ring again and the world would get even more confused.

Right in the middle of things the dream with the General disappeared just as though it were an ordinary nightmare, and Pandora was someplace else.

Someplace weird.

Way up in the air someplace; clear blue daytime sky all around in every direction and the ground way below her.

The TV tower, that's where she was! On top of the TV tower. And why else was she here if it wasn't to call her daddy?

"Daddy!" she shouted. "Daddy, I'm here! Come get me, Daddy!"

Nothing. Nothing but the ground and the trees all around her on the low horizon, and the brightness of the sky everywhere out and above.

"Daddy Daddy come save me Daddy you're my only hope!"

And she heard her voice echo back to her, which was a very new thing to Pandora.

And sure enough: a light in the sky, bright grey even against the brightness of the daytime sky, and in a moment Pandora could see it was a tall figure standing on the bright disk of a UFO flying saucer, and the figure and the flying disk came closer and closer came down to her—

Till it was close enough for Pandora to see.

When she saw she almost screamed.

Because what she saw wasn't what she expected —wasn't her daddy at all.

The one on the flying disk was old Walt Fulton.

When he was in earshot she shouted at him.

"Get out of here you old Walt Fulton old earthling man!" she shouted. "You aren't my daddy and I don't need you anyway!"

And the saucer with Walt Fulton on it kept a-sailing toward her, but the old man himself—he wasn't sailing anywhere. Oh, he still stood on the flying saucer. But Pandora could see how he was crumbling and all dejected inside, and she felt like an awful louse for saying mean words at him.

But what else could she say? The old man kept getting in her way when she was looking for her daddy, and she wasn't about to put up with that.

No way.

No how.

He was right here, now, him and his saucer were only a couple-three feet away from Pandora floating in the air beside the tip-top of the TV tower. He looked like he was about to die.

"Go away, old man!"

And just like that, he did.

And Pandora woke up.

It takes the helicopters too damn long to get there.

Too damn long! Twenty minutes, thirty, and where the hell are they? They should have been here already. He could've had the transport chopper warmed up if he'd known it was going to take this long!

Macdonald knows something's wrong, something's up, so he gets on the radio and he starts asking questions. Loud and hard.

Nobody has any answers. The helicopters are on their way—that's all he can find out.

Damn it.

Mike Peterson didn't like the idea of arresting a little girl—not at all. But how could he do anything else? No matter what he felt, he was a man of the law. He'd been a lawman all his adult life! When the FBI called and told you it was a matter of absolute national security that you go up the hill and arrest a little girl and you were a sheriff who took his work dead seriously—what the hell were you supposed to do?

Peterson did what he saw as his duty, even though he thought it was wrong.

Seriously wrong.

He pulled the cruiser into Pine Junction, took a good look around. He didn't like what he saw.

He didn't ever like it, when you got down to it. It was a tiny, mean-hearted, cramped little place that probably wouldn't even've got its name on the highway exit if it weren't for the TV station being here. But there was something more about it that morning —something distinctly ugly. Foreboding, that was the word he wanted. The damned place felt exactly the way Green Hill used to, back before everything changed out there.

He parked his cruiser, climbed out. Began to wonder if he'd been wrong to drive out here by himself and without backup—he hadn't even thought to tell anyone where he was headed before he left the station. If he got into trouble out here it might be hours before anyone so much as figured out what had become of him.

Bad.

He was going to have to be more careful about

things like this. He wasn't used to having the authority to take his own assignments; till the old sheriff retired he hadn't been in a position to go tracking after dangerous nonsense without someone at least telling him it was his to handle first.

And then he saw Pandora.

And the moment that he did all the things that had worried him a moment before suddenly seemed petty and selfish.

She was still dreaming when he saw her.

Dreaming of her father. He could see that, just like the FBI agent said: the girl (and she was a girl, even if she was clearly and undeniably not a human being) was dreaming, and her dream by some unknowable magic was plainly visible for anyone to see —anyone but anyone who walked into the Pine Junction town square could see exactly the things that she saw in her dream. And Peterson saw the Space Alien girl here sleeping on the bench; and ghostly all around her, floating in the daytime air, was the girl all over again, but high up in a tower, and she was shouting. Almost screaming.

"Daddy, Daddy, I'm here! Come get me, Daddy!" she shouted. "Daddy Daddy come save me Daddy you're my only hope!"

Peterson tried to imagine what the father of the Space Alien girl would look like—and found himself unable even to begin to imagine. When he tried to age her face in his mind, tried to imagine, her features shifted ever so slightly and made male—his mind's eye refused to make an image for him.

Just refused.

He couldn't think why; he'd never had much trouble imagining strange things when he put his mind to it. It was a talent of his, thinking strangely.

"Little girl?" Peterson wasn't really asking a question—more like he was trying to get her attention. "You've got to come with me, miss. I've had phone calls from the FBI, the military—any minute now I'm sure the CIA will call. They want me to take you into custody. I don't see any way I can rightly refuse them."

"Her name is Pandora." This from the cameraman. "Could you speak up a little, Sheriff Peterson? You're speaking so quietly that the microphone isn't picking you up very well."

Peterson recognized that cameraman. Sherwood Smith. He'd been with the station, what, three years? Something like that. Always friendly enough. So why couldn't he turn that damn thing off for a little while? Peterson didn't want the whole world watching him carry poor Pandora out to the cruiser. He didn't want to do it, much less have the whole world see. But he knew what'd happen if he asked the guy to turn the damn thing off—he'd end up as a sound bite on *News Watch,* and they'd say he was trying to repress the news, and he was damned if he was going to let them do that to him.

"Pandora. . . ?"

No answer.

"I've got to ask you to come with me, Pandora."

Didn't respond. Didn't so much as move a muscle. *She must be too deep asleep,* Peterson thought. *She must not be able to hear a thing I say.*

He didn't want to have to carry her to the car. He really really really didn't want to—not just because he wasn't keen on arresting little girls (never mind how she was a Space Alien and all; Pandora was a little girl plain as day, and you didn't have to sit down and explain that to Mike Peterson) not just because he wasn't keen on arresting little girls but because something down in his gut told him that taking her into custody was *wrong*—and not just wrong but liable to cause a disaster he couldn't begin to imagine.

He stepped close to the girl, leaned over her. Whispered: "Pandora?" She didn't answer any more than she'd answered him before. *I'm giving her over to her enemies,* he thought. And he almost turned right then and walked away.

But didn't. He couldn't; it wasn't in him to turn away from the trust that was his job. No matter if he'd hate himself for doing it.

The very worst thing of all for Macdonald is when the helicopters come soaring over the hill like space-age cavalry—and keep right on going.

Right over them.

Right past them.

And when Macdonald gets on the radio and orders them down, they just ignore him.

Three big fast helicopters—that's the new model, isn't it? *Damn,* Macdonald thinks, *damn it those birds look good.*

As they sail over his head.

Macdonald feels the bottom falling out from under his already screwed-up world. Something is very, very wrong.

Hightower. McNamee.

"Oh shit," Macdonald calls to Yolen. "We need to see this. Get me a CNN feed."

Arms so carefully beneath the still-dreaming girl—one beneath her back, one still in the air below her legs. And hesitated there before he came into contact with her, afraid to touch her for no reason he understood.

But whether he understood or not, he was right to pause.

He would have been even righter to turn and run and never look back.

Because when Mike Peterson tried to lift Pandora his arms didn't press against her back and legs; instead they pushed up and through her. Not right through her, as though she were a ghost painted light against the air, but up and into her like pushing through hard gelatin. Like she was there mostly but not completely, here enough to touch but not quite enough to hold. Not nearly enough to lift.

Lift.

Peterson wanted to scream, what with the way his arms felt all deep inside where Pandora wasn't really and if she wasn't here where was she?

Where?

She was here, she was plainly here enough that Peterson could feel his arms inside her body feel the working of her heart against her biceps but she couldn't feel look at her look she was still sleeping fitful still dreaming of her daddy look at her expression she was smiling all thrilled and excited as though she'd found someone she'd lost too long ago to remember but now here he was she'd found him O Joy! O Joy! Reunion—

But that was her joy, not Peterson's. He was too busy trying to get his damnable arms out of the thick never never move gelatin that wasn't quite Pandora, and he was afraid that if he moved too suddenly he'd hurt her, and if he didn't move fast enough she'd be back in the world and the two of them couldn't *really* occupy the same space not at the same time when they were both really *in* the same time (Peterson, a man with considerable experience where Weird Things were concerned, understood about time and Pandora instinctively) if she woke and came back to *now* the two of them would explode or something nasty, Peterson just knew it.

His elbows free. His forearms. His wrists. His hands.

He was backing away. He didn't mean to back away; didn't plan or premeditate it. But he did it. Back all the way to the camera, where the cameraman groused that he was in the way, and stepped aside and kept moving and moving back.

He was afraid? He didn't think he was afraid, but it was something like fear that he felt. And it surely made him want to get back into his cruiser and keep moving!

But how could he? He couldn't just turn around and run. And if he could, he wouldn't let himself.

He heard Pandora shout: "Go away, old man!"

and for half a moment he thought she was talking to
him, and if she was did that mean that she wanted
shut of him? Didn't it mean he could leave in good
conscience? No, no there wasn't any way. She was
dreaming, still dreaming, and it wasn't Peterson she'd
shouted at but the broken old man standing on the
flying saucer. (Flying saucer? Old man? Peterson
was amazingly confused. He wished he'd spent more
of his attention watching her dream and less in trying to lift her from the bench.)

    The old man looked familiar—very familiar. But
Peterson couldn't remember for the life of him where
he'd seen that face before.

    And then it didn't matter what Peterson did or
didn't do, because there were helicopters everywhere
in the sky, so many of them so big so frightful that
Mike Peterson himself just wasn't an important part
of the equation anymore.

Pandora woke all sweaty and miserable—sweaty and
miserable and tired and confused and not rested at
all. Like—like she'd been working or something, instead of trying to get a nap. Which was why for the
longest moment she didn't register the helicopters or
the sheriff cruiser or the TV camera or the people
watching or any of the eleventy-dozen signs all
around her that she'd got herself into some mighty
deep dip by taking a nap in a town square in the
middle of nowhere.

    In fact, it wasn't until General Hightower and the
seven of his deranged air police jumped off the helicopter and charged her *charged her* with their rifles
drawn bayonets and everything wasn't till she realized she was about to die that Pandora got up off her
duff and *ran* for it because her life depended on it
which it certainly did! Pandora saw Hightower and
she remembered her dream, remembered the terrible scene in the dark hallway back home in the barracks, and she ran, *ran* straight toward the TV
camera, and as she ran she turned to face the video

lens. And because her heart was still in her dream with her Space Alien daddy she could never find, she screamed: "Daddy Daddy save me Daddy they're trying to get me Daddy *help me!*"

And then she was past the camera and the cameraman and running for her life.

Running.

Past the sheriff and his cruiser; past the building that housed the TV station and the tower that stood beside and behind it.

And back into the woods.

There wasn't any time for Pandora to think about the strangeness of the woods before she plowed into them, but she sure wished there was.

Because the woods behind the TV tower were kudzu woods—pinewoods invaded by kudzu vine. In another year or three if the coldest part of winter didn't kill it the vine would grow so tall, so thick, its weight so heavy that it would starve the pines. Two years after that the kudzu weight would crush the rotting trunks, and there'd be no forest, just an alien vine-choked field.

But now there were pine and kudzu both, and because the vine had trees to cover, the netted mass of kudzu hung like a carpet up above the ground.

High above Pandora's head.

Everywhere around her now.

The woods were covered with kudzu vine, covered and crowded and suffused. The thick green leaves—big as Pandora's head—crowded everything everywhere that wasn't trees, pressed close against one another above and around her until the day wasn't light but dim and green as the kudzu stole the sun. She wanted to slow and stare and wonder at the horror of the thriving choking green, but there wasn't time. Wasn't time to watch her step in the knotted roots; only time to keep running no matter how she stuck or stumbled in the great green mass.

But even if the kudzu was hard on Pandora, it was

worse for the APs. They were taller than she was—
too tall to run under it, the way Pandora did.

Then suddenly the green went thick and closed in
all around her, and an instant later vanished as she
broke through to a clearing. . . .

No. It wasn't a clearing: it was the edge where the
kudzu woods met a roadway. And if Pandora didn't
get out of it and back into the cover of the forest the
air police were going to shoot her down for sure.

Bolted across the road—

—and damn near got herself killed.

Of course she nearly got herself killed! She didn't
look both ways before she crossed the road! No one
ever taught her that, because they didn't think she'd
ever need to know, but they should have, because
Pandora damn near ended up pasted to the front
bumper of Mike Peterson's sheriff cruiser.

Damn near.

It would have killed her, too, if it weren't for Peterson's reflexes kicking in so fast. And the cruiser's
brakes taking such a thorough hold, and (praise God)
the tires grabbing the clay-dirt road and dragging the
cruiser to a stop.

Pandora stood dumbstruck for the longest time,
staring at the cruiser's windshield the way an opos-
sum stares at headlights just before it dies.

The sheriff leaned out his open window. Shouted
at Pandora. "Don't just stand there," he hollered,
"unless you want them to catch you. If you want a
ride, get in. If you don't, get moving!"

Pandora blinked.

"In. . . ?"

"In the car," Peterson said. He reached cross the
front seat, opened the passenger door. Later Pandora
remembered how the nice voice on the TV always
said she should *Never get in a car with strangers,*
but that moment with the air police bursting through
the kudzu to capture her Pandora didn't think at all
—she got in the cruiser with the sheriff and slammed

the door shut as the sheriff floored the gas, and the cruiser roared as it tore down the dirt road.

The road was like a dirt-floored tunnel cut deep into greenery so thick that she could hardly see the sky, and behind them there were APs shooting, screaming, threatening to kill them both, trying to kill her *blam blam blam!* Shooting as the cruiser sped away into the green.

"Get down!" Sheriff Peterson (Pandora read his name off badge, that's what it said, SHERIFF MIKE PETERSON) shouted as the cruiser's back window exploded into a shower of minuscule glass cubes.

As green tunnel took a sharp turn to the right, and the tires screamed as Peterson spun the wheel. When they were clear of the bend he let out a deep shuddering breath, and the sound was a gasp and a sigh and the wind that sifts out of the lungs of a corpse, and for a moment he seemed to relax.

Outside the cruiser the green tunnel grew denser and denser until it seemed to close in around them. Then suddenly the canopy above them disappeared, and Pandora saw four helicopters—two with military colors and a little one with the letters WLBO stenciled on the side—pacing their car from above.

General Hightower hung from a ladder below one of the helicopters. He had a gun in his free hand, and when he saw them he aimed and fired at the roof of the cruiser. But his shots went wild in the wind.

"He's going to get us," Pandora said. "One way or another."

Then suddenly the woods grew thick again, so thick around and above them that broad daylight looked like green dusk.

And suddenly Peterson slammed on the brakes.

Slammed on the brakes and cut the engine, and just *was* there, stock-still and quiet as you please.

Macdonald is watching *News As It Happens* on CNN in the middle of this Godforsaken Tennessee corn-

field when he sees Hightower descend from the helicopter, and suddenly it's all too much for him.

Just too damn much.

He can't take it anymore.

So he does something stupid.

Very stupid.

He collars Estes—because there's something between Pandora and Estes, some frail connection Macdonald can see but could never explain, and that's a
hope, at least, a thin hope in a situation full of futil-
ity. Macdonald collars Estes and grabs the humvee
Eisen and Collier came down in, and he goes for the
washed-out bridge.

This is the stupid part: that bridge isn't fit for
walking across, let alone driving over with a humvee.

Even if he *could* walk across—not a good idea,
but possible—what would be the point? It's five miles
from that bridge to Pine Junction. He needs to be
there *right now,* not an hour from now.

So he does something stupid with the humvee.

Like this: barreling down the washed-out road,
gathering all the speed he knows how to gather. By
the time the humvee bursts through the great white
Bridge Closed sign they must be doing a hundred,
hundred twenty miles an hour (there's no way to
know for sure; Macdonald has enough to juggle without watching the speedometer).

Through the sign, and the humvee bounds up and
off the last jagged slab of paved road, into the
air. . . .

Moving so fast that they sail right past the spot
where the bridge picks up again on the far side of the
gap.

This is probably just as well, since the whole
damn bridge—what's left of the whole damn bridge—
groans and trembles as they land on it, and the hunk
of road beneath the humvee's left rear wheel drops
right out from under them.

It's only luck that the half ton of stone and mortar
that falls down onto the highway doesn't kill anyone.

Not that Macdonald stops to check. As if he could! They're still moving at close to a hundred miles an hour, bounding and pounding across the rutted pavement, over the crevices that look down onto the rushing traffic that is the interstate highway. Not even a humvee has brakes enough to stop them before the far end of the bridge.

The groaning is louder, now. As though a metal beam down inside the stone were threatening to give way. Well, that's okay, Macdonald thinks; we're almost across; it doesn't matter now—

He should never have thought such a thing, of course. Thoughts like that tempt fate too dearly.

As now.

As the whole roadway tilts out from under them as it collapses, as the—

As the front tires slam into the fractured pavement on the far side of the bridge—

The tires slam into the edge, jerk straight up. And for a moment they're watching the sky—and down again, on the far side of the bridge. And thank God for four-wheel drive, because it's the front drive that pulls them up out of the void, onto the road—

And suddenly it doesn't matter what happens to the crumbling bridge anymore, because they're across and free and Macdonald glances back to see that the roadbed didn't fall down onto the highway, but it's leaning down toward it, *way* down toward it, and somebody better close that road before some truck finds out that the clearance is now nine feet where it used to be fifteen.

As the humvee roars up out of the washed-out road toward Pine Junction.

"Get Yolen on the comm," he tells Estes. Estes looks very very pale—quite an accomplishment, all things considered. "Get her to give you blow-by-blow what's showing on CNN. I want you to tell me if anybody goes anywhere."

. . .

When the engine was quiet Peterson turned and looked at Pandora.

"Be very quiet," he whispered. Pandora didn't know what he was getting at; she raised an eyebrow at him. "They've got to be tracking us with directional microphones. If they've got the new ones they'll be able to hear us talking—even in here, even under all these trees."

And Pandora sat stock-still in her seat, watching the dim green woods silently, staring up into the strangling-thick canopy above. . . .

And saw a leg, a man's leg, squirming and wrassling through the tangled vines and branches. And screamed.

Peterson sat bolt upright, startled, looking like someone had shoved a hot poker where a poker never ought to go, and saw the AP himself lowering hand over hand toward them.

And started the engine, pushed the accelerator to the floor, and put that cruiser in *gear*.

As the APs (and there were lots of them, lots and lots, all of them just an instant behind the first one) got their feet on the ground and their rifles pointed at Pandora shot her shot her right between the eyes *no!*

No. That AP tried to shoot her, but by the time he got that round out its barrel they were *gone*, and the bullet wasn't going through her eyes, but smashing through the rear passenger window, making more of those square little chunks of glass go flying every which way.

Thank God.

"They're following us," Peterson said. Actually he shouted it, which was necessary because of the way the wind was rushing through the broke-open back and side windows. He gestured toward the windshield, toward the green up above and ahead of them. "Following, hell. They're there before we are. They know where we're going." And just then there was a break in the tunneling branches, and Pandora could see how he was exactly right—there were four helicopters lined up along the road ahead of them, going where they were going before they even got there.

They're going to get me, Pandora thought. *And they'll get the poor sheriff, too.*

Peterson shifted gears and pushed the accelerator back down to the floor, and the cruiser went flying and caroming down the suddenly twisty dirt road; and all the sudden they were right over the edge of a cliff going *boom* roll roll roll *boom* over the edge—no. They weren't, he made the turn, the right rear tire kind of lost it for a moment lost its grip out over the edge made them go all tippy but then the cruiser whipped 'round and they were on the road again flying anyhow even if they were still all four tires on the dusty road.

It didn't do a damn bit of good. The helicopters were still up there above them.

Two long breaths, and they were around the bend. And on the far side of the bend was a railroad swath with train tracks running down the middle.

And on the tracks there was a train.

A great long train that trailed off forever in both directions. It was hardly moving.

And there was nowhere for the cruiser to go.

Except maybe backward. But how could they go backward with the APs coming that way on the ground? Wasn't any use, even if Sheriff Peterson could get the cruiser turned around on the narrow road (now that he was stopped he was trying to do it, but with the way the cruiser was so long and the road was so skinny it wasn't going well) as the helicopters began to circle up above them, shooting and blasting at the cruiser with their big guns, and it was over, they were going to die this way, right here, right now, they were going to die.

As the humvee came slaloming around the bend.

• • •

As they come around the corner Macdonald sees the helicopters circling the police cruiser, shooting at Pandora and the sheriff. Hightower hangs from a rope-and-chain ladder beneath one of the helicopters, shooting wildly at the cruiser with his service revolver.

Hightower!

That man has got to die, Macdonald decides: *got* to. He swears Hightower won't leave this place alive, and he means it.

He tells Estes to duck into the back of the humvee and see what they have for firepower. Takes the microphone off the clip on the humvee's dash. His voice booms out through the loudspeaker on the humvee's roof: *"This is Jake Macdonald speaking,"* he says. *"Put down your gun, Hightower, and present yourself for court-martial arrest. —That goes for the rest of you, too. I want those helicopters on the ground, and I want to see all of you come out of there, single file, hands in the air."*

And suddenly Hightower—who's been laughing maniacally as he shoots at the pair in the cruiser— goes beet red and angry. He screams—no, that's not a scream, it's a war cry, a challenge bellowed from the throat of a man who knows nothing but the lust for murder.

"Jake!" Hightower shouts. "If you try to stop me I'm going to kill you, Jake. I swear to God I am." And he laughs like the devil incarnate.

Macdonald pulls the humvee alongside the cruiser as Estes comes back with two rifles and half a dozen clips of ammunition.

Two rifles? Half a dozen clips of ammunition? How the *hell* are they supposed to hold off the kind of firepower Hightower has in those helicopters with two guns and six clips of ammo? Macdonald swears again, takes one of the guns, and starts shooting. He aims at Hightower, at the helicopters' rotors—and damn near gets one of the rotors before Hightower sees what he's doing and waves the 'copters down.

Three of the helicopters—all of them except the civilian chopper with the news crew beaming its signal up to CNN—come down on the road on the far side of the train, penning them in. Bad news: they're outmanned, outgunned, and trapped.

"Get on the comm," Macdonald tells Estes. "Get us some reinforcements—I don't care if they have to close down the highway to get here, I want them here. Now. Tell Yolen to make sure it happens."

Three of Hightower's deranged air police rush them while Macdonald is giving orders—the sheriff manages to pick off one of them, but the other two damn near overrun them before Macdonald looks up, sees them coming, sees they're wearing flak jackets tougher than his bullets, and wastes half a clip of ammunition making sure he blows the brains out of both of their skulls.

Dirty business. Makes a spectacular mess. The kind of mess that plays real bad live on CNN.

The President is going to be *pissed*. Seriously, seriously mad. There's going to be hell to pay real soon.

Macdonald reaches back into the hummer's cab, grabs the mike off the dash.

"Give it up, Hightower," he says. *"There's no way you're getting out of this alive."*

Hightower stands up and laughs, but Macdonald can see he's shaken. Of course he's shaken; he just lost two men who served with him for years. It won't matter that they were low-life scum who should've gone to courts-martial years ago, not to Hightower, because service is like that: the people you serve with are your people, and what the hell they've screwed up in the rest of their lives just doesn't matter.

"You're dead, Jake," Hightower bellows, spraying the humvee with a dozen rounds from his machine gun. "I swear to God you are."

Macdonald isn't impressed. The man's a fool: he's shooting without cover. Macdonald takes careful aim, tries to blow his brains out—and damn well would've done it, too, if the bellowing maniac hadn't picked that moment to stand tall and bellow another challenge. As it is, Macdonald's shot catches Hightower just above the heart, and that's no damn use because he's wearing a flak jacket. The force of the bullet sends Hightower sprawling, but that doesn't matter. The round would've knocked his wind out, maybe bruised him up a little, but there's no way it could've took him out.

Estes puts down the comm. "They're coming," he says. "It's going to take a while to shut down the highway, but if we can hold out there's plenty of help on the way."

Macdonald nods. He isn't sure how long they've got. Maybe all the time in the world, if Hightower's men are as stupid as he is.

But they aren't that lucky, of course. With Hightower down the APs show a little common sense: two of them go left, two go right. They scuttle into cover and begin trying to circle around.

"Shit," Macdonald says. He tries to pick off the APs, but it's no use. They're in deep trouble, any second now. He looks over at the little-girl Alien, who looks scared out of her mind; at the sheriff, who's reloading his pistol. "How you doing over there?"

The sheriff shakes his head. "Not good," he says. The windows of the cruiser are all gone; the engine block is fuming and smoking—it looks like the cruiser took a few rounds from the helicopters' GE cannon right through its hood.

"This is going to get hairy in about two minutes," Macdonald says. "If they can get into the rock over there—" he gestures right "—we're meat. And I don't think we can stop them."

The sheriff and Ken Estes glance at the rocks, and both of them can see it's true: the rock would give rifle cover from a vantage that covers everything the helicopters can't. As they watch, one of the APs makes a scuttling run for the rocks—and Ken Estes only barely manages to pick him off.

"There's a little cover here between the cruiser and the humvee. We all need to get between them and stay low."

It isn't much of a strategy, but it's all there is at that moment. They're lucky none of the APs has thought to try using the helicopters' cannon on the ground—it wouldn't take the big guns long to take apart the hummer and leave the four of them corpses in the slag.

Then suddenly the two who went right rush them from the woods as the second one who went left makes a run for the rocks—and it's no damn use, no damn use at all, Estes covers the rocks as Macdonald tries to take out the charging pair *and his gun jams* JAMS God bless it why would anyone leave a piece of junk like this lying in a humvee where someone might have to use it?

"I need help, Estes, gun trouble," and it's over, yeah, Estes manages to take out the suicide assault but it's still over and they all know it, the damned AP in the rocks has them nailed, *nailed.* Macdonald pushes Estes and the girl into the hummer. "Stay low," he says but it's not going to do any good, the inside of that thing is no cover at all even if it's all they've got, and he grabs the sheriff playing Shoot-Out at the OK Corral with the AP in the rocks, and he shoves him into the hummer but it's no use, no use, the AP gets the sheriff through the shoulder just above the heart, he'll live if he's lucky maybe not if they don't get help soon real real damn soon and then there's the sound of thunder inside Macdonald's head and the world goes black.

When the tall man died Pandora knew it was almost over. Any second now they'd kill Uncle Ken, and a moment after that she was going to die, too.

She could feel it: there was death in the air, and it was coming for her.

Three bullets slammed into the side of the humvee. One of them ricocheted around in there with them five times—it almost hit her twice.

Uncle Ken looked around, looked desperate. And then suddenly there was inspiration on his face, and Pandora knew he'd found something like hope.

"Pandora," he said, "I want you to make a run for that train. It's the only way out of here. Make a run for it, I'll cover you."

Pandora wanted to say, *No, no, I can't desert you,* but Uncle Ken stopped her the moment she started to object.

"You're important, Pandora. Important to the whole damned world. You've got to get out of here."

And she wanted to tell him he was wrong, that she was just a girl, just a little girl who probably wasn't even a Space Alien, but then the bullets started flying, hundreds and hundreds of them, and she was too scared not to run.

Later she felt like she deserted Uncle Ken, and that bothered her a lot. But she managed to do it, maybe because none of the APs expected her to try to run: she ran the fifteen feet from here to there in an instant, grabbed the side of an open boxcar door, pulled herself up and in, and disappeared into the quiet darkness of the train.

For three long minutes she thought she'd gotten away safe and sound for sure, and everything was going to be okay, okay, any second now she'd be at the next town to get out and find Uncle Ken and the good guys and turn herself in.

But it didn't work out like that.

Because five minutes after Pandora slipped into the boxcar she heard the sound of a helicopter above her. And then the big cannon started firing rounds that tore holes in the walls and floor around her, shaking the whole damn train, and Pandora screamed, screamed in absolute terror of the end she knew had come for her—

As her Guardian Angel kicked in.

And something went *wrong,* seriously wrong, and where Pandora should have fallen a moment away from danger, she and the whole train went soaring out of time.

As the world disappeared.

It was a long time before Pandora found it again.

S I X

Among all the stories of haunted engines and bewitched contrivances that have filled our collective ear since man first entered the age of great machines, the tale of the Awful Lady may be the most curious. For where most such stories pit man and machine—after the pattern of the ballad of John Henry—the story of the Awful Lady describes not rivalry but—symbiosis?

No, not symbiosis. Something darker and less nurturing.

There is a lady derelict, the tale goes, who haunts the nation's railroads. A bitter, hateful ghost who isn't ghost at all but rather a living woman who slept too long inside the boxcar where she'd stowed away, and so was trapped forever in the distance between cities.

In some tellings she's trapped by her own stubbornness, waiting for the train to return to her original destination. In others she's the victim of a curse that prevents her from leaving.

It's said train conductors sometimes see her glaring at them hatefully through night-dark windows—late in the evening when the passengers sleep as quietly as the train rolls across the midnight landscape. Now and then a passenger wakes to report an old woman clawing through the trash receptacle at the far end of the dining car. Sometimes people hear her screaming, angry and frustrated—but no one who's ever heard that scream has found its source.

Perhaps (on reconsideration) the tale of the Awful Lady *is* in the mold of John Henry. But if she is John Henry's analogue, she's taken to the logical extreme —a woman not only pitted against a mechanical rival, but defeated by it; a prisoner of the train that rolls forever.

As she lay on the boxcar floor Pandora and the train cut loose in time sailed across possibility. When they came to rest they floated in a place where time bends constantly upon itself and cause takes on a preternatural meaning: Pandora and the train fell into the place spacefarers call *The River of Our Destiny*.

Those who understand such things say the *River* is a place below *place* where mutable *time* and acausal *cause* flow through the fate of the worlds to produce our circumstance.

Pandora didn't understand.

What she saw wasn't a river or time or cause or acausality: she saw a train adrift through hell, and she hated that.

She really really did.

Yolen and the cavalry come charging over the Pine Junction hill with guns drawn and humvees roaring

—too damn late. The battle's already over. Peterson is half-dead in the dirt; Macdonald is beside him, unconscious with a hole in his shoulder half the size of Texas; a bullet grazed Estes's skull as he covered for Pandora, and he's dizzy and bleeding like a fountain. Hightower and the helicopters have disappeared into the sky.

From page one of
The Wall Street Journal

ALIEN ARMADA
ENTERS SOLAR SYSTEM

Astronomers at seven western-hemisphere observatories report the presence of a fleet of alien starships just inside the orbit of the planet Mars. "We spotted them last night, a little after midnight," said Dr. Alexandra Rodgers, Professor of Astronomy at the University of Southwest Virginia at Bristol. "It appears that they're moving in the direction of the earth." Rodgers was uncertain how long it might take the armada to arrive. "They're on a course that'll bring them into collision with this planet in a matter of days," she said, "perhaps less. They're moving very quickly. If this is where they're going, they'll have to decelerate—and how long that takes depends on the power and tolerances of their equipment, and on the amount of thrust stress the Aliens themselves are capable of withstanding."

On the train it looked like this:
Pandora lay on the boxcar floor, breathing. Just breathing. It was all she could think to do.

When she glanced sidelong out the open boxcar door, she saw the most amazing, terrifying sight.

She saw the sky of hell.

It was a dusky grey haze—a weirdling, impossible, unreal haze like no sky anyone anywhere had ever seen or will ever see: it was a sky made from grey mother-of-pearl and stale brackish water.

It was a sky shining with the light of ten thousand days and nights blended in on one another; it was every sky Pandora'd ever lived beneath, focused and diluted till it was all those times at once.

Where am I? Pandora wondered. *What's happened to the sky?* She could feel the train moving, gently rumbling as it rolled along its tracks; but the rumbling made no sound that she could hear.

An hour after Pandora disappears into forever, the Aliens show up.

Above Wright-Patterson.

Thousands and thousands and thousands of them.

As she watched the weirdling sky sidelong through the open boxcar door, a feeling came over Pandora. It was like—like everything was okay just as long as she could lie here perfectly still, but if she so much as moved a muscle horrible things would begin to happen.

It was an amazingly perceptive intuition. For she was exactly and precisely right, and if she'd listened to it just a little longer her life might've been very different.

But how could she? How could Pandora know that the Awful Lady waited on the far end of the boxcar, watching Pandora and hating her just as she'd hated her for a long, long time—despite the fact that Pandora had never set eyes on her?

Pandora saw something like lightning flicker across the darkling sky, and she sat up to get a better look—forgetting the intuition that told her not to move.

And her world went mad.

As the Awful Lady screeched and screamed and leaped, and Pandora turned to see a monster charging at her from the darkness at the far end of the boxcar.

A monster.

And that was exactly right, too, because the Awful Lady *was* a monster. She was a terror, a horror, and the moment Pandora saw her she knew that awful woman meant to kill her.

Of course she meant to kill her! There was death and decay in everything about the Awful Lady. In her eyes so bloodshot red, that red so radiantly sanguine that it seemed to shine. In the grey-brown rags that were her clothes—a skirt, a blouse, a sweat-soaked overcoat too heavy for the warm Tennessee air. In her hair, that hung unruly, in greasy ropy hanks snared with bits of debris; and what color was that awful awful hair, grey or brown or—or was it any color at all but the color of death?

Pandora screamed. She would have run if there was anyplace to go—but there was noplace. Just the darkness at the far end of the car, and boxcar doors that opened out to hell.

"I'll kill you!" the Awful Lady screamed as she launched herself up off the boxcar floor. "Kill you kill you *kill* you!"

And then she was in the air, and Pandora had to run, and there wasn't any way to go but out the door. Where the train was moving at two hundred miles an hour through a place that was no place at all.

It's after Pandora's disappeared, but before the Aliens appear in the sky above Wright-Pat. Yolen and Estes are in the ambulance with Macdonald, and they're taking him (partly against his will) to a hospital.

"Find that train," Macdonald says.

And Yolen and Estes promise that they will—but no matter how they try, no one finds it.

No one but CNN.

Again.

As Pandora sailed out into nothing she saw the ladder made of rungs bolted to the outside of the boxcar. And she tried to catch it as her left hand slapped past that high rung, slapped past and in the instant it took her to realize that she had to grab the ladder had to climb the ladder in that single solitary instant as it already got to be too late to save herself Pandora realized what she had to do.

But by then it was too late.

Too damn late.

Her hand was already gone; the rung way out of her reach.

And Pandora plummeted to the ground that wasn't ground but the firmament of hell.

Until half a breath before she shattered against rushing hell Pandora managed to get hold of the bottommost rung; and though that wasn't enough to save her legs from crashing dragging tearing painfully against the jagged rock of hell, it was enough to let her pull herself up out of the void.

Barely! She had to hold on for everything she was worth to keep her hold on the rung with her legs dragging against the rocks of hell that wanted to tear her away, and she held on, held on and dragged herself out of hell onto the side of the train.

Both hands, now—Pandora had both hands on the bottom rung of the ladder.

The Awful Lady stood above her, watching from the open boxcar door. Laughing at her! Twice she tried to spit on Pandora, and would have, too, but the wind of the train's passage was so fast that it blew right back in her face.

Serves her right, Pandora thought as she pulled up onto the second rung. When she had both hands around it her feet stopped scraping across the ground of hell, and she knew she was going to be all right if she just kept climbing.

Except the Awful Lady got really angry when Pandora reached for the third rung, and she started kicking Pandora's hands, trying to stomp her fingers and make her lose her grip, only that her legs weren't long enough so she sidled onto the ladder and stepped on Pandora's fingers.

Stomped on them real good, grinding them between the heel of her boot and the painted iron rung of the ladder, and for a moment Pandora was sure that she'd lost her grip and she was going to tumble down to hell and die, but she didn't, she held on, reached around the Awful Lady's stinking grimy legs to grab the fourth rung, and no matter how the Awful Lady kicked and hurt her Pandora held on.

And then the train lurched.

So hard the boxcar banged against the one in front of it, and then into the one behind, and the Awful Lady lost hold of the rung above her head and nearly went flying out into hell—

No, she didn't lose her grip, not completely, she managed to grab on to the edge of the boxcar door and pull herself back up into the boxcar.

Pandora saw the Awful Lady having trouble and she saw her chance—and took it. Before the Awful Lady caught her balance Pandora was up the ladder, climbing past the open door, over the top, onto the roof.

Dvorkin throws off his headphones, pushes away from his terminal. "Okay," he says, "I've got it. I've got McNamee pegged."

Macdonald doesn't want to hear about it. They're on the road from Tennessee to Washington, and he's depressed, and he's tired, and his shoulder hurts like hell but he's got too damn much to do to take a pain pill, and he's got to go talk to the President as soon as he gets back to DC.

He doesn't want to *hear* about McNamee.

But he has to.

"What is it, David?"

"I finally managed to crack open McNamee's secure storage on the net." Makes no sense to Macdonald whatsoever. Nor to Yolen, to judge by the look on her face. "Computer storage. Files."

Dvorkin beams when he says the word *computer*. Macdonald sincerely wishes that he wouldn't grin that way; Macdonald's mood is so black that he finds the put-on cheerfulness unpleasant.

"What did you find, David?" It's Yolen who asks. Just as well that she does; Macdonald was about to ask himself—and a lot less politely.

"McNamee's a conspiracy nut. Some of the stuff I got out of his files—incredible. It looks like he's convinced that the government's been infested with Aliens since the sixties. Lots of documentation—none of it very credible." He looks away, and for just an instant his bright mood dims. "There's a three-page rant square in the middle of it all—something about McNamee's old boss, Chris Imershein. Looks like McNamee thought old Chris was an Alien or some such. I think McNamee set him up for the helicopter crash that killed him."

The room goes quiet for a long moment that lasts until Yolen sighs.

"Why am I not surprised?" she asks. "Everything I hear about this bastard—"

Estes—sitting till now quietly at the far end of the command center—clears his throat.

"What exactly did you want to know about General McNamee?" he asks. "I know a little bit about him."

Bingo.

"Tell me everything," Macdonald says. "Tell me all you know."

Macdonald *knew* there was an important reason to collar Estes, drag him onto the team. And this is it.

Estes tells the whole long story of his time at Wright-Patterson; the argument with Anna; what happened when her father—General McNamee—learned that she was pregnant.

There's something strange in the man's usually sunny voice as he speaks. Guilt? Bitterness? Regret? —All those things, mixed together.

And something else in his voice, too—Macdonald isn't sure what it is, but he can hear it.

The strangest truth about the Awful Lady is that it isn't her fault that she's so pinched and shriveled and mean inside.

She didn't commit an act so terrible that it turned her into a horror; she didn't insult some dire fiend and bring its curse upon herself; she didn't do anything but be born in the wrong time and in the wrong place and to the wrong parents.

Parents, that was the thing.

And not just her parents, but everyone who ever knew her, back when she was a child.

There was something about her, then—something small and proud and insolent. It drew the attention of everyone who saw her on the streets of Chicago; and with their attention it drew their ire. The Awful Lady's parents beat on her mercilessly, and did worse things than beat her. Unspeakable things, they did unspeakable things that scarred her forever and ever.

Scarred? No, not scarred. There were few literal scars of her childhood on the Awful Lady's hide, and those there were had little to do with beating or abuse. Her parents were too careful of what the police might say if they found her broken or bloodied. As were the three strangers who set hands on her in the course of her adolescence. But even if the Awful Lady's upbringing left no scars on her, it wrote true tales on her face, and deeper into her soul. There was no one who saw her the year she turned seventeen who could not read the story of her past; and of those who read only one who did no cry to know. (That one found her in a dark and quiet place, and she did the Awful Lady worse than anyone ever had done her before, not excepting her mother.)

The truth is that the Awful Lady herself is the victim of Awful Ladies just like her; and because abuse isn't just a terror but a lesson, she learned some terrible truths.

And they are truths, for all that they're terrible and ugly. It's true beyond denial that violence is a powerful tool; that pounding the life out of something or someone small and unprotected soothes the corruption in a poisoned heart; that the world most often steps aside and lets the strong devour the weak.

And day by day she learned to exercise those lessons; and now near the end of her life the Awful Lady lives consumed by the knowledge of them.

Still: at the base of her the Awful Lady is a victim. Down in her heart she always was and always will be a small child beaten and abused, abandoned to the hands of the parents who despise her.

"Okay, where do we pick up McNamee? Can you track him down from those files?"

Dvorkin shakes his head. "Not a chance. I broke his security good—but not that good. He'll know I've been in there." He pauses. "There may be something in this mess that'll tell where he is. I only scanned a bit of it—there's too much to read all at once. Eight megabytes of text, maybe more. But even if there is he'll be gone before we could get to him."

"Find out what you can. If you see anything in that mess that you could use to track him down—*do* it." Macdonald turns to face Ken Estes. "Estes—I want you to go talk to this daughter of McNamee's. She'll know where he's hiding if anyone will."

The Awful Lady went after Pandora, of course. Up the ladder, over the top, into the rushing air that ripped across the boxcar roof.

Pandora was ready for her. At least as ready as she could be without a gun. She didn't try to hide, or run. Running was too dangerous up here, and any place she could have hid would have left her especially vulnerable when the Awful Lady found her.

Instead she walked two cars down, turned back, and stood facing the direction she'd come from.

Same direction that the Awful Lady came following.

"I'm not afraid of you," Pandora shouted when she saw the Awful Lady climb up over the edge. "I don't know who you are and I don't know why you want to hurt me. But I'm not afraid, you hear?"

But it didn't matter what she said, because the words all got lost in the wind.

"I'm not afraid."

This time the Awful Lady had heard her.

"I don't care if you're afraid, you little witch. I'm going to kill you once and for all. I'm going to kill you *dead* this time!"

Which was really scary even if Pandora did know that dead was dead and if you got killed you were dead and that was that.

"You can't scare me, mean old lady," Pandora lied, "I ain't scared of nothing nohow."

Pandora stood with her back straight and her expression calm, looking as tough as she could.

And then a bat came flying out of hell, screeching and screaming all the length of the train. It swooped right over Pandora's head, wailing and flapping not six inches above her, and she thought for sure she was dead and buried.

An instant later it was gone.

But it took her calm with her when it went. And that was the worst thing it could have done to her.

Because the Awful Lady saw.

Saw Pandora shriek, duck, and cry like a baby when the bat startled her. And all her scared-of-the-world-gone-amok slipped out of her at once. And she cried.

Which was the one thing you never ought to do in front of the Awful Lady.

Never ever ever.

Because, well, because it touched something inside the Awful Lady when she saw someone cry like that; only it touched her sort of backhanded and backward because of all the terrible things that happened to her. And when the Awful Lady saw you crying all hopeless and defenseless like that, what she saw was herself.

She hated herself more than anything else in the world.

Hated how she'd wailed so pathetically when her mom and dad had beat her; hated how she'd lie for hours pitiful and delirious if they hit her hard enough to knock the wits out of her head. Hated most of all how she never had the stomach to *show them a thing or two, all right!* which was what her dad always said just before he did the worst things to her.

When the Awful Lady saw someone like Pandora crying like a baby, she got this awful need.

Need? Was it a need?

No, it was more like a compulsion.

Or even like being possessed.

When the Awful Lady saw Pandora crying what she thought was *I'll show them a thing or two, all right!* And then it was like this script took over, and she wasn't really boss of her no more.

The script went like this:

"I'll kill you, you little witch!" and then she screams, and she leaps, and when she lands with her hands around the throat of the little one she only shakes her to death for a moment, because you don't want to choke them so long they die because how do they learn when they're dead?

No way.

Not dead? —that's wrong. *"I'll kill you, you little witch!"*

Well, dead is the point, but you want to teach 'em good first, right? Right. So you take the hands away from the throat, no, you take one of the hands away from the throat and use the other to keep a collar on them, and you haul back with the free hand and *hit!* Open-handed at first, and then when you build up a little momentum, then when you got it like you got the beat, you tighten up your hand and make a fist out of it, a fist to pound their ugly little face into a pile of red *jelly!*

Yeah!

Like that.

It's not a pretty thing to watch, the Awful Lady in high dudgeon.

Only, well, it doesn't play out like the way it's supposed to.

Because Pandora wasn't as small or as helpless as she looked; and because she had an angel around her, even if she was in hell.

For instance: the hands didn't hit the way they were supposed to, but kept on going *right through* Pandora, well not right through her as though she was a ghost, but damn near like that. A little hesitation, a little catch like into red jelly—and through. But not red jelly, but something weird weird weird, because red jelly wasn't electric like that, only red.

Even caught up in the script the way she was, the Awful Lady got a little sick with herself on account of that electric tingle when her hands went into Pandora. But that sick wasn't half as bad as when Pandora pushed away and got up on her feet and grabbed her by the great dark coat.

And hit her with a rock-dense fist, right between the eyes.

The Awful Lady fell slumped flat on the roof and started whimpering when Pandora hit her. One good punch, no more, and the Harpy on the Train in Hell turned into a crybaby. So strange! Hadn't anyone ever hit her back before?

Pandora couldn't begin to imagine.

For a long time she stood on the train roof watching, still afraid that the Awful Lady would get up on her feet and attack all over again. But she didn't. Not for as long as Pandora could stand there watching her, and longer; and after a while Pandora began to feel bad for her crying like a little baby, and despite the fact that she knew it was dangerous she stepped close to the Awful Lady and stooped down to talk to her.

"What's the matter?" Pandora asked. "Are you okay?"

That didn't get an answer, maybe partly because the Awful Lady was crying so hard and so loud that she couldn't have heard a word Pandora said.

"Are you okay?" Pandora reached across the space between them, touched the filthy shoulder of the Awful Lady's coat. "I'm sorry I hit you," she said, which was a plain old lie that Pandora didn't recognize till she heard herself say it. She wasn't sorry one darned bit, because if she hadn't hit the Awful Lady back the Awful Lady would have kept on beating her till she busted something.

Absolute fact.

"I'm sorry you feel bad," and that was somewhat truer, because Pandora wasn't one to want to watch another person hurting. "Please be okay."

The Awful Lady kept on crying and crying. Pandora kept on feeling worse and worse.

"I feel so bad," Pandora said. "I'm going to cry if you don't stop crying."

And that broke something open all over again.

"I hate you," the Awful Lady said. Very quietly, at first, but after the first couple of syllables it was lots louder. "You meant to hurt me just like that, I know you did."

Pandora shook her head. This wasn't what she wanted.

"I didn't," she said. "I really really didn't. I don't mean you any harm."

"Liar," the Awful Lady said. "Liar! You hit me all the time. You cut me with your knife. You killed my dog when I was six!" And she lunged up at Pandora,

got her hands around her throat, and started choking all over again.

Pandora tried to say, *I never saw your dog, I never made you bleed, it wasn't me you're thinking of someone else*—but there wasn't any way she could have gotten the words out with her voice choked off and all.

"I'll make you see," the Awful Lady said. "I'll teach you how to be."

Choking harder now, and Pandora couldn't get any air. So she put her hands on the Awful Lady's wrists, and pulled them, pulled them out and away. . . .

And something went so wrong.

Terrible, terrible wrong.

Macdonald sits in the President's office.

He's sat here many times before, but rarely with so little to show for his work. Macdonald is not a man accustomed to failure—but he's found precious little success since Yolen first noticed Ken Estes disappearing from the records.

The President is calling him on the carpet.

"They look like a war fleet, Jim," the President says. He's talking about the Alien armada that showed up over Wright-Pat two hours ago. There's no need for the President to be any more specific; Macdonald understands. He almost always understands what the President wants—they've spent many, many hours working together.

Macdonald nods. He thinks he knows what's coming. He isn't looking forward to it.

"It's still possible that they're only here to get Pandora."

Macdonald and the President have been talking about this since the Aliens first showed up on the telescope pictures. They're both certain that it's Pandora who's brought the Aliens—but why are there so many of them? And why warships? Why so much hardware to rescue a little girl?

"I still want Pandora back," the President says. "And quietly. No more soldiers on TV shooting at little girls!"

Macdonald has an urge to object, to remind the President that he just damn near got himself killed protecting that little girl. But the President knows that the same as everybody else who saw the shootout on CNN. He isn't chastising Macdonald, and Macdonald would be a fool to respond as though he were.

"Yes, sir, Mr. President."

"But"—and Macdonald knows as he hears that word that the twist of the knife is coming—"but Jim, it's too big. It could be war. I need to give the generals room to plan for it. I've got to take this away from you."

The President is taking authority for situation away from Macdonald.

Macdonald knew it was coming, but even so the words hit hard, harder than the ache from the hole in his shoulder.

"Yes, sir."

The President is right, of course. Macdonald is more than enough for tracking down Pandora, tracking down the project—but he's no strategist, no tactician, nor is he any longer skilled in the arts of war. And he knows better than to pretend to be. As does the President, who knows the trouble Johnson and Nixon brought on themselves micromanaging Vietnam.

But damn it, Macdonald has a job to do, and it bothers him considerably to lose authority in the middle of it.

"I want your people to keep looking for Pandora. —The brass are so obviously unsuited to the task that I wouldn't dream of letting them near her again." He clears his throat. "And that time thing about her—if there's anything more you can learn on that, well, God bless you. But it's past time for contingency planning. We need our boys in the air. And if they're in the air, the brass need the elbow room to see after them."

"No argument, Mr. President."

It's nowhere near as bad as Macdonald was afraid. "Now, what's this about physics? About time? You say you're making headway?"

And Macdonald tells the President. About the grad student down in Florida who saw Pandora appearing and disappearing on television, saw a few fine details and odd bits of light—and slapped her forehead, and *knew*. . . . And she was right, too. She's just about managed to duplicate the Pandora effect in her laboratory.

As he recounts the sequence of events it comes to him that this is exactly the trouble with classified research: that ideas grow in the light of day. That the breakthroughs happen not *here* inside the Pandora Project, where two dozen physicists toil night and day for a lifetime, but over *there*, where a young woman slaps her head and *knows* what's right, just because she's the one who's best made to add all the bits of evidence together. And the more anyone claps the lid of secrecy down on knowledge—the more secrecy there is, the less knowledge there is.

When he thinks it that way Macdonald realizes that it's so simple, so straightforward that any fool ought to know classified research is boneheaded nonsense. Nothing new to him; it's his *job* to reach down into the government and collar fools like that.

Trouble is there's just not enough of him to go around.

Pandora grabbed the Awful Lady, trying to choke her by the wrists, and she *pushed* with everything she had.

Which turned out to be a little too much.

Because it sent the Awful Lady flying.

Right off the train.

Onto the firmament of hell.

The Awful Lady screamed as she realized where

she was—and the sound of her scream was a thing that stayed with Pandora as long as she lived.

PRESIDENT
CALLS UP RESERVES

WASHINGTON (AP)—The President today issued a terse order declaring a state of national emergency and calling up all available air, land, and sea reserves and National Guards. White House spokesmen refused to comment when asked to explain the significance of the order. They did not respond to questions concerning a possible connection between the mobilization and the Pandora crisis.

Live televised address by the American President to his people, carried worldwide over seventeen radio, and television, and satellite networks:

"My fellow Americans, I'm here with you this evening to share some disquieting news.

"The Alien armada first publicly reported this morning has reached the United States. The Aliens have taken up positions above Wright-Patterson Air Force Base in Ohio. They have, through means unclear to us, cut off all travel and communication to and from the base.

"Their intentions are unclear to us, but we have every indication that they are not friendly. Efforts to communicate, negotiate with them have borne no fruit.

"I have therefore with great sadness called up the entirety of our nation's reserve and National Guard units, and as of this moment I am calling on all NATO and bilaterally allied nations to send all necessary assistance.

"In the meantime we will continue our efforts to communicate with the Aliens. Unfortunately, the evidence has begun to suggest that they hear and understand us perfectly well, but are not interested in responding.

"I ask that every American remain calm and prepare to participate in the effort to preserve our nation."

It's a bad, bad day for Dvorkin. The news is terrifying; Macdonald's mood is even more frightful, if that's possible.

And still: there's a job to do. This is no time for hiding in a bunker someplace—no matter how appealing the thought of it might be.

Dvorkin steps out of Macdonald's office and sees the two women waiting in the anteroom. "I recognize you," he says, nodding to each in turn. "Eisen and Collier."

They both look uneasy as sin, and rightly so—Macdonald's waiting room is no place he'd want to be himself, if he hadn't known the man a dozen years.

And of all the days to wait outside Macdonald's office, this may well be the worst.

Eisen stands, extends her hand. "Mr. Macdonald? You wanted to see us?"

Dvorkin shakes his head. "No, I'm Dvorkin. I work for the man." He frowns. Is Macdonald liable to want these two anytime in the next few hours? Dvorkin could use some help; he's just managed to isolate the block of Pentagon basement offices that Mc-Namee's been running his terminal out of. Good, bright, observant eyes; sharp, fresh minds—Eisen and Collier are just the sort of help he could use. And besides, they're pretty, and Dvorkin has always appreciated the company of attractive ladies. Trouble is Macdonald is liable to come storming out of his office at any moment, and just maybe he'll be looking for these two. And if he does there'll be hell to pay. . . . No. Not a chance. Macdonald's in there with Yolen, and they're up to something; by the time they're done not even Macdonald will remember why he drafted these two. "Come with me," he says. "I've got work for you."

For a long time after, Pandora sat on top of the train, watching the hell sky shift from dim to light to dark. After a while the sky of hell metamorphosed into the nighttime sky above west Tennessee, and a helicopter came down through the night to watch her. And watched and watched and watched. At first Pandora thought it was a military helicopter, like the one that brought the General to hunt her in that little town she ran away from. And then she saw the cameras, and the letters CNN stenciled on the side, and she knew that they were friends.

She waved to them—to the people in the camera. And she shouted *"I love you!"* and she hoped that they could hear.

And someone inside the helicopter waved back, which was pretty damn wonderful.

LARRY KING LIVE:
WHAT HAPPENS TO TIME AROUND PANDORA

Larry interrupts his physicist guest, who's spent most of the last half hour attempting (fruitlessly) to explain Pandora to the Live Global Audience.

"We've got a bulletin," Larry says. "We've got a live report from Arkansas. Just a moment — There! Look at that!" The image of Pandora sitting atop the train appears on television screens all around the globe. "She's waving to us!"

And she *is* waving, too. She's waving, and she looks hungry, and tired, and bedraggled. But there's something in her eye, something in her expression—something that makes everyone who sees her think, *She loves us.*

And perhaps she does.

"She's beautiful," the physicist says.

"Yeah," Larry says. "She is."

. . .

Yolen looks up at Macdonald as Dvorkin leaves the room.

"You think it'll come to shooting?" she asks. "Is this really going to happen?"

Macdonald looks out the window for a long, long moment. It's a thing he does by reflex when someone asks a question he doesn't want to think about. Lately he's been doing it a lot.

"I hope not."

It's a nonanswer, and Yolen knows it. Hell, they *both* know it. And they both know that Yolen won't settle for it.

"Do you think it will?"

Macdonald shrugs. "We do what we have to," he says. "The President has called up everything, everything he's got. We're watching. Trying to figure out how these bastards tick. And we've got people working on the Pandora problems. What else can we do?"

And that's still an evasion, even if it is less of one. Yolen just looks at him.

"They don't look friendly, Jane. They listen to everything we say, they watch everything we do. But they don't say a word."

"You do, don't you? You think they're going to attack."

Macdonald doesn't say another word.

There isn't a chance McNamee is still in the basement.

This is what Dvorkin thinks as he rides the security elevator down down down into the netherworld of offices deep beneath the Pentagon: *McNamee is gone.* What they'll find in the block Dvorkin's isolated will be nothing but a dead-eyed terminal and a week's worth of Domino's pizza boxes. (Everyone at the Pentagon eats Domino's pizza—Dvorkin has never understood why. He finds the stuff repulsive. When it's Dvorkin ordering, the pizza comes from Mario's.) And cigar butts—Dvorkin remembers that from his search of McNamee's original office: the man chain-smokes wretchedly cheap cigars. The ashtray on McNamee's desk had been full of cigar nubs all chewed up and slobbery; even so many hours after McNamee had run from the room, the stink of stale fetid tobacco smoke had been enough to choke Dvorkin.

If there's anything to find down there in the basement, it'll be a hint as to where the man has gone.

That's what Dvorkin thinks as he and Collier and Eisen ride the elevator. He's wrong, of course.

After a while the sky of west Tennessee metamorphosed into the desert night over Arizona, and Pandora fell asleep on top of the train beneath a pitch-black sky scarred with stars like diamonds.

The moon rose as the train traveled the track that runs alongside I-10 through southeast Arizona, and Pandora woke to see a place in the mountains that looked as alien as her dreams: tall, sharp, dusty mountains that looked like jagged piles of loose pale dirt sown with great rugged geologic rocks. There were no plants, no weeds, no flowers, trees, nothing, but there was terrible erosion. In places the looseness of the dirt and the sharpness of the wind and the violence of the uncommon rain conspired to heap great piles of sharp boulders high up on the hills, and Pandora almost laughed when she saw them—they looked like toys some colossal toddler left behind in disarray.

And suddenly Pandora and the train were someplace else entirely.

Chicago.

In her dream and on the train out of time it was dawn in the winter in Chicago. Or maybe it wasn't winter yet but it would be soon, because it was colder even than when she was at the highest windiest part of the mountains crossing to New Mexico.

And it was snowing.

Snowing!

Pandora had never felt snow before, hadn't even seen it in person. The scientists were very strict about that; if there was snow in the courtyard, they said, then Pandora had to stay inside. And Uncle Wally enforced that rule, even if he did think it was dumb.

Strange, marvelous stuff, that snow. Pandora opened up her mouth to let a flake sail down onto her tongue—and when it touched her she felt a tingle run all up and down her spine.

And felt sleepy.

As the cold deepened, and the snow waned, and the trains around her on every side were cattle trains loaded tight with herds of smelly animals.

So many cattle. They were here for the slaughter, weren't they? Once Pandora had read someplace that Chicago was a city of slaughterhouses.

There were pools of melty snow down by the train tracks, already starting to ice over as the temperature dropped.

Pandora felt so sleepy. And the ice and the cattle for the slaughterhouses depressed her, and the depression made her tireder. Pandora thought she could hear Uncle Wally calling to her as she drifted off to sleep: *Get yourself inside, child. Or you'll catch your death of cold.*

They're in the corridor of an abandoned wing of the Pentagon basement, not far from the office that housed McNamee's terminal.

"What exactly do you want from us?" Collier asks.

"I want your eyes," Dvorkin says. "I want you to look around, see what you see. We're looking for a general—Daniel McNamee—who's gone over the deep end. If you see anything here that makes you think you might know where he went, tell me."

"How am I supposed to know. . . ?"

Dvorkin shrugs. "Just follow me and keep your eyes open."

That's when the door opens, and McNamee steps out with his service revolver in hand. He doesn't threaten them, doesn't tell them to turn around or put their hands up or anything like that. He levels his revolver, aims, and shoots.

When Arne Starr was a kid he always wanted to be a superhero. Like in comic books. *Hulk will smash!*— that was his favorite, *The Incredible Hulk*. Arne would read *Hulk* five times over, every month. Arne didn't like it much when Hulk would lose his temper and stomp his feet and kick over buildings and cars and cities and stuff. But how important were things like that in the long run? Everything wore down sooner or later, even cities, even the world, really, the world was going to wear out eventually, Arne read all about that in his science class. And Arne knew how underneath Hulk's temper tantrums Hulk was sweet and lovely as a three-year-old, and didn't that count for something?

Arne thought it did.

And he thought this, too: he wanted to grow up to be a superhero like in the comics. Somebody so big and so strong that he could *help* Hulk, and be there to help him not hurt anybody when he was temper-tantrumed. That was what Arne wanted to be able to do, and he knew in his heart that if only he could, he'd be very, very good at it.

But he couldn't, of course. Because there were no such things as superheros, and even if there were he wasn't strong enough to be one. Even if Arne *did* read comics, and even if he *did* want to be a superhero, he wasn't crazy.

Just special, was all. And if he maybe wasn't as special as he liked to think, he wanted to make himself as special as he could.

At first when he was younger he thought the best way to be special was to draw his own comic books, because then he could do his own superhero stuff, even if he couldn't make it real. So he studied hard, and he learned to draw—

Then he saw the blue angels, that time they did the expo over the stadium at the 'Niners halftime show. And after that—well, who the hell wanted to draw comic books when there planes to fly?

And Arne is a pilot, and that's that. A navy fighter pilot, and not just a fighter pilot but a damned good one. Navy and the air force together didn't make more than three air-to-air kills in Iraq—mostly because the Iraqi pilots didn't have the cojones to fight.

And two of those kills were Arne's.

That was mostly luck, of course. There weren't many fighter jocks who got to *see* enemy aircraft in Iraq. But it was skill, too, and talent. And Arne knows it damned well.

Which is why Arne isn't afraid when the call comes that Sunday morning. No matter how the voice on the other end of the line makes it sound like it's the end of the world and they're sending Arne on a suicide flight. Arne isn't scared, and he wouldn't be, no matter what.

Smash!

They're sending him all the way to Ohio.

Ohio! All the way to Ohio from NAS Miramar, here in San Diego! And it isn't any damned exercise. Not with the call at four-thirty in the morning; not with the sound in that lieutenant's voice.

It occurs to him as he stands in the shower rinsing away the slick lathery soap: occurs to him for just a moment to wish he'd asked Major Jones exactly what the hell it was going on. But only for a moment. Arne is a pilot, not a news junkie. Arne knows there just isn't any sense following the news, trying to second-guess orders before they get to you. They come when they come, and sooner or later there's a briefing.

It's Collier who saves them.

By screaming.

She doesn't scream in terror, doesn't collapse in fear (which Dvorkin is damn near ready to do himself): when she sees the gun she screams and she leaps. Before McNamee can pull the trigger she's off the ground, in the air. All over him. And when he shoots, his bullet flies wild into the ceiling.

Collier is a very, very brave woman, Dvorkin thinks. Amazingly brave.

But if she manages to save their lives she doesn't manage to bag their man: McNamee was on the airforce boxing team back when he was young. And Collier—no matter how brave she may be—is no match for him.

"*Aliens!*" McNamee screams. "*Aliens!* I knew you'd come for me! But I've got you now."

And he just may have them, at that: before Dvorkin and Eisen get enough of their wits about them to give Collier a hand throttling the bastard, he's shoved her away, gotten his balance. Leveled his gun and started shooting.

Dvorkin grabs Collier's arm, pulls her back out of the room. Rolls into Eisen, pushing her out of the doorway. And slams the door closed as the revolver blasts and shards of wood go flying everywhere.

There are a thousand thousand things Ken Estes has on his *I want to do* list that come in ahead of going back to see Anna McNamee. But what the hell was he supposed to do, tell Macdonald to stuff it? Hah! Whatever ugliness waits for him in the convent with Anna (a convent, yes, a convent, twenty minutes on the phone and Ken had managed to find that out: her father sent her to a goddamn convent to have his baby)—no matter how bad it got with Anna, it couldn't be anywhere near as bad as trying to argue with Macdonald.

And still.

Ken is in the helicopter Macdonald called to carry him back to Ohio, and in an hour or two he'll be landing somewhere near the convent. And he wishes like hell he was someplace else.

Any goddamn place at all.

Because it hurts like hell when he thinks about Anna.

Oh, he doesn't think he loved her, so it shouldn't hurt because of that. But they were together damn near every hour Ken had to spare for most of the last six months, and even if that isn't love it's something that matters a lot more than Ken wants to admit.

Even to himself.

But the thing that really makes him hurt isn't anything to do with how he feels or doesn't feel about Anna McNamee.

The thing that makes him want to break right down and cry is his baby inside her whom he never meant to love.

Pandora saw the Awful Lady two more times while she rode that train. If everything were causal the way it is in the workaday world, that wouldn't have been possible. After all, the Awful Lady had fallen off the train into forever where it connected with hell, and only people like Pandora—trapped anomalously with time—can cross the gap from here to hell.

The Awful Lady Pandora saw staring at her when she woke on the train top was a dozen years younger than the one who'd tried to kill her not too long before.

"Who are you?" the Awful Lady asked. "Tell me, tell me this time. Tell me who you are."

Why isn't she still trying to kill me?

"I'm Pandora," Pandora said. "But you know that already, don't you?"

The Awful Lady scowled. "I don't know you." She pursed her lips. "I never seen you before that time."

Pandora thought: *She doesn't remember.* And then: *Amnesia!*

Which was wrong, of course. But Pandora still

hadn't caught on about the Awful Lady being out of sequence with her.

A dog howled somewhere in the distance. The Awful Lady cringed at the sound—cowered, ever so slightly—until the howling became a mournful sound, and now mournfully pathetic. And as the howl became more piteous the Awful Lady's expression became hungrier and hungrier, till finally she looked as though she could no longer contain it—

"Stop that!"

The Awful Lady looked puzzled. "I don't understand. . . ."

"Looking like you're about to kill something."

"What's that to you?" the Awful Lady said, scowling. "I kill what I want to kill. Mind your own damn business."

Pandora ignored her. She didn't care what the Awful Lady did or said, as long as she didn't try to hurt Pandora. The train was in the Rockies again, and it was cold up here. And Pandora was sick and tired of being cold. "I'm going down into the boxcar," she said. "Good-bye."

Pandora climbed down the ladder of rungs, into the boxcar. As she swung through the boxcar door she heard the Awful Lady swish over the side and begin to climb down toward her.

I wish she'd go away, Pandora thought. *I wish she'd go away and never come back.*

There was something else in the boxcar—Pandora could hear it breathing. There, in the corner— the far corner toward the front. Something small, in the shadow. Pandora stepped toward it cautiously, certain that at any moment the thing would leap from the dark—

—leap from the dark—

No.

It wasn't angry. It was the dog. The pretty white-hair terrier mutt she'd sat beside on the ridge above the highway in Tennessee. The dog the monster gutted and left to die.

He whimpered when he saw Pandora. Whimpered and whined and eased forward to sniff her hand and lick her fingers.

"Doggie!" Pandora said. "It's good to see you again, doggie. Are you okay? Why are you whining?"

And she stooped closer, to check where the doggie had had his insides all spilled open before. And saw a bloody scabrous mass not yet entirely healed over.

Back behind her she could hear the Awful Lady make this choking noise.

"Doggie is my friend," Pandora said. "I know him from before."

And she thought: *It was doggie I heard howling before, and when doggie sounded sad, the Awful Lady looked like she wanted to kill him. I'm not going to let her hurt doggie! I can't!*

And suddenly Pandora had an awful intuition, and she knew she had to turn to face the Awful Lady before she screamed and leaped—

Too late.

By the time Pandora turned the Awful Lady was already in motion, diving into the half dark where the doggie lay still nuzzling Pandora's hand—

Pandora grabbed Awful Lady's collar as she rushed by, and pulling her down onto the floor, and now the Awful Lady screamed indignant and outraged, and her fists flailed out hitting everything, the floor, the wall that they'd bounded up against together, Pandora—

—and then one of her blows hit doggie. Hit him *hard!* And right under his pelvis beside his busted gut, and doggie screamed in agony and wailed and wailed. . . !

And Pandora got so mad. So *mad!* She just stopped thinking, she got so mad. Nobody was going to hurt her doggie while Pandora was around to stop it, and anybody who tried was going to be damned good and sorry.

She lifted the Awful Lady by the collar, then

slammed her down into the boxcar floor, lifted her up, and pounded pounded pounded her against the wall of the train.

The Awful Lady's eyes rolled up into her head, and her neck went floppy slack to let her head roll back and forth. Her tongue slid out her mouth, so her jaw clamped down to bite it every time her head went forward. Pandora saw all that, and she knew it was time to stop. But she couldn't. Her blood was up, and every time she thought about stopping she thought about poor doggie, and she thought about what the Awful Lady would do to him if she let her go, and that got Pandora's blood rising all over again.

And she thought about the General, hitting her and hitting her. And she knew that she'd turned into something as bad as him.

And it made her want to curl up and die when she thought that. But it didn't make her stop. Not till the Awful Lady started to look a funny color, and Pandora got afraid she was going to die, and she let go of the greasy stinking collar of the Awful Lady's overcoat as the Awful Lady crumpled to the ground.

The Awful Lady shuddered and heaved a great sob, and she rolled away into the corner and started crying.

Pandora felt like dirt. She was dirt, and she knew it—she tried to do the right thing but it never came out right because she was so awful.

Awful, awful, awful.

Even if she had saved doggie.

She turned to look at doggie in his shadowed corner. "I've saved you, doggie, see? Saved you from the Awful Lady!"

But doggie was gone away into time, just the way he'd come to her.

The helicopter lands gracefully on the convent's great green lawn.

Ken opens the helicopter's door a moment after it lands. And hesitates. Is there something he's forget-

ting? He'd swear there is—but how can there be? He
owns nothing but the duffel in his bunk in the barracks on Wright-Pat, and for at least a day now
there's been no way he could have gotten to that,
even if he'd tried.

The truth is that he very literally has nothing to
forget—nothing but the uniform that covers his hide,
and there's no forgetting that.

And more: the reason that he hesitates in the helicopter's open door is that he doesn't want to face
the one who waits inside that convent for him. But
there isn't time to hesitate! No matter how much
Ken wants to: there isn't time because there's an armada of Space Aliens poised over Wright-Patterson,
not fifty miles from here, and it's war any second
now, and everybody knows it. And McNamee (asshole paranoid bastard UFO nut that he is) has got
hooks deep into the Pentagon's machinery, and two
or three times an hour he's ordering all-out assaults
on the Alien fleet, and there's no telling what he'll do
if Macdonald doesn't get a collar on him soon.

Soon.

There's a woman in the convent, and Ken doesn't
want to admit to himself how he feels about her because if he did it'd just set him up all over again—set
him up like a clay pigeon on a shooting range. And
he doesn't want that oh God no he doesn't.

But what can he do?

Not a goddamn thing but keep moving. Because
he has to.

Macdonald told him to lie.

Macdonald said: *Tell her you're there to see her.
Tell her you love her! Tell her anything you have to
—just make sure she tells you where her goddamn
father is.*

Ken wanted to look him in the eye and say *No*,
but he didn't have the nerve. What he'd said wasn't
No at all. He said, *Yes sir!*, and he saluted before he
left the room.

Trouble is Ken has never been much good at lying. No talent for it, no stomach for it, no idea how to begin to tell a lie anyone might believe.

Three nuns wait for him at the door.

"I'm here to see Anna McNamee," Ken says. But they already know that; he told the nun he spoke to over the phone that he had to see Anna. And it's hard to imagine that the convent gets many other visitors who arrive by helicopter.

The nun on the left smiles, and her eyes sparkle; when she speaks Ken recognizes her voice. "She's eager to see you," the nun says. "Anna is such a delightful young woman."

Ken thinks that delightful isn't a word he'd necessarily use to describe Anna McNamee, but he thanks the nun all the same. And he follows her and both of her sisters into the convent.

The next time Pandora met the Awful Lady was the first time they met, and the last time, too, but Pandora still hadn't caught on about how that worked.

Pandora was back up top of the boxcar, and they were rolling back into the Chicago stockyards, and the smell of hogs for slaughter was ripe and thick around the train. The train slowed but didn't stop, not quite—the train never stops entirely while Pandora is aboard it—the train slowed and Pandora spotted a lady derelict wandering among the trains. She thought, *That looks just like the Awful Lady.*

But it can't be the Awful Lady. The Awful Lady was down in the boxcar below her.

Isn't she?

Pandora decided she had to see. She pushed off the roof, onto the ladder of rungs, and climbed down into the boxcar. As she descended the smell of death and filth that came from the pigs grew sharper, denser, and twice Pandora had to choke back her bile to keep from retching. She hated that smell most of all.

The boxcar was empty, and it smelled of pig shit and urine and dead things left to rot, just like the rest of the rail yard, but worse. How could pigs live in this? Even if they were pigs. Pandora thought about bacon and wondered how the hell she ever managed to eat that stuff that used to be animals that lived in their own shit.

Where the hell was the Awful Lady? There was nothing in the boxcar but filth and stink and a layer of gooey pig crud ground into the floor.

Then the train lurched back into motion, suddenly and unpleasantly, and it damn near threw Pandora off her feet into the disgusting stuff on the floor. . . .

A sound in the doorway, and Pandora knew it was the Awful Lady come to revenge herself once and for all, and she whirled around to face her.

And it was the Awful Lady, but not like Pandora expected—she wasn't angry or vengeful looking, just a crabby old lady hobo trying to climb up onto a moving train.

Then the Awful Lady saw Pandora, and she growled. "What are *you* doing here?"

Pandora didn't answer. She stood in the boxcar waiting and watching as the Awful Lady climbed up onto the filthy boxcar floor. And then she noticed the pile. A pig pile, right there where the Awful Lady reached for a handhold into the train—

"Your hand—"

But it was already too late. *Squish,* right through it, Pandora could hear the sound from all the way over here. And look how the pile oozed like molten lava on a science show now that the dried-up crust was too busted to hold it, and Pandora couldn't help herself, she had to puke, then and there she had to puke even though she hadn't had a bite to eat in— how long? Since back at Walt Fulton's cabin. Long, long time. Which meant she didn't have anything to puke up, but she puked anyway, dry heave and dry heave and dry heave as she steadied herself against the boxcar wall and that wasn't steady enough be-

cause again and again the train jolted and she nearly
lost balance and tumbled headfirst into the shit.

Into the shit.

And then she finally got a grip on herself, and
forced herself to stop trying to puke even though her
body didn't want to—

—something was wrong outside, she could see
that from the corner of her eye, outside was changing
and changing, and suddenly out of nowhere they
were in a lightning storm, and there was rainwater,
rainwater scattering in through the open door, rainwater spattering over the Awful Lady still squirming in the shit trying to get into the train, rainwater turning the crud on the boxcar floor into a slippery wet
mass—

—look how Chicago disappeared all around them
as the train slammed and lurched and banged as they
went from *now* and *then* to *when*—

—as the Awful Lady screamed—

—as Pandora's gut found some impossible reserve, and choked up something bilious and black
and that tasted of death—

—as a dog howled mournfully at a nonexistent
moon—

—as the boxcar shuddered to pieces and collapsed all around them, only to reappear whole and
intact a moment later—

—as lightning struck the boxcar and the world
went bright and dark and bright, and the dog
screamed in agony and fear and the Awful Lady
yowled in triumph as she hauled herself aboard the
train and Pandora blacked away and fell senseless
onto the shitty shitty floor.

"It's okay," Dvorkin says to Collier and Eisen. "He's
trapped in there. All we have to do is keep him
pinned down while we call in reinforcements."

Eisen nods. "How do we do that?"

Dvorkin takes a pen, a scrap of Post-It paper from
his pocket protector. Writes on the paper. "Here," he

says, "that number will get you the phone on Macdonald's desk. Run down to the security station by the elevator, call him. Let him know where we are and what's happened. He'll know what to do."

"She's in the convalescent ward," the nun tells Ken as they walk the sparkling-clean halls. "Tests today. For the baby. But she's eager to see you."

Somewhere in the endless night their foul shitsmeared boxcar became a pretty new car with clean floors and open doors on both sides. But Pandora and the Awful Lady remained together in that car that was this car, and the dog was still somewhere out of sight but close enough to hear his howling.

And the rain drove on and on through the open doors, washing Pandora and the Awful Lady and the floor that needed no washing. Pandora shivered in her dream, and her body shivered with her, but the cold and the wet and the wind were not enough to wake her.

Nothing was enough to wake her. Not till the sun rose up through the raining sky bright glaring sunshower through the wet, and the light and the water were too much—she had to roll over to get away from them. And the tiny bit of waking it took her to move in her sleep was enough to tell her that she was taking a deep chill, and had better move herself if she didn't want to die of pneumonia or strep or whatever Space Aliens got instead of them.

No matter how bad she was beginning to think of herself, Pandora still wanted to live. So she forced her eyes open, forced herself up. Smelled the pig slime still clinging to the part of her face the rain hadn't been able to rinse, and wanted to crumple up and puke all over again, but she couldn't because she didn't have the energy and besides the rain was on her face now and even as she smelled the stink it rinsed away.

Rinsing now from her sopping-wet clothes.

So much rain. Cool, cool rain, steady and hard as a shower on high. Where were they that it rained as heavy as this? Pandora tried to see out the open box-car door, but the rain was too heavy. All she could see through the door was rain and more rain and the bright sun above them.

She crawled toward the back of the train until she was clear of the door. When she was clear of it she sat back and watched the rain driving through for the longest time.

Looked past the rain, and saw the Awful Lady watching her. Watching hungry and covetous as she sat all bundled in her great filthy coat.

Was the Awful Lady going to come after her? No, she was just sitting there on the far side of the rain, watching and wanting and maybe planning or something.

Maybe. Or maybe she was just as cold and weak and sick as Pandora.

So much rain, Pandora thought. *It's going to flood out there.*

Then the rain stopped—just as suddenly as it had come on them in Chicago. And the world cleared, and Pandora could see out—

—see out across a flooded plain that stretched into forever.

Water to the horizon on both sides of the train, and way out there a feeble strip of grey sandy land.

Like the train was Noah's ark or something. It wasn't possible, no matter how time came unhinged. It didn't happen, and it couldn't happen, and if it did happen there wouldn't be train tracks over the water anyway.

Pandora leaned out the open boxcar door and looked down to see where the hell they were.

And saw the causeway.

And laughed! How silly, to mistake a railroad causeway across some great lake for the ultimate biblical flood!

"Stop that!" the Awful Lady shouted.

"Oh, 'stop it' yourself," Pandora said. "Look how beautiful it is out there! Look at the sky so blue and the lake so clear and look there, look at that bird in the sky, what kind of a bird is that? —And the air, so warm and clean; like the rain had washed a million years of mud away from it. Look out the door and enjoy it and stop being such a crab, huh?"

The Awful Lady didn't take that well at all. She made a grating noise down deep in her throat.

Pandora ignored her. She got to her feet and stood in the doorway surveying the world. There was a tiny sailboat out on the lake; as Pandora watched, a flock of water birds rose up from the lake to sail into the air.

If I knew how to swim, Pandora thought, *I'd jump out of here.*

And suddenly the Awful Lady screamed, and Pandora turned to see her lunging toward her.

Oh no you don't! Pandora thought, but she was wrong about that, because the Awful Lady's hands hit her just above the kidneys, and if Pandora hadn't had a good hold on the edge of the doorway she'd have fallen out of the train. Her breath gasped out like it wasn't coming back, and her feet went out from under her, but Pandora didn't fall. She got her other hand around the boxcar wall, grabbed hold of one of the steps on the ladder made of rungs. And held on for dear life as the Awful Lady hit and shoved and kicked her.

The Awful Lady gave her a terrible beating, but Pandora didn't let go of the boxcar wall, not even when the Awful Lady found a place under her arm that made her scream to hit it.

Didn't loosen her grip for an instant.

But she couldn't take the Awful Lady hitting on her forever, so she turned right into the Awful Lady's punches, and pushed herself out of the precarious position at the edge of the boxcar floor. Which let the Awful Lady hit her nose and mouth and stomach over and over again—

—*bang!* everything around Pandora went *bang!*
as the train lurched against itself, and as the Awful
Lady hit her Pandora saw they were moving again
through time and space, and the endless sea of water
in the bright of day was now an endless sea of wheat
beneath a moonlit sky—

—hit her nose and mouth and stomach over and
over again, but Pandora took the beating, because
that was the only damned way she was going to get
her hands on the Awful Lady and put a stop to this
nonsense once and for all.

Her left leg back around the door, onto the floor.
And now her weight was firmly braced against the
wall, and she could face the Awful Lady without fear
of getting thrown out into the night.

Let go of the rung on the outside wall, turned to
face the Awful Lady suddenly as she could manage.
Pushed aside the open claw-hand fist that was about
to rake across her face, and punched that Awful Lady
hard as she could, right at the center base of her rib
cage.

Which made the Awful Lady scream all full of terror and surprise and indignation, like she never had
nobody she was beating on turn and start beating on
her—

—but that was always the way with bullies, wasn't
it? Wasn't it? They weren't ever anything in a fight,
weren't ever up to anyone who'd fight back at
them—

—hit the Awful Lady *hard,* because she was
damn tired of being hit, and then and there Pandora
didn't give one good goddamn if she hurt that Awful
Lady, didn't care if she broke her like a used-up
doll—

—didn't care if she killed the Awful Lady, because
the Awful Lady good and goddamn well *deserved* to
hurt for what she did to Pandora—

—*hit,* hit and hit again—

—as lightning all around them flashed to light the
sea of wheat—

—but later, later Pandora began to hate herself for what she did in the boxcar flashing dark and bright as lightning shot and thunder boomed.

Later she thought back about the Awful Lady lying on the boxcar floor looking up into Pandora's eyes all terrified and small, looking at Pandora like she was a murderer come for her, which in a way Pandora *was* because she didn't care one whit whether she killed the Awful Lady just then, she just wanted to make sure once and for all that the Awful Lady never laid a finger on her ever ever again—

—and the Awful Lady was on the floor, and Pandora was going to hit her once and for all, was going to hit her in the throat just below the chin and break her there, *break* her—

—and the memory of that face looking up at her from the floor and the desperation in those eyes and the helplessness so visible painted on the Awful Lady's face, they're things that haunt Pandora forever—

—but before Pandora could follow through the blow, before her fist so much as touched the Awful Lady's throat, lightning struck the train one final time, knocking Pandora off her feet.

Only this time she wasn't holding on to anything. And instead of falling against the wall, the way she would have hoped, she fell right out the boxcar door, into the infinite wheat-brown sea.

"Ken!"

Anna is as pretty as ever Ken has seen her.

So pretty that it hurts to see her. And it surprises Ken what he's feeling, when he sees her sitting up in the hospital bed, smiling at him as he walks into the room: he's feeling glad to see her. Even after all the water that's passed under the bridge, he's feeling like he missed her something awful these last ten days when he thought he'd never see her again. And he doesn't ever want to lose her forever ever again.

And he knows he's in trouble.

And he knows he can't lie, even if it was Macdonald who told him to do it.

"Hello, Anna."

He doesn't know what to say after that.

"I had a test, Ken. They tell me she's a girl."

Ken wants to curl up and die.

Maybe.

Maybe he's not sure what he wants to do.

Maybe he wants to cross the room and hold her, because he loves her, because what he feels for her and what he feels for their child—what he feels means it isn't important that she got her daddy to toss Ken in a pit and throw away the key.

Maybe.

But there's this for sure, no matter what he feels: "I'm here for the government, Anna," Ken says, not so much because he's as cold as it sounds to say it as because *not* saying it will be leading her on, making her think he's here just for her. And he doesn't want to lie like that. Because he couldn't live with himself if he did, and if Macdonald steps on him for telling the truth, then that's what it costs to keep the faith. "They want you to tell me where your father is."

And it's like he's hit her with a sledge.

And when he sees it on her face Ken almost does die, right there in his tracks: he almost dies because no one who ever hurts a body like that should continue to live. And Ken knows it.

"I thought you loved me." It's a whisper; so quiet that maybe she didn't mean to say it at all.

And then the thing that surprises Ken most of all.

Because it comes from him.

"I do, Anna." Not even meaning to say it, not even knowing he would; the words just well up from inside him, and when he hears them he knows they're true, he knows that the words own him like nothing else ever could. "I love you."

And after that he can't ever be the same.

. . .

Dvorkin keeps expecting McNamee to make his break for it while he and Collier—unarmed and scared witless—watch the door. Even with Dvorkin and Collier on opposite sides of the door the way they are, poised for one of them to ambush McNamee as he tries to shoot the other—even with the best plan Dvorkin can think up, the possibilities are very ugly.

Possibilities, hell: probabilities.

And he keeps waiting for McNamee to make a break for it. Come out shooting hard and fast and to hell with aiming, if he just shoots fast enough they're both screwed and Dvorkin is seriously afraid why don't they get the hell out of here what's taking Macdonald so long already? McNamee is a serious problem, but he isn't worth Dvorkin's life, not to Dvorkin.

So where the hell is Macdonald already? It's been what, half an hour? At least that—and then Dvorkin looks at his watch and sees five minutes have passed since Eisen took off down the hall heading for the phone.

Damn damn damn.

And then they round the bend down at the far end of this hall: Macdonald, Yolen, Eisen. A squad of MPs in tow.

"What took you so long?"

But Macdonald probably can't even hear him from there. And if he could he'd ignore the question.

In just a moment (well, it's not just a moment—in fact it's not a moment at all, it's a fucking eternity as Dvorkin's standing next to the door that's liable to explode in a hail of bullets, hail of bullets any goddamn moment now) in just an eternity Macdonald and Yolen and their half-dozen clean-cut clean-living MPs are there, looking the door over so quietly, so carefully, and then blowing the thing away with a submachine gun.

Not a moment's hesitation: they blow out the door and go rushing through, those MPs do. No worry; no fret; no obvious forethought. It's as though

they do this so often that they've long ago choreo-
graphed every step of their violent ballet.

Which perhaps they have.

It only makes sense, after all: when Macdonald
calls in the MPs, he calls in the best.

There's only one problem.

Which is this: When the MPs go rushing through
the door to *Get McNamee, damn it, get him alive!*
they don't manage to *get* him.

Because he isn't there.

The nuns have left them alone, and Ken sits in the
chair beside Anna's convalescent bed.

"I've got pictures," Anna says. She leans away,
reaches for the papers on the nightstand opposite
Ken. And Ken feels another thing he forgot: desire.
Not desire like when he was seventeen and it made
him shaky because he wanted it so bad. More like—
like just the wanting is a thing to savor, and it's good
to be near her and he wants to be near her forever.

"Pictures. . . ?" *Pictures of what?* he almost
asks, but doesn't.

"Baby pictures, silly. The woman with the—
sonagram?—one of those machines, she took pictures of the baby inside me for the doctor. And she
let me have these two."

They aren't pictures that she hands to Ken, not
exactly. They're thermal printouts like from a fax
machine or a cheesy terminal.

And the image that Ken sees—it isn't the image of
a baby. Well, yes, it's a baby, it's Ken's baby, and he
loves her, only, well, she doesn't look human exactly.
More like a face hugger from *Alien.*

"She's pretty," Ken says. And he tries real hard to
mean it—but it's hard to mean it because it's just not
true, and Ken's such a lousy liar that he doesn't believe himself, not for an instant.

Anna laughs and laughs and laughs.

"Ken! She's *supposed* to look like that. That's

what a baby looks like when she's four months along."

And then Ken's laughing, too, because laughter's infectious, especially when it's Anna laughing, and isn't it funny when you think about it? . . .

"I love you," she says. And when he looks in her eyes he knows that she means it.

And he means it just as much. Maybe more. "I love you, too."

"But I can't tell you where to find my daddy. Because I love him, too, and I'll never betray him."

It's exactly what Ken expected. And it doesn't bother him: *screw* Macdonald. And screw him twice if he tosses Ken into a pit and throws away the key.

"It's okay," Ken says. "I didn't think you would."

She bites her lower lip. "Are you going to be okay. . . ?"

Ken shrugs. "What can they do to me? —I'll be fine."

He tries to sound as sure as he can when he says it. Maybe he doesn't do as well as he'd like to.

Or maybe he does just fine: if Anna hears his uncertainty she shows no sign of it.

"This picture is better," she says. "She looks more like a baby here."

Well, sort of like a baby. Ken can discern the outline of a skull, and maybe that's where her eyes are. Or maybe it isn't.

"She *is* pretty," he says. And this time he isn't lying. She really *is* beautiful, his daughter is. Well, maybe he's a bit deluded, maybe he's a bit enchanted with his own. But isn't that only right in a father-to-be?

It certainly is.

And then this comes over Ken, and it's the third thing that surprises him:

Baby like that ought to have a daddy, he thinks. *Baby like that shouldn't have to grow up with her mama alone.*

The words chill him to the bone.

He doesn't want to think them. Doesn't want to hear them.

But he does, he really does.

"We can get married, if you want," Ken says. And no matter how there are people who would say he proposes for all the wrong reasons, it's the right thing to do, and he knows it when he does it, and he never ever ever regrets it.

Aliens!

Imagine that! Fighting Space Aliens—blasting UFOs out of the sky like, like the cockpit was some real-to-life video game!

Smash!

Like he really *was* something out of a comic book.

Arne can't wait.

Barely has the patience to stay in formation. *Sure* doesn't have the patience to slow for the refueling tanker when they're up over Missouri. But what can he do? The last thing he wants is to run out of gas in the middle of his big chance to play *Space Invaders* with real equipment.

So Arne thinks about the Aliens, just to distract himself. Thinks about their ships.

Most of the briefing had been on their ships. Ships? As in spaceships? Arne isn't sure that's the right word for any of them. The big ones are enormous—so big that it looks like there is room to stuff whole cities inside them.

Fifty of those—*fifty* spaceships the size of cities— hovering in the air up above Wright-Pat.

Arne feels awful for the poor bastards who got stuck inside that base when the Aliens sealed it off. If it was him in there . . . Arne shudders. What the hell are the Aliens trying to do, anyhow? Starve them to death?

The next size down is tiny in comparison with the city ships, but still awfully damn big. Long and tubular, like cigars the size of a trucks. Trucks? Yeah, that's it exactly: they look like semi trucks floating around in the air.

Don't move any too fast, those floating sausage trucks. Arne has a feeling that if it comes to shooting, they'll get themselves way out of the way.

The other two Alien fliers are the ones that look dangerous. Both of them round, like flying saucers—the naval intelligence colonel who briefed them said that was probably because they weren't depending on lift, just thrust, and Arne can believe that when he thinks about what he saw them moving around on the video they ran during the briefing. The big ones are about the size of an A10 ground support jet, and armed like them—except they have bomb bays, too. Hard to figure how there's room for bombs inside fliers that small, unless maybe they're very small bombs.

Small bombs.

Arne tries to imagine what the hell the point of small bombs could be. And finds that he can't.

Unless they're little bitty nukes?

Jesus.

The other kind of flier is even smaller. Much smaller, in fact—it looks like it's big enough for one man, an engine, and a hell of a lot of gun power. Moves even faster, maneuvers even more dramatically than the larger fighter. So damned small it'll be hell getting a shot at the thing.

Looks like it'll be a terror in a dogfight.

Hell, any of them will be hell in a dogfight. Even the big city ships.

Because every single one of them has those damned shields. The same shields they have up around Wright-Pat—something strange and alien and so damned tough that no one has been able to make a dent in it, not with anything, not jackhammers, not tank cannons, not even with the five-thousand-pound bomb they tried dropping on the damn thing.

Nothing they did made any difference to the shell over Wright-Pat in the least, not even though they'd been trying to blow a hole in to the poor bastards stranded inside the base since just after the Aliens closed the place off.

Arne doesn't know how the hell he's supposed to cope with shields like that. And (being fair) neither had the NI colonel—he'd been pretty honest about it, too. "I understand we're working on a counterbalance. They tell me to tell you this isn't a suicide mission, and that there's a reasonable chance the shields won't end up being a problem for you." That was about when the briefer coughed, looked away so he didn't have to see their eyes. "I can't tell you anything about that. Truth is I don't *know* anything about it." What he didn't come right out and say was, *For all I know that may be handing you a line.* He really had that look about him—he really looked like someone who'd just told a lie by leaving out the truth. Makes Arne a little uneasy, and Arne isn't a guy who gets uneasy on an ordinary basis.

Anna looks about to faint dead away.

"Did I hear you right?" she asks.

Ken thinks how that's not a very romantic way to respond to a proposal of marriage. But it isn't lost on him that maybe he didn't propose in the most romantic possible way.

"I think so. I—I said . . ." And he chokes when he tries to say it again. "I want to—"

"Yes!"

And after that, well, even if he has any regrets, what can he do with them?

Not a goddamn thing.

"I can't wait to tell my daddy," she says. "I'll tell him first thing. He'll be so happy!"

And Ken thinks about the color of his skin, and he thinks, *Like hell that old Irishman'll be happy to have a black son-in-law.* But he doesn't say a word about it. Trouble like that comes knocking often enough; last thing he wants to do is go looking for it.

And besides, it'll be God knows how long before she can talk to the old man. And God willing he'll be in jail by the time she does.

In jail and harmless.

Ken hopes.

And then the phone rings.

I'm not out of my mind, Dvorkin thinks. *I'm really not out of my mind.*

Macdonald is pissed.

Collier is bewildered.

Yolen is bemused.

McNamee is *gone.*

The room is empty.

Oh, not empty of everything; there are discarded Domino's pizza boxes scattered across the worktables, piled heaping high above the room's wastebaskets. Three dead-eyed terminals, not a one of them in working order any longer. And the pile of dross beside the paper shredder—it's genuinely impressive.

But nonetheless the room is empty: empty of people.

"Are you sure this is one man we're looking for?" Collier asks this. Collier the brave one: she has a sharp eye, Dvorkin thinks. "None of these boxes is more than a day or two old. I don't think one man could eat this much in so little time."

"I think you're right," Eisen says. "Look at the terminals—each one of them is adjusted differently. Look how far back that monitor is over there. And this one, look at the keyboard—it's braced on a folded coffee cup to lie at an even steeper angle than it's designed to take."

Yolen nods.

Macdonald isn't even paying attention. He looks pale and exhausted. The blood has stained its way through the bandages on his shoulder again.

• • •

It's six hours later when the techs finally figure out how McNamee managed to get himself out of the locked room.

Too late by then. Much too late.

Dvorkin wants to kick himself when he hears: McNamee was there all along.

Right there in the room. Inches from them.

Behind the wall opposite the door.

The wall that wasn't a wall at all—just a façade McNamee pushed away and walked around the moment that the room was empty.

"Any word from Wright-Patterson?" Macdonald asks into the telephone. It's the first thing he says into the phone after he dials, and dialing the phone was the first thing he did when they got back to his office a moment ago. He wants information as soon as he can get it, Dvorkin thinks. It's understandable that he wants it. "All right. Call me the moment you hear anything—*anything.*"

He swears as he puts down the phone.

"Nothing?" Yolen asks.

They all know the answer before Macdonald shakes his head. "Not a whisper. How many of them on Wright-Pat? Ten thousand? Twenty? They must be scared out of their minds."

Bluegrass country: a sea of not-quite-green south and east of Cincinnati. Arne has never seen anything else that looks exactly like it. Not the deep green of forest; not the russet dusty shades of the dry west; certainly not the grey and white of a city from the air.

How long has he circled above north Kentucky, south Ohio? Twenty minutes, at least. His orders have kept him far away from Wright-Patterson, but twice now he's peered out into the distance and seen . . . he isn't sure what it was he saw. But he saw it as his circle brought him nearest to Wright-Pat, and didn't recognize it, could hardly even make it out. But he saw it! Saw it even if there was nothing on his radar, and what the hell doesn't show up on the radar of an F18A Hornet? Something bad, that's what. And the techs goddamn well better rig up something that can see it, or this war isn't going to last ten minutes.

Then flight control directs him in to the greater Cincinnati airport, which is actually across the river in Kentucky—the flight controller tells him where it is in great detail. But he doesn't say what the hell he's doing sending a Hornet into a civilian airport.

Maybe because he doesn't have to.

Because Arne can see for himself as he swings 'round to land, as he nears the airport: it isn't a civilian airport anymore.

The passenger jets are gone.

There are fighters everywhere crowding every available bit of the field, and not just navy, not just air-force jets, not just American jets: there are aircraft here from all around the world. Lots of them Arne recognizes. More than a few he doesn't.

As though all the world's airpower had gathered itself together for one final battle. *This really is the end of the world, isn't it?* That's what he thinks: he thinks of something someone told him once, or maybe he heard it on Sunday-morning TV—about how at the end of the world all the world's armies will gather in one place, and when they were done the end would be on them.

And here they were, all the armies of the world's skies.

And he lands his jet as smoothly as he can with these thoughts in his head, and flight control points him at a spot where two dozen mechanics are doing maintenance on navy jets. And he gets out of his jet, and finds his orders. Finds his bunk which is half a seedy hotel room four miles from the terminal. And falls asleep on the edge of the bed, even before he thinks to take off his flight uniform.

But he doesn't sleep well.

Just the opposite, in fact: Arne dreams night-mares.

Of things Alien and blood-hungry and vicious, blasting him from the sky; of battles playing over and over and entirely juxtaposed. Now forward through the battle, now all events out of sequence, now in sequence but backward and some of the most important parts don't happen but the consequences still follow just as though they did. . . .

He wakes three hours later shivering and cold but drenched with sweat. Notices that there's now another pilot—yes, a pilot, look at the insignia on the man's jacket hanging in the closet, he's a navy pilot from a carrier based in Norfolk, Virginia—there's another pilot snoring uneasily in the room's other bed. Arne feels out of uniform, sleeping like this in his flight suit where another officer can see. But he's too damn tired to care, and even if he weren't so tired he's frazzled from the nightmares.

So he shucks off his shoes, and he gets under the covers, and he tries again to get some rest.

But his sleep is no better. And his dreams are worse.

"Okay," Macdonald says. "It's time to put this show on the road again."

Yolen—still sore from hiking through the Tennessee cornfield, and not about to let Macdonald forget it for a moment—groans.

Dvorkin knows there's something really important to do, right here, right now, maybe in another part of the Pentagon someplace where maybe Macdonald won't be able to get ahold of him for a while. . . ?

"Forget it," Macdonald says. "I'm going to need everybody. *Everybody,* David, including you."

Dvorkin feels himself redden. Is he really that easy to read? Or is Macdonald really that good at reading people?

He clears his throat. "Where are we going?"

"Ohio."

And he doesn't have to say another word.

Because they all know they're going to the front.

And they all know why, too.

"Daddy!" Anna says, and Ken feels like he's falling, falling hard and fast and forever never landing never hitting bottom just falling falling falling forever. . . .

How long? How long since she picked up the phone? Only a moment. Isn't there something about a how long you have to wait before you can trace a call? No, that was with the old telephones. With the new ones you can tell where the caller is before you pick up the phone.

I've got to tell Macdonald. Macdonald will know how to trace that call. And then we'll know where the old bastard's hiding.

Ken looks around, hoping maybe there's another phone somewhere in the room—and there isn't, of course.

"Daddy, we're going to get married! Isn't that wonderful news, Daddy, Ken wants to marry me!"

She's so caught up in talking to her father she doesn't see Ken trying to figure out how he's going to get the old bastard, and now look at her face, look, she's all crestfallen, Jesus Lord what's old man Mc-Namee saying to her?

"Daddy. . . !" And then she starts crying.

And it's like to break Ken's heart, hearing her cry like that.

And he has to leave, has to leave the room to go find a phone to *call Macdonald!* but look at her, look at her hurting like that, how can Ken leave her alone when she hurts so bad?

So he doesn't.

He stays there, holding her hand, patting her shoulder, just *being* there for her all through that awful call and for a long while later after she drops the receiver and stares numb listless wet-eyed at the wall.

After a long time he kisses her on the cheek, and he tells her he'll be back for her. And he goes out to the helicopter and calls Macdonald. And tells him how to find her father.

They're on the big fast helicopter, Macdonald and his team.

Heading west.

Dvorkin sits at a mobile terminal, engrossed. Every now and then he laughs quietly. He's been like this since Estes got through to them twenty minutes ago.

He looks up from it, smiling.

"McNamee calls her twice a day, every day," he says. "The phone-company records trace back to a secure mobile line—no way to tell where he is or where he's been from that. Even if we knew a little more about the line he's using. But that doesn't matter—we've got the equipment to trace his connection all the way back from the convent if we catch him live. All we have to do is put an ear on every circuit that goes in or out of the place. Sooner or later he'll call her again. And then we have him."

Macdonald chuckles. "I like it." He looks across the cabin. "Any word on Pandora?" he asks, but he knows the answer to that as well as Dvorkin does—because Dvorkin would have told him the moment there was news. "Anything at all?"

"Nothing."

Macdonald frowns, shakes his head. He looks worried. Worried for the girl? For Pandora, the Alien?

Dvorkin finds it hard to imagine, Macdonald getting all sentimental and mushy-eyed over a little girl Space Alien. But that's the thing he sees, looking the man in the eye.

Stranger things have happened. But not many of them.

All through the night as Pandora lay broken beside the train track she imagined her Space Alien daddy, holding her hand, comforting her. As the moon set, her dream shifted: it became the dream she always dreamed when she was little. That was a dream she missed maybe more than anything else in creation.

"All of you, keep your eyes open," Macdonald says as the fast helicopter nears Wright-Patterson. "If you see any sign of McNamee, get me on the comm right away. Don't let him out of your sight."

Cincinnati International Airport: that's what this used to be. Amazing, Arne Starr thinks, how a place can be so entirely transformed in the course of a week. The civilians are gone; the passenger jets are gone. Even yesterday's big C130 transports are gone. All there are here are fighters, fighter-bombers, and combat planes—so many wings of them that Arne can't begin to count.

So many planes, pilots, so many insignia . . . there are pilots here, people Arne's met these last twelve hours, people from places he's never even heard of. Qatar? Brunei? Guangdong? Taipei? It isn't just the brass that's scared. It's everybody. The whole damned world is here to fight the last damned battle at the end of the world. . . .

No.

It's not that bad, not really. Is it? The Aliens haven't threatened to blow up the world or anything, Have they?

Arne tries to think about the question.

He doesn't *think* anyone has heard anything from the Aliens. Or at least: if they've said anything Arne didn't hear about it.

So why is everybody assuming that they're hostile?

What if they're just there to rescue this little girl he's heard so much about?

And then he thinks of the armada hanging over Wright-Pat, and the thousands of fighters they've sighted coming in and out of the floating carriers.

And he can't imagine for the life of him why they'd need so much just to help a little girl.

And he wonders what the hell the world did to piss them off so bad.

And he wonders when the hell it'll start. When they'll send him up; when the Aliens will either at-tack or withdraw for reasons as unknowable as those that've brought so many of them here.

And something way down inside him doesn't want to know the answers to any of those questions.

SEVEN

No modern mythography could ever be complete without an Alien invasion.

After all, we all in our most secret hearts know the reasons why the Aliens draw designs upon us. No one has to tell us that every extraterrestrial encounter, every bigfoot sighting, every Alien abduction hides behind it: the Aliens mean to invade.

Their impossible light ships are scouts advanced before some terrible battle. They carry away our people to learn the ways to murder us. They lurk in the dark among the stars, gathering strength to steal our world away. We do not say these things out loud. There is no need: giving such things voice only perpetuates the dread. But no matter that we're silent, we all in our imagination know the truth. We could not be who and what we are if we did not.

And it's no great wonder that we imagine such terrible things, for there has scarcely been a year in human history that someone somewhere did not stand ready to attack his nearest neighbor—and never a time at all when some threatened tribe didn't feel the need to build walls against the waiting enemy. Invasion is so basic, inevitable, perpetual a part of the human circumstance that our hearts are born knowing and dreading the possibility.

But we live in a world where the threat of nuclear holocaust pins vast armies in their barracks, where mundane violence is paralyzed against itself. Because it cannot bear the worst possibilities before it, the popular imagination sees Alien invaders ready to rain down on the planet at any moment. There's a logic to this displaced anxiety, after all: what are all invaders if they aren't *Alien?*

Alien invaders indeed.

In meteor storms; in swamp lights; in St. Elmo's fire. In landing lights of quiet aircraft that fly low in the dark.

Our tabloids foretell the extraterrestrial assault often and in graphic detail. But the tale finds its truest form not in the tabloids or our folktales—but rather in our theaters.

In movie houses, on late-night TV: this is where we see the Alien armada come to steal our world away with its spaceships and death-ray guns and strange unfathomable cannon. Our cinema knows them as we do not dare imagine: they are the demons of our waking dreams; the invaders of our Zeitgeist; the captains of our destiny.

The Alien lurkers wait to devour us entirely and whole. Our imagination knows they are our destiny.

When Pandora was very very little she had a dream. It wasn't just one dream. More like—it was a recurring dream, but it didn't come the same every night.

Every night as she'd fall asleep the details would change.

It was like this: Pandora was a baby, and she could see herself who was a baby, and wrapped in blankets so firm and warm she'd sail through the air —it wasn't like flying, exactly. More like—like some magic force would carry her and hold her, and she'd sail through the streets of the old old city in the night so beautiful so peaceful so far from the awful poking prodding white-coated monstrous men who were her waking life. And gradually the beautiful old city would give way to a strange and wondrous place that must be heaven; and after she'd sailed through the kingdom of heaven for a goodly time, she'd come gently to the ground and land and slough away her blankets and there in heaven she was free to play to live to thrive and heaven and the world that was heaven loved her, and everything was good.

After forever in heaven she'd fade away to deeper sleep; and in the morning she'd wake knowing that no matter how horrible the world was, there was hope and love and light because heaven loved her.

As she grew older the dream changed.

Nightmarishly.

The greatest sign of this was the decay of the beautiful city in her dreams outside the window outside her crib. As the months went by it grew darker, and danger seethed from the bricks, the mortar; leaked down from the eaves.

But Pandora sailed safe inside her bundled blankets, and she knew she was safe even if she also knew that danger waited to devour her.

For months she saw the city decay. Night by night; house by house. And then something horrible happened: one night as she drifted through the air and the beautiful rotting seething city segued her to heaven—that night she saw the blight had somehow reached inside the kingdom of heaven; and so quickly! The lush hills and valleys so sudden withered brown only showing sparse streaks of dying

green; the land the ground the very soil that was the
firmament of heaven that loved her—it was tainted
now with something sinister and yellow.

Something that made Pandora think of bile.

And she screamed, and her blanket shuddered
loose and sloughed away even though she still hung
in the air.

And before she could fall to the ground, she woke
screaming and alone and afraid in her crib.

Uncle Wally came to comfort her after only a moment. And she loved her uncle Wally, and she knew
that she needed him more than anything else in the
world. But even so, after her dream betrayed her she
never had a place in her heart that wasn't hardened
to the world and ready for the most terrible thing
that was possible.

Which maybe was for the best.

The helicopter only takes twenty minutes to bring
Ken to the landing field at the camp outside Wright-
Patterson. But it gets complicated after that: it takes
him most of two hours to find Macdonald's tent
among so many others. Not just tents, not just trucks
and humvees and tanks and artillery but people, too,
he sees marines mixed in with regular army mixed in
with folks from at least half a dozen different National Guards. All of it disorganized, all but out of
control. Oh, there's a command someplace, and
when Ken finds command they give him directions to
find Macdonald, but command just isn't working,
that's the trouble. Probably because the mobilization
hasn't had the time to catch its breath yet.

When Ken finally does find Macdonald's tent, it's
almost deserted. Nobody inside but Janice Eisen and
Sarah Collier, who know as little about what's going
on as Ken does.

Ken steps out of the tent, bums a cigarette from a
passing marine. Lights it and waits.

But not for long: he's on his third drag when
Yolen rounds the corner of the humvee on the left.

Macdonald and Dvorkin are only a moment behind her.

"Where the hell have you been?" Macdonald wants to know. Except he doesn't wait for an answer; walks right on by, into the tent, doesn't even bother to tell Ken he should follow.

Ken crushes the hot end of the cigarette between his right thumb and forefinger, winces when the heat gets through to him (he's lost the calluses he had when he smoked more regularly), trails Macdonald into the tent.

Passes through the tent flap in time to see Dvorkin go directly to the mobile terminal in the back corner of the tent. Sees him begin typing codes.

"He still hasn't called her," Dvorkin says. "I wonder if he knows we're listening?"

Macdonald shrugs. "Could be." And then he does a double take. Not at Dvorkin and his terminal, but at the secure fax beside it. "Hot damn," he says. He looks at Collier. "How long ago did that come in?"

Collier shrugs. "Five minutes?"

Macdonald lifts the fax from its cradle. "Kansas," he says. "Her train. Rolling through Kansas." He turns to Yolen. "We need to find that train—we can't afford to lose her again. Get everything we can get ahold of. Yeah, I know that isn't much; I know almost everything is on its way here. Whatever's left in Kansas, we'll use that."

Arne wakes again.

Sees the time written digital on the bedside clock.

Rolls out of bed.

There's a briefing at ten, but Arne doesn't have the stomach for it.

Stomach.

Yes—his stomach. His stomach hurts. He needs some food.

He needs to go to the galley, which three days ago was the cheapest cafeteria in the greater Cincinnati airport. And find something to eat. And find some coffee.

Coffee most of all.

He gets to his feet. Bathroom: shower, shave, put on yesterday's uniform. Which is disgusting from the long flight. There wasn't room for an overnight bag in the cockpit, and even if there had been, there wasn't time to pack one before the folks at Miramar pushed him out the door. He had clean underwear, at least; someone in logistics already saw the trouble coming, had a dispensary running out of the Hertz Rent-a-Car desk.

He's almost awake as he steps out the motel-room door (even if they *did* commandeer the damned thing into a barracks, it's still a sleazy-cheap room in a third-rate motel). He's awake, and he's hungry, and he's wrung out from an awful night and an awful day before it.

Two minutes standing in the sun pacing, wishing he could have a cigarette even though he quit smoking six years ago, wishing for a cigarette because times like this were when he used to smoke—times of waiting and waiting for the world to drop the other shoe. Two might-as-well-have-been-forever minutes waiting outside what used to be the motel's front office—and then the staff car comes to get him. Actually it's not a staff car at all. It's a Dollar Rent-a-Car airport shuttle, commandeered for the duration same as everything else was commandeered for the duration, because it was handy and it was necessary and the air force knows how to take what it needs in an emergency, and my-oh-my isn't *this* a sight more comfortable than a humvee? Damn right it is. Screw humvees: would have been a lot better if the government had invested in airport shuttles. Arne would have told them so if they'd've asked, but of course they didn't. They never do.

The staff car stops at what used to be Arriving Flights. Lets Arne off, picks up two Italians. (Arne recognizes their uniforms from the NATO War

Games three years back.) He wanders into the terminal, looking for the galley that used to be a cafeteria.

Finds it. Wanders down the serving line where everything looks disgusting, but he's hungry, damn it, he has to eat or his stomach is going to take him apart. So he finds himself a cup of coffee, two small boxes of Wheaties, and a carton of low-fat milk, and wanders toward a table where he can sit alone in a corner and watch the jets landing and landing.

And he eats.

And the jets land in waves.

So many jets.

Arne wonders how many of the pilots inside those jets will be alive a week from now. And then he forces the thought away from him, because there's nothing but despair from thoughts like that.

"Mind if I join you?"

It's Andrea Robin. *Lieutenant Colonel* Andrea Robin. The first familiar face he's seen in what, two days? She isn't a friend, isn't even someone he knows well. But she's an acquaintance, at least. Fighter pilot from back at Miramar. And right now even the company of a friendly stranger is welcome.

"Please do," Arne says, And he smiles—or tries to, more accurately. He's in an awful awful mood, and when he tries to smile, what he manages is, well, not a handsome expression.

The lieutenant colonel sits, begins to pick at her eggs and toast. After a moment Arne goes back to watching the arriving jets.

"They've taken every airport for three hundred miles around," she says. "And every last one of them is as busy as this."

Arne turns to look her in the eye. "Really? Every airport in the state?" And he tries to sound like he's surprised, tries to sound like the information matters to him. Because it's something that *would* have interested him yesterday, or the day before, or the day before that. But right now he just doesn't want to know. He wants to soar up into the sky and blast the

Aliens from the air. He wants to fight! He wants to get it on with, get it over with, get it done with. . . .

(. . . *except the real truth is nothing like that. The fact is that Arne's scared out of his mind. That he's pretty goddamn sure that he's going to die the minute he's in firing range. And he wants to live, not die, and part of him wants to get up into the sky and run like the Iraqis always did over the gulf, but Arne's got more backbone than that. He wouldn't run. He wouldn't even let himself think about running. And so he thinks of fighting, and he thinks of glory, and he thinks of victory, because if he thinks about those things hard enough he can't hear how scared he really is. . . .*)

. . . done with. Get on with it, already!

"Really," Andrea Robin says. "Not just every airport in the state—all of them in Kentucky, Ohio, Indiana. Some of them in Illinois and Pennsylvania, too. They need that many for the jet traffic they're getting. They'll need them more when the fighting starts."

Deep behind his eyes Arne can see the battle already hanging in the air; see a thousand thousand jets bursting asunder, flowering in flame. In his heart he can hear the pilots of those broken planes, screaming and screaming at the fire and the falling sky.

Pandora dreamed her flying dream again as she lay unconscious beside the railroad tracks near the highway. For the first time since she was a tiny tiny, she dreamed that she flew bundled in blankets, floating far and away along a river of magic in the air, sailing quickly and carefully now above a highway though before she'd flown through city streets.

When the flight was over she sat in her dream in the warm fireplace room in the pretty cabin in the woods, and she was bundled in blankets. She sat before the fire old Walt Fulton had built after he'd dragged her in from the icy stream early that eve-

ning. And in the dream it *was* that evening—no, not
that evening, that night. Late late that night, in the
deep dark middle of the moonless night after the day
she'd took breakfast in Walt Fulton's homey house,
seen the spaceship, fallen plunging into the icy water, and finally talked the night away warming from
her chill.

It was the middle of the night, and she woke, and
the old man sat in his fireside chair watching her.
Watching so intently, as though she were some arcane book he had to study carefully.

Pandora hated it when people stared at her. It
made her feel—like a reptile in a zoo. And she wasn't
any reptile!

Even her mommy wasn't any reptile.

But there was something about the old man's
staring that didn't bother her so much. As though
maybe somehow it was all right for him to stare? No,
not that. More like, like even though it was staring
and intrusive and not very nice and even rude, there
was something about the old man that made up for
him staring at her.

Pandora didn't know what it was, couldn't imagine how anything anyone could make it okay for
them to stare. But she thought it anyhow—no, felt it
more than thought it. *Intuition—this is intuition. Of
course! It's natural. All Space Aliens have good intuition. I am an Intuitive Being.* Which was maybe a
little much, maybe a little conceited or something,
but when you got right down to it, Pandora—lost and
alone and hated by everyone and unconscious on the
roadside—Pandora didn't have a whole lot going for
her right then. If her ego gave her comfort by inflat-
ing herself—well, if it did, what harm was that? It
touched no one but Pandora herself.

"Old man," Pandora said, staring in the dream at
Old Walt Fulton watching so intently, "old man, tell
me how you loved my mother."

The old man frowned. "I never loved her, Pandora. I told you that before."

"But you knew her! I know you did. You must've liked her—how could you not have liked her, seeing as how she was my mommy and all? Tell me about that. What was she like? What was it like to talk to her?"

The old man shook his head. "I'm human, Pandora. And it isn't in anybody human to like anybody or anything like—*that*. Just the sight of her would make my hair stand on end! Horrible, horrible. She was always gracious to me, and kind to me, and the truth is that I owed her my life. But how could any human being appreciate the company of anything as —*disgusting* as your mother? It isn't possible. I'm sorry, but it isn't. I didn't." Pandora stared at the old man, insulted and astounded. Her mouth had fallen open almost the moment he'd begun to speak. It was her *mother* he was talking about! How *dare* he? But he did dare, and kept on daring. "She was—she was very nice and like that. She was never mean to me. She was never mean to anyone—not that I ever saw. But I hated her. No—that came later. I didn't hate her then. Not while she was alive. But I sure didn't like her, I'll tell you that."

Pandora was fit to be tied—furious with the old man despite the fact that she knew he was a dream and this was a dream and the old man never said any of these things she heard from him now.

"Old man—you vile, foul, lowly terrestrial human—" these were strong words, and stilted and wordy enough that Pandora would never have said them if she were awake to think about them before speaking "—you are an evil thing, old man. I hate you with all my heart."

The old man blinked, confused—as though he found her venomousness confusing. Or maybe it was her language that confused him.

And Pandora listened to her words that hung in the dream air around her for the longest time. And listening, she heard.

Hearing, she realized that they weren't true.

Whatever bad the old man did, he wasn't foul or vile or lowly; just an ordinary man caught up in the strangest circumstance, doing the very best he could to carry himself with a clean conscience. And even worse than that, she realized when she heard her own final sentence, Pandora didn't hate the old man at all.

She loved him, in fact.

And she knew that she loved him, and accepted him in her heart.

But she didn't accept and she didn't admit what her heart already knew beyond a shadow of a doubt:

And what she wouldn't admit was the reason that she loved him.

The strangest thing, as Pandora wakes.

It starts like this, and it keeps going—on and on into the bright/the sunrise/the glow at the far edge of the horizon, like a terrible nightmare daymare dream where she wakes into the world that is stranger and more awful than the world should ever be:

Pandora lies in the dirt that is the shoulder of a two-lane highway. Lies at a crossroads, near a train. No, not a train—at first it's only a train track. A train track and a crossroads not thirty feet away. There is nothing but nothing else in this far nowhere of wheat fields and flatness and endless sun-bright sky; no man woman nor child; no tree; no building of any kind anywhere in sight.

It is a terrible, desolate place. It frightens Pandora.

She sits up. Pushes herself out of the dirt at the crossroads. Stares at the wheat, the train track, the horizon, all of which seem to cower beneath the overwhelmingly bright sky. She wonders where she is and how she's ever going to find her way home from a place as desolate as this, and she can't begin to think.

The road and the track and the wheat are desolate and endless, but there has to be some traffic along them, doesn't there? A truck on the road, a freight train on the rail, someone who can take her to town and help her call the police or somebody, anybody who has the sense to call the good guys instead of General Hightower.

So Pandora sat in the dry, scrawny wheat, waiting all through the morning for a truck or a train or a car or someone to give her a ride, but there was no one. The day wore on until the sun rode high overhead glaring down at her like an angry desert sun searing her Space Alien skin; and there's nothing, no train, no truck, nothing; and oh but she's thirsty with no hope of water in this place of brown dry wheat and cloudless rainless sky; and the sweat trickles down her forehead to well and tickle on her brow, and when she forgets to wipe it away it runs down into her eye to sting!; and she wishes wishes wishes that she'd never left the base, after all, she should've killed the General dead so he couldn't touch or threaten or frighten her ever again and why oh why can't she just go home?

O how she wants to go home.

And there's still no train, and Pandora waits. Her skin hurts so bad in the fiery burning sun. But how can she hide it? —There's no shade, no shade anywhere for miles.

Only the wheat. And what shade is that? It's not enough, but it's something, and the sun on her skin is unbearable, so Pandora does the only thing she can think of. She crawls into the wheat and lies flat on her back to let the sun shine on the cloth of her air-force-drab shirt, and she tucks her arms beneath her to hide them from the bright. Turns her face down into the dirt to let her hair take the sunshine.

After a while she realizes that she's crying. By then she's been crying for a long time. She isn't sure how long. She thinks, *How can I cry in the dry in the bright, how can I cry when there is no water? I'll dry to death if I don't stop.* She tries to quit, but it's no use. After a while she breaks down into sobs.

Eventually she falls asleep, still sobbing.

When she's been asleep an hour a National Guard transport truck comes roaring down the highway that runs parallel to the train track. Pandora is too deep asleep to hear it, and the soldiers inside the truck—who are looking for Pandora, and if they were paying attention they'd have found her—don't look into the grass where Pandora lies hiding from the sun. The Guardsman and Guardswoman in the truck aren't paying attention at all, in fact. They think it is a fool's errand that sends them wandering through the empty Kansas wheat fields.

Perhaps they're right.

An hour later Pandora wakes alone and thirsty and miserable in the Kansas wheat, and she despairs. *That stupid train isn't ever going to come,* she thinks. *Someone closed the road a hundred miles from here.*

She stands up, looks out at the dizzy-bright afternoon. And sets out to walk across the plain.

Just before the dusk turned dark entirely, Pandora saw the truck. Broke-down along the side of the road, way off in the distance. The driver put on his tail lights to guard against the dark, and Pandora saw them like they were a beacon calling to her across the endless fields. She hurried toward the light, but the distance stretched forever.

When she finally got to the truck she found the two National Guards bickering so heatedly with one another that she couldn't get their attention, no matter how she tried. Pandora behind the truck, waiting and waiting for them to quit shouting so she could turn herself over to their custody. But damned they never did! They kept screeching back and forth, and no matter how Pandora cleared her throat, they never heard.

And it finally came to her that the two National Guards were oblivious, plain and simple, and if Pandora was going to turn herself in to them she was going to have to do it herself. *Well,* she thought, *why not?* And she did what she should've done in the first place: she climbed in the back of the truck, sat down on the floor, and made herself at home.

After a while the National Guard who'd been stooped over the engine shouted, "It's done, god-damn it—now will you get off my back?"

The other one didn't answer.

Pandora shifted onto her knees, stole a glance out through the window that looked in on the truck's cabin. She saw the woman Guard with a comm set wrapped around her head, and she was speaking into the microphone—so softly that Pandora couldn't hear a word she said. Then suddenly the woman's eyes went wide, and a moment later she pulled off the comm set and let it fall to the ground.

"New orders," she said. "We've got to go to Ohio. Right now." The man Guard looked at her like she was out of her mind.

"You're out of your mind," the man Guard said. "This truck is barely running. It won't make it through Missouri, let alone all the way to Ohio."

"I'm serious," the woman Guard said. "There isn't time to argue. Just get in the truck—I'll drive."

The man guard scowled. "What's with you? You're acting like it's the end of the world."

"It *is,*" she said. "And the army needs you there. Now get in the goddamn truck!"

Somewhere on the road Pandora found the provisions crate. She almost started crying when she saw what it was—she was that hungry. MREs with water from sealed plastic bottles! Pandora was so hungry and thirsty that her hands shook as she tried to open the MRE wrappers—it took five minutes to open the first packet.

The truck only broke down once more on the trip from Kansas to Ohio. That was a miracle, Pandora thought—it was like the woman Guard had a magic touch with the truck, to keep it moving all through Missouri, Illinois, halfway through Indiana. When it finally did break down—seven miles outside Indianapolis—they were only stuck for the few minutes it took the service-station mechanic to do something with clamps and hoses under the hood.

"Whole damn thing is just about shot," the mechanic told the man Guard, "but it'll get you there. That's what you really need, isn't it? You got to get there."

"Yeah," the Guard told him. "They need us there, I guess."

The mechanic nodded stoically. "You save the world," he told the Guards. "I know you can."

And back onto the highway, and across the midwestern plain.

Somewhere in Ohio Pandora heard the woman Guard shout something about Wright-Patterson Air Force Base. It took her a while to realize what she was talking about because Pandora never thought of it by that name, but finally it did: the woman was talking about the place where Pandora had spent almost her entire life. *We're going home! They're taking me home!*

Pandora got so excited when she realized that. She couldn't wait! But when they got to the outskirts of the base she saw a spectacle that turned her eagerness to terror.

Because there was an Alien space armada three thousand ships strong hovering over her home.

It's a war, Pandora thought.

Like Operation Desert Storm those two whole months on CNN-TV—airplanes and tanks and humvees all over everywhere, and everyone in sight dressed up in uniform, and above them, spaceships crowding so close in the sky—like *Star Wars* where Luke in his tiny fighter took on the whole Empire. . . !

That's what this was, wasn't it? Operation Desert Storm vs. *Star Wars*.

The one spread across the ground, ten thousand tanks and trucks and trenches and big artillery guns, the other crowding all the air above them.

Pandora watched the Alien armada as her truck wound 'round and 'round and back and forth through the maze of makeshift dirt roads in the camp outside the base.

She hardly even noticed when the truck came to a stop not far from the fence that looked in at Pandora's mommy's hangar.

The hangar and the barracks where Pandora spent almost all of her life. She looked down from the sky and saw the hangar, her barracks in the background—and she almost cried for joy.

"There's some sort of a shell over the base," someone told the woman Guard. "You can't see it, but it's there. Hurts if you touch it, and no way you get through. Nothing gets in, nothing gets out."

I could get in, Pandora thought. *I bet I could. I bet he's wrong.* She was out of the truck, halfway to the fence. Pretty soon someone would look up and spot her, she thought—but she didn't care. *That army guy is wrong,* Pandora thought. *The shell isn't invisible. I can see it when I look at it all squinty-eyed and careful.*

It was absolutely true, too: Pandora could see a faint glitter just inside the chain-link fence.

So-pretty glitter. Like blue-white snowflakes dancing up and down in a wind, only snow is made of puffed-up frozen water and this was electron stuff like fire only different.

It's time, Pandora thought. *Little bits of time swirling back and forth. It feels hard to the soldiers because they can't go through it—not any more than they could go through yesterday.*

She didn't know how it worked, not really. But she'd lived with time amok all her life, and she had a strong intuitive sense of the ways it operated.

"Hey! There she is!" That was the man Guard Pandora had rode with all the way from Kansas, finally clearing the gunk away from his eyes and noticing her. "Somebody grab her!"

Pandora ignored him.

"Pandora!"

Uncle Ken? Yes, it was, it really was him. Pandora knew his voice. She'd know it anywhere, even here in the battle just about to happen, standing right beside the fence that was the center of it all, so close to the Alien shell that all she had to do was turn and her elbow would brush against it—

"Pandora, stop!"

She could see him in the corner of her eye, pushing through the people who crowded around her. When he was close enough to touch, Pandora wrapped her arms around him and she gave him such a hug! And she cried and cried and cried.

And then there were air police all around them, jostling them, shoving Uncle Ken out of the way and grabbing Pandora to haul her away to a terrible fate.

But something went wrong.

Pandora flailed against the APs, and as she did her elbow brushed against the fence against the fence. Through a broken chain-link to touch the impenetrable shell.

And her Guardian Angel came into contact with the Alien as the spacetime shell the world exploded in a cascade of light.

Sometime later (no, not later, it wasn't later, or maybe it was but maybe it wasn't, but what it was for sure was some *other* time) sometime other Pandora woke in the early morning in the dirt inside the fence. Inside the impenetrable Alien shell. Early early in the morning, maybe spring, maybe fall, maybe it was a cool dewy day in early summer.

She was on the base, inside the fence, and as she looked up Pandora knew something was wrong—with the hangar where her mommy's body lay in state. It was wide-open and dead empty even though it should never be open. Pandora ran to it, ran to see what fiend had defiled her mother's remains—

And found nothing.

Nothing but an empty hangar and a mountain of debris.

The hangar door was broken away, torn from its mooring—its twisted steel panels lay scattered on the floor. The hangar's walls were scarred with burns and bullet holes; parts of them looked as though they'd melted. Others looked as though they'd shattered of their own accord.

A hole big enough to drive a tank through in the wall at the far end of the hangar—Pandora imagined a tank rolling through that wall, its big gun tearing away the hangar door—

No.

It wasn't a tank that tore this place apart.

There was a reason for the ships up there in the sky; there was a reason for the battle scars here in the hangar; there was a reason why the bodies of her mother and the two lizardoid men were gone.

And whatever was behind that reason Pandora knew it would come for her soon.

I'm not afraid, Pandora thought. *I'm not afraid!*

She could see her barracks—her *home!*—just outside the hole. It was battle-scarred, smashed, and hardly even standing, but it was home, and Pandora cried for joy when she saw it.

Even if it was a ruin.

She hurried to the barracks, and found the big back door to the new wing—the door that was always locked and chained and the chains welded permanently shut—was torn away from its hinges, and inside there was an awful mess. One wall all broke in; here on the right a line of holes where a machine gun tore through the plaster. And there was Uncle Ken's room with its furniture busted up into shards of wood and scraps of fabric.

But that was nothing beside what Pandora found when she rounded the corner.

And saw the blood that covered the walls, the floor. Blood all over everything in the hall where the General had tried to rape her.

Pandora started running when she saw the blood. She had to; it was just too much for her—the walls, the floor, everything painted, smeared, and spattered with red-turned-brown; and who?, and what?, and Pandora didn't want to know she didn't want to see she just wanted to *run!*

Run forever.

But what she ended up doing was running right through it all, deeper and deeper into the barracks.

Which she shouldn't have done, because everything everywhere was wrecked, all jagged metal splintered wood and any moment now she'd skewer herself if she wasn't careful—

—and there were corpses everywhere in the corners, in the wreckage, oh Pandora didn't see them didn't see anything didn't see her uncle Wally dead bloated rotting she didn't see because she didn't look, didn't have the heart to look because they were dead and she loved them dead everywhere murdered by the Aliens who loved her but she didn't see wouldn't see closed her eyes and *screamed* still running—

"Pandora!"

Uncle Wally! That was Uncle Wally's voice!

Uncle Wally was alive!

"Pandora, stop!"

And she opened her eyes.

And saw her uncles huddled in the galley, waiting for the end.

Uncle Wally was coming across the room, catching her, steadying her, keeping her from losing her balance. And he gave her such a hug! Uncle Wally cried and cried as he patted her back, cried and cried for the joy of holding her, just the way he used to when she was a baby.

Pandora cried harder and louder and longer.

"I missed you, Uncle Wally." Pandora said, and she hugged him even tighter. "I missed you so much!"

She held on to her uncle for the longest time. And then they went to the galley table and sat with her other uncles. And all of them drank coffee, even Pandora. And they talked and talked and talked.

Pandora told about her adventure out across the world and time and back again. Her uncles took turns telling about the awful things that happened after she left: how the General and his deranged air police broke out of their quarters, tied up their guards, and left the base, taking Uncle Wally with them; how Uncle Wally came back two days later shot up so bad he should have died, but didn't; how people came from Congress, the Pentagon, the White House, the United Nations, and everywhere to over-run the barracks, but couldn't get in because Macdonald had put them under even tighter security than they'd had when the project was a secret; how just when things began to quiet the Aliens showed up above them, sealed off the base, and ransacked everything looking for Pandora. (Uncle Wally said he tried to tell them she was gone, but they didn't listen.)

It was scary stuff to talk about, but it was so good to hear them, to see them—so good that the scary parts just didn't matter.

And then, after the sun had set and Cookie lit up candles (there wasn't any electric left since the Aliens closed off the base) and broke out the disgusting-but-thank-God-because-they-were-better-than-nothing MREs; after they'd all of them finished eating and pushed their tins away; after the conversation had died away because there was nothing left to say, nothing left to do but wallow in the presence of folks well loved and nearly lost—after everything

the light of all lights descended on them from the
sky.

With the light there came a thunderous roar—
loud as worlds broke open, bellowing with pain.

"Dear God," Uncle Wally said. Pandora could
hardly hear him through the din.

He looked terrified—like he'd seen a ghost. Or
like he was about to become one.

"It's all right, Uncle Wally," Pandora told him. She
almost said, *I know who it is, I know what it is, it's
my daddy come to save me come to take me to the
stars, don't worry Uncle Wally I won't let him hurt
you,* but she held her tongue instead. She wasn't
ready to say what she suspected. Not till she was
surer. Instead she went to the window, looked out at
the light so bright it ached her eyes to see it.

And saw what she knew she'd see: the spaceship
come down for her. Come down to take her back to
her people who she'd never known but always loved.

"It's beautiful," Cookie whispered somewhere
close behind her—they were all crowded close behind her, looking through the windows to see the
spaceship with its wondrous-bright circle of pure
white light that hung like a halo—but underneath,
not from above, a halo below the fuselage where a
rocket has a ball of fire. . . .

"It *is* beautiful," and that was Uncle Simon, who
sounded all choked up and about to start crying all
over again, like he had when Pandora had found
them all huddled up in here.

As they watched, the spaceship settled to the
ground, and the light beneath it dimmed, and in a
moment a section of its wall drew down to become a
ramp.

And a figure appeared in the doorway.

But it wasn't Pandora's father: it was her mother
who stepped into the open doorway.

And waited there.

Mommy! Alive!

Pandora didn't understand, and for an instant

that seemed to last forever she just couldn't believe
what she saw through the galley window. What miracle of Space Alien technology could make dead
Mommy alive to walk, to wait, to come for her who
was huddled in a broken bunker at the center of a
battle about to happen?

It was impossible. Even for Space Aliens!

Wasn't it? . . . Pandora bit her lip. And remembered old Walt Fulton's spaceship, remembered the
curtained window that looked out onto a grave with
his own name on it.

And here was Mommy, standing out there waving
to Pandora. Waiting for her.

And she knew that it was time to say good-bye.

No matter how much she loved her uncles. No
matter how deep and dear the bonds between herself
and them: the place for a little-girl Space Alien was
among her own.

She started crying all over again.

"I love you, Uncle Wally. I love you all!" And
something big and awesome in her heart didn't want
to go, no matter how she knew that she had to. Uncle
Wally hugged her, patted her back. All of them
hugged on, and most all of them cried. "I'll come
back to see you! I promise!"

But she wasn't sure she would, or even could.

"It's all right, Pandora," Uncle Wally said. "You
know we're here for you."

And none of them were sure how true that could
be, either, because there wasn't any question about
the secret air-force project built around Pandora being over.

When she knew she couldn't bear *good-bye* another moment, Pandora left the barracks.

She stepped out the door of the barracks, turned
to see her mother—alive, breathing, waiting. . . .
Pandora's heart almost broke. Not because it was a
bad thing, but because the sight of Mommy was a
thing that filled her heart with joy beyond capacity.
She raced to Mommy across the grass and the bro-

ken pavement; despite the APs on the far side of the invisible shell firing their guns into the air to warn her away.

The APs didn't matter. There was no way they could shoot her through the shell.

Nothing mattered, in fact—nothing but Mommy waiting on the spaceship's ramp.

Pandora paused and stood before her mother for a long strange moment when she got to the end of the ramp. Adoring Mommy's unearthly form; looking into her enormous wet segmented eyes.

"*Mommy,*" Pandora said.

And her mother seemed to smile. And she reached out to take Pandora into her long, membranous arms.

Pandora cried and cried to hold her, but she didn't know why. It didn't bother her, the way Mommy's skin felt slick and slimy, just the texture of raw cow-gut tripe in Cookie's kitchen. She was Mommy, after all! She wasn't gross; she was *special.*

Mommy was Mommy, and it felt so good to hold her that Pandora could never have found the words to tell about it.

After a while Mommy led her to a double-wide seat inside the lander, and they sat together no more than a moment before the pilot closed the hatch.

And they flew away forever into the sky.

Mommy put her arm around Pandora as the ship rose off the ground. Pandora cuddled close to feel the cool slickness of Mommy's fleshy white body against her cheek. When she pressed, the flesh gave way like a loose sack, but Pandora didn't care.

She told herself she didn't care, anyway.

But it was harder to ignore the *crinkla-crinkla-crinkla-croo* sound Pandora heard through her ear pressed against Mommy's breast. The more she heard the sound, the more it unsettled her till finally she realized that the clammy dampness of Mommy's tripe-soft skin made her feel queasy, too, and deep inside her most secret heart she knew she'd lived too long among Earth humans to grow easy with the sound of an Alien heart that beat like something made from crumpled cellophane.

She knew that from the moment she heard the sound.

Maybe she knew from the instant she felt her mother's touch.

But it was years before she could admit it to herself.

"There she goes," Macdonald says as the Alien lander rises away into the sky. "We've lost her."

There's regret in his voice. And something else, too. Satisfaction? Yes, Dvorkin thinks: that's it exactly. He sounds as though he's happy for her. He sounds as though he's glad she's found her way back among her own.

What Dvorkin feels is relief.

"Just watch," Dvorkin says. "Now the Aliens will head back into space and never speak to us again." He read a science-fiction book like this once: it told how the Aliens were so much nobler, so much wiser than mankind, and how they left the human race to the world-bound fate it so richly deserved.

Only it doesn't happen like that.

Because the Aliens don't go away.

Because they aren't wise or noble or well-meaning or anything of the sort.

Pandora watched the world soar away below them through the lander's great portal windshield. The ground seemed to spin away at an impossible speed at an impossible angle; the clouds rolled past her wildly, and now the armada all around them, every ship so great and mighty and strange because it was so Alien, even to Pandora.

Then suddenly all motion stopped, and there was a great ship before them.

My daddy's ship, she thought. It had to be her daddy's: look at the shimmery walls of light, hear the thunderous music of its engines; look at the great rounding towers that stretched infinitely up through the sky. . . .

And then the view disappeared as the lander floated through a portal. A moment later Pandora's seat shuddered ever so slightly, and Mommy said that meant that the air lock was secure.

Home, Pandora thought, *I'm home!* But the words echoed hollowly inside her head, and where there should have been a joy beyond all knowing in her heart, there was something thin and sad. Pandora didn't admit it to herself—no more than she admitted there was something about her mommy that made her skin crawl—but deep inside her secret heart she knew that it was so.

There were a bunch of questions Pandora meant to ask as Mommy walked her through the corridors of the spaceship that was big as a mountain. Like, how could Mommy be alive when Pandora had seen her dead? And where was her daddy? It was Daddy she'd counted on all this while, but Daddy wasn't on the lander—just Mommy and the snake-faced pilot.

But every time Pandora tried to ask, Mommy interrupted her, and then they were hurrying to the ship's doctor even though Pandora wasn't feeling sick or anything. But snake-face said it was the captain's order, and when Mommy asked him what the captain meant by it, snake-face told her to ask the captain for herself.

And when they got to the doctor Pandora got a terrible surprise—because the doctor was an abductee, an earthling human abductee like old Walt Fulton. He frowned when he saw Pandora, looked her over, drew a little of her blood, and asked her how she felt. She told him she felt fine, and he seemed to take her at her word.

And then he did something—well, something strange. He put cuff-thick bracelets on Pandora's wrists, and something like a hockey mask on her head. And threw a switch that sent light bursting everywhere around them.

Mommy caressed her back. "It's all right, Pandora. You're safe now. You don't need the time sink to protect you."

The doctor nodded. "She's well rid of it," he said. "It was decayed as though it'd held her for a century. Another week or two, it might have hurt her."

When the doctor was done Mommy led Pandora to the crew-quarters deck. As they went past Mommy's quarters she told Pandora that if she ever needed anything all she had to do was speak to the door of that room, and the door would summon Mommy.

"Am I going to stay with you, Mommy?" Pandora asked, and as she heard herself ask the question she realized that she dreaded the answer.

"No, Pandora," Mommy said. "You're too old for that. The captain has assigned you quarters of your own."

Quarters of my own! Pandora thought. Her own private room aboard the spaceship! It was a dream, she knew it had to be a dream, but she didn't pinch herself because she didn't want to wake from it.

They went down a long beige corridor, and another, and another.

"Mommy," Pandora asked, "how did you get to be alive again? I don't understand. I *saw* you when you were dead."

Mommy made a long burbling noise that maybe was a sigh and maybe wasn't. "The ship's doctors," Mommy said, "reassembled my corpse and called my *self* back from beyond to fill it. How else, child?"

That didn't make any sense to Pandora, but for the life of her she couldn't think of any way to ask the question that would get her a better answer.

Then Mommy stopped beside a door, and said this room was hers.

"Tell the door to open," Mommy said. "It knows to answer to you."

Amazing, Pandora thought. *Amazing how everything about you can change in a single afternoon.*

She told the door to open, and Mommy showed her everything inside the room: the big wide bed, the bookshelves on the walls, how to pull the desk down from the wall, how to operate the bathroom. When she was done Mommy stood waiting in the doorway, just *watching* Pandora for the longest time. Till finally Pandora started to cry—not because she was sad or afraid or anything, but because there was just so much *wonderful* a girl could take all at once.

When she was done Mommy said she had to leave. She kissed Pandora all slimy on top of the head before she went.

When she was gone Pandora wandered over to her bed—just for a moment, to see how comfortable it was before she looked through the bookshelves for something to read. Only she never managed to get to the bookshelf, because the bed was so comfortable and Pandora was so exhausted that she just didn't have it in her to get up.

She slept that way—sprawled haphazardly on the bed without even the blankets—for hours.

When she woke she turned to look out her window at the beautiful blackness of space—but it wasn't space she saw when she looked out that window. It wasn't even dark, in fact. It was bright clear beautiful blue sky, and when she looked down over the edge of the window she saw the base and the hangar where they'd kept Mommy and right next to it Pandora's barracks.

We aren't going away, Pandora thought. And she wanted to know why, but she was partly afraid to ask.

Two hours ago Macdonald took delivery of a very special rocket launcher. Most of this device is an ordinary ground-to-air missile, but its warhead—its warhead is *special*. Seven technicians—some of the best the Pentagon has at its disposal; skilled, talented craftsmen commandeered from a black project—seven technicians and a brilliant physics grad student from MIT slaved day and night to assemble the warhead on this rocket in almost no time at all.

Macdonald thinks this rocket may be the last best hope for the human race in the War Against the World. He tells this to Ken Estes as they stand watching the technicians assemble the rocket's last fittings.

"This thing," Macdonald says, "is going to save our bacon. Mark my word."

"If it's that sure a thing, why the hell don't we fire it *now?*" Ken asks. "If this is our only hope, why the hell are we sitting on it?"

Macdonald closes his eyes. Sighs as though he's had this argument more times than he wants to remember—which he has. First on one side, when he argued with the President. Then on the other, after the President had showed him how he'd been wrong.

"Because *they* haven't started shooting yet. Even if they have sealed off Wright-Pat. Until they start shooting, there's still just this much chance they aren't hostile."

Pandora went to ask Mommy why they hadn't left the sky above the base. It took her a while to find Mommy's room—Pandora didn't remember her way around the spaceship very well, and she ended up going around the deck three times before she remembered Mommy's door.

"Mommy. . . ?"

"Is that you, child?" Mommy burbled all phlegmy through the door. "Come in, come in."

The door opened and there was Mommy sitting at the desk with the computer terminal that didn't look like a terminal.

"I looked out the window, Mommy. And I saw Earth! We're still right by the air base! I thought we were going home. Didn't you say that last night? Didn't you say we were going home?"

Mommy shook her head, but Pandora wasn't certain that meant no.

"Did I see right, Mommy? Are we still by Earth?"

Mommy waited a moment before she answered. "You saw the truth, child."

"But we can go now," Pandora said. "You've saved me, right? Can't we go?"

"No, Pandora, we can't," Mommy said. And Pandora got that awful chill again, the same terrified chill she got every time Mommy spoke. It made her feel like crud to feel that way—her hair standing on end, all grossed out and queasy—just from listening to her mommy. But she just couldn't help herself: Mommy made Pandora feel all yucky and—*alien.*

She loved her mommy, though. A girl just had to love her mommy! It wasn't right not to!

"But why, Mommy? It's dangerous here, with all these guns and tanks pointing at each other."

Mommy spent a moment looking at Pandora. Was she . . . considering? Pandora couldn't read Mommy's expressions yet. She wasn't sure she'd ever be able to.

"The humans had you for too long, child. All the time they had you they had the secret of space and time. They know enough to puzzle out the mystery."

Pandora tried to understand, but she just couldn't figure. What was so bad about humans having the secret of space and time? There were abductee humans all over the ship they were on—Pandora passed a dozen of them in the halls while she was looking for Mommy's room. She had a feeling there were even more on the other ships. And the old Walt Fulton, the man Pandora met in the woods—he was human, and he didn't just have the secret of space and time, he had his own spaceship, too.

"What's so bad about that, Mommy? I know lots of humans. Most of them were nice to me."

Mommy nodded slowly. Did that mean like it did when a human person did it? "They can't be trusted, child. The humans on this world are feral, and very dangerous."

Pandora's ears filled with a rushing sound that terrified her. It took Pandora a full minute to understand what upset her so—understandable when you consider that she'd never had to look at things that way.

"Mommy, *feral* is a word for wild dogs. And it isn't even fair to them! I knew a wild dog two times. Humans aren't animals. They're *people!*"

Mommy didn't answer right away, and when she finally did she sounded impatient. "Nevertheless, child. They are feral and now they have a secret that we do not dare allow them. It isn't safe."

Pandora had an awful intuition—an intuition so bad that she didn't want to know if it was true.

But how could she ignore it?

"Mommy," she asked, "what are we going to do, Mommy?"

She was still waiting for Mommy to answer when the captain's people called the two of them into the his private sanctum.

Visitors, the door said. It still unsettled Pandora that the doors could talk. *Reed and Marlock of the Captain's staff.*

Mommy made a burbling noise as she turned to face the door. "Admit them," she said.

The door opened to reveal two uniformed Space Aliens.

"The captain summons you," the tall squiddy-looking Alien said, stepping through the open door, looking Mommy in the eyes. He nodded to Pandora. "Both of you."

Some kind of trouble they're going to take us to, Pandora thought. *Something awful.* But when Mommy got out of her seat to go with the captain's Aliens Pandora turned and followed—what else could she do, under the circumstances? She'd already run away from a world. It wasn't in her to run away from the whole universe.

So she hurried to keep up with her mommy with her legs so long, and she took Mommy's hand with its worms instead of fingers, and the mouth down at the center of what should have been her palm kissed Pandora's hand as it held her.

"I love you, Mommy," Pandora said. "I love you very much."

"I love you, too, Pandora."

And Pandora meant it, she really meant to mean it. And so did Mommy! But Pandora's ears saved the words from both of them, and lots of times afterward Pandora heard them, over and over again.

And much as she wanted to think anything else at all, she knew that both of them were lying. Partly because of something subtle that she learned to hear in her mommy's voice; partly from the way the words echoed emptily inside her heart.

There were two impossible things Pandora saw when they got to the captain's sanctum. First of those was the captain himself—a big, muscley, brown-furred grizzly bear of an Alien. Long, sharp fangs—and a kindly twinkle in his eye. He winked at Pandora when he saw her step through his door, and picked up the skipper's cap (just like the one Skipper wore on *Gilligan's Island*) that rested on the table beside his overstuffed chair. And set it on his furry head.

"Just for you, Pandora," the ursine captain told her. "Just to make you comfortable."

Which made Pandora giggle in spite of herself.

The second impossible thing in the captain's sanctum was Walt Fulton, the old-man earthling she'd met in the cabin in the woods in Tennessee—only now he was young, not even middle-aged. And he wore the uniform of a Space Alien lieutenant.

And all Pandora could think was *no no no* because she knew damn well what was coming next. Because she'd figured it out a long time ago, even if she hadn't admitted it to herself.

"This, Pandora, is Lieutenant Walter Fulton. Lieutenant Fulton, I present to you Pandora."

And then the captain sighed.

And Mommy, who'd stepped in a moment behind Pandora, made this awful fluttering noise—a sound that had to mean something bad, even though Pandora couldn't figure what exactly.

"Macdonald—I've got a bead on McNamee."

Macdonald looks up from the intelligence reports he's reading. He looks pleased.

"Where is he?"

"Right here in the camp."

Macdonald nods. "That's what I thought. Those APs Estes described—the ones who tried to arrest Pandora—they sounded like Hightower's goons." He sets aside the intelligence reports, crosses the tent to look over Dvorkin's shoulder at the terminal. "Can you track him from here?"

Dvorkin shrugs. "Maybe. I've got some equipment. Not sure what use it'll be tracing a signal like this."

Yolen's comm set flashes, begins bleating sharply. "What. . . ?"

Yolen works the switch, turns on the feed. And blanches. "No time," she says. "No time for McNamee. —The Aliens just made their move. Artillery needs Macdonald to supervise his rocket."

Macdonald swears under his breath. Massages his forehead with his left hand.

"David. Ken Estes. Take Collier and Eisen, see if you can find where the call is coming from. Find McNamee—Hightower will be with him if we're lucky. Call me when you locate them. Keep an eye on them till I get there."

It was the strangest thing, Pandora thought—to see an old man she'd met just days ago suddenly transformed three dozen years younger. Had they cured

him of old age when they brought him on the ship?
Was that possible?

No, Pandora thought, *it's like with the Awful
Lady. Walt Fulton is out of order in time.*

The same thing happened to her uncles sometimes when they were around her—only with them
their hearts and their heads usually stayed in time
line with her, even if their bodies got old or young.
Was Walt Fulton like that? Did he know her? No,
look at him: he didn't even recognize her, except
maybe from a picture on TV.

He doesn't even know who I am, Pandora
thought, and it made her so depressed, because she
had a good idea already who he was and why the
captain had all of them in here. She didn't want to
think how he was going to take the news if he hadn't
had a clue of it.

And looking at him, looking down into his heart,
Pandora thought he didn't have a clue.

Arne is asleep when the call comes.

"Scramble, Starr."

Arne (who wakes today no more alert than he
woke yesterday) is confused. "Huh?"

"Aliens, Starr. Thousands of them. You're up in
the air as soon as you get here. Get here now."

And the phone goes dead.

"Right," Arne says. He lets the receiver fall back
into its cradle.

Walt Fulton turned to smile at her when the captain
introduced them—well, sort of. He smiled till he saw
Mommy hovering over Pandora's shoulder, and then
he—well. He didn't sneer, exactly, because a sneer is
something someone does intentionally. More like his
face filled with involuntary revulsion, and he looked
like he was going to get sick or run away or something, only instead he forced his smile back into
place and said, "Good *morning*, Krant! It's good to
see you again. And you, Pandora—I'm especially

pleased to make your acquaintance. I've heard a lot about you these last few days, I'll tell you."

He was lying about something, that was for sure.

The captain cleared his throat.

"Pandora," he said. And then said nothing for a good long while, as though whatever it was he'd meant to say was wedged in his throat. "I understand you've been looking for your father, Pandora."

Pandora nodded. "He was why I ran away," Pandora told him. "I ran away so that I could be on TV. And then my daddy could see me and save me from Earth! —Only he never did. It was Mommy who came back to life and saved me."

Sadly, slowly, the captain shook his furry head. "I think your father might've tried to help you, Pandora, if he'd only known."

"Really?"

The captain nodded. "I know him well," he said. "I've known him many years. He a passionate, compassionate young fellow. I admire him considerably."

Pandora felt all glowy inside. "But how come he didn't know?"

Mommy groaned. Pandora turned back to look and saw that she was all a-tremble. Beads of phlegm hung like tears from her arthropoid maw.

"He does not know because I have not told him."

She is crying, Pandora thought. *Listen to the despair in her voice.* Pandora stepped back to hug her, to comfort her, but Mommy pushed her gently away.

Which made Pandora feel pretty awful. But she didn't say anything on account of how Mommy looked ready to shrivel up and die herself.

"But *why*, Krant? You've made an obligation on him that nothing can untie. Three quarters of her genetic material is his directly; she's more his child than yours. As anyone who looked at her could see! And you've left him seventeen years of Pandora's life ignorant to answer the obligation he never knew he'd made."

Mommy only shook her head and rephrased herself. "I did not tell him. I *would* not tell him."

Walt Fulton was beginning to look alarmed, like it was finally settling through to him what everyone else in the room had already figured out.

"Krant," the captain said, "what you've done was not only wrong. It was illegal."

Mommy shook her head yet again.

"Pandora is my child. She is dear to me." And with this she reached out and pulled Pandora to her protectively. The tentacles of Mommy's hand reached down to hold her, to caress her.

"The child's in no danger. But you, Krant—your liberty is at stake."

That was when Walt Fulton lost his composure. "Who?" he demanded. *"Who is the father?"*

But he already damned well knew who the father was, just like the rest of them.

Mommy spat. Pandora had never seen her spit before, except in the vision of when the ship was crashing. It surprised her to see it, and surprised her doubly to see it here in the captain's sanctum. After a moment she spat again, and hissed. "You are."

"What?"

The captain coughed. "I found the record in the computer easily enough, once I knew to look for it. Quite a job! Three full days' work for one of the big processors, knitting a sample of your DNA in with hers. And then another month she spent tinkering with the rough design." He glanced at Mommy. "Till I met Pandora, Krant, I had no idea you were such a hand with genetic sculpture."

"What?"

And all Pandora could think was: *He is, he really is my daddy. That's why he was waiting for me in the cabin in the woods; that's why he came back to try to help me with his spaceship.* She closed her eyes, and shut away the room and the people and everything. And she thought: *I was so mean to him.*

*He's my daddy and he loves me and I was so mean
to him.*

But she didn't think through the last little bit of
the equation. Didn't think how the Walt Fulton/
Daddy she knew from the cabin in the mountain was
an old, old man, mellowed and tamed by time.

All she could think was *Daddy Daddy I'm so
sorry Daddy!* As she opened her eyes and said exactly that.

"Daddy I love you Daddy, I'm sorry Daddy. . . !"
and she ran to him, to hug him, to love him as he
looked up at her mommy and *screamed:* "What have
you done to me, you slime-drenched *witch?*"

He pushed Pandora away. A little harshly, maybe,
but not really rough.

And the silence in the room hung thick as sand,
but drier and scratchier and more menacing.

"Oh my God, Pandora," Walt Fulton said. "What
have I done to you?"

But it was too late for that, because her heart was
already broken. And she fell on the floor and crawled
away across the carpet to the room's darkest corner,
and she cried and she cried and she cried.

Walt Fulton followed her there. "I'm sorry, Pandora," he said. "I'd do anything in the world to help
you forgive me."

She wanted to forgive him, but how could she
when it hurt too much to speak? Hurt too much to
do anything but sob and sob.

"Pandora, I'm so sorry." And then he stood up,
and spoke to the captain. "I need some time, sir. I
need to get out of here and clear my head. I want to
take a scout and get *away*—for a few hours. Till dinner." He knelt again to look at Pandora up close, to
touch her shoulder, to try to get her attention. But
she just didn't have it in her to *give* him any attention. "Pandora, I'll be here for you at dinnertime, and
if you're feeling better we can talk."

The captain cleared his throat again. "There isn't
time, Walt. The attack is already under way."

For half a moment Walt Fulton looked surprised, confused—and then suddenly he turned angry.

"Well then, goddamn it," he told the captain, "you'll just have to destroy the earth without me."

And he turned away and left the room. And even though he said he'd be back in a few hours, Pandora knew it would be half a lifetime before she saw him again.

Ten minutes after the telephone wakes him, Arne Starr is on the runway of the greater Cincinnati airport (which isn't in Cincinnati at all, nor even in Ohio, but across the river in Kentucky), queueing up for takeoff. It's a hell of a queue; there are more jets here than Arne has ever seen in one place. A dozen times more than he saw on the runway at NATO exercises.

Still, the line moves quickly. Four jets at a time: synchronized pairs of them lift off the runways that point in all four directions. The jets of every second wave roll up and away in broken-S takeoffs, each jet looping up and around as it pulls up from up from the runway, banks forty-five degrees, pulls nose up into a high-g turn, and gets the hell out of the way so that the next wave can get up—

—into the air.

Arne's in the air, and the scene is absolute madness. Madness! The sky is crowded as a busy runway, crowded in every direction, crowded from here to eternity—

But it may not be crowded for long.

Because it isn't just a mob scene, it's a bloody mob scene.

The Aliens are slaughtering us.

And it's true, too: everywhere there are jets and Aliens in the sky near one another, the jets exploding, plummeting to the ground in fiery glory.

And right there, right then—right from the moment he looks out at his sky, Arne Starr knows he's going to die today.

And he's right, too.

Destroy the earth without me.

They're wandering the great sprawling camp—Dvorkin, Ken Estes, Sarah Collier, Janice Eisen. Linked by comm sets even though they're physically spread out across two miles of cacophony and confusion.

The sky above Ken Estes is a screaming terror. He does his best not to look up; it scares the hell out of him, the sight of all that blood and thunder.

And then Ken hears it as he walks an endless field of ordnance tents.

He'd know it anywhere, anytime. Even here and now, with the world a screaming battlefield for a hundred miles in every direction. How could he ever forget that voice, after that night a week ago, when the old man found out about Ken and Anna? After the screaming, the threats? After the old man tossed Ken into the Pandora Project and threw away the key?

No way.

No way Ken could ever forget.

General Dan McNamee's voice: a shrill harangue plainly audible over the thunder.

"I don't *care* what the President says," McNamee shouts. "The President is a chickenshit. The only goddamn thing we got that's going to take those Aliens out of the sky is nukes. And if you don't want to send them up, I'll send them up myself."

The voice that responds is Hightower's. "You heard the man," Hightower says. "Arm that thing. That's an *order,* son."

And Ken discovers the most amazing thing: that even here in the battlefield, here in the middle of hell on earth screaming booming planes blasting everywhere from the sky, even here and now where the world is coming to an end—there's something that scares Ken worse than any of that.

Holy shit.

Hightower and McNamee with a nuke.

Ken whispers into the comm: "Get over here," Ken says. "Get Macdonald. Right away. I've found Hightower and McNamee. They've got a nuke."

When Walt Fulton was gone—when *Daddy* was gone —Mommy turned to follow him.

She didn't get more than two steps before the captain cleared his throat. "Hold, door," he said— and the door, which till that moment had been sliding open, suddenly rolled shut.

Mommy turned back to face him. Her gills were pulsing, swollen angry blue.

"I can't let you go, Krant. You've given no account of yourself. This is a serious matter—not something you can shrug away and ignore."

Mommy hissed. It didn't mean, Pandora thought, like it'd mean if a human person hissed—maybe there was a little anger in it, but mostly she seemed to hiss and spit when she was at the verge of exasperation. When she was frustrated, or maybe embarrassed. Which she must've been right then, because she spat three times into the soil by the captain's potted plant (was that a plant?) and twice she missed it.

"I will give you no account," Mommy said. "This is no concern of yours. Nor of Wal-ter Fulton's! Unhinge the door and let me free."

"You're wrong, Krant. Fulton has an obligation. And no way to answer it."

Mommy screeched—and Pandora thought that it probably meant pretty much what it would have meant if a human had made that sound.

"What would you have me do, Groau? Renounce the child? Very well then, I renounce the child. *Now leave me free!*"

And the door opened, and Mommy stomped away

in about the nastiest huff Pandora had ever seen from anyone.

The truth is that in a very real sense the Space Aliens are right to destroy the earth.

Never mind the bloodthirstiness of the people of our world; never mind the terror of atomic weapons set loose upon the universe. The most frightful thing of all to them is the secret of the stars—and that secret lay trapped inside Pandora all those years she spent in her barracks on Wright-Patterson. And even if the addled scientists who surrounded her were helpless to discover the secret, the earth was not. Indeed: even as the jets and fighter scouts soar and blast through the skies above the American heartland, Macdonald's graduate student—the young woman who built his unwieldy but oh-so-astrophysically-elegant missile—sweats and trembles still working in her laboratory, for any moment now she will unlock the deeper, more dangerous secret of time unwound to space.

The insight she needs is *that* close—she can feel it weighing on her, waiting for her to realize what down in her heart she already knows. And when she does, the key to time and space will unfold, and when it does, no more than two or three years of trial-and-error experiments will put stars at elbow and foot for all mankind.

This is a thing that the Space Aliens find disquieting.

Threatening.

Justifiably so.

I renounce the child.

Pandora tried to follow, but Mommy went too quickly—she was gone before Pandora could pull herself up off the floor.

And besides, as soon as she started to get up the captain motioned that she be still. And Pandora wasn't one to argue with one as big and bearish and angry looking as the captain was at that very moment.

Arne switches from the takeoff controller's comm channel to the one set aside for airborne communication. And nearly busts an eardrum. The channel is one long feedback squawk—no, that's not feedback exactly. It's the sound of two damn many pilots trying to talk at the same time—there are too many of them in the sky, too damn many trying to use this channel. But what the hell can they do about it? There are only so many channels to go around.

It's the same on his radar panel: so many lights that they all merge into one impenetrable white mass.

Fuck this. Equipment is useless. And he turns off the comm, and he turns the contrast on the radar panel till its image fades away entirely.

And Arne Starr flies computer blind on reflex into the brilliant noontime sky crowded with Aliens and dying jets.

It's a seriously stupid thing to do. Even under the circumstances. Even for a hotshot pilot like Arne.

But it works.

When it finally sank through to Pandora just exactly what it was Mommy had said, she started to cry all over again. *Renouncing* Pandora! Why would Mommy want to do a thing like that? Like, like she was an idea, and not a person, and Mommy had suddenly changed her mind. —No, like the captain had put her in a position where she *had* to change her mind. Or something! And why would the captain do a thing like that? Unless he was just a hateful *thing*, and Pandora really didn't think he was, because nothing hateful could have a twinkle like that in its eye. Could it?

When she looked up she saw the captain staring at her.

"*Why?*" The question came out almost before

Pandora could think it. "Why did they go away? Why did you let them? Why did you make them?"

The captain sighed again, shook his head. "I don't know what I can tell you, Pandora. I wish that I could tell you something good."

"Why did my daddy say that about blowing up the world? You aren't really going to do that, are you?"

The captain didn't say a word. Not a word! He just sat there stooped down with his arms braced on his hairy knees, staring at her with his big round eyes.

"*Why?*"

Pandora had spent all her life alien to the world and hardly a part of it. But now—well, now was different. She *was* an earth person—at least partly. On her father's side. And there were lots and lots of people in the world she loved. She didn't want to see it blown to bits!

"I'm sorry, Pandora. I'm very, very sorry."

"You can't," Pandora said. "I won't let you!"

The captain's eyes went wide. He almost seemed to chuckle.

"And how do you propose to stop us?"

It took Pandora a long time to think of an answer. "I just will, is all. Mind me, damn you!"

The captain frowned. "You know," he said, "I think you may be serious. And I've got an notion—it isn't sane, but I have it still. I think you may well be a threat to us, if you decide to make an obstacle of yourself." He looked up at the door and growled. "Door! Summon Smith and Wzyn. Have them seal Pandora in her quarters."

EIGHT

Spaceships, Sasquatches, Satanists; Space Aliens, Haunted Cancers, Ghost Trains. Millennialist Nightmares and Shopping Mall Vortexes: An amazing day that dawns to find these things inhabiting our folklore. Consider them as a whole and they describe an all but unmistakable reforging of our communal id.

They describe a people who have remade their most essential nature—and become a thing not imagined in our own nightmares.

They describe ourselves.

There is no great mystery behind this metamorphosis. We are the product of our times, and this is an age where steaming clanking mechanical contrivances have given way to invisible miracles like electricity, atomic radiation, and electronic information.

Only in the strangest fantasy could mankind live three generations beneath an atomic hammer of doom and *not* rebuild its most fundamental self.

And only in our strangest nightmare could we conceive our own man-made apocalypse and see the world as once we did.

Sift the words through your mind's ear: *atomic hammer of doom.* Savor them. Hear with your own heart how they've touched and changed every event these last three generations—from the most trivial quandary to the most monumental reconsideration.

The atom hammer is very likely the most significant icon in our contemporary lore, no matter that it is fact and not only legend. It distills and binds together all of our contemporary circumstance, true and untrue, mythic and mundane. It is as much a part of our collective heritage as are the witch lore and demonography of Europe's Middle Ages.

Oh, it has a heritage. Thor's thunderous hammer, so central to Norse myth; and Zeus, too, could cast lightning onto the world. Yet more than these, our foreboding doom traces itself back to the Apocalypse of Revelation—and farther, to the flood that led Noah to Mount Ararat. And evolves still again from that heritage: for where before our doom lay in divine hands, now we carry it uneasily upon our own shoulders.

Is it any wonder that our spirit wearies beneath the weight? That our myth becomes misshapen and bizarre? That our hearts swell with confusion and unease?

Arne flies on instinct and intuition, without the F18's comm or radar, without its eyes or ears—flies through a lunatic sky crowded with death and destruction.

Seven times in the last ninety seconds he's had Alien fliers in his sights, and he's blasted away at them with the F18's big General Electric cannon.

And the rounds hit home! Arne saw them hit—saw something like red fire where the shells connected.

But after a moment the redness went away, and it left behind no sign of damage.

This is a sucker's game, Arne thinks. *We're all going to die—just a matter of time. Sooner or later one of these guys is going to get in a lucky shot, and I'm history.* Twice already he's felt the Aliens getting a bead on him, and he evaded just in time to miss getting it but good with that death ray of theirs. *What the fuck are we doing here? Dying for show?*

Arne doesn't want to die. He will if he has to, and maybe he has to, but he sure doesn't want to die for no damn reason at all.

I feel like a kamikaze.

And he thinks: *Kamikaze.* The thing about kamikazes isn't just that they killed themselves—which they did—the thing that makes kamikazes worth remembering is that they took ships down with them. One plane for a whole damn destroyer—sure, the kamikaze died. Sure, he was a suicide pilot. But if he took a ship down with him it didn't matter so much. Because one pilot, one plane—they aren't much of a price to pay for a whole ship.

I could do that, Arne thinks. Look at the Alien carriers so high in the sky; look at them so badly defended. As though the Aliens don't even consider that a jet could fly so high—let alone attack.

Arne eyeballs the distance, bites his lip. Maybe the Aliens are right. Even for an F18, those damn things are up there.

Loops up and around, avoiding the beam of an Alien ray. Takes a pointless shot at a pair of Aliens just above him.

And just keeps going—up and up and up.

Ken Estes stands terrified outside an ordnance tent beneath an infinite battlefield sky.

Where are they? The rest of the team is taking forever to get to him. And they need to *hurry,* damn it, because any second now old man McNamee is going to come out of that tent, and he's going to see Ken, and he's going to kill him.

Either that or he and Hightower are going to blow up the world.

Ken Estes doesn't want to die. And he's going to, one way or another, if Dvorkin, Collier, Eisen—if they don't *hurry, damn it.*

Then suddenly there's a screaming roar from the nearest battery of artillery. For half an instant Ken thinks it's McNamee and Hightower, that the paranoid lunatics have gone and done it, and that's it, that's the end of the world, they're gone and in a moment the atom rocket will blast and they'll all vanish in a puff of subatomic vapor, all of them, all of them for miles and miles around vanish once and forever till the end of creation—

No.

No, look, that isn't any nuclear missile: it's Macdonald's weird contraption. The thing his grad student built for him. Shooting up off the ground, burning, sizzling with red electric fire. . . .

Up, up through the air, across the battlefield. Is it going up to hit the Space Alien carrier? No, look how shallow the arc. It's already leveling off, heading down again—

Straight down toward Wright-Pat.

What is Macdonald trying to accomplish? There's no way he can hit the closed-off base with that thing; there's that shell over the whole place, the Alien shell—

The Alien shell.

Macdonald's rocket slams down into the dome of the Alien shell, and everything everywhere goes red with that same impossible fire.

Reel forward:

Hours in time; miles across the land.

Look into the bunker deep deep down below the deepest White House basement.

Look out along space and time until you find the briefing.

The briefing that's almost begun.

The President has found his seat, and taken it; the Vice-President enters through a secure door at the far end of the room. A moment later the Secretary of Defense follows him—and now two or three others whose titles would obscure the fact that they've a good deal more authority than the VP or the SecDef.

The one called Jake is here, too. That is the name that the generals who give this briefing give him: Jake.

They call him Jake, and they do not like him. Not one bit.

Jake works for the President. The generals have seen enough of him at briefings like this one to grow used to his presence. But not even Jake imagines that they'll ever grow to appreciate him.

He's dressed appropriately enough, but there's no mistaking that he's much the worse for wear. Look at his eyes as he stands away in the corner, by the velvet drape that hangs near the large door opposite the one through which the VP made his entrance. His eyes are tired and worn, bloodshot.

"Mr. President," General Booth says from the podium. "Mr. Vice-President, Mr. Secretary." She nods as she calls each out by title, and nods to the others whose titles aren't relevant. And then she clears her throat as she turns toward the man by the door. "Jake," she says. "Good to see you again."

There's no one in the room who misses the fact that she's lying when she says that. The discomfort, the dislike in her voice as she speaks to *Jake*— they're palpable things.

Jake smiles a predatory smile.

"And you, General," he says. "It's good to see you, too." His voice is just as full of things unsaid—but it's something very different that he isn't saying. Something personal and intimate, as though they once were lovers.

And different because the tension between them is nothing reminiscent of a lovers' quarrel. Perhaps . . . perhaps it's that they were once both a part of something that they cared about and believed in. Something more important than either of them.

Something (perhaps) that one of them left behind.

Something that Jake left behind.

Booth clears her throat.

"General Hershey has asked me to brief you on the events over Wright-Patterson Air Force Base this afternoon," she says. As she speaks the wood paneling that is the wall behind her rises like a curtain—revealing a row of video monitors. Three of them flicker to life. "Behind me," Booth says, gesturing, "behind me you can see the video portion of this briefing. On the right, the CNN footage shot from Xenia, Ohio—a little town just east of Dayton, not far from Wright-Patterson." She coughs, reddens. "I understand you're already familiar with this footage, Mr. President." Absolute fact, and to the serious embarrassment of the intelligence agencies: when events are in motion the President finds CNN more timely and reliable than his intelligence feed. Which it may well be. But certainly military-intelligence types (Booth among them) will tell you that their information comes sooner and more accurately. Regardless, their arguments have never persuaded the President to give up CNN. "Here in the center, DoD footage broadcast from the encampment just outside the base. And on the right flight-camera footage from several planes—most of it synchronized to match the first two."

This is hell, Ken Estes thinks. *It really, really is.* And though he's wrong, the confusion is only natural, given the circumstances. Look at the sky burning red everywhere with the impossibly red electric fire.

Look how it spreads out from every Alien spacecraft above the world, look how it closes every gap to fill the sky.

This is the end. It's over.

He's wrong about that, too.

Look at the red that covers Wright-Patterson, now burning—is it really afire? Does it truly burn? The red engulfs everything it touches, but look down into it, look for the charring, the evidence of combustion—and there's nothing.

Half a dozen of the Alien fighters plummet to the ground—one of them not more than twenty yards from where Ken stands. That closest one shatters when it hits, explodes—and when the explosion subsides the wreckage burns on unnaturally, shimmering bright red, so bright it hurts Ken's eyes even though it's day.

Ken doesn't even notice when the tent flap opens somewhere behind him.

"What the hell is going on out here?"

Doesn't even think to run when he hears that voice too damn close behind him.

Not good.

Not good at all.

"Answer me, *boy*. What the hell is going on out here?"

And Ken turns, not even thinking, not even realizing who he's turning to face. Turns to answer a persistent question, to face someone who wants his attention and won't go away till he gets it—

McNamee.

Looks over his shoulder, points at the glowing wreck. . . . "Look for yourself, damn it. Over there. Alien, crashed—"

And McNamee sees him.

And Ken realizes what he's brought on himself.

I can't stay here, Pandora thought when the door to her room whispered shut behind the two Space Aliens. *I've got to do something.*

But she couldn't think of anything to do. She was locked in her quarters, and no matter how she pleaded with the door, it wouldn't open.

My daddy will do something, Pandora thought. *He's got to save the world.*

Her daddy was a human, even if he did have his own spaceship. He had to save the world!

But she knew in her heart that he wouldn't.

He isn't ever going to come back.

Pandora couldn't know about the temporal anomaly that would catch Walt Fulton's scout ship a moment from now as it launched from the flagship's bay —but she was Fulton's daughter, and she'd spent so much of her life twisted up in time that she had a powerful sensitivity to the fates. She knew when things went permanently wrong.

And an instant from now, they were going to go about as horribly wrong for young Walt Fulton as they possibly could.

The CNN correspondent screams faintly from the turned-down speaker of the monitor on the right— his shouts just barely loud enough to hear beneath Booth's voice. "They're coming! Thousands of them, thousands swarming like hornets—!" and that's the image that fills all three monitors as their cameras pan the sky: fighter ships. Uncountable thousands of Space Alien fighters bursting from their carrier ships, occluding the blue of the sky with the fire-bright exhaust of their engines and the metal grey of their many airframes. And for as long as that moment lasts there isn't a heart in the room that doesn't shiver and skip three beats—no matter that all of them have seen this footage more than once before.

When Booth speaks again she's all but breathless. "We didn't have a lot of warning, here," she says. "The attack was about as much of a surprise as they could make it under the circumstances—no small accomplishment. After all, they'd waited seventy-two hours for us in plain sight in the sky over Wright-Pat.

We *knew* they were there for us, and we were sure enough that they were hostile. But we had no idea that there were so *many* fighters in the carriers. We still don't know how they managed to carry so many; the volume of fighters seems to be greater than the capacity of the carriers that launched them."

The Vice-President coughs into his hand. Asks for clarification. "I don't understand," he says, "what exactly do you mean with this stuff about volume and capacity?"

Booth touches a button, freezing the images on their monitors. Hits another that turns on a fourth monitor. It shows the image from the second monitor—right this moment it's centered on the great mother ship that took Pandora. Which is convenient: Booth takes her electronic wand, touches the image on that ship on the fourth screen.

Immediately—magically, almost—the computer that controls that monitor zooms in, expands the mother ship to fill the screen.

"Here, Mr. Vice-President," Booth says, "look closely at this ship. How many of the fighters would you say it could hold—take a guess, looking at it. Imagine that the entire ship were full of them."

The VP shrugs. "Four hundred? Five hundred?"

"Good guess," Booth says. "That's almost exactly what we'd estimated the ship might hold before the battle started. It was our worst-case estimate; we didn't imagine that the entire ship could be filled with fighter craft, but we felt we had to prepare for the possibility." She frowns. "We were wrong. This carrier launched nearly fifteen hundred fighters—at least that many. The film analysts are still recounting; they keep finding more of the damned things."

The Vice-President has a look on his face—a belligerent look, almost. As though he were refusing to believe her.

It wouldn't be the first time.

"How can that be?" he asks. "Are these things inflatable, like beach toys? Or what?"

The faintest chuckle rolls across the room as the Vice-President says *beach toys*.

And it *is* funny, the way he asks the question. Not that Booth can afford to laugh: the VP may not be among the nation's great minds, but he's one of the best friends the Pentagon has. *Nobody* in uniform makes fun of the VP. Not where the brass might see it, anyhow.

"We don't know, Mr. Vice-President. All we know is what we have on the videotape: hundreds and hundreds of the fighters pouring out of every carrier."

There's an awkward moment of silence as Booth waits for the VP to ask the next question, but he never does. Eventually Booth restarts the videos, goes on without him.

"You!" McNamee screams. And he doesn't hesitate an instant: he grabs Ken by the collar. Hauls back his fist and flattens Ken's nose. "Hightower," he says, "I found something outside the tent. Measly peckerwood who thinks he can mess with my little girl."

And he starts to drag Ken (half-senseless) into the tent.

And Ken sees what's inside. Sees the mobile rocket launcher that isn't any ordinary mobile rocket launcher. How the fuck did old man McNamee get a portable nuke away from security?

There's no way to answer the question, and even if there were, there isn't time: because Macdonald has come 'round the bend—Macdonald, Dvorkin, Yolen, Collier, Eisen, all of them running at the tent, and five squads of MPs just behind them—

"Let him go, McNamee," Macdonald says. "Put your hands above your head. Don't do anything sudden. Or I'll kill you. I will, I swear it."

And what's Ken to do? His head's still spinning like a top. His arms and legs are made of gelatin. There's blood filling his sinuses, leaking out his nose. It's even in his eyes somehow—he has to keep blinking it away or the world gets dim. He does the only thing he *can* do: he falls to the ground. Tries to pick himself up once he's fallen. Which is no use—old man McNamee's punch hurt him even worse than it felt. He's too disoriented, too woozy and off balance to find his legs.

"You're going to be sorry for this, Jake," McNamee says. "I swear you will."

Do these two guys know each other? There's something—familiar in the way McNamee calls Macdonald *Jake.* Ken isn't sure; maybe he's just imagining it.

Still on the ground, Ken watches Macdonald walk up to McNamee, stand maybe two feet away. Sees him level his gun point-blank at McNamee's gut.

He's going to kill him, Ken thinks as he stares up into the space between the two men. Isn't there enough blood here already? Blood burning, blasting into vapor up in the sky? Blood in Ken's eyes? Blood all over the damn place. Ken doesn't think he can cope with any more. *I've got to get up. I've got to get away.* And he tries again to push himself off the ground. Almost manages to do it—until his left elbow buckles, sends him back face-first into the ground. Smacking his nose all over again, and now there's even more blood.

What did that old SOB hit me with, a rock?

Fist like a rock, at least.

One of the squads of MPs shuffles past them into the tent. Their sergeant swears when he sees the mobile nuke inside it.

"How the hell. . . ?"

Macdonald, looking into the tent over the man's shoulder, swears back at him. Angrily. "How the hell do you think he got it? Same way he's been able to put through orders no one ought to be able to make. The man has hooks so deep into the Pentagon it'll be thirty years before we find the last of them." He smiles. "Isn't that right, Dan?"

McNamee looks annoyed at being called by his first name. He doesn't say a word.

"Get a tech team in here," Macdonald says, "get them to disarm this damn thing before it hurts somebody."

"Yes, sir."

Another voice, from inside the tent. "All clear, sir. Empty except for the missile."

No!

It just isn't so, and Ken knows it. He heard several voices from inside that tent. He heard the old man talking to Hightower! Ken marshals everything he's got. Gets himself halfway up, sits looking up from the ground.

"That's wrong," he says. "Hightower was in there with him. I heard others, too—half a dozen, easy."

McNamee swears again. Hauls back and kicks Ken in the gut, to shut him up. And it does shut him up— thoroughly. Surprises the hell out of Ken. He didn't think the old man had the nerve to try something like that with a gun leveled at him.

"Hightower," Macdonald says. He stoops over, looks Ken over, checking to make sure he's alive. "Christ Almighty." He pats Ken on the back. Looks up, nods to the second squad of MPs. "General Belisarius Hightower is around here someplace," he says. "Find him. Fast. Arrest him. Do anything you need to to bring him back here—kill him if you have to, I don't care. Yeah, you heard what I said." Then he turns back to face McNamee. Maybe he's going to ask him what they thought they were going to do with a nuke? It doesn't matter. Because he can't ask it anymore. Because when Macdonald turns back to face McNamee, the man is *gone.*

Pandora watched the fighter spaceships—hundreds and hundreds of them tiny in their distance as they launched from the great wide bays of the mother ships. Every one of them sparkled bright electric, from the spacetime shield that surrounded it.

Destroy the world!

Pandora shuddered as she watched the beginning of the end.

The CNN correspondent is screaming again. Screaming and screaming as the American jets fall from the sky. One after another after another after another, they fall like clay pigeons—like targets. Shattered, thrown effortlessly from the sky.

They hit ground exactly as clay pigeons land: as rubble.

"The other thing we weren't counting on," Booth says, "was their guns." Her expression changes subtly as she says this; she's clearly disquieted, perhaps even horrified. And rightly so. "We lost a quarter of all the planes we had in the air in these first five minutes. Not just the ones in the air over the general vicinity of Wright-Patterson; *all* our planes everywhere over North America." She turns to the monitor again, points, enlarges one of the Alien craft as it fires on an F16. "We *still* don't know what they were firing."

As she speaks five jets—three American F16s, a British Tornado, and a French Mirage—appear on the CNN monitor. And almost as soon as they appear an Alien fighter swoops into view, pursuing them. In an instant the five jets explode into flame and plummet to the ground.

Booth freezes the CNN monitor.

"There," she says, "another perfect example. Look closely at the Alien fighter. What did it fire?— Nothing. Nothing physical, no radiation, no laser, nothing. Nothing we can see. Oh, the pilots could tell when the Aliens shot at them—one of them described it as 'hearing the death ray.' But we still don't know how. There's nothing the analysts have found as they've gone over the spectrographs of this part of the battle—nothing. A slight disturbance in the infra-red—say, about as much heat as you'd see from a warm breath on a cold night. Easy enough to see, but nothing that ought to take down three F16s, a Tornado, and a Mirage."

Macdonald starts to order the second and third squads of MPs to hunt down McNamee—and then reverses himself.

"No," he says, "that isn't safe. This damn thing—" he points at the missile "—McNamee's armed the firing mechanism. Had to, to get it out of command and control. I want you people here, and I want you to watch this damned thing like it was worth your life. Because it *is* worth your life—yours, mine, every damned life for fifty miles in every direction." He looks at Yolen, Dvorkin. Ken Estes only now beginning to pull himself up off the ground again. "*I'll* go find the SOB. He can't be gone far. Yolen, Dvorkin, Estes, Collier, Eisen—come with me. I'll need you if he puts up a fight."

Pandora tried to look away. Because she didn't want to think about what the captain was trying to do, and she sure didn't want to see it happen. But she didn't have it in her not to watch! She had to know, to see. . . .

See the explosive fire blooming out of those three F16s blasted from the air.

See the missile zipping out from under the wing of the Alien fighter and across the sky toward the mobile power transformer in the center of the camp outside Wright-Pat; see the seven-story cascade of blue-white sparks as the bursting transformer erupted.

See those great artillery shells sail high across the sky toward Pandora in the mother ship, see it strike —only to vanish into time as it struck the spacetime shield.

It was only beginning, and already so much destruction, so much violence, so much hopelessness— none of the earth artillery could touch the Aliens. The jets were useless, too—none of their weapons

could pierce the spacetime anomalies that shielded
the Alien fighters.

It's over, Pandora thought. She could see it happening already, and there was nothing that could
stop it: in an hour the earth's defenses would lie in
ruins, and the Alien armada would lay waste to the
world.

Arne Starr doesn't get very far above the battle before a wing of Aliens catches on to what he's got
planned and moves up to intercept him.

Fast, those Alien fliers. Damn fast. One moment
Arne's got the sky to himself, and there's nothing
between him and the sitting-duck carrier at eleven
o'clock; the next the Aliens are all over him, and if
he hadn't jinked his jet when the hair rose on the
back of his neck, they'd have burned him right out of
the air.

Christ.

The six Alien fighters herd him back down into
the battle, one shot at a time.

I'm meat, Arne thinks. *They're shoving me into a
trap.* There's no way out, and Arne knows it—there
are just too damn many of them, and not even Arne's
Sidewinder missiles seem to make a dent in them.

And then, just as the trap begins to slam shut
around him, something happens to the sky.

The whole damned sky.

"This is where it all started to change. See the missile there, coming up out of the battery at the gates
of Wright-Patterson? See the peculiar apparatus up
in the nose where the warhead ought to be? That's
no ordinary missile. Where most missiles have
bombs or gas or biohazard in their warheads, this
one has, well, a contraption. Hard to call it anything
else if you've seen it up close. Even here on the
video—"

As she speaks the missile reaches the apex of its
flight, turns back down toward the ground . . . but

now it's above Wright-Patterson, and it isn't just ground it's heading into, but the faintly sparkling shell that covers the base.

"—even here on the video you can see the tubes and wires. I'm told that there wasn't time to build the device a proper enclosure, and that the engineers weren't especially concerned about ballistic drag—given the distance of the target."

And the missile hits home.

Hits the summit of the spacetime shell that covers Wright-Pat.

And everything, everything everywhere on all three monitors goes red impossibly red with electrifying light.

They find McNamee a lot faster than Macdonald could have hoped.

Trouble is they find him on McNamee's own terms—and it's hard to imagine that those terms could have been worse for Macdonald and his crew.

Down a long row of tents, just past an enormous red electric fire that isn't fire and isn't electric and maybe isn't even all that big, but it sure looks big, right then, right there Ken looks at it as they pass and it looks enormous. And as he's staring at the fire Ken hears a cough he'd recognize anywhere, anytime —a cough that always makes him think of a distant round from an AK47, and how the hell could he ever forget a sound like that? He couldn't possibly forget, not even if he lived a thousand years.

"Down that way," Ken says. "McNamee's behind that tent on the left."

Then, before Macdonald can so much as react to what he says, a door slams.

And a truck engine roars to life.

And before any of them knows what's happening to them, the truck is roaring 'round the tent, tearing the rope and canvas from its moorings, plowing through—

Coming right at them.

With a vengeance.

They try to scatter. All of them but Ken Estes. Ken—he's had one too many from McNamee already. Ken is *mad*. He stands his ground, stares McNamee and his truck right in the eye. Shakes his fist, and in his heart he's threatening to tear the old SOB limb from limb.

Perhaps he's shouting, perhaps he's telling McNamee what he thinks of him once and for all. Perhaps he's finally standing up for himself.

It doesn't matter in the end. Because there's no way to know what Ken may or may not say; the truck's engine drowns out all other sound. And besides, what does it matter what Ken Estes says? He's a man, and the truck is a truck. It plows him down, and he dies.

Simple as that.

Red, red everywhere burning blasting electric nuclear thermodynamic raw blinding blasting red, the sky goes red as the aboriginal blast at the center of the cosmic egg, fire come to consume the world consume us all O woe the end is upon us I'm a dead man, Arne thinks.

Only he isn't dead—not yet.

He isn't sure why. An explosion this big should have shredded his F18 in an instant. But it didn't, and it's been what, fifteen seconds? Twenty? And he's alive and he's flying and God the brightness hurts his eyes. . . .

And there's an Alien, right in his sights. A big one. Arne fires three rounds at it from the GE cannon—

And damned if he doesn't blow the thing from the sky.

Holy shit, Arne thinks. And he doesn't try to understand his luck: he follows it through.

Keeps his finger on the trigger. Blasts three more Aliens from the sky.

What the hell is going on?

Then it comes to Arne:

The fire.

The red fire has something to do with the shells that surround the Aliens—the ones that made it impossible to shoot the things. The fire burns, the shells are gone, the Aliens are sitting ducks.

Arne blasts another out of the sky—and another and another after that. It isn't hard. The Aliens are disoriented by the red fire that isn't hot and doesn't burn. And so accustomed to fighting from behind their shields that they don't understand how to evade.

Two minutes and Arne's managed to kill a dozen of them, using his cannon as though it were a machine gun and the Aliens were infantry. Three minutes and the rest of the jets have caught on—the ones that managed to survive the first round of the battle, the new ones soaring up to join them.

It's going to be a massacre, all right, Arne thinks. *But not like I thought.*

Nothing at all like he'd thought, in fact.

The carrier on the DoD monitor quivers for a long moment as the red fieriness consumes it—and begins to drop.

Stops abruptly.

And then it begins to rise.

And rise.

All of them, all of the great mother-ship carriers rise away rise high up into the sky—and keep going.

It isn't quite as simple as it seemed at first, with Ken Estes and the truck.

Because as McNamee and his truck plow through Ken Estes, they push into the red electric fire behind him.

And as they do the strangest thing begins to happen.

Because the red electric fire *isn't* fire, and it isn't electric, and it isn't even red, exactly. It only seems that way.

What it really is, is time.

Time gone berserk, made material. Or not material, exactly; if energy is matter at the speed of light squared, then this unearthly stuff is the product of some tangentially similar relationship between energy and time.

It's an exceedingly unnatural substance.

And what it does when it absorbs McNamee and his truck and Ken Estes's corpse—that's perhaps the most unnatural thing of all.

Red electric time that isn't red isn't electric flares as McNamee plows into it—explodes to engulf not only McNamee, the truck, and the corpse but Macdonald and the living members of his team, too—and a couple of the tents along with them.

And then, suddenly and incredibly as it began, the red spectacle *stops.*

Just like that.

Snap! —and nothing moves. Nothing—not even Ken Estes's corpse, which hangs suspended in the air, where only an instant ago it had bounced and bounded on the truck's front bumper.

And then time rewinds, and it's starting all over again.

The sky is alive with fire and light, and in his mind's eye Arne is back on his old block in junior high, reading *The Incredible Hulk* for the ninety-ninth time.

Hulk will smash! Arne thinks. And three more Aliens explode gloriously and plunge toward the earth.

From her place high above the battle Pandora watched the sky explode, saw the exploding red subside into sputtering red fires made of time. Half a dozen of those fires burned and sputtered all through the battle, like the embers of a bonfire smoldering in fits.

. . .

"In retrospect it looks as though we were luckier than we could have hoped to be. Almost every bit of the technology the Aliens use depends on that 'peculiar spacetime effect' that the physicists keep talking about. —Heh. 'Spacetime'—where do they get words like that? Everybody else just calls it the Pandora effect. Which sounds right to me!" It's almost as though Booth forgot where she is, and only now suddenly remembers. At least that's her expression as she suddenly falls silent: she looks embarrassed. She coughs, turns back to point at the zoom-in monitor. Draws a box around the screen with her wand, and the image zooms out to show a long view of the sky over Wright-Patterson.

Everything everywhere in the sky above the base is red.

Burning, fiery red.

"What the device in that missile did was short-circuit the Pandora effect. Not the way you'd short-circuit a lamp or an engine—deeper than that. What was the phrase that the physicist used in that report?" She steps back to the podium, shuffles through her papers. "Here it is. 'If our device works as we think it will, it will short-circuit the ether underlying the whole of southwestern Ohio.' And it did exactly that. As well as we could possibly hope—and a little better. Because we didn't count on how many of their machines depend on the Pandora effect. Look, here." She gestures toward the video monitors, where the red fire has begun to subside. "See how the Alien fighters all dip ever so slightly as the redness subsides? The analysts say that's happening as their auxiliary engines are cutting in. They point out that the Alien fighters maneuver very differently from this point forward—you can see it yourself if you look closely. Far as we can tell, their auxiliaries are ordinary jet engines, not a whole lot different from the ones on our planes."

• • •

High above the earth and away from the planet at right angles of time, young Walt Fulton in his lone scout tries to return to the scene of the battle.

And something goes very, very wrong. Because the red fire isn't just the Alien shields gone awry; it's time and space gone cockeyed. And spaceships that depend on bending space and time are helpless against it.

And Fulton, utterly unaware of what he's flying into—Walt Fulton and his scout ship fall out of the universe we know entirely.

When they fall back into the universe, they're a billion light-years away from everything they know—out in the dark pit of space beyond the stars, in that awful place beyond the reach of the first light of creation.

And there begins the tale that lies hidden behind this one: how Walt Fulton and his scout ship fell across space and time and possibility to fly out into the black deep of space so far from True Center that the first light of creation has not reached there yet.

How cannibal space pirates found him there so near their lair, and did to him things that few could bear to hear . . .

But this escapes the scope of our telling: Walt Fulton lived again to sail among the suns, and sailed them—sailed beyond the last of them.

And when, years later, he recovered from his ordeal and bent space and time to take him back to Pandora where he'd left her on the battlefield, what he found was the red fire that made time impenetrable for a hundred hours in every direction.

On the far side of the red fire there was nothing for miles and miles and miles around—nothing but death, ruin, and destruction. On the near side there was no Pandora, for she was lost to time and the world all the while she rode aboard the train adrift across the years.

. . .

"It wasn't just their engines that depended on the Pandora effect—their shields did, too. See the three fighters going down here? Without the Pandora effect they have no shields. And their pilots don't know evasive tactics; with their shields they just haven't ever had to learn evasion."

It's obvious what she says is true. Because the sky everywhere on all three monitors is filled with slaughter.

Hulk will smash!

There are Aliens, Aliens everywhere dying and dropping to the ground.

It's like it never happened with the truck. Ken Estes stands alive and whole and defiant, shaking his fist at McNamee bearing down on him, and the rest of the team stands behind him. . . .

Only it's different now. Because even if Ken's body has forgotten the brutalization it received pounding and pounding on the bumper of the truck, his mind remembers. His heart remembers.

Even if time has looped and Ken is whole and hale, even if his death has unhappened, he hasn't forgotten it.

How could he forget? How could he ever?

No way. Never.

And so he jumps aside as the rest of Macdonald's team scatters—

All of them but Dvorkin.

Poor Dvorkin.

He's confused, see. He doesn't understand that the events he knows have disoccurred. Sure, he sees the truck—but he's too confused to realize that he's going to *die* if he doesn't get the hell out of the way.

Poor Dvorkin.

Well, there's this for him, anyway: he never knows what hits him. He's too confused to realize that he's dying till, well, like in the old joke:

Q.: What's the last thing that goes through David

Dvorkin's head before he's splattered across the bumper of the truck?

A.: His nose.

Pandora felt an awful jolt just as the redness outside her window reached its brightest.

Falling! We're falling!

And then there was a great ominous roar as the ship's descent came to an uneven stop. A sound, a shudder—rocket engines? Pandora imagined great rocket engines detonating somewhere down below her, and wondered if a ship this big could use a rocket in an emergency. Could a rocket really hold a mountain off the earth?

Pandora couldn't imagine how.

But they did. The rockets beneath Pandora held them in the air—and now slowly, steadily began to lift them up.

Up into the air and away from the world forever.

Hulk will smash!

Two dozen; three. Arne loses track of his kills. But he doesn't stop. Doesn't even slow down. How can he? There's a war on. If he stopped and thought about what he was doing he'd be lost.

Snap!

Just like that, and Macdonald and his team once more stand whole and hale surrounded by red-flickering time-gone-mad.

And McNamee and his truck bear down on them.

Bear down on Macdonald, more specifically.

Because this time it's Macdonald who's the odd man out—everyone else has already scattered, the instant time coagulated *here* and *now*. Oh, Macdonald tried to get the hell out of the way, too—he isn't a man who's easily confused.

But even if he's a man able to put aside his own confusion, he's just as bound to his fate as any other.

And when he tries to run for it, he finds that he's entirely unable to move.

Poor Macdonald.

For him there's this: he dies struggling, knowing his fate, understanding his doom—but refusing to accept it without a fight.

"I told you you'd be sorry, peckerwood!" McNamee shouts.

And then Macdonald dies.

Pandora watched the battle closely as she slowly rose away from it.

Not because she wanted to see which way it went (she had an awful feeling about what was going to happen, and she didn't want to witness it) but because it was better to watch her world fall apart than to close her eyes and only listen with blind dread.

Better to watch the missiles soar again and again from the batteries that launch them; better to watch jet planes and Alien fliers blast one another from the air.

No great trick to that; there were jets everywhere in the sky outside Pandora's window. American, Canadian, NATO jets; Israeli, Saudi, Kuwaiti jets; jets from places as far away as Russia and Japan. The amazing part wasn't that they were there, those jets of so many nations—though that was a pretty damned amazing thing, all by itself. The amazing thing was that they were picking the Alien attack ships out of the air as quickly and as thoroughly as a flock of swallows devours a swarm of gnats.

"We sent up a lot of surface-to-air missiles. Most of them made no difference at all—even without their shields, the fighters have no trouble getting out of the way of a big missile. And the carriers—they're easy enough to hit, all right. But none of the missiles seemed to have much effect. Not even the ones that managed to break through a carrier's superstructure. But one of them hit home, sure enough—and what it

hit was the carrier we'd pegged for the flagship."
Booth points her wand at the zoom-in monitor. "It
did more damage than we could have hoped. When
the folks in artillery saw what they'd done they were
ecstatic." She frowns. "But later we were very sorry."

Snap!

Collier and Eisen die as a team, just as they
worked as a team these last few days. They've both
seen Macdonald, Dvorkin, Estes die: they know the
routine. They know there's no escape.

And both of them accept their shared fate—with
dignity. Yes, dignity: that's exactly what there is
about them as chortling McNamee and his nine-ton
truck plow the women into the ground.

Such dignity. Such grace.

Smash!

The Alien drops like a rock, and Arne looks up to
find his next target. And there's nothing! Nothing
anywhere. Even most of the Allied jets have left the
sky.

What the hell is going on? he wonders. And then
he remembers the comm channel—he shut it down
because it was making too damn much noise. He
goes to turn it back on, to get whatever orders there
are that he's been ignoring—and that's when he sees
it.

Firefight. North of here—that's Wright-Patterson,
isn't it? The closed-off base? Yes, that's it exactly.
The battle is winding back down to its center. If he
wants some of the action, he needs to go find it.

The missiles kept coming toward Pandora, wave after
wave after wave of them. From the same bank of
launchers that broke the spacetime shell, from batteries just like it scattered across the camp. Ordinary
missiles; artillery rockets; great cannonlike devices
Pandora couldn't quite identify.

And some of them found targets in the big mother

ships—tearing great holes in the hulls they struck, and God knew what damage deep inside. That ship, up there, look at it, Pandora thought. Billowy cloudlets of smoke spilling from it, and now and again a lick of flame, and if somebody didn't do something soon, probably the whole ship would burn and everyone inside it would die.

Pandora was so pleased that it wasn't *her* ship going to blazes that she forgot all about the last volley of rockets.

The rockets speeding through the sky straight toward her.

The ship managed to pick five of them out of the air with some kind of an antimissile gun—something that made Pandora think of the Patriot antimissile missiles like on CNN over Saudia during Desert Storm. *Smash boom bash ka*-boom *crunch!* That was five of them so loud she could hear right through her glass—but the sixth one, that was another matter. Because the sixth one came in right behind the fifth, so close that the antimissile computer must've mistook it for the tail end of the one in front of it. Right through the wall! Right into the ship's engines, right in there she could tell because suddenly they were falling even faster! Pandora felt it, right through her chair, through the floor beneath her—and right after a great fiery blast blew out the gaping hole below her.

In a moment the engine compartment caught fire, and a thick funnel of smoke rose up across the outside of her window from the floor above, and soon the smoke became a fire raging outside her window. She watched it grow hotter and wilder, blazing out the ruptured hull, into the air. . . .

The walls and floor of her room were made from something special; they kept the heat away from her for the longest time. Long before her room began to warm there were smoke stains on her window, and the outer surface of the glass gradually distorted, and finally the floor itself began to warp.

And then it was warm.

And her ship began to fall.

Steadily, quickly.

Till suddenly gravity went loose all at once as they fell freely to the ground.

"Without their shields the Aliens are sitting ducks."

Indisputable fact: All three monitors are alive with the red fire that surrounds the Alien fighters as they explode and die. If the ammunition holds up! But the A10s are in the air now, and the wide-bore guns on an A10 go on and on and on. And even if the A10 was designed for ground support and turning tanks to shrapnel, it's more than a match for the Aliens who have no shields.

Another five minutes and the Alien fleet will be nothing but debris.

But it isn't going to last that long. Because already the Aliens have begun to break and run; already the fighters stream into their carriers retreating into the sky. . . .

All of them, all of them running for their lives.

All of them but the crippled carrier, that even now settles defeated to the ground.

"Per your orders, Mr. President, we tried to board, capture, and salvage." Is it regret in Booth's voice as she says this? —Was the order a thing that went against her better judgment, something she came to rue?

Perhaps.

Perhaps her expression is not regret at all, but rather quiet anger.

Certainly it's sadness on the President's face. As to whether it's regret, well, who can know? A man with responsibilities as wide as the President's must keep his own counsel when all is said and done. Who else but he must weigh the whole of the nation—the whole of the world!—against its parts?

And still—it must weigh on him indeed.

For the attempt to take the Alien flagship brought

disaster down on everything from Cincinnati to Indianapolis, from Columbus to Fort Wayne.

"Yes, General Booth. Those were my orders.
Please continue."

Snap!

Jane Yolen is a woman of transcendent will.

Her fate comes for her exactly as it came for Macdonald: she sees, she knows, she understands. She
stands brave before the truck that comes for her, and
when she turns to step aside, her legs betray her.

But where Macdonald is a brave man born to
struggle to survive, struggle and perhaps triumph,
Yolen is another creature altogether.

Yolen is She Who Will Not Be Denied, and no fate
could ever master her. When she finds herself unable
to move, she reaches down into her heart, reaches
into her endless well of determination. And despite
the fate that binds her to that spot, Jane Yolen walks
away from the truck bearing down to murder her.

Trouble is, it doesn't end so simply.

Sure, the truck roars right past Jane Yolen, leaving her unscathed. But in its wake roils fate denied,
and this in a place already fiery with sanguine time
gone mad: and don't you just know it? Something
has to give.

The way it gives is like this: Time blasts out in
every direction from where Jane Yolen should have
been—time accelerated beyond all knowing, beyond
anything anyone anywhere anywhen in the universe
has ever known, perhaps *will ever* know.

And isn't it just like fate that time-on-speed
catches Jane Yolen in its violet, violent explosion?

It is indeed.

Time-on-speed engulfs Jane Yolen, and she begins
to age fantastically. Years wash across her face in a
matter of moments; years, years, and more years still
—till finally, suddenly she dies.

Dies of old age.

The strangest thing about Jane Yolen's fate is that

even though it's age that kills her, she dies even faster, even more suddenly that Dvorkin did.

Dvorkin takes some satisfaction in this.

Later when Pandora thought back about the battle in the sky over Wright-Patterson, it seemed to her that the big Alien spaceship must've had an incredible number of safety devices. How else could it be that she scarcely felt the war she saw destroy that ship—not till the very moment it struck ground and crumpled like an aluminum can under the tire of a truck.

With Pandora still inside.

When Arne gets to Wright-Pat, what he sees is positively bizarre. Five, six dozen Allied jets in a low-grade firefight with half that many Alien fighters. These Aliens aren't the same cannon fodder Arne has been picking out of the sky for the last hour. They're —smarter. Look at them, evading, thinking—these pilots know their stuff. God knows how they learned it where none of their fellows had, but they do know it, and they're putting it to use—they've got the better half of the action over Wright-Pat, despite the fact that they're outnumbered two to one.

At the center of them is one of the big Alien carriers. The carrier is wounded—worse than wounded, it's dying. Sinking quickly to the ground. Even now, as Arne watches, it touches dirt, its superstructure begins to collapse under its own weight—

And as it goes down a final volley of fliers bursts from the big ship.

And suddenly Arne and the other jets are outnumbered.

Seriously outnumbered.

After that there's no time for thinking. Half a dozen Aliens on his tail, and all he can do is run for his life—and wonder why the hell there aren't any reinforcements.

Twice Arne manages to loop end over end, come up behind the Aliens, and blast one out of the air.

But it doesn't matter—not much. Because there are lots more Aliens than these, and easy replacements for both of the two he kills.

But the thing that worries him most of all isn't the Aliens. Not directly. The really scary thing is that he's running out of fuel, and there's no way in hell to gas up under the circumstances.

Hightower.

Macdonald made a serious mistake when he sent a squad of MPs to find Hightower—and not only because following McNamee led to his death again and again beneath the tires of McNamee's truck. Underneath the bluster and the bullying, deep inside the fat that bloats him like a hog prepared for slaughter, Hightower is dangerous; the fact that he's a swollen pig of a man doesn't neutralize his talent or intelligence. All six of the MPs Macdonald sent to follow him are not adequate to bring him back; no army of MPs could be enough to capture him. Even Macdonald himself would be hard put to put Hightower in irons.

Worse, where McNamee only means to run for his life and his freedom, Hightower has a darker plan in mind; of those two Hightower always was the one with—*vision*. From the instant he disappeared from the tent that held the missile, Hightower meant to return.

And he does exactly that.

He comes back to the tent just a moment after the last of the MPs Macdonald set to watch the missile settles into his duty. And Hightower waits, watching but unseen, until a spectacular explosion low overhead shakes and burns the sky—and all the MPs stand agape, staring wide-eyed at the exploding Alien above them.

In that racket no one even hears Hightower shoot the MP who stands guard before the missile's electronics access hatch.

And as the explosion continues and redoubles, no

one sees Hightower hurry toward the dead MP. No one sees him push aside the access hatch and grab the three carefully chosen wires he'd marked an hour before.

Wires Hightower tagged and arranged because he knew that it could come to this.

"Stop right there. Right now."

Hightower laughs and laughs.

Because it doesn't matter—not one bit. Not anymore.

Because Hightower has the wires. And the wires —held just so—the wires are a dead-man switch.

"Don't try it," Hightower says. "If you scare me I might let go of the wires. And if I let them go, the missile goes up—and we're all history."

Low over Cincinnati, and the Aliens are all over Arne —blasting and blasting, and if he wasn't flying frenzied evasion he'd be dead already.

Soon, soon. If the fuel gauge were honest he'd be dead already.

Very low, now: Arne can read the sign above that big low building ahead of them: BRIARWOOD PET MOTEL. Big pretty-looking place.

Which is about when Arne looks up and sees the Alien right on top of him.

Literally.

Not more than what, two feet above him. Maybe less.

What's he trying to do, ram me out of the air?

It doesn't matter. Whatever the Aliens are up to, it's bad news for Arne. He needs to move—fast. But there's no place to go! Aliens above him, ground so low below—

And Arne does the only thing he can.

He dives.

Straight toward the ground. Straight toward the Briarwood Pet Motel.

The Aliens start blasting away behind him, but it

doesn't matter anymore; Arne's out of the kill zone of their weapons—

—the kennel, the kennel he's about to hit the kennel—

—he doesn't need any goddamn Aliens to kill him; he kills himself just fine, thanks—

—and manages to pull away at the last instant. Well, almost; the F18's scissor-V tail section takes a few shingles off the Briarwood's roof. But it's mostly intact, and Arne's still in the air—

But the Aliens aren't quite so lucky. One of them hits the kennel with its death ray, blasts a hole wide enough to drive a thruway. And the two close behind Arne are *too* damn close. And they aren't half the pilots Arne is; when they try to pull up to follow they slam into the kennel's big front office.

In the carnage and the confusion the kennel catches fire and burns to the ground. Not that it really matters; the place is hopelessly overinsured.

It was only the bottom of the great ship that collapsed. The very bottom, where the burned-out engines were. Maybe two, three levels above it—levels evacuated only an instant after the missile hit, when it became obvious that the fire would spread, and how.

It was no mistake that the third level—the level with the officers' quarters, the secondary bridge, the minor galley—it was no mistake that the third level survived the landing more or less intact. Those who designed the ship knew perfectly well that the third level would become an important nerve center, and they reinforced it against the worst possibilities.

Pandora's room was in the third level. It should have come through the landing well enough. But it didn't.

Because the fire in the low decks had already warped the ship's superstructure, and the very worst of that deformation was where the fire was hottest—just below Pandora. The safety controls in her room were plenty enough to protect Pandora, but they weren't enough to save the nested mass of beams and girders caught directly in the fire, because there were no such safeties down in the gridwork between the engines and Pandora. And when the ship struck home just inside the fence that marked off Wright-Patterson Air Force Base, those beams and girders gave way.

The trouble for Pandora came when they took her floor away with them.

Arne rolls, straightens. Points the F18 toward Wright-Pat, hoping against hope that there's something in the air between here and there that can pick the Alien vultures off his tail. It's a poor hope, and he knows it—but it's the only hope he's got.

All his days Walt Fulton worked to find a way back to his abandoned daughter.

He could have gone to the detritus of the battlefield and tried to resurrect her—as he'd been resurrected more than once himself, and as the ursine captain had resurrected Pandora's mother, Krant, above Wright-Patterson. And more than once he tried! But it's no simple matter reassembling a body atomized by a thermonuclear explosion. Even for an armada of Space Aliens it's a considerable task.

And Walt Fulton by himself was no Armada—though there may be those who would try to tell you otherwise.

So he tried and tried again to reach Pandora before that ultimate moment. But hard as he worked, time around that battle would not bend—no matter that he worked his whole lifetime to bend it.

And then, when Walt Fulton's hair was grey and his eyes were weak, it finally came to him that he had to travel longwise through the years to reach Pandora. Round about and patiently through time: which is why Pandora could meet Walt-in-his-dotage in the woods before she ever knew him.

. . .

The way it turns out Arne's only hope is no hope at all.

Because they're all over him, the Aliens are all over him, and they've got him in a killing box over the camp outside Wright-Pat—and hard as he tries, there's just no getting out.

Hightower's having the time of his life.

And who wouldn't be? So much attention! Two, maybe three hundred soldiers poised on his every word; their eyes riveted to follow his every gesture. Hightower glories in it. After all these years locked away in a barracks on Wright-Pat, he glories in the attention he so richly deserves.

"What do you want, Hightower?" General Simpson, all but prostrating himself before Hightower. About time! Long overdue! Simpson was the SOB who cashiered Hightower after the Korean War. If there was time Hightower would teach the bastard a thing or two, he would.

But there isn't time, and there's too damn much going on, so Hightower ignores Simpson. There's nothing the man can do for him anyway. Hightower is here to be the *cojones* of the world. He's here to watch, to see, to know when the vile goddamn Alien filth needs to be burned off the face of the earth—because there's no one else in the world who has the nerve to push the button, not after all these years.

No one but Hightower.

But Hightower will do it when the time comes.

Nuke 'em good, too.

Snap!

It's starting all over again. The truck, McNamee, Ken Estes standing defiant before them—like a broken record come back to its original ring, time in the fire is back where it began: with death.

Ken Estes's death.

Only it doesn't happen like it's supposed to this time.

And the reason it doesn't happen right is Arne Starr.

Arne Starr, way cool hero pilot of the battle's fiercest F18, changes destiny when his fate folds him into the obscene providence that binds Macdonald and his team.

Like this: The Aliens have finally tagged Arne, and he's going down in a blaze of glory glory glory he's going to *die* his plane dropping like a rock after that last shot from the Alien gun blew out the bay of his one surviving engine. Dropping like a rock, only he's not heading into bare ground, he's heading into the camp outside Wright-Pat—heading right into that bright red fire—and what does it matter? Die splattered across an empty field, die snuffed by a bright red fire, it's all the same when you get down to it.

Isn't it?

It is.

Except, well, this here fire is *special*. It isn't fire, isn't burning, isn't even really red although it looks that way. What it is, is time, and not just time but time gone mad, and when Arne smashes into McNamee's truck he dies just as dead as he would have otherwise. But Ken Estes doesn't, and McNamee—McNamee finally gets his.

The impact with Arne Starr's falling jet stops McNamee's truck right where it is. And McNamee, who's never been as careful with the details as some might think, isn't wearing his seat belt.

Bad move, that.

Because McNamee isn't wearing his seat belt, the impact of the plane sends him sailing right out through the truck's windshield.

The battle turned real for Pandora when her room split in two.

Split itself wide down the middle of the floor, and suddenly all the sound and smell of war was right there with her, booming and screaming and stinking every bit as bad as if she were in the trenches beside her uncle Ken. Scary at first, just a little scary and unsettling—the scent of gunpowder, and that was blood, wasn't it? And something bitter, like a chemical for cleaning. Except that there was nothing clean about that smell.

Then an artillery shell landed in the dirt just outside her window, and the ground and the ship around her exploded in a hail of stones and dirt. Up through the gaping breach that was her room's floor, and if she'd been standing *there* instead of *here* she'd be torn to shreds, just like the books on the bookshelves.

And Pandora screamed.

I've got to get away, get away, get away.

If she hadn't been too terrified to think she might have realized that even if she could get a million miles away, getting there would be infinitely more dangerous than being here. It was a battlefield out there! They were shooting, and bombing, and any moment now the MLRS would go off again and a thousand tiny rocket bombs would turn that field outside her window into a wasteland.

No matter how bad it got, it was safer in here than it was out there.

But Pandora was too scared to think clearly. She jumped down through the crack in the floor, onto the battlefield, and she *ran*—fast as she could through the shooting and exploding and the fire, as jets and spaceships blasted one another in the air above her, and look, look all around the ship, there were tanks moving up to encircle the spaceship—

Pandora *ran* like her life depended on it. Didn't look where she was going; didn't try to go no place but *away*.

Snap!

And now it's Arne Starr alive again and all bewildered behind the wheel of the truck.

And McNamee—McNamee stands cowering before the truck that is his death waiting to happen. Isn't that always the way with bullies? Isn't it? They can dish it out, but when it comes time to take it, they shiver in their boots.

Not that it matters, not in the end. Because when you get right down to it, cowards die just as dead as brave men; and their graves aren't especially distinct.

The last thing that passes through old man Mc-Namee's head before he splatters against the bumper of the truck?

The hood ornament. What did you think?

Pandora didn't look where she was going as she ran across the battlefield. Not any farther than it took to look where one foot had to go to follow the one before it. What would have been the point? Everything was war, destruction, violence for a state and a half around in every direction; any place she could run was just as bad as where she was. Main difference being that so long as she kept moving, Pandora made a harder target.

Or so she thought with the tiny corner of her mind that was clear enough for thinking.

Maybe she should have thought some more. Maybe there was someplace on that battlefield that was safer than the rest. More sheltered, at the least. Certainly she should have minded where she was going.

Because as it was, she headed right into the path of the looped spacetime collapse that killed and killed Macdonald's team.

Killed and killed and killed them beneath the tires of a truck.

And then maybe it was no accident that brought her running straight across the battlefield into the worst of all the hells that war had to offer: maybe it was the fates who guided her.

At the very least, the fates were part to blame.

Because what happened to Pandora when that bolt of red diffuse spacetime flux struck her like a shaft of unreal lightning—what happened to her then was indeed ordained. It had to be: it was at the root of every strange event that had come to pass in the week she'd already lived.

When Pandora was fifteen feet from the red time-fire that burned around Macdonald and his team, a bolt of red lightning that wasn't lightning shot out of the time-blaze and struck her, knocking Pandora senseless. When her vision cleared it was a week before in time—and a world away in circumstance.

Mommy's hangar stood before her intact, undamaged; seeing it, Pandora knew where and when she was. Knew her mommy lay in state inside it, dead but uncorrupting.

And she knew what was about to happen all around her. And she knew what she would do, what she had to do—and she knew that she would do it no matter that it meant the worst.

Late late night, dark and all but moonless. And wounded by time rifted twice or more times with Pandora's passage: somewhere behind her in the warm June night there blew a cold winter wind awakening to welcome her. She thought she felt a wisp of snow settle into the back of her neck.

Uncle Ken screamed somewhere in the distance.

From that direction—from the far side of Mommy's hangar.

From the barracks.

I've got to save him, Pandora thought. And she ached a little inside, because she'd thought just that a week ago, and the thought had led her to that moment with the General, beating her, *touching* her. And she didn't want to live that moment again. No matter what, she didn't.

But what could she do? It wasn't in Pandora to let anyone be beat to death like that. Not if she could do a thing about it.

Uncle Ken came out of this okay, she thought. *I*

know he did. She'd seen him three times since this
moment, and she knew he was alive. But what if he
lived because Pandora *now* had saved him in this
then?

She tried to think of anything else that *could*
have saved Uncle Ken from the hateful APs. But
there was nothing: no one in that whole wing of the
barracks but Uncle Ken and the General and the APs.

And Pandora.

She shuddered. And ran toward the building as
fast as she could.

Across the road that ringed the row of hangars;
across the field that lay between Mommy's hangar
and the road.

I'll save you, Uncle Ken! —and thinking that gave
her even more déjà vu. *Just try all you can to live
long enough to be saved!*

Around the hangar, and there was home, just as
she'd first left it. As though she hadn't even left it yet,
which in a way she hadn't, because somewhere else
in the barracks there was another Pandora running
to the rescue—and doomed. *There's nothing I can
do for me. I know what happened to me. There
wasn't any saving.* Which made her feel very sad.
But what could she do? There was one who maybe
she could help, and one who she couldn't. She had to
do the one she might accomplish.

Along the barracks' outside wall till she came to
the new wing. And now that she was here no damn
way to get in at all—not a solitary window facing
toward the outside world. And the only door was
chained and bolted shut.

She couldn't even see what part of the hall this
was. Couldn't know for sure if she stood by the General trying to pound Pandora's brains into the terrazzo, or by Uncle Ken's room where—

—where Uncle Ken screamed the second time,
and she could hear the APs, too, APs shouting and
swearing and pounding on Uncle Ken—

And she just stopped thinking, was all.

She stopped thinking about the wall and the door and the bolts and the chains. And she ran to the door, and she yanked on it, hauled away at the handle with every iota of hysterical strength she had. . . .

Pandora wasn't human.

But all her life in one way and another she'd measured herself as though she *were* a human little girl. And because she had, it never had occurred to her that she was strong enough to rip a reinforced steel door away from its concrete mooring. It'd never even so much as occurred to her to test herself to see if she could do it. After all, she was Pandora. She was gentle and demure and sensitive and friendly, and it wasn't in her to play at ripping doors from their foundations.

But she was plenty strong enough to rip steel like it was paper.

Stronger.

And the door came away like so much torn aluminum siding.

And there were the APs, now out in the hallway. One of them holding Uncle Ken as two others beat him with their truncheons.

"Put him down," Pandora said.

The two with the truncheons looked like they'd heard a ghost whisper in their ear. Which maybe they had, when you consider all Pandora's circumstances. Those two pulled back right away, and good for them because she didn't want anybody calling her bluff.

But the third one, the one who held beaten sagging Uncle Ken for the others to batter—that one just laughed.

"What are you going to do, little girl—hurt me?" And laughed some more. "I'm afraid."

If you were smart, you would be. But she didn't say that, because it would have been a challenge, and she didn't want to challenge him. Just wanted to stop what he was doing. So she walked right up to him,

and grabbed his hands where they had Uncle Ken
pinned upright. And she pulled them away. Firmly,
directly, but no more roughly than was necessary to
unhand him from Uncle Ken.

Well, maybe she hurt him a little. But not on purpose! Just, well, his left arm made this funny popping
sound as Pandora pulled it away, and as soon as it
did she realized that she'd pulled him away at the
wrong angle, and she would have said sorry but already the AP was bellowing in rage, letting go of Uncle Ken and hauling back to smash Pandora a good
one with his fist that wasn't broken.

And she felt very sad, because she really didn't
want to have to fight or hurt or even threaten anybody, and she was trying very hard to be nice even if
a certain amount of force was unavoidable. And what
she was going to have to do to stop the AP's fist
wasn't nice, and it wasn't going to be any accident,
either.

Which was to grab it in midair. And drive it off to
the side, into the cinder-block wall. Where it made
the sickly crunching sound that Pandora knew damn
well it was going to make.

And the AP screamed. And fell to the floor beside
Uncle Ken.

And boy did she feel bad for that. But what could
she do? Not a damn thing—she couldn't think of a
single, solitary thing. It wasn't like he was going to
try to play nice with *her.*

Uncle Ken lay prone on the terrazzo, gasping for
air. Pandora knelt to speak to him.

"Uncle Ken. . . ? Are you okay?" Which was a
stupid question, because he was plainly *not* okay.
"Are you going to be all right?"

Uncle Ken started to talk, choked, and then nodded instead. Spent a moment catching his breath,
and whispered: "They didn't break anything—not
yet. Just my air gone. That's all." And gasped. And
gasped.

Which was when Pandora looked up and saw that the two APs were still in the hall, watching them.

The sight of them made her unspeakably angry for no reason she could name. "Get out of here," she said. "Out the door"—she gestured toward the door she'd broken—"and go away. And never come back. If I ever so much as see you here again I'll kill you, I swear it."

The APs got, and fast. It was always that way with bullies, Pandora thought: they were the biggest chickenshits where it came to coping with things more dangerous than themselves.

A scream from down in the hall and around the corner—no. Not a scream, but a scream suddenly choked off, and then a sound like—

—like—

That was *her* scream. Pandora's scream, when the General *touched* her.

No.

And again she just stopped thinking. Stopped thinking and got to her feet and ran to the far end of the hall and rounded the corner just in time to see—

In time to see the General and the ugly hungry look etched into his panting face—lust and hate and anger all twisted up together.

And she knew that he *wanted* her. Wanted to do things to her that two people bound forever together ought to think carefully before they try—but where those two consent their love to bind them physically together, the General wanted to use that act to work his hateful rage out upon her body.

Wanted the Pandora she'd been a week ago; the her who'd just disappeared from his grasp. And did not care one whit that Pandora so reviled him.

She wanted to kill him when she saw that. Of *course* she wanted to kill him.

And she almost did, too.

The General looked up, still panting and hungry. And saw her staring at him.

"There you are, you miserable little slut. Thought you could get away from me, eh?"

Pandora wasn't afraid. How *could* she be afraid of something as ugly and little and mean inside as the General was? She'd seen too much. Lived too much!

"Stay away from me," Pandora said. "I'm warning you!"

She meant it, too.

"Warning me of what, Alien bitch?" The General laughed. "What're you going to do, cry at me?"

He was close enough to touch, now, if she'd wanted to touch him. Which she didn't! She didn't want to lay a finger on him. And even more than that she didn't want him laying a finger on *her*.

"I'm warning you again—back away. Or you'll be sorry!"

The General only laughed—and reached for the collar of her shirt and the waist of her slacks, and started to tear them away—

She felt his hand reaching in to rip her clothes, reaching in to touch her where she wasn't about to let that man *touch* her . . . and suddenly everything was a blur. Not like usual, with time fading out around her and the world going away. Like—like every angry thing she'd ever thought or felt had all burst out at once, and she hit the General with her fist, and with the other and the other and the other, and she could hear bones and things breaking as she hit too hard in places liable to bust, and the General fell limp to the terrazzo floor but she still couldn't make herself stop, she just kept thinking about what he'd done to her that made her run away from home and what he was about to do to her if she didn't stop him, and she was hitting and hitting and hitting—

And there was blood spattering everywhere across the walls, the floor, and still she didn't stop. She couldn't stop—just didn't have it in her till the last little bit of pent-up fury was gone.

And the General lay motionless, *broken*.

Panting, catching her breath. Seeing what she'd

done. To the General. To the walls, the floor—blood splattered everywhere on the walls, spilled thick and deep on the floor.

I'm a monster, Pandora thought. *A bloodthirsty monster.*

The world went quiet, and began to fade away.

I hate me.

Pandora hung her head and wandered through the barracks aimlessly as time sifted forward all around her.

Hate me hate me hate me.

Not paying attention to anything around her, not people, not walls, not anything. And none of it mattered: everything and everyone faded before her as she stepped near. Stepped through.

When time came home again it was night on the battlefield and Pandora stood in a smoldering ruin that had been her barracks home.

Caught in the cross fire.

Shooting outside; now and again she could hear an explosion. Pandora looked up as she turned a corner, saw a great gaping hole in the ceiling—and saw a rocket trace its light across the sky.

"Uncle Wally?"

She wasn't going to panic.

Not if she could help it.

Here uncles were here someplace, hiding in the dark. Or they'd run away when the shell went down. Or, or, wasn't there an air-raid shelter down beneath the galley? Pandora had a dim memory that there might be.

They were okay. They had to be!

She was sure of it.

And still. Still.

In her imagination she saw them in every darkened corner: her uncles beaten, broken, bodies charred in the fire that followed the explosion. . . .

And then she got to the galley.

Saw where the missile struck.

Square in the center of the galley wall.

Right through the window where yesterday Pandora stood watching Mommy's spaceship with her uncles crowded close.

If they were here when the rocket hit, they're dead, Pandora thought.

She felt sad and quiet down inside as she walked to the hole in the barracks wall. Looked out at the battlefield.

It was all but over, wasn't it?

The spaceships were gone from the sky. All of them gone but her daddy's great spaceship wrecked and dying a quarter of a mile across the battlefield. Smoldering, glowing here and there where the war had rent its fuselage. Before it lay the broken hulks of a dozen dozen tanks, those and more tanks still fighting, tanks full of soldiers still trying to board the wounded ship.

Pandora thought about her mommy who *renounced* her, thought about the captain and the snake-face pilot who brought her up into the spaceship. The doctor, too. Were they still in there? Were they alive? She had a feeling . . . that spaceship. It wasn't going to be there much longer.

Look at the strange clouds of smoke curling up from its crushed engines; look at the unsettling greygreen light that shone up through the gap where the fuselage touched earth.

It's going to explode, Pandora thought. *It's going to blow up so big that it takes the whole base out with it.*

As she watched, the light from beneath the mother ship grew brighter, hotter. First yellowish; steadily up through orange. Toward red.

It's going to destroy everything. Everything for miles and miles around.

It occurred to her that she ought to run and hide. Ought to find some kind of cover if she was going to survive the blast. But she just didn't care enough to run, because she kept remembering the General as she pounded and pounded him, as blood went every-

where as bone shattered and his head lolled back and
forth across the terrazzo floor. . . . She was a killer
with blood on her hands who hated herself too much
to care if she lived or died.

Hate me hate me hate me.

She hated the General for what he did.

I'll kill him if I ever get the chance, she thought. *I
swear I will.* But when she thought those words she
hated herself even worse, and then she looked across
the battlefield to see the General standing on a plat-
form beside a missile, surrounded by a thousand
soldiers, and she knew that if she really wanted to
she could find a way to kill him.

But she didn't have the heart.

She looked up into the dark, away from the battlefield. And saw the light.

High in the sky, yellowish and fire bright. Growing larger and larger as she watched.

Fiery like a rocket, Pandora thought. *Like a
rocket falling toward me.*

And it was a rocket, descending quickly on a
plume of fire. In just a moment it was close enough
to see.

When Pandora saw her eyes went round-wide-
open, wide as they could be.

Because it was her daddy's ship: old Walt Fulton's
spaceship from down inside the stream in Tennessee.
Pandora would have known it anywhere.

The soldiers watching Hightower are beginning to relax—just a little. The battle is winding down; the big
Alien carrier is on the ground, and hundreds of tanks
surround it. Grotesquely green light seeps up from
the ship carrier's underside, and as the moments
pass the light grows bluer and bluer as the heat of the
flames grows more intense. Everyone who sees the
ship can tell it's going to explode soon.

The battle is over. Hightower is still holding the
trigger wires on the side of his tactical nuke, and
maybe, just maybe, the soldiers begin to think, the

crazy asshole bastard will let the techs disarm the thing. *Maybe.*

And maybe not. That's the kind of nut Hightower is: you can't ever be sure what he's going to do.

Now the wounded Alien carrier opens like a blooming rose, and after a moment a ramp finds its way to earth. And in a moment there are Aliens moving down the ramp with their hands held high above their heads, toward the ground.

Surrendering.

A tall bearlike thing in the skipper's cap leads the Aliens slowly, steadily down. Behind him are all manner of unrecognizable extraterrestrial monsters, and human men and women, too.

It's over. The Aliens have surrendered, and it's over. Someone lets out a sigh of relief, and the sigh spreads to consume the entire company of soldiers who stand watching Hightower.

And then Hightower sees something—on the far end of the battlefield. He points with his free hand, and every last one of them men and women guarding him turn to see what he's talking about.

"There she is," Hightower says. "That bitch. That goddamned Alien bitch! Get her—get her now, God damn it, before she gets away!"

A couple of the MPs look like they're thinking about it, but none of them do. They aren't taking orders from Hightower, even if he is a general. They're supposed to arrest the man, not carry out his instructions.

And then it's too late. Because there is a rocket ship settling to the ground, and the Alien girl is climbing aboard the ship, and now the girl and the ship sail away into the sky.

And General Hightower—Hightower just can't take it anymore. He's screaming, trembling with rage; he looks like a man about to go berserk.

"She's getting away," Hightower shouts. "Getting away!"

And he forgets himself. And lets go of the wires.

. . .

Pandora waited. And she watched.

Watched her daddy Walt Fulton's spaceship settle to the ground; watched its door ease open as General Hightower screamed in impotent rage.

Watched old Walt Fulton, the old man and not the young one, as he climbed down the ship's ramp. Walked the distance from the ramp to the broken wall. Climbed in through the wall, crossed the galley to where Pandora stood.

"We've got to go, Pandora," her daddy said. "It isn't long before the big ship blows."

Pandora blinked her eyes, tried to respond. But it just wasn't in her, no more than it had been in her to run for her own life.

"Pandora. . . ?"

And then he started to cry, because he could see how she was broken inside. And he lifted her in his arms where she went all limp like she was a rag doll. And he carried her into his ship.

A couple minutes later Pandora felt her daddy's spaceship rise up into the sky to carry them into forever. As they rose the big blast threw them across the sky, but the ship still kept on rising.

It's a tiny, tiny nuke as nukes go. Ten, maybe twenty kilotons. Strictly for battlefield use, such weapons: they have no strategic value.

But my oh my they can do wonders to a battlefield.

Pandora was broke inside for a long, long time. But she was a person, people aren't stone that breaks and stays broken; they're living things that take a wound and recover—or die.

And because she didn't die—because her father knelt beside her bed, feeding her, seeing to her, all but forcing her to breathe—because she lived, in time she came again to thrive.

. . . .

One hundred hours pass.

Radiation dims above the battlefield that is no longer any battlefield.

The time-fire here begins finally to dim; it's fed all these hours on the fiery explosion, and now finally that fire fades away.

The ground stirs, breaks in that spot across the glassy plain—there, over there. Four days ago a barracks stood in that spot. Now there is only the glass breaking away to clear the entrance to an underground shelter.

Wallace Turner is the first of them to reach the surface. Two dozen others follow him—climbing up from that hole in the glass ground. Men and women who've spent so many years inside the Pandora Project that they've forgotten the feel of the light of day.

And in the foreground the time-fire sizzles, sputters, and goes dead.

General Dan McNamee, freed from the time-fire, screams as he sees the desolation that surrounds him, Macdonald, Macdonald's team.

He takes his gun from its holster and raises it. And there's no question in the mind of anyone who sees him do this: McNamee is going to start shooting. And there's no time loop to pull them in and out of death anymore: if he kills them, they're going to die dead.

And Ken Estes—standing behind McNamee, where he's just crawled out from under the broken bumper of the truck—Ken Estes just can't take any more.

"Oh man," he says, "get a life."

And tears the bumper from where it hangs loose beneath the truck's grille.

And clubs McNamee over the head, but good.

When she'd slept ten days and nights in the cot aboard her father's spaceship, Pandora finally spoke.

"Where are we?" she asked. It hurt her throat to speak.

Her father looked startled but pleased.

"A million miles beyond the moon," he told her, "spinning 'round the sun."

It wasn't hard to tell he loved her. Look at the way he watched her, looking like he ached with pride!

"How did you find me? Why are you so old? Where have you been?"

Her father smiled. "I've been trying to reach you almost all my life," he said, making a laughing noise that sounded full of pain. "I told you I'd be back, didn't I? Back there in the captain's cabin? It wasn't easy, but I did it."

It was a long time before he told her more.

ABOUT THE AUTHOR

ALAN RODGERS is the author of *Fire, Night, Blood of the Children,* and *New Life for the Dead. Blood of the Children* was a nominee for the Horror Writers of America Bram Stoker Award; his first story (actually a novelette), "The Boy Who Came Back from the Dead," won a Stoker and lost a World Fantasy Award. During the mideighties he edited the fondly remembered horror digest *Night Cry.* He lives in Manhattan with his wife, Amy Stout, and his two daughters, Alexandra and Andrea Rodgers.

Those who would like to reach the author by electronic mail can write to him on GEnie at the address "ALAN.RODGERS". (Stated as an Internet address, that's "alan.rodgers@genie.geis.com".)

RICHARD CHRISTIAN MATHESON

CREATED BY

From a startling new voice in fiction comes a savagely
written thriller of greed, ambition...and terror.

"Quick-jab-to-the-viscera style...brilliant."
—*San Francisco Chronicle*

"[*Created By*] gets the reader into a wrestler's grip
and will not let him go."—Peter Straub

"A masterly fable, told with insight, wit, and
welcome venom...this is Hollywood Hell...
devastating."—Clive Barker